Second Pass

A SIL Novel

By

Ken Ludden

authorHOUSE

1663 LIBERTY DRIVE, SUITE 200
BLOOMINGTON, INDIANA 47403
(800) 839-8640
www.authorhouse.com

This book is a work of fiction. Places, events, and situations in this story are purely fictional and any resemblance to actual persons, living or dead, is coincidental.

© 2004 Ken Ludden.
All Rights Reserved.

No part of this book may be reproduced, stored in a retrieval system, or transmitted by any means without the written permission of the author.

First published by AuthorHouse 07/08/04

ISBN: 1-4184-8356-7 (sc)

Printed in the United States of America
Bloomington, Indiana

This book is printed on acid-free paper.

Cover art and design by Ben Love.

Prologue

NASA made space travel popular—then disasters began. Concurrently, elderly outnumbered youth, creating a powerful political force and a demanding and unpleasant world for the young. Reading was replaced by video news, books, and information. Anti-education lobbyists believed science caused extended life expectancy and slavery to the elderly. NASA needed support to maintain funding.

Dr. George McVee, Senior, was recognized for discoveries and inventions. A celebrity before entry into NASA's astronaut corps, NASA promoted his first mission to regain interest. Broadcasts showed McVee with his son standing before the towering shuttle. Georgie held his father's oxygen tube. McVee later returned to a hero's welcome.

Space Industries Laboratory (SIL) was built as the International Space Station became obsolete. SIL was a spherical station that housed 3,000 at capacity. Its mission was research, but it housed many commercial enterprises. McVee was one of the first on board, more for star power than for work. He broadcast a popular weekly television series from SIL.

A year later, McVee was awarded the Nobel Prize. With fanfare surrounding the award, every television station broadcast the ceremony live.

McVee became convinced he didn't need to follow NASA's script. He promoted education and literacy, and created violent animosity. NASA viewed the Nobel Prize ceremony as a way to regain credibility. Every public relations person went to work, building McVee's celebrity.

The night of the award delivered the highest Neilson rating in history. Officials and leaders watched with pride. As the broadcast was in progress, backroom meetings among Congressmen carved out new funding for NASA in anticipation of increased public support.

McVee was called to the stage. He kissed his wife and tussled his son's hair. The standing ovation seemed sincere, though orchestrated by NASA public relations managers. He strode across the stage and was greeted by other Nobel winners. The award was presented. He bowed crisply and set the trophy down. He pulled a folded paper from inside of his belt. Unfolding the oversized paper he revealed his acceptance speech—printed in large letters.

The audience booed, the camera scanned the speech as network executives tried desperately to pull the camera. But the camera was scripted to stay on McVee for three minutes; it took ninety seconds to cut to commercial. The damage was done. NASA funding was in peril and people argued about education, reading, science and other contentious topics of discord.

Dr. McVee was sent to SIL the next week; the president instructed his staff to get rid of him. McVee wasn't allowed to speak or answer questions. He stood, again, with his son holding his oxygen tube. Little Georgie saluted and smiled, but his father was grave as granite.

Two weeks later SIL exploded. Only a few scraps were found, as rescue quickly became salvage. The crew was declared dead. NASA funding was cancelled. Science sank deeper into the abyss of hostile public opinion. Bands of people attacked scientific facilities, destroying billions of dollars of equipment. Pharmaceutical companies were attacked and sabotaged. People lied about their scientific affiliations to remain accepted.

Georgie's mother remarried and tried to get Georgie to focus on anything but science. But Georgie did not believe his father was dead. He worked hard and joined the science underground. Against his mother's wishes Georgie got a full scholarship to MIT for their BS/MS/PhD program. A cult hero for the scientific underground, whispers followed his every step at MIT.

He told his best friend about some discs his father had given him, telling him they held hope for the future, and if he studied hard enough, he would be able to understand. With prompting, Georgie opened the discs and made a startling discovery—Dr. McVee sabotaged SIL and caused the explosion. His utopian dreams mixed with bitterness toward a scientific community that exploited and abandoned him and produced a madman set to create a world in which he reigned supreme. It was then discovered that SIL was now on an eccentric orbit that passed near enough Earth for travel every eighteen years.

It is thirty-six years later, and Georgie is now Dr. George McVee Junior. Life on Earth and SIL has evolved into complex tandem political situations, churned into separate but equal frenzies as time nears for—Second Pass.

Chapter 1

"Mr. Kiterage, you will follow procedures or I'll have you removed," bellowed Chairholder Sylvana, veins accenting the vertical lines of her temples. Several in the Assembly started shouting at each other and at the Chairholder, the rest murmured under their breath. The chaos was punctuated with angry shouts directed at the Chairholder by the opposing Borns. Many Firsters defended their party's leader, adding to the melee. "Order, ORDER!"

"You lied to us at elections! Broken promises, tyrannical rule! You're a fraud! You'll never win my vote in the next election," snorted the outraged Samson Kiterage, as he swung himself out of the Assembly chamber. At the doorway he turned and yelled, "She'll have us all compromised. Don't allow her to intimidate you just because Commander McVee is sick. Think of The Principles, of our heritage! Silians -- refuse compromise!" He swung his body out of the doorway and let go, heaving himself down the central hallway toward the Finders Station.

"Order!" Sylvana called, waving loose hairs from her eyes. "We're going to vote on citizenship rights before we adjourn, and I'm willing to hold the session for an eternity to get it done. Now, Germaine, your findings please."

Germaine Wilson floated up to the speaker station and cleared her throat. She knew that opposing Sylvana would bring a tirade against her and possibly result in her rations being threatened, or expulsion as she had done to Kiterage, but she took her position seriously and remembered well the last conversation she'd had with Commander McVee. "Chairholder Sylvana," she said with resignation, "if you please. I must echo the sentiment of Mr. Kiterage's stance, if not the demeanor. SIL was designed as a haven for those who seek refuge in space, those who seek to escape the prejudice and division of Mother Earth." Several of the delegates hissed at the reference to Earth, while those who sided with Sylvana booed loudly until Sylvana gave the clacker another strong whack.

"Let her speak!" she commanded.

"Thank you, Chairholder," she said resenting the need to show respect for the wrinkled woman at the dais. "I acknowledge the feelings of Firsters and Borns. I myself was born on SIL to

Second Pass

Firster parents, and I was raised without hope of rescue. I never understood why rescue was so desperately sought by my parents, for I never knew Earth. SIL is my home and has been good to me. I respect Commander McVee for his work, but I don't believe that accepting new citizens as equals is wrong, nor do I see it as potential disintegration of Silian values."

"What do Borns know? You'll bring destruction to us!"

"I've warned you for the last time," Sylvana proclaimed. "I, Chairholder of SIL, declare Silence Rulings in effect."

"She's crazy," whispered a man in the crowd. "She can't mean it."

"Don't argue with her, and I'd keep my mouth shut if I were you Adam. You wouldn't look handsome with only half a tongue," the woman next to him said as she caressed his elbow with her hands.

"Don't worry, Isa," he said, "I couldn't imagine life without being able to speak my mind to you!"

"Germaine, continue," Sylvana said as she glared at the Assembly. She knew she had them now, and her reputation told them her threats were good.

Germaine looked at the little tyrant, wishing her dead. *Why can't she be sick instead of Commander McVee*, she thought. "My vote is for full and equal citizenship, full access to all vital supplies, but probation periods on entry into the Eye Chamber and all sustaining production areas." She pushed herself back to her original place, stabilizing herself with her jets.

"Are there any more Sentiments to be presented by the Assembly?" Sylvana leered over the crowd. As she counted the votes mentally, there was a near even split, which meant that she would be able to sway the Overseers to the Firster position. Delighted that old McVee was ill so he couldn't give Commander Directory to the assembly, but aware that she must get them to vote before they had too much time to think. Bur first, she had to sway a vote more, or two if she were to reach her goal and appear to be innocent of swaying the Assembly. "If not, then we will give the floor to Finder Malanga's first sponsor. Elizabeth Dunn, come forward."

The young girl looked to her right and left before she started her forward motion to the speaking station. She had never before been to the Assembly, and was not sure she could make herself speak over the fear she felt gripping her throat. Chairholder

Sylvana was a terror, she had heard, and was capable of making people say things they didn't mean at all. Malanga's orders were clear, and her preparation had been deeply ingrained. The meditations were now starting to come to her rescue as a cool calm traveled the length of her body. Elizabeth was inwardly grateful that Malanga had selected her as first sponsor, for her training already, though only four years into it, had given her gifts nobody else seemed to posses. She was at the speaking station before she knew it, and, with trembling hands, took a pad out and held it firmly so she wouldn't let it float away from her. She looked up with her eyes at Sylvana, seeing the wrinkled old crone through her nest of red hair. *Look beyond the eyes, follow the light within them to the core*, she recited her lesson in her head, looking not at the old face and it's gnarled anger, but through the eyes to the inner being, so vulnerable that it needed to protect itself with such a harsh exterior, and she saw a child crying with fear, lost in a sea of hopelessness and catastrophic change. She assumed this was the terror Sylvana had felt when she thought she would perish on SIL as it sped off course after the explosion. Whatever it was, this terrifying old hag suddenly became a small child, and Elizabeth knew just what to do.

"Madame," she said shyly, using the old term. There were a few gasps in the crowd, but she kept her warming eye on the center of the old woman's forehead, while looking her directly in the eyes. The wrinkles seemed to ease for a second, until muscles turned the eyes to ice. Sylvana knew what she was up against with these Finders, but she also needed their statement on medicine to further her cause. She would use them, but not allow them entry into her soul. And Elizabeth spoke softly, "Madame Lauretta, allow my gratitude to be in your presence, First Captain."

"You will cease with the salutations and get to your message, and be quick about it!" Sylvana cut herself off before she hurled insults at this evil witch. "Speak!" she commanded.

"Speak I cannot, but read I will," Elizabeth said as she lifted the pad to her eyes, rather than lowering them. "Assembly, strength of SIL," she read, "accept my first sponsor to take my place as I treat your ailing Commander. I, Finder Solange Malanga, am requested by Chairholder Sylvana Lauretta, First Captain of SIL, to inform you of the differences between medicine as practiced on Earth and our own Silian practices. Our new citizens will be accustomed to various medical practices no longer used on

Second Pass

SIL. They will expect medication in the form of chemical additive and interruption therapies such as surgery. I am fully trained in these, and have trained several new doctors in these practices before the art of Finding was developed.

"It will be difficult for new citizens to become accustomed to our atmosphere, diet and weightlessness. As we saw in our first visitors who stayed here, there will be periods of severe diarrhea. disorientation, nausea, depression and sudden changes in mood. They will have aches in their legs and arms, and many will experience temporary depression as their bodies become buoyant and lose their gravity resistance composition, and longer term depression from their loss of orientation via gravitational pull. They will not understand why they should forgo rigorous exercise in their first two years, while watching others who have been here longer work hard to develop the physical strength they are themselves loosing. We must stand by our new citizens and offer them assistance in their transition."

"So," Sylvana interjected, "we will need to offer them special forms of medicine. How will this be compensated? Do we offer them extra rations and exchanges, or do they receive free care?" Her smile was hideous and arrogant. She looked over the crowd as they realized that full, equal citizenship would cost Firsters and Borns some of their rations and exchanges. She knew well the training each of them had, training that all must be shared for survival. And she knew the anger born of long decades of hopelessness and hard work, surviving against terror of slow, breathless death in the void.

"Madame Lauretta," Elizabeth said softly, "there is more to this report."

Sylvana swung her gaze to Elizabeth, newly unsure. "What more could there be?"

"Don't let new citizens steal our rations and exchanges!" cried a man in the crowd.

"Equality is unfair," another yelled the familiar Firster phrase.

"Let her speak, Finder Malanga has saved us all, she is wise," said a voice familiar to all. The crowd hushed and turned. Sylvana swung her head around, nearly setting herself into a spin. Her bony fingers clutched her speaking station and she hissed as she saw Commander McVee in the distance. Her hatred inflated now to desperation, she needed to take a vote quickly or all was lost. "We will now vote!" she declared.

"But you cannot vote," McVee said as he drifted toward her. "Not yet. Let the first sponsor finish, then you can vote."

"You no longer have control here, McVee," screeched Sylvana, "I am duly elected Chairholder. We vote!"

The sound in the chamber grew as people mumbled their sentiments. Some were yelling slogans and phrases, others were asking for quiet. McVee floated up to Sylvana, who backed away from him, shifting her control from her clutch on the speaker station to her jets. "We vote!" she yelled.

"There is only one more statement, Chairholder," Elizabeth said calmly into the amplifier, "and it won't take long to deliver."

"Read," said McVee.

"No! I forbid it!" yelled Sylvana.

"Commander Directory!" countered McVee, Sr. All heads went to Elizabeth still talking among themselves. Tension was heightened by the call of Commander Directory. In the many years of the Assembly there had never before been such serious calls made. Commander Directory is one of the most serious powers afforded to the Commander and, as everyone was well aware, McVee had shown what seemed to be unreasonable restraint over the years of fighting with Sylvana, not once calling Commander Directory. And likewise Silence Ruling was equally rare, making this historic moment vibrant and uncertain. Why, when Silence Ruling had been written into law it was imagined that it would never be used. No situation any of the Overseers could imagine would call for such drastic measures, but they had installed it because of their own experience with unimaginable things becoming reality. That both of these had been called within a short time made everyone nervous. Debate created its own sound, like tempestuous waves breaking against the hull of a ship, rising, falling, swaying, and anger was its inevitable nausea. The sound grew from rumble to roar as the two leaders locked eyes.

Elizabeth hummed low the unifying sound, and others joined her automatically, joining in the trance-inducing hum. They quieted and she again raised the pad and read, "To make the transition of new citizens quick, and to assure their adaptation is swift and deep, it is my recommendation to start them in the ways of Finders immediately. First days are long forgotten when the body is acclimated. There is no need for special medical attention other than in extreme cases."

Sylvana's face contorted with shock and horror; she was ruined by this. All Silians revered Finder Malanga and had each, in some way, benefited directly from her new healing methods. She had helped the Chairholder herself to develop the confidence needed to hold and enforce her leadership position. Gratitude had no relevance in the rage she now experienced, and the only loyalty was to her own agenda for the Assembly. Equal citizenship would destroy everything she had been working toward, and jeopardize her position in the future. All would be lost. Elections were next due less than a year after the arrival of the new citizens, and she would never be able to win the majority of them with her Firster program. Thought became motivation, and hatred action, as Sylvana coiled and then jetted herself to Elizabeth, kicking her in the head as she sped by, then turning and grabbing her by the hair, pulling her head back. "Guards, split this woman's tongue! Silence Rulings are in effect, she has spoken without permission of the Chair!"

The guards started toward Elizabeth slowly, unsure. If they disobeyed the Chairholder they would be punished severely, but they couldn't bring themselves to such harsh treatment.

"Stop!" ordered Commander McVee. "There is no jurisdiction which allows the instigation of Silence Rulings here. Silence Rulings are only to be in effect in times of peril in face of complete destruction of SIL. What is this lunacy? What are you afraid of, Chairholder? Does equality threaten? For the second time, Commander Directory!"

Sylvana, defeated by his higher authority, tasted rage in her throat. McVee was supposed to be dead; and she the leader of SIL. She had been bending the rules for months since McVee was debilitated, and had gotten away with near murder several times just to silence her foes. McVee could ruin her forever by calling her on impeachable offenses, of which she was blatantly guilty. She now had nothing to lose, and she had prepared for this moment, playing scenario after scenario in her head, winning each battle of the wills by various means, always maintaining her power. She jetted to him quickly and, as she approached, pulled a knife out of her sleeve, falling at his chest with a desperate lunge, but he shifted to take the blow in his arm instead.

Blood floated up and outward from his arm as shock overcame his face. Sylvana righted herself with more facile jet work, but was confronted by three men. She swung her knife menacingly at them, though they did not flinch. Elizabeth was at McVee's side, jetting him out of the door and toward the Finders Station to tend his wounds. Sylvana, restrained by the men, screaming insults and threats. Heads shook in disbelief. Jiimson, leader of Assembly Firsters, gathered a group of supporters to free Sylvana floating en masse toward her captors, grabbing them to break their circle. Jets hissed and couples locked in battle twirled recklessly out of control. More Firsters joined in Sylvana's defense, while more Borns joined to equal their force. Suddenly there was a shrill scream, as a knife plunged into Sylvana's heart. Her gasping body floated spastically in the center of an expanding group of bodies, frozen in fighting positions. She grasped frantically at her throat and at the air around her. Blood flowed from the wound and out of her mouth, forming dancing globs and bubbles, shimmering in the artificial light. Urine ballooned from beneath her robes as she gasped a final breath of air, ending with a frightful spasm and then peacefully floating limbs whose motion was paralleled by a spinning knife. First Captain, Sylvana Lauretta, Chairholder of the Assembly was dead; her assassin would never be identified.

* * * * * * *

The glow of the LOL communications relay station at Associated Labs in Cambridge lit skin green, and at four o'clock that morning no other light was lighted. The rumbling of the satellite dish shook the floor, but no guard would think that odd or go to check, particularly the one on duty as his coffee had been laced with mild sedative rendering him unconscious. The two men worked quickly and quietly, decoding the secure transmissions from Chairholder Sylvana to the Earth station.

"D'ya tink shes gonna snuff'm?"

"Quiet, whisper you dummy."

"But da guard's out, man, he can't hear nuthin."

"I told you, idiot, this room is seismically monitored, and your low voice can trigger a response. In the unlikely event the tapes will be checked, we can't afford to compromise our position by leaving any kind of mark."

"Man, you talk all dem big words 'n shit, but you don't know fuckin nuthin. 'Sides, wid all your security clearance and bullshit you don't need to be sneakin any fuckin how. If ya want my help, ya gotta listen to me just like I gotta listen t'your sorry ass."

The older man sighed and rubbed his eyes, tired from the green-lit screen, and regretting having hired this thug in the first place. But, Sylvana had made it clear that she deemed it necessary, so he was stuck. That is, stuck if he wanted the reward she promised. And he knew the reward was real and attainable. So he smiled, and patted the ape on the shoulder.

"Don't mind me," he said, "I'm just tired. You're doing a good job. Sorry I was short with you." He hated being contrite to this beast. "How are your studies coming?" he asked to change the subject, hoping it would quiet his companion.

"Real neat, man. Did'ja know my talkin is Brooklyn? I jus is talkin my way of talkin, and teach says its Brooklyn. Ain't dat some shit? Do whole family talks like dis too! Guess weah some kinda special, huh?"

"Well, that's great. But shouldn't you be practicing what she is teaching you? I mean, you could try it with me, like extra study, like I'm your tutor." He hoped to get him to agree, both for ease on his ears and to be reassured that progress was being made. He'd never due like this, and the stakes were too high to risk anything at all going wrong.

"Nah. I talks like I talks wid ju. Don't worry man, I be ready."

The satellite dish rumbled to a new position and a new message appeared on the screen. The older man looked at it, read it, then froze. "Shit!" he cried.

Tapping him on the shoulder, the other man said, "Uh, scuse *me*, whadabout de sizemo crap? Dat was a preddy loud shit dere!" And he chuckled at his retaliation.

"No, look at this. It says Chairholder Sylvana is dead! She was murdered!"

"Whadafuk? Who done dat?"

"There was a fight in the Assembly Chamber. Commander McVee was stabbed in the arm, and Sylvana was killed." He thought about the implications of this. The best part was that she wouldn't be taking her cut of the money, but she also wouldn't be there to direct from the inside. And that Jiimson was not to be trusted, assuming, of course, he would take her position. But laws on SIL were not very logical, and the lines of succession to the Chairholder position were not clear to him.

He looked at the big oaf, now pawing the screen as if rubbing it would make the message clearer. He needed this guy's help more than ever now. He laughed out loud at the thought that he was now in charge. Jiimson, according to Sylvana, wasn't in on all of the details of their plan, just the ones concerning loading dock procedures and shuttle transport capabilities. With a grin he said, "I guess I have to promote you, buddy."

"Promote me? T'what?"

"You and I are the only two who know the whole plan," he said with conspiratorial conviction even though it wasn't true, "and now we have to carry it out ourselves."

"Whadja need me to do now, man? I got lotsa stuff to do already. We still gonna do the protection? I like dat. You ain't gonna take dat away from me?" he said with a threatening fist under the other man's chin.

"Nothing of the sort," he said, removing the fist, "of course you're going to do everything we talked about before. But now, you will be my partner. You've got to increase your studies, get the speech created quicker. You'll be important in many more ways now, and we must have you giving the correct image."

"Whadabout da money, man? I godda have more now."

"Of course you will, we all will! Sylvana's dead, so there's no cut for her."

"Hey, I like dis. Dis'll work, yeah!"

"Now, let's get out of here. I need to think, and that guard will be waking up soon. Besides, I have to get to my desk at the regular time in the morning."

The two men turned off the monitor and quietly left the building. Nobody saw them leave.

* * * * * * *

The hallways in the Social Agency Building had floors hard and polished so every shoe fall made its loudest click, tap, whack, squish or clunk, often to the embarrassment of the building's newcomers, particularly when rainy days added a watered squeak. And the doorways were far apart, with no courtesy of a bench, alcove or displayed art to welcome humans to this officious home of bureaucracy. The sterility devoured humans with over high ceilings dwarfing people into vulnerability; bow willingly before power or be collapsed by it. The power, silent and

Second Pass

invisible, bordered the hallway behind the parade of closed doors to each side. And it didn't matter how many people were in this building working or pleading their cases, those doors shut all noise in, leaving an echo chamber hall. It was as if all of the life in the building was sucked into the powerful offices, used by the officials to dominate the lives they manipulated from behind their big, heavy, polished desks. Even their polish was the result of the life force of faceless workers who came in the dark of night to break their backs for little pay making this powerful world seem banal.

After 5:00 pm, when work stopped, there was no difference in the hallways; signs or sounds of life couldn't exist in that silent vacuum. But in some offices, some people worked on. Some were new to their professions, as yet uncorrupted by the infectious malady of chronic non-productivity, who worked because of what the job was or should be. They received no overtime for their troubles, and praise for their productivity was rare. In fact, if they did accomplish part of a project, management grinded them down to ineffectiveness with endless procedural alterations, slowing them to align with the sedentary sloth of bureaucracy.

Dr. George McVee, Jr., Director of Space Industries Lab Placement Office, called SIL-PLACE by insiders, often worked past 5:00. He seldom got home before 11:00. Placements had to be made, accommodation modules custom built to owners' specifications, registrations and records updated, vaccinations prescribed and monitored, passports issued and the endless dilemma of citizenship settled. And then, only then, after months and sometimes years of agonizing, slow paperwork, a person went to the final review board to get an answer. Passage through this maze of waiting was accompanied by endless interviews, and George had to review all of the papers, letters, forms, videos, financial records, immigration information, State Department clearances, background checks and medical histories. With only two hundred places left to fill before the upward limit of 1,248 new arrivals, three years just wasn't enough time.

The first 15 years had been slow. Letters came inquiring about SIL, requests for brochures and application information, steadily from the beginning, but it wasn't until the three-year mark that the avalanche descended. Plans had been naïve to the task. It is rare that a government agency exists for nearly two decades before it first gets to see if it is workable, and there was no pre-existing test case against which to plan or project. Seventeen million brochures had been sent, and six million application information packages produced two million five hundred thousand actual applications - over half of them in the last year. The staff struggled under the strain and complained plenty to George. George picked up the overflow for morale, he told himself, which meant guilt. He'd needed three prescriptions for stronger glasses in the last six months, had developed an acid stomach and a fatigue twitch in his right cheek late each evening, which increased until his eyes burned out of focus and he admitted defeat for that day.

Fitting eight hundred new residents on SIL was no problem. It had been originally built to house up to three thousand with future module connectors, and had plenty of space. The problems arose from vacationing visitors who would go early in the pass and return late, SIL resident transfers after thirty-six years in space, SIL visitors to Earth who would return before the pass ended, and the rotation of shuttles. The early years of the space program provided back-up vehicles, facilities, and plans; today there were no back-ups. It had to be worked out, built, and then it had to work. George would work on the problem more tomorrow. Eyes burning, twitch jumping, he turned off the lights and entered the hall chasm carrying his shoes both to avoid the sound and also because it felt good. Once outside of the building and heading toward his car, the cement on the garage floor was cool and restorative to his shoe-confined, heat-ripened feet.

There were always six cars on his floor of the parking garage. He didn't know to whom the other five belonged, but they were there, always in the same places. He no longer noticed them, and didn't even look up when he heard a car engine start as he walked. It was either the headlights or the screeching wheels that made him look up. The car was barreling toward him, right toward him, accelerating as it neared. He jumped out of the way, briefcase and shoes flying, and ended up on his back between two cars he'd pinballed between on his descent to the floor. In the distance wheels screeched and someone shouted an obscenity from the level below.

George got up easily with only slight pain in his right elbow and left hip, fumbled around gathering his papers and shoes and walked to his car. He discovered the origin of the pain in his hip when he reached into his pocket for keys. He didn't care that the keys cut him, or bruised him when he fell on them, he cared only for home where leftovers would quickly be heated to inedible

Second Pass

temperatures and then cool as he watched his autovision disk of the days events. And he prayed Shandor wouldn't call, come by or, as was his latest annoying habit. He would be waiting in his garage, then follow him into the house and chatter endlessly while George tried to listen to his phone messages, cook his dinner, and watch the news. He liked Shandor, but he needed to have just one moment of his own life to allow him to register that he had indeed existed that day, if only for just a few minutes.

Shandor had never matured, would never mature. Tom did his best, but you can't raise a child when he's an adult. Shandor's childhood as an orphan in servitude to others on SIL made him fiercely independent and immature. Tom worked hard to pacify severe regret that he'd missed his son's childhood, reminded daily of that fact by the cheerfully seditious young man. How odd that the carefree joy of childhood, so surely missed in a child without it, was infuriating in an adult, and then again inspiring in the elderly. But Tom had made his choices and must live with the results.

George was caught short by this thought of results. Results, like shadows, were connected to you by the illumination of day, and were obscured by darkness, the shield. He wound his way home on the two-lane road through McLean's posh neighborhoods toward Great Falls, staring into darkness. Results would come in any day, maybe today. He would find out if Liz was pregnant, if he was a father. Would they marry, he wondered, or just live together in a kind of efficient arrangement only two scientists could endure, raising a child with rigorous effort to avoid the mistakes their parent's had made? Was all of life a controlled experiment? Calculate risks, establish criteria, create a pure sample, add stimulus and watch results, checking them against your hypothesis. It is impossible to escape methods learned in prolonged higher education. Becoming a Ph.D. accomplishes the droning of life; years of intense study cement habits of the discipline, in his case astrophysics, into every part of life, rendering you useless in many aspects of common humanity. The lack of attention to clothing or hair, like Abel's mark, along with the abundance of pens in his pocket, marked him as a physicist. The world saw physicist, son of a scientific celebrity. All of the personal mythology the press created when SIL was found and he was reunited with his father launched him headlong into the world of politics and social science. He wanted to be just a man, nothing more. *A man with an average life didn't have to....what? Didn't have to what?* He would never know what average felt like, nor would his own child, if there were to be one.

Liz had missed her cycle without stress to blame. They'd lived as a couple now for fifteen years—in different houses. It never occurred to them to move in together, or to make any other outward changes to reflect their relationship. Two houses gave them room to live their differences instead of suffering them. Bickering about time spent together didn't enter their world. Each understood the other's work, and knew it was important. They worked together all day, every day, on separate projects, and then caught up with details when time permitted. George and Liz would have it no other way, which made it frightening to contemplate consolidating households to raise a child.

Distracted by a noise, a buzzing or flicking tap on his windshield, he noticed a yellow flier stuck under his wiper blade. When he stopped at a crossroads, he reached around to the front and grabbed it, dropped it onto the passenger front seat, and promptly forgot it as he turned and entered his neighborhood, looking carefully at his garage to see if Shandor's car was around. Surprisingly, it wasn't, thank God. He pulled into the drive, electronically opened his garage door, and parked while the door shut behind him. He grabbed his ruffled pile of papers, his shoes and his empty brief case and turned his attention to his stomach as he entered the house.

The front door opened sluggishly due to the usual large pile of mail delivered through the slot in the door. He stepped over it and skillfully dumped his armful onto the couch, threw his jacket on top, picked up Slava, his hunger- and affection-starved cat, and proceeded to the kitchen. The clean shelves and empty sink brought a smile - Sienta, the housekeeper, had been there today, a fact always forgotten until he got home, and she had the blessed habit of preparing food for the week. He hadn't asked her to, she developed the habit over time as she examined remnants of his meals left in the sink. She first chided him about his diet and encroaching middle age, then prepared little treats. Once she went to the store and brought him fresh fruit and milk, refusing to accept payment. That soon became a regular event, so he gave her a raise since she only accepted money on payday. Over the years she became his cook and housekeeper, and he kept giving her raises.

Second Pass

She had lost all of her children in the earthquakes and never had more. She wouldn't talk about it or about their father, who seemed never to have been in the picture at all. She just adopted George, and Shandor who came with the package, conspired with Liz and kept their lives healthy and clean. She didn't care for George's mother, didn't approve of his stepfather, but took personal interest in any part of their private lives she got word of, unable to distinguish between tabloid rumors and facts confirmed by George, Liz, Shandor, Tom or George's mother, whom she only spoke to to find out little things about her newly adopted family.

The opened refrigerator door showed a series of containers with little notes, all in Spanish, explaining, he imagined, what to do in what order; he didn't speak Spanish. Sienta never stopped believing he would one day speak it, and like a high school language teacher who speaks nothing but the language studied to *non-comprending* ears she spoke, wrote, and gestured to him in Spanish. So long as he looked at her when she was speaking and grunted some sort of reply, she was satisfied. Important information was delivered in heavily accented English with a look of pity that he couldn't get it in the only true language, as if he were deprived the real meaning in the less adequate English. He remembered his run-in with Tom in the library, and their argument about languages of origin. But, there was no English note, only the Spanish food instructions, which meant she didn't know the pregnancy test results.

His food heating, and the cat meditatively eating, he settled down with the pile of mail on the foyer floor. From experience he knew most of it would merely be put in a pile to go to the office. People often sent letters about SIL business to his home, which he didn't mind, but they could wait until morning and the attention of his staff. He sorted, only half looking at the envelopes, waiting for the phone to ring, for Liz to call with the test results. Half way through the pile (seventeen letters for the office, six magazines, twelve ad brochures and pamphlets, four bills, and two personal letters, one from his mother and the other from Soloman Gould) he noticed the front door was open and Slava had run out. "Damn it cat!" he yelled as he raced outside to retrieve him.

Slava, an indoor cat with few 'natural' instincts, never took advantage of the wide openness of his front yard, but always ran for freedom in a small, dark hiding place. George looked under the pyracantha and under the holly, usual places for the errant escapee, but Slava had not gone to either of his usual spots. George started calling his name, looking around the garage door, drainage spout and in the unmowable grass too close to the side of the house. He then heard a pathetic little meow from inside the garage, under his car. "Slava, you nutty kitty, come here." But the cat didn't emerge from under the car, so George knelt down and tried to reach, effectively shooing the cat further under the car. "So, you want me on my belly, do ya? So much for my shirt, Slava. You know how Sienta hates us to mess up our clothes, well, your fur, my clothes." George ooffed onto his belly and crawled under the car.

As he reached for the cat, his cuff caught on a hanging wire. To free his cuff, he reached with his other hand, not wanting to jiggle the wires too much and cause himself another repair bill. As he reached for the wire, he looked where it came from and froze. It was connected to some sort of device that looked an awful lot like a bomb magnetized to the bottom of the chassis. He held his breath and gingerly freed his cuff, grabbed the cat, and slid carefully out.

Once inside, he closed the door and picked up the phone to call the police. But the phone had no tone, even when he depressed the disconnect several times quickly.

"Hello? George?" the voice spoke to the air.

"This is George."

"George, it's Liz. Why do you sound so funny?"

"I just had to chase the cat from...Liz, I have to call you later, gotta call the police now."

"Wait, George. Why do you need to call them?"

"I'll call you later." He hung up the phone, instantly realizing it was the wrong thing to do. But he dialed the police and told them what he found. They would be right over; don't answer the door or go anywhere near the car. He found these terse comments and a few other things, like the fact they slammed down the phone in a hurry as he overheard them yelling frantically to a squad car in the background, both overly dramatic and truly terrifying. The phone rang.

"Hello?"

"George, you can't just..."

"Sorry Liz. The cat ran under the car and I found a bomb there."

Second Pass

"I doubt the cat planted a bomb under your car, George. I think you're working too hard."

"No, it must have been the guys in the garage when I left work. Maybe they were trying to run me down, if they're the ones who planted the bomb... Liz? Did you go to the doctor?"

There was a long pause filled with breathing and false starts. Liz was trying to figure out what weirdness George was telling her and break the news to him. It wasn't at all the way this had gone in her head.

"What?" George said to the stammering.

"I'm pregnant, George. We knew I was," she rationalized.

"I didn't. Did you? Really?

"Well, sort of. My body has felt strange to me. So, what's this about guys in the garage?"

"Liz, you can't just tell me you're pregnant and then change the subject! That's great! I mean that you're pregnant is great!"

"And you can?" Liz countered.

"Get pregnant?" George was mystified.

"No, dummy. You can tell me about this bomb and garage guys and then shift to my test results? I believe you are the pot calling the kettle black, sweetie."

"Oh, I did do that, didn't I? Oops! What a weird conversation. Should we start over?"

"No, not start over. I'll come over. Be there in ten minutes."

"Don't go near the car. I mean the police said. Shit, park across the street and come in by the kitchen door. This is crazy."

"I will, and I agree."

"What?"

"Never mind, George. I'll be right over." The phone clicked off.

George sat in the living room and stared at the shadowed wall. He wanted to be more worried about the bomb than he was, and more excited about the baby. But he wasn't. Life just didn't excite him that often, or, more precisely, compared to the dreams and excitement of his youth, today's feelings were all tepid. Losing your father, that's something. Believing he is alive when the world says he's dead, that's something. Hoping to be vindicated, then it happens, that's something.

Nothing could possibly ever move him again like the day the odd signal from deep space became his father's return, than the day he again saw his father. Entire lifetimes are lived without such strong stuff in them. Eternity is spent in an instant of hope, or hope dashed completely by reality, and the world just goes on, minding its own business. Hell lies between not having and not getting; the instant of embracing one's fate. The undoing of youths' dreams leaves dream carcasses to mock the newly formed man. Bitterness is forbidden if you're healthy, and renewed dreams are chided by groups of the matured that never had dreams to forfeit to age. Love's panacea blanket has too many holes to warm you in all ways warmth is needed, and if it could, then where is it found, anyway?

And, to bring a new life into this? It was just another thing that couldn't be. that was. He would accept it, prepare for it, and use his early memories as guides. It has to be possible to avoid repeating the past, otherwise nature's generosity of dashed dreams remembered would serve no purpose, and nature always has purpose.

Smoke from the kitchen, from his forgotten and burned dinner, woke him from reverie. Swearing his way to the kitchen he grabbed some bread and a banana and yelled a 'fuck you' at the notes from Sienta on the refrigerator door, but then thought better of it. She had nothing to do with any of this. So he apologized to the door through the jumble of mush in his mouth.

The police came. Liz came. His home was snatched from him as a barber cuts away your hair, just doing his job. There were calls to make, calls to take, forms to fill, and the most ridiculous questions to answer; the more ridiculous the question, the more often it was repeated.

The police left. The bomb, made of common materials impossible to trace, hadn't been entirely attached, or he would have been dead. No fingerprints were found. He sat at the kitchen table across from Liz, staring at the card the police had left, and next to it the infodisk of agencies available to watch over him, to drive him, to render him impotent by enveloping him with hired body guards. Goons! Of course, 'you don't need to take these precautions, but it is recommended in this case,' they had patronizingly said. He swiped the pile away, disgusted.

"I'll get you a tank ale," Liz's back said to him as she started for the refrigerator.

Second Pass

"I hate tank ale," he grumbled.

"You love tank ale, and you're acting like a spoiled brat. But you are adorable. Like a baby. Did I say baby? No it must have been someone else." She plunked the ale down in front of him and hugged his shoulders.

"I'm sorry Liz," George said as he picked up the ale, "and I'm sorry to you to, buddy." He knew he was talking to his ale, but didn't care if crazy was added to this moment's irregularities. He continued addressing the bottle. "I don't hate you - why, you've been one of my closest friends! For years!" He looked up at Liz and kissed her embracing hand. "This isn't the way I thought we would celebrate if you were pregnant, you know."

"I know, but I am pregnant, and you had better figure that into your quixotic decision about hiring a Neanderthal companion, I mean body guard." She chuckled.

"What do you mean by that?"

"Well, if someone is out to get you, or me, or us," she said patting her stomach, "I don't want to be caught unprepared. We have a family to think about now, don't we?"

"Liz, let's handle this one thing at a time." He held his hand up against her protest. "I know the events of today are related, and in the continuum things don't happen as isolated incidents, but there is a whole lot of shit to process. I don't mean that our child is shit but today everything just feels like shit so I said shit, and we should talk about these things as separate issues to consider before we lump them together and come up with a final decision. Whew!" He took a long draught of his ale. "Love this stuff."

Liz smiled. "So, Mr. Professor, Doctor, sir, now that I have the benefit of your lecture, let me give you mine." She held her hand up just as he had, though his protest was only raised eyebrows above the snout of his ale bottle. "I am pregnant, and we decided, long before all of this 'shit,' and I don't mean the baby is shit but you started it so I said shit too, that we would have this child because he or she will be so unbearably lucky to have such distinguished parents and the world is in dire straights without another little George/Liz clone. And while I am pregnant I intend to continue working and being productive and don't want the added stress of worrying if your buns, which used to be much cuter but will still do quite nicely, are on the line waiting to be picked off by some weirdo assassin. Lecture over." She took the mug from his hands and swallowed, mimicking him, eyebrows and all.

George let out a bellowing laugh and manhandled her onto his lap. "Did I tell you I loved you today?"

"Too much shit," she smirked.

"Oh, yeah. Guess I'd better not then." She wopped him on his head. "Hey," he stood, nudging her out of his lap, "since everything is related here, let's discuss shit while we sort the mail. Deal?"

"George McVee Junior, you are impossible."

He leaned against her. "Oh? You are in error, ma'am. I'm quite possible." His kisses were protested as the Harlequin's in an operetta.

"George," Liz looked down into his eyes, "do you really want to sort the mail now? I mean, right now?"

"I guess I could let Sienta do it in the morning..." he kissed her.

"It would be a shame if she had nothing to do..." she took his hand and started to walk down the hall to the bedroom.

"Of course, I hate to shirk my responsibilities, but it's been quite a day..." he pulled off her sweater as they continued walking, "so much shit."

"And she will understand," she said as she unfastened her bra. "Besides," she turned to unzip his pants, "she'll want something to do since she missed all the commotion tonight."

"We mustn't leave her out," he said as she unbuttoned his shirt.

"Plus, she'll have to get used to doing more now that I'm pregnant and helpless," she said as he assisted her skirt doffing wriggle.

"Perhaps she can choose the agency to do surveillance," he said as he kicked off his shoes.

"Of course she can," Liz smiled, "I knew you'd see things my way." She kissed him as they fell on to the bed.

Chapter 2

Ronald Stevens stood at the head of the long, polished conference room table. His suit was immaculately pressed and fitted, the usual silk handkerchief smartly showing its reliably perfect triangle above his breast pocket. Associated Laboratories was known for its lax dress code, and even at the meeting of the Board there were many who simply wore shirtsleeves and no tie. Board members were chosen for their accomplishments as was the staff at Associated, more for merit of their work than for longevity at the firm. It was also uniquely defining that many members were younger, an apparent departure from the assumption that most scientists were elderly. But, when membership came to a vote by all Associated employees, the elderly always voted for the younger men, knowing that their age-tapped strength was better spent on their projects, rather than negotiating the world's political realities as they applied to Associated.

So Stevens stood out. He was an outsider, recruited from the law/investment firm Wilson, Jones, Stevens and Cooke, which owned Associated. By interpretation of the regulations, he had in fact worked for a long time on Associated, having been the senior partner assigned to Associated for more than fifteen years, and it was he who was chief negotiator with the government when it had been discovered that Associated was not the home for the elderly it appeared to be, but a working physics laboratory of the greatest, and oldest, scientists alive.

He first met George upon his return from SIL, as the senior Military Press Corps Officer, assigned to handle press for the returned crew, and the arrival of Shandor. He was quickly snatched up by the firm as a senior partner, ignoring the fact he had no law degree. He handled public relations during the tumultuous years following the discovery of SIL, since that discovery was the direct result of technology developed at Associated. The public was won, however, not by Stevens' work, but by the great and global relief that SIL had been found, and the startling fact that most of its inhabitants were alive and well. Even so, Stevens' photo appeared more often than any other in the autovision programs and daily news infodisks. He became the symbol of Associated, much by his own design, when it was hailed as the savior of the lost SIL crew. And yet, despite his popularity and identification as Associated representative, there had been an arduous battle when Joseph Conroy, new Vice President of Operations for SIL Inhabitation at the time, pushed his nomination as Board President when Solomon 'Sol' Gould retired. It was Gould himself who led the opposition to Stevens' election, vehemently campaigning against him. If he hadn't gotten the flu, most of the disgruntled Board members still said, Stevens wouldn't have been elected. But fate had worked against poor Sol when he got the flu and lost this battle by an absence of four days that critical week.

Defiant in his position, Stevens had taken over with little grace, forcing changes that often impeded the work being done. He was not a physicist, he was an economist with an honorary doctor of law degree, and had no concern whatever about the actual work being done. His only concern was whether that work would position Associated for continued grants and public support. Some said he didn't even know what was going on, and couldn't understand it if he did know about it. His good looks had only sharpened as his hair turned perfect silvery white, and the immutability of his control grew with each new grant and endowment he secured. His arrogance shone in his gloating smile as he stood before the assembled Board, all seated before him, his voice booming with slick confidence as he made his announcement this morning.

George had gotten the call at six, asking him to come to Associated at eight for an emergency Board meeting, dealing directly with SIL. Liz was groggy from their celebration of the new child, and told him to go ahead, she would join him after the meeting. As George was dressing to leave, Sienta had arrived, seen the mess and marched straight to the bedroom. Her intention was to scold George for leaving the mail on the floor, not eating properly and, worst of all, not calling her when the bomb was found and the police came. She had been aroused when some news reported called her at home in the middle of the night to get background on the story about the bomb. George chuckled at the ill fate of that reporter who, undoubtedly, got a Spanish tirade too fast to understand even by most Spanish speaking people, filled with recriminations and assigned shame, as was Sienta's way. Instead of her grand entrance, to her dismay, he just kissed her on the forehead and said Liz would explain everything. The last thing he saw was Liz shaking a threatening fist at him for dumping that task on her; he chuckled all the way to Associated.

Second Pass

"Good," Stevens exclaimed, "McVee, Junior has arrived."

"George," George said, "please. Call me George."

"Too confusing, McVee, Junior," was the dismissal "we wouldn't know who was who, would we? So, today, ladies and gentlemen, we have some interesting news from SIL. About five hours ago, First Captain Sylvana Lauretta was murdered during a heated argument in the Assembly Chambers on SIL. The argument was between Firsters and Borns regarding the citizenship rights of the future inhabitants of SIL."

"How was she killed?" demanded Conroy. "How do we know it is true?"

"Joseph, calm down. She is dead, of stab wounds to the heart they say, and we know it because of an encrypted message received on our government communications relay at four fifty-two this morning. We have no reason to doubt the report." He put down the paper he was reading from, and looked around the table, hands raised palms up before him, fingers spread as he shrugged. "Does anyone doubt the validity of this report?" He looked around defiantly. "Other than Joseph here?"

There was mumbling around the table, mostly members speaking to themselves, trying to figure out the implications of this news, assuming it was authentic. There had been a great deal of discussion about the new citizens lately. Stevens and George were on opposite sides of the debate. Stevens wanted to utilize every seat on each shuttle with new citizens or visitors to achieve 'maximum opportunity;' George wanted to have a few empty slots on each flight for a contingency 'to assure shuttle availability in emergencies.' The Board of Associated, only involved in communications between SIL and Earth, monitoring of shuttle flight paths, and docking, didn't seem to think it was their place to dictate anything about who, or how many, went on the flights. Since the day Stevens became Board President, there were more and more politics; scientists do not like politics.

"Was there any word from my father?" George asked, suddenly worried about him. He knew of his father's illness, but had been assured by Paul there was no real danger. But George Senior was the political opponent of Sylvana Lauretta, and any fight surely would have effected his father, or perhaps been caused by him.

"There is no word of or from him," Stevens said checking his paper again, "but he may have been involved."

"What do you mean 'may have been involved'?"

"It says, and I read, 'Just before the murder occurred, Commander McVee was rushed from the Assembly Chamber to the Finder Station,' which, if I understand correctly, is what they call their medical facility, 'for medical treatment.' Otherwise, there is no mention of him." With a smirk, Stevens put the paper back in its folder and closed it with finality, opening another folder, extracting a paper and about to commence on a new topic.

"Not so fast," said Jules Rosen, a fairly new member of the Board, "shouldn't we get a copy of that?"

"Well, Rosen," Stevens coughed uncomfortably, "it is classified, uh, has classified references at higher rating than all Board members have. Now," he began again, but was interrupted this time by George.

"Mr. Stevens, there is no classification rating too high for me to see. Give me a copy please."

Stevens looked lost for a moment, and straightened his tie to cover the moment. He looked at Joseph Conroy, to his left, and then down at the table. "Yes, McVee, Junior," he cleared his throat, "we'll see you get a copy. I've only one copy here. See me after the meeting."

"I'll see it now. Give me your copy and I will read it in your presence and return it. You can dispense the photocopy to me later." He held out his hand.

Stevens bent down to Conroy and whispered back and forth with him for a moment. Then turned to his right and said something to the legal counsel for the Board, who scowled deeply, loosing his chin into his chest as he thought. In a moment, he looked up at Stevens, shrugged and shook his head no. "You must show him, Stevens. To withhold it is illegal."

"But it is marked confidential to my attention," Stevens countered.

"I'm sorry, Stevens, Dr. McVee has the authority to see it, even if it is so marked."

A great sigh of resignation came from Stevens' down turned head, blowing the paper he was about to read from. He returned it to its place, took the other folder and handed it to George.

Opening the folder, George read the short paragraphs:

"Chairholder Sylvana Lauretta was murdered at 2:23 SSP. She was stabbed in the heart by her own knife. The incident occurred during a fight, which started during a heated Assembly debate on new citizens' rights on SIL. Elizabeth Dunn, apprentice to Dr.

Second Pass

Malanga, the SIL medical officer, had just read a statement by Dr. Malanga, outlining the Doctor's position on medical services for newcomers to SIL. She had been interrupted by Lauretta, when Commander George McVee, Sr., intervened, overruling Lauretta's interruption. When the final sentence of the statement was read, Lauretta lunged at Commander McVee with her knife. Just before the murder occurred, Commander McVee was rushed from the Assembly Chamber to the Finder Station for medical treatment.

"Tensions have increased between the Firsters and Borns political factions on SIL, with this latest confrontation over new citizenship rights bringing hostility and much argument on the Assembly floor. Firsters believe that the original intention by Commander McVee to eradicate all references to Earth, along with all learning of earthly ways, is noble and should be adhered to, going as far as to try to deny access to SIL by new citizens. Borns, who have never known Earth and aren't familiar with the perceived ills coming from earthly society's socialization methods, wish to share their world with many, expanding society on SIL, and developing the newly formed orbital nation into a truly vital force in societies of humans. Dr. Malanga's statement, which so angered Chairholder Sylvana was: 'Our new citizens will be accustomed to various medical practices no longer used on SIL. They will expect medication in the form of chemical additive and interruption therapies such as surgery. I am fully trained in these, and have trained several new doctors in these practices before the art of Finding was developed.

"It will be difficult for new citizens to become accustomed to our atmosphere, diet, and weightlessness. As we saw in our first visitors who stayed here, there will be periods of severe diarrhea, disorientation, nausea, and sudden mood changes. They will have aches in their legs and arms, and many will experience depression as their bodies become buoyant and lose their gravity resistance composition. They will not understand why they should forgo rigorous exercise in their first two years, while watching others who have been here longer work hard to develop the physical strength they are themselves loosing. We must stand by our new citizens and offer them assistance in their transition. To make the transition of new citizens quick, and to assure their adaptation is swift and deep, it is my recommendation to start them immediately in the ways of Finding. First days are long forgotten when the body is acclimated. There is no need for special medical attention other than in extreme cases.'"

George looked at the paper again, rereading it carefully. "You will deliver a copy of this to me before the end of our meeting?"

"I will have it copied, and a copy given to you," Stevens said through tightly clenched teeth, looking then at the legal advisor with smoldering anger.

"Thank you," George said lightly, "and is there any other reason for this meeting?" George wanted to get his copy of the transmit and study it. His father had been injured, and he wanted to go to the ComRelay station at Associated and speak to SIL. He planned to ask his best friend, Paul Dunn, to find out what was happening, exactly. It was good luck that Paul's daughter had been present at the time of the murder. He would know what was happening with Commander McVee. Paul had experienced some frustration in his work because of the ill sentiment toward him and his wife, BQ, by Firsters. The very senior scientific community were also the core group of Firsters, making Paul's work even more difficult and often sabotaged. As a result, he and George had spent many hours at the ComRelay trying to guess at the true picture of things on SIL. George, with the highest security clearance possible, had seen all of the communiqués from SIL and often had more accurate information than had Paul.

"There are some very pressing issues, McVee Junior, that need to be addressed," Stevens said with a fresh smile and new papers in his hands. "We must discuss the transport vehicle placement status. Your latest numbers simply aren't high enough. Remember, we will not have another chance to populate SIL for another eighteen years. We must take full advantage of the opportunity, as I see it."

"I am not prepared to discuss that today, Mr. Stevens," George held his anger back as much as possible. "It is not fair to assume that I travel with all of my papers and research on me, particularly to an emergency session. If you want to schedule a meeting, please contact my office and they will be happy to do so."

"Uh, George," Joseph Conroy said with a slight grin and arrogant point of his finger, "surely you could take a moment to speak 'conceptually' with us on the matter. Would that be asking too much?" His deceptive little boy looks had no effect on George, who remembered well his attempt to sabotage the original mission to find SIL. Years of working together on SIL inhabitation had done

Second Pass

little to ease the tension between them, though many people told George he was silly to hold such a grudge for so long.

"There is no 'conceptual' discussion, more than a rehashing of our old debate, Joseph," George said calmly, "nor is there any indication you have changed your stance significantly. I, for my part, have not changed mine either. So there seems to be nothing to discuss here."

"Well," Stevens beamed his broadcast grin even broader, "let's see, there were 204 inhabitants at SIL's last passing, and the current population is 402, not counting the 56 currant pregnancies."

"Stevens," George interrupted, "where are you going with this?"

"Just bear with me, McVee Junior, you'll see in short order," he straightened his tie and continued. "Since that time, Mr. & Mrs. Dunn stayed and subsequently gave birth to twins, there have been 112 births to the first inhabitants, 116 births to children of first inhabitants, eighteen of the newborns died in their first weeks of life, fifteen other citizens have died of disease and old age, and Shandor left and came to Earth. That makes the current population 402, if my information is correct."

"What's the point, Stevens?" George asked with irritation.

"The point is, in terms of your last assignment roster, you allow for only 1,248 new citizens of SIL, with 312 temporary visitors from SIL to Earth, 27 citizens leaving SIL to reside on Earth until the next pass, 208 ambassadorial visits and exchanges, and 312 temporary visits from Earth to SIL. This leaves the final total population of SIL 1,623 until the next pass. Is this accurate?" He asked in a condemning tone, indicating that George was either stupid or crazy.

"Assuming there are no deaths between now and then, and remember to subtract one for Captain Lauretta leaving 1,622, and there are currently 56 pregnancies which are expected to go healthily to term, with no indication that any of those newborns will come to Earth. So, the correct figure is 1,678." George was able to rattle off the figures with speed and accuracy after having spent most of the past two weeks working and re-working the numbers.

"Yet," countered Stevens, "I see that this only accounts for 15 large shuttle runs in the four month period. We have six large shuttles, each capable of making five trips within that time.

According to my calculations, and acknowledging that two of those trips will be used by the ambassadorial missions, three for hauling fuel, and seven for transporting supplies. Why, McVee Junior, I count a total of 27 trips. We could award another 312 citizenships if we achieved full utilization. I consider this shortsighted."

George was red with anger, and started to walk around the table toward Stevens. "You may call my office to schedule a meeting regarding SIL transport, citizenship rosters and any other matters you wish to discuss." He was nose to nose with Stevens, who smiled like a damned fool. "And I believe this young man," he pointed to a messenger entering the room with an envelope, "has my papers?"

"For Dr. George McVee, Junior," the young man read the name without recognition.

"Thank you," he said to the messenger who turned and left, "and thank you all, Ladies and Gentlemen. I have important business to attend to." And he was out the door.

He fumed as he stormed down the hall toward the LOL ComRelay room. He had explained time and again that the small shuttles transporting the arrivals and supplies between the space station and SIL were overtaxed as it was, and the reserve three large shuttle trips, even if they had been full, would have left an impossible backup of people on the space station, with many possibly risking what was being called "improper delivery," which meant they would either never get to SIL at all, or get stuck on SIL never to return for 18 years until the next pass. Those large shuttle trips, only three in a four-month period, were the reserve for emergencies. Stevens knew that damned well, but he was publicly stating more citizenships were actually available than were being offered. He called for an investigation of George's office by the Federal Government to look into the shortfall. This had kept George at his office until late every night for over two weeks. He had been inundated with complaint mail on top of a new surge of inquiries about citizenship. Each letter had to be read and answered, and the first shuttle flight wouldn't leave for another 34 months.

George flashed his id badge at the laser scan eye and swung through the doors to the ComRelay station. There was a melancholy romantic quality about the sound of the dish rumbling from orientation to orientation. And it gave him great pleasure to see Liz's space coordinate system displayed electronically in

Second Pass

a 360-degree panorama. They had had a party to celebrate the installation of the display panels, and Liz was given a plaque of merit for having invented and refined the deep space system. He took personal pride in the entire setup, knowing that his invention of the Low Orbital Lens (LOL) was the main feature of the entire system.

He never was particularly neat around his living quarters or his office, but he inspected every inch of the shining marble floor and light-blazing electronic display panels. He found a dark green toothpick on the floor, which he picked up and deposited into his pocket with disgust. He would have to remember to discuss this with Woody. Woody was a good custodian, but he was older and sometimes missed things, so he wouldn't be hard on him, just sharpen him up a little.

He took a deep breath, shook the tension out of his shoulders and approached the relay station, excited to talk to Paul and find out what was happening with his father.

* * * * * * *

Solange Malanga pulled back from the monitor screen, head held high in the air, and took in a deep breath. Elizabeth knew the prayer posture well and allowed her silence in which to make her prayers and promises. The arts of Finding were tied to the forces of the void and the powers above; prayer was one of its key components. The act of praying, so different from what Elizabeth had learned at home, was truly an act of loosing the self to the larger nothing. She watched her master in prayer, examining her long graceful neck, the taught muscles of her jaw and the masterfully tied mass of hair, which floated just above her scalp. Her shoulders were slightly forward and her arms straight, holding herself at the Internal View Port. The body, slightly withered from age, was, none the less, supple. "Stretch and save," Malanga always reminded Elizabeth who disliked the two-hour daily stretch required of Finders. She remembered the early days of her Finding studies, when Malanga still had color in her hair and was not yet allowed the longer tied hairstyle afforded leaders. They would do the tandem stretches while talking about Finding, and the methods of the Seek. Those days were heaven in memory, seeming to stretch beyond the time her body had been granted its consciousness, days of perpetual revelation.

"Hemareflux," said Malanga, startling Elizabeth out of her reverie. "We must get him to the centrifuge immediately or he will pass. Quickly, Elizabeth, jet his stretcher." The command made, they sped the stretcher holding Commander McVee's body to the centrifuge area. "Preemptive: Medical!" shouted Malanga repeatedly all the way to the room, scattering people out of their way as they sped through the passageways.

When they arrived at the Centrifuge room it was in use, the large tray speeding around the parameter with a single person on it. Elizabeth hit the switch to begin its slowing process as Malanga prepared the Commander's body for its session. As the tray slowed, Jiimson, standing in the middle of it with a jump rope dangling from his hands, started yelling at them to turn the thing back on.

"Preemptive: Medical!" Malanga shouted without looking up.

"No way, Malanga," shouted Jiimson. "You can't save him, and you know it. He's too sick." He reached for the tray switch to reactivate the centrifuge.

"Do not touch that switch," Malanga warned, "I have called Preemptive: Medical."

"Ah, but I can overrule you, Solange," he used her first name as a sign of disrespect. "When Chairholder Sylvana died I became Chairholder, and as such I can overrule your hysterical rulings." He chuckled at his new power.

"But not when life is at stake!" she yelled at him. "Commander McVee is in hemareflux and must be gravitized or he will die. Stand aside, Chairholder."

Jiimson didn't budge, though he didn't turn on the switch either. He locked eyes with Malanga in defiance. If he could hold her such for long enough, McVee might die, which would greatly improve his power and make his goals more easily attained. Malanga, recognizing his tactic, calmed herself completely, handing the stretcher over to Elizabeth. She floated to the center of the room, eyes on Jiimson all the while. When she reached the center post, to which the guide wires of the centrifuge tray were connected, she held her hands in classic pyramid position and hunched her shoulders.

"What are you doing?" demanded Jiimson. "Is this more of your witchcraft? I command you to halt, woman!"

Elizabeth watched, knowing what Malanga was doing, but had never before seen it done, nor truly believed it was possible.

Second Pass

The transportation of electromagnons was a theory Dr. Malanga had developed, and was herself just beginning experiments in it. From Malanga's posture, Elizabeth knew she couldn't even hear Jiimson's bellowing, and wouldn't stop if she could. Commander McVee's life was at stake, and Malanga would do anything, including die herself, to save him.

* * * * * * *

Paul's page beep sounded as he was transferring genetic material between two vials. He had been interrupted several times by Machmood, who was clearly trying to anger him. All of the arguing, and Lauretta's murder, had people showing their political affiliation in anger and with posturing. Paul ignored his page and continued the transfer, making a mental note to answer the page when he was done.

The microscopic syringe loomed huge on the monitor screen, and the pinkish liquid, while actually only a few molecules in size, looked like a full drink tube. He made minute adjustments to the simulator controls, positioning the injection to hit at the heart of the cell. Machmood tapped him on the shoulder, ruining his approach.

"Damn it, Machmood," Paul hissed, "you've been trying to disrupt me all day. Now why did you do that?"

"Sorry, Paul," he replied with amusement in his tone, "but there is an urgent message for you to report to the ComRelay in central control room 2N." He gave his most innocent expression, "I wouldn't have disturbed you otherwise." He shrugged and tilted his head, more smug than contrite.

"Thank you," Paul said through clenched teeth. "I'll leave this as is, if you would please refrain from touching anything."

"What would I touch? Me? Ruin an experiment? You're starting to sound insulting, Mr. Dunn. Do you mean to insult me?"

"Of course not," Paul said with an artificial smile, playing the game that began when he arrived on SIL, "you are trustworthy, Elder Machmood." He bowed and jetted out of the room.

When he arrived at the ComRelay, he could see George's face on the screen through the window of the door. As he swung into position before the camera, he grinned for his friend. "George!" he said with a laugh, "what brings your face to SIL? So glad to see you."

"Hi Paul," George said, "sorry to interrupt, but I am worried about my father. We heard about Lauretta. The report mentioned your daughter in connection with him. Can you fill me in? What happened?"

"Uh," Paul realized he didn't really know what happened, other than gossip's version. "I don't know, George," he began.

"Paul, I have top clearance and you can tell me, whatever the security restrictions on you are," he said, still indignant from his run-in with Stevens.

"No, George, it's nothing like that. You misunderstood. What I mean is I don't know! I was in the lab when it all came down. I've told you before that I'm pretty unpopular here, you know. The Firsters are trying to prevent any new citizens from being fully empowered, trying to create a lower class from the beginning. It's terrible for the Borns—the accusations, the politics. And for me and BQ and our kids it's worse. You wouldn't believe it. We're the first Earth transplants; we're being watched. Anything we do is used as reasons for not granting citizenship, full citizenship, to those not originally on SIL. Like I said, it isn't even much better for the ones born here to parents who were originals. Change is the most feared commodity around. It's crazy!"

"But, what about my dad, Paul? What does this have to do with him? I read the report and it seems he was injured."

"I don't know, George. Look, I was in the lab, which I always am when there's an Assembly meeting. These old guys prevent me from getting anything at all done on regular days. When the Assembly meets, they nearly all go, leaving the lab available. I don't have much choice but to work during the meetings if I want to accomplish anything. And about your dad, I know he is at the Finder Station, and Elizabeth is helping Malanga with him. Wait, let me call down there and find out," he put the image on freeze and went to the intercom, and keyed it for private connect with Finder Station. In a few minutes he learned Commander McVee was in very bad shape with hemareflux , was at the centrifuge trying to reverse it. He sighed and reactivated the interrupted link.

"George, here I am again. He's in serious condition, but they didn't say why. They told me he's at the centrifuge trying to reverse some hemareflux problem he's having. It seems he was cut and his blood flow is suffering." An alarm went off behind Paul, and an all call sounded.

"Security to Centrifuge! Security to Centrifuge!" The announcement repeated steadily.

"Did ya hear that?" Paul asked.

"I can't make it out, what's happening?"

"They have called security to centrifuge. There must be trouble. Listen, George, I'll go down there and link back with you as soon as I can. Can you stay at Associated for a while?"

"Damnit, Paul, I hate being here with all of the shit Stevens is putting on me. But, sure, I'll stick around. Maybe I can go bother Liz," he said with resignation.

"Maybe you'll get lucky in the supply room," Paul chuckled, "worse things could happen."

"That reminds me, Paul," George couldn't believe he'd forgotten about the pregnancy, "Liz is pregnant."

"She's...WHAT? When did that happen?"

"Listen Paul, I'll fill you in on all the details, but first go see about my dad." George was getting impatient.

"Right," Paul said, "link back with you ASAP." He was gone.

George killed the relay link and erased the tracer image. He had been burned several years before when he and Paul had been on link and the tracer, used for security searches only according to its developers, when they discussed Lauretta's erratic behavior. The next morning, Joseph Conroy confronted him about the political atmosphere on SIL. The topic is always discussed at Associated, but this time Conroy was quoting things Paul had said, and George knew Paul hadn't told anyone else, even BQ according to him. Ever since, he dumped tracer images the moment transmission was ended, a thing few had the security clearance to do.

He nearly knocked Woody over as he pushed through the double doors. "Hey there, Woody, I nearly knocked you over! Sorry 'bout that," he said with a smile.

"No problem from you," Woody replied, then twisted his smile into a grimace, "but every body around here seems to think nothing of pushing me around or knocking me down. People are so rude these days. I hate to sound like the geezer I am, Georgie, but it used to be much more civil around here."

"And tidy," George said, reaching into his pocket. "Look what I found!"

Woody looked at the chewed toothpick he presented. "Look, Georgie, your mom wants me to keep an eye on you, but cleaning your pockets is not in my job summary!" He grinned the words from insult to playful nudge.

George laughed out loud. "Not my pockets, silly," he said, "I found it on the floor when I got to the ComRelay this morning. You're slacking off I believe, perhaps you need a rest?"

"Let me see that thing," he yanked it from George's fingers, "and such a nice green color too. Now why would anyone want to chew up a fine piece of forest-violation like this?" He grimaced at George menacingly, "What do you mean, a little rest, son? No way I'm about to retire. No siree!"

"I was thinking about sitting down for a coffee in the canteen. How about it?"

"Your bill?"

"My bill?"

"Okay then. Just don't be criticizin' me job," he slipped into his native brogue as he stuffed the toothpick into his own pocket. "This'll give the little woman a tad to worry me over," he said with a wink, "me pockets *arrrre* herrrr business. What's in'um, and ooonder'um!" He slapped George on the shoulder, guiding him toward the canteen.

* * * * * * *

Many hurried through the passageways to meet the security call. Junctures were tricky to navigate with hand jets as each tributary brought more volunteers careening toward the trouble. Collisions were forgiven in advance in emergencies, though the rule about taking every precaution to avoid adding injuries to responders in emergency situations was vehemently quoted by those receiving the impact. A smile would follow from those who wanted to avoid confrontation. Paul ran into several people, inflicted no injuries, nor received any, and continued toward the Centrifuge Chamber with the growing mob, a fixed smile on his face. He couldn't imagine with this many responding who the victims would be. But he knew Commander McVee, Finder Malanga, and his own daughter were in the Centrifuge. Accidents in space were harrowing, since there were such limited resources. Breeches of the station's outer skin were nearly always fatal to at least one person, though the early problem with meteors had finally been taken care of by an electromagnon shield created years before. He knew this was not this sort of emergency, though others responding wouldn't have that information.

Second Pass

The entrance looked like a beehive with many bees simultaneously trying to deposit pollen. Legs, butts, and arms protruded from the cluster of bodies in a waving mass like sea grass, with new arrivals simply adding more density to the mass. Paul surveyed the situation, knowing he would never get inside, and decided to back track and enter from the side through the Assembly Chamber, which had been closed off after the murder and remained shut. He felt no compunction breaking through the protective tape, throwing the doors open wide as he entered the Chamber.

He looked across the room. The tray spun at full G, blurring the figures on it. A streak created by his daughter's red hair verified she was assisting with Malaga and the Commander. He couldn't see any great trouble, other than the medical emergency he'd been informed of. There was a group of people struggling off to one side. He jetted to them to discover Jiimson trying to turn off the motor spinning the tray, while others prevented him.

"Give up, Jiimson," Stetler, the new head of security yelled as he struggled to hold fixed axis with the flailing Jiimson, who's torso was pinned in a bear hold.

"I don't have to take orders from a punk like you, Andrew," Jiimson snorted.

"Yes you do! I'm Head of Security and I'll see you're denied privileges in the future."

"Ha!" snorted Jiimson, "I'm Assembly Chairholder now and I'll not have my authority challenged by Security, Head or otherwise. You've no jurisdiction over me now!" His eyes opened wide and then he crumpled into flotation posture.

"What happened?" Stetler said, brushing back sweat soaked blond hair with his muscular forearm.

"Got'im with a pressinject tranquilizer," said one of the men. "It's old and so it took some work getting in position, but the jugular's pretty darn quick, isn't it?"

"You shouldn't have those," Stetler said almost with a whine, showing how overwhelmed he was in his new position. "Report to Security when this is over."

"Common, Andy, just let it go," said another man in the crowd, "there's taking your job seriously and taking your job seriously. Give the guy a break."

"Report to Security!" Stetler yelled at the first man.

"But he saved the situation!" yelled the other man.

"You report to Security too, then! I'm in charge and will have to show you I mean business!" He struggled with Jiimson's bulk, floating them toward the door. "Make way! Make way!"

Paul asked several people what was going on, and pieced the story together. Malanga had interrupted the new Chairholder from one of his first exercises of privilege, having the exercise tray to himself, and he tried to pull rank on her. She had Commander McVee with her, which gained sympathy of those nearby and Jiimson was thrown off the tray. But Paul wondered why Jiimson would be so stupid. He might be the new Chairholder, and granted he was second in line to Lauretta who hated the Commander, but surely the Commander would have been respected. Since the situation was life -threatening, there was no question he should let him on the centrifuge tray. Paul knew first hand how people were crazy since the murder, and Jiimson was making a very bad impression as the new Assembly Chairholder, indeed.

Hemareflux was on everybody's lips. Paul knew it was serious, but didn't understand it at all. Yet, since there was nothing else he could do, he could at least report that much to George, so he jetted back to the ComRelay.

Twenty-two minutes, spent in bored frustration with the sometimes sluggish ComRelay, was underscored by the certainty Machmood would have disrupted Paul's work by now, somehow, and in a way perfectly explainable. Paul called back to the centrifuge room, and to the Finders suite to gather what information would be forthcoming, only to be disappointed bitterly. SIL Communication Control intercepted every attempt to reach the two facilities, interrogating him about just why he wanted information. The usual contempt for Earth transplants was no longer hidden behind politeness protocol since Lauretta's murder, and outright hostility hissed in every word spoken to him. He took a deep breath, dreading the time to come. It would only get worse as Second Pass approached.

Finally George's face appeared, quizzical and attentive. "Well?" he nearly yelled.

"Hold on, George," Paul said as he anchored himself to the foot straps beneath the ComRelay, "I've gotta get situated here. There's so much lint on these Velcro straps they hardly hold. There, I think that's got it," he twisted his sock-clad foot beneath the strap. "I wasn't able to find out anything. Commander's being treated, Malaga's there with my little girl, working. But, its..." he shook his head in frustration.

"What? What's wrong, Paul. Is he alive?"

"Oh, he's alive, that's sure. They say it's hemareflux, so it could be pretty serious. At his age it may be fatal, but he didn't have to wait long to be treated, so my guess is he'll pull through."

"Why was security called? Is someone trying to murder him too?" George's voice was high with the tight anxiety constricting his throat.

"No-one was trying murder him, well, at least not exactly."

"What does that mean, Paul," George was angry and the vagueness of the reply, frustrated at the distance between him and his father.

"It means that Jiimson, who became Chairholder when Lauretta was murdered, was causing a commotion in the exercise room. His first official duty as Chairholder was to claim his rights to solo time on the exercise tray, if that tells you anything about his qualifications for the job, and he refused to relinquish the tray for the Commander."

"Why didn't security just throw him off? Where were they?"

"They were there, or I should say, he was there. It's Andrew, oh, I guess you wouldn't remember, he was just a little grabber when you were here last. Andrew Stetler is the new head of Security for SIL. His dad, Arthur, left his post when he'd had a few minor strokes, so Andrew took over. It seemed like he would have a couple years of experience by the time the new arrivals created any real call for Security, or so everyone thought. New Chairholder, new Security chief. God, what a mess!"

"But you haven't told me what is going on there," George was angry now, "Paul, you're the only way I can find out!"

"Don't yell George!" Paul countered, "I've had a hellofa fucking day, a hell of a fucking few years here! You can't imagine how unpopular me and my little family are."

He took a deep breath as he looked at the screen. George had aged, in gravity so it showed in startling ways to Paul's view, which had been changed to that of the perpetually gravity-free who's age doesn't show by sagging or wrinkling. George was right, of course, and Paul was his only link to the world of SIL. "Sorry, man, I know I'm the only way you can find anything out here. What was going on was this: Jiimson and Andrew were facing off. Jiimson didn't want to give up the Centrifuge, probably not realizing the Commander was in dire health, and was trying to turn it off so he could get back on. They were fighting by the switch."

"What do you mean, fighting by the switch? Where was my father? Is he okay?"

"I told you, your father was on the tray with Malanga and Lizie were with him. They had gotten Jiimson off of the tray somehow before I got there, but Jiimson wanted to get back on so he was trying to turn the switch off. And I don't know how the Commander is. All I know is they were still working on him." Paul showed his most earnest face to George to confirm his intention to relay as much information as possible.

"I know you are doing the best you can Paul," George responded, "you can understand how I feel, can't you? SIL's so far away, my dad..." his voice thickened under the weight of worry, vainly wishing Paul into actions he himself would take if there, actions only he could take. "You okay?" Paul asked.

"Yeah, I'm fine. So there's nothing to find out, even if I were on SIL. Thanks for trying, Paul," he said as he reached for the sign-off switch. Paul held up a halting hand.

"George," said in a warning tone, sharply as if a command, stopped George, "we need to talk. There are things going on here, things more dangerous than anyone is admitting."

"What things?" George asked with half disgust, half doubt.

"SIL's falling apart, George. Not the ship, she's fine, but the community. Remember how impressed we were at how well everyone got along, how easily disputes were settled and how survival required people to work together even when they disagree? People are now at each other's throats with deception and hostility. Prison has become prize, a prize everyone wants to control. The selfishness is nauseating; they feel they've nothing to lose. And I am their favorite scapegoat, me and my family. Did you ever feel hunted George? Watched by the predator ready to pounce and tear you apart?"

"The closest I've come to that is nearly getting run over the other day in the parking garage, then finding a bomb under my car. But, no, I guess not."

"A bomb?" You've got to be kidding, man. Who's out to kill you?" Paul's disbelief echoed in his raised tones.

"I'm not kidding. Liz wants me to get security, so does my mom."

"Well it sounds like they know what they're talking about. I think you should too."

"I will, don't worry. If it weren't for the kid and all I wouldn't, but now I have things to think about other than myself." George tossed it out like chucking a food wrapper. "When do you think you'll find out about my dad?"

"Wait one second, friend," Paul chuckled in disbelief, "what's this about 'the kid'? Did you get Liz knocked up?"

"Yeah, I guess I did," George said smugly, "I forgot all about that for a while there. She's pregnant! My kid! How about that?"

"Way to go George, now you get to change dirty diapers like I did! Only you won't have to chase them through the air! You'll have gravity to assist you. You wouldn't believe the mess... Are you getting married?"

"Why?" George said defiantly, "There's no reason to get married. We don't want to change things too much, I mean, it's just a baby and we have our work to do."

"God, George, I forgot how stupid you can be. Don't you remember what happened to you when you were a kid? Don't you want some stability for junior?"

"Most of the trouble when I was young was due to my parents' incompatibility. I'd have been better off if they hadn't been married; you know that. Besides, times are different now. Liz and I are different. My mom and dad didn't have a clue about being married, family, kids, none of it."

"George, you don't see how much the same you are as your parents were. You just can't see it."

"What the hell d'you mean by that? You don't have any idea what goes on here. SIL is too far away." His sudden anger made others in the room look up, and convinced Paul he'd hit on a major nerve.

"You're right, George," Paul said falling into the diplomatic role, automatic now, by which he survived. "Don't get all pissed, man, I was just... Never mind. You know what's best. I'm happy for you." They both knew Paul was backing down to save the moment. It was an admission of how much things had changed over the past fifteen years, and how they had lost touch with each other's reality. Regular ComRelay contact was not like being there, not at all.

The rest of their conversation, which was awkward and short, was a hesitation waltz of politeness and sidestepping potential emotional land mines. They talked the required length to fool themselves into believing they had settled their differences, which they hadn't. Paul would dutifully call when news of George's dad was available, as he said he would, as he would when anything major, whether personal or otherwise, occurred. He always had; so had George. And now he sat pondering friendship as previously he pondered questions of astrophysics, intent to get to the bottom of the puzzling relationships between people. Like celestial bodies, they had patterns of movement, movement effecting changes in its counterpart, affected by the slightest fluctuation in the norm. They had been friends from the beginning, though Paul's initial attitude of inferiority to George's celebrity had been annoying, real friendship later purchased by bonds of mutual ambition and inescapable life pain. Without Paul's help he wouldn't have found his father, without SIL Paul wouldn't have found Sallie, without George's self-pitying depression and Paul's phobia of space they wouldn't have found themselves able to nurture each other.

Time changes things, or things just change. Either one really, doesn't matter which. SIL's history set it apart from the beginning—apart from society, apart from government. Commander McVee took it for his personal experiment, snatching lives out of the hands of those who lived them. Had he created a monster or a paradise? Historians will dispute that for eons. For however SIL started, it failed to continue on its intended path, pulled by events and egos into becoming a nation unto itself, the infant in the sky now taking its first steps. Like all things naïve, those who abuse and take advantage, teaching bitter lessons to produce cynical wisdom and defensive self-protection, would force SIL to adulthood. Friendship simply isn't important to an emerging nation, nor family, nor justice. Self-preservation is all as would-be tyrants and conquerors line up their forces to do battle over this vulnerable child nation.

Chapter 3

Jun-Jun listened to the door latch click and then the muffled sound of his mother's jet burst sending her down the corridor to work. Free at last he jumped into his waiting warm suit, suffocated his cotton socks by adding two pairs of thermasox, put on the ultra violet protective goggles, and smeared grease over his exposed facial skin and onto his brown hair. The grease darkened the hair to a glistening black, which nearly matched his dark eyes. He was small for his age, with a lithe, athletic body. His gamin looks, he found, made people go along with him, follow him into play or prank, and it even seemed others were afraid of his rejection. He didn't really wonder about this, being the son of the 1st Officer and Communications Chief he just assumed others were below him. Slapping his hands together to bring blood heat to his fingers, he spoke into his private computer log. "Junior Bryant, 2nd Pass minus 3 E-years, 14th day of Balan, 7th hour 26th minute. Save in file "ED-Private": "Going to outbay #22 for free-lock experiment number 7, to be assisted by Erica Dunn. Where the past six free-locks have been successful in that no loss of life occurred, dramatic visualizations were achieved and sense of exhilaration was experienced. Heart rate each time has leapt to treble normal exercise high rate, blood pressure surge lasted less than twenty minutes, headache follows experience for 12 to 18 hours. Sleeping and dreaming after free-lock are intensified. This intensification seems to be a permanent change with a gradual heightening of the effect between free-locks. No other ill effects recorded. Today's free-lock will last for 30 seconds. Out."

The computer responded with the password protect check sequence, as expected. But when Jun-Jun turned to leave, the computer prompted him for a voice validation sequence, which he didn't expect. He hurried through the sequence finding the computer would accept his voice as valid only if he spoke in a lower than normal tone. He made mental note of the need to have the voice module recalibrated, and jetted hurriedly to outbay #22.

Erica's eyes rolled away from her watch, settling on her tardy mate with bored recrimination. "You are always late, Jun-Jun, always! How can the computer keep an accurate record if all of the times we record are off by ten minutes? You really don't understand the scientific process at all."

"Common, Erica, I am not always late. My computer is off; it made me do a voice validation sequence. I'll get it fixed tomorrow. Are you ready?"

"Me?" she laughed, "I hardly need to be ready to watch you try to kill yourself. Question is, are you?" She looked him up and down, from greasy head to thick-socked feet, wondering why he was so enamored of this particularly messy experiment. She had always wondered if his experiments in free-lock weren't just a death wish or some daredevil curiosity into the extent of his masculine prowess. She didn't understand, but he was her best friend so she went along with it. Besides, she found pulling him from the outbay, holding his limp, cold body close to warm it and blowing in his mouth to resuscitate him sexually stimulating, a secret she kept even from her diary.

"Ready, able and willing, you red-haired devil." He tried to kiss her on the cheek, but she squirmed away.

"Get away from me with that nasty grease all over you," she protested.

"But you don't have any problem with it in resuscitation. What's the problem, it's just a kiss."

"You know very well I do it later to save your worthless life, Mr. Experiment," she said coyly, "and if you had any other way of gaining consciousness I certainly wouldn't do it."

"When are you going to free-lock, Erica?"

She stopped to consider. She had promised, as a basis for the experiment, she would run the same number of tests as he did so there would be a set of data for male and female subjects, but as she watched him die each time she lost conviction. The thought of his cold lips on hers made her shiver. "You finish your series first, jumping out of sequence might effect the data, then where would we be?"

"You aren't going to chicken out are you?" he said with an eyebrow menacingly raised.

"Of course not," she said, her eyes going quickly to the medical scanner in her hand, busily checking his vital signs and entering initial settings. "Well," she said checking the screen once more, "looks like we're ready. All set?"

"Sure am," he smiled confidently. "Let's get started!"

Second Pass

She steadied him as he entered the outbay compression lock. It was a tight squeeze only because he couldn't allow any of the grease to get on the lock's opening and, since grease was on his head and hands, he rolled into a ball while Erica jostled him through the opening with care. Weightlessness had always been a fun game while they were growing up, and most kids on SIL were skilled at maneuvers, which made adults cringe or rush to the rescue, but now it was a problem. A slight touch caused an extreme rebound, and a finger caught for the briefest moment could create an unintended movement of catastrophic result. She watched his location, her own, monitored the pressure of each grip and rate of release while trying to stabilize her position by wedging her feet. He got in the bay, no grease on the rubber concealing ring. She locked the outbay cutting off verbal communication while Jun-Jun started his meditation.

Youth overlooks potential death in the way idealism is replaced by resignation in the elderly, yet each is perilously close to death. Death is a constant; reactions to it vary predictably according to chronological station. Erica looked through the thick, tinted window. Here, where life and death perpetually viewed each other through a thick piece of Plexiglas, death's eyes were now joined by those of her best friend as he lifted his head from reverie and, snapping the tether securely to his belt, gave her the signal. Seeing it, she punched in the sequence for opening the outer door to space.

Jun-Jun went instantly pale as his air was sucked into the frozen vacuum of space. The purple cast to his skin came from the tint of glass, yet shook Erica every time. The first time produced panic in him; he wildly waved his arms around and gasped for air, eyes bulging. It had been an accident. The door was open for only 12 seconds that time. A careless technician had bumped the controls when Jun-Jun's helmet was not yet connected to his safe suit. His limp body had been rushed to the Finders, who gradually warmed him and brought him back to consciousness, amazed at how fast the body temperature was sucked into the ice of space on the side of SIL away from the sun. The speed was exactly as fast as the air expanded into nothing. But Jun-Jun had had a profound experience, one shared with Dr. Malanga at great length. He had seen his own death, and his life after death. Trembling from fear was replaced with wonder—a sure knowledge that dying wasn't really that bad at all. Now he left it open for 30 seconds, no more by Erica's jurisdiction over the controls, though he would have preferred longer experiences of death. Erica's insistence that after more than 30 seconds the body would explode and re-entry into life would be useless with an exploded body convinced him as much as he had little choice in the matter, since she was at the controls inside SIL as he willfully died outside.

She shut the outside door and re-pressurized the bay, the purple corpse floating still as cloud, awaiting her resuscitation and the animated conversation sure to follow. The shroud of purple left as the door swung it's tinted window open leaving a gray limp body to remove as carefully as she had placed it moments ago. Free of the rubber ring, but now covered with grease herself, she locked lips with her friend and started blowing into his mouth, then forcing his exhale with her rhythmic bear hugs.

She began to worry after fifteen breaths. The unresponsive body became an ungainly burden, legs and greased arms floating limp in a kaleidoscoping mass impossible to hold from any angle, but she kept up her pump-blow-pump-blow with tears floating in little balloons away from her desperate face. With a loud sob she let go of the body and covered her face with oily hands, she was a failure to her friend and a murderer. A sharp crack of blinding light flashed her to darkness.

An instant eternity later she was looking into Jun-Jun's eyes, huge and close, innocently staring at her asking the silent question "Why?". So this would be her hell, an eternity of staring into the beautiful innocent eyes of the friend she'd murdered. Her eyes locked in horror at the sight an anguished scream came, and enveloped her. "NO!" the scream echoed over and over into the emptiness of her death.

The eyes changed, corners wrinkling as if the face held a smile, growing closer until she felt a kiss on her cheek. "Sorry I knocked you out," Jun-Jun said, "I guess I spasmed when I came back, I think my leg kicked you in the head. You were unconscious for about two minutes, Erica, you scared me."

She regained her conscious mortal form and pushed him away. "Get away from me. You gave me the scare of my life. I thought I was dead! And we aren't ever going to do this stupid free-lock again, EVER!" She shook with tears, hugging herself.

"What's the big deal? We can't stop the experiment now, we're just getting started."

Second Pass

"You find someone else to shoulder your murder rap. But it won't be me. Do you hear me Jun-Jun? It won't be me!" He tried to get close to her, but she kept him away like a terrified animal.

"I don't know what you're talking about," he put his hand to his head, "my head is throbbing, but I'll tell you, this was the best, Erica, the very best yet! I saw things you wouldn't believe! I went farther into the tunnel this time, I nearly got to the end. It was so..."

"Do you know what is at the end of the tunnel? Do you!" she screamed to interrupt him. "It's death, Jun, DEATH! When you get to the end you are dead! Don't you see? All of the euphoria, the 'great visuals' you talk about - it's about being dead. And if you get to the end of the tunnel, I will be responsible for murdering you! I won't do it, Jun, I refuse!"

He looked startled. Of course he had realized the addictive sensations he so loved were the result of the air and heat being sucked from his body, but he hadn't thought he would actually die. She was right; it was dying that brought these sensations. "I..." he started, but ended with a sigh.

"Why do you want to do this? Why?" she demanded, sobbing.

"Well, I was just thinking of Commander McVee, I wanted to be like he was."

"That doesn't make any sense at all. He never died, you idiot."

"But my mom and dad told me about the Commander. When he was an outlaw. You remember from our history class, don't you? How he hid in the ship out-structure to keep from being caught? How he discovered the Eye?" He looked searchingly at her, unable to conceive that she didn't understand.

"Jun-Jun, he never left the ship's atmosphere. The Eye had sealed off the rupture in the outer hull; we learned that in engineering. I don't understand what this has to do with you trying to kill yourself at all. You're crazy!" She strapped on her jet pack to leave, but he grabbed it from her.

"Wait, Erica, wait!" He spun her toward him, causing them to revolve as a pair. "My parents told me he was willing to go into space, to die. He was going through the out-structure to the place of the blast to die if he needed to. He was going to find out what was out there. Well, I've always wanted to be as brave as he was. I was named after his son, you know."

She looked with disbelief knowing she was crazier than he, unable to harbor ill feelings, but still unwilling to continue the experiment. "We can't do this any more, Jun-Jun. I can't. You are taking this Commander hero worship too far and I can't be part of your death. Why don't you do some of the other things he did if you want to be like him so much? You could develop better O_2-producing plants, or work for the Assembly to help him form the type of laws he wants for here. Why, you could work in the Chapel - anything! He is a hero, but that isn't worth dying for."

He knew she was right, and knew too he wouldn't find anyone else to help him free-lock. "Why are you so upset this time? Everything was the same. It didn't matter the last time."

"You're wrong, it wasn't the same. I couldn't resuscitate you this time."

"But you did! Here I am."

"No, I didn't. I gave up. I worked and worked at it, squeezing you and blowing into your mouth, but you didn't respond. I left you for dead because I was too weak to bring you back. You came back on your own somehow."

"You're right," he said quietly. "I did."

"What?" she wasn't sure she'd heard him.

"I did come back on my own. I was in the tunnel, in the light, going to the warm. I saw me and you here, you were so desperate trying to bring me back, but I was too far away. I saw you give up, I saw you stop. That's when it happened, right at that moment."

"What happened? You're scaring me."

"I had the choice, I knew coming back was the right thing. I saw it all, everyone on SIL, the future and the past. I saw the whole thing and saw how I fit into it, that I still had things to do. I decided to come back then, to finish what I needed to finish, what I'm here for."

His tranquility echoed in the soft high pitch of his voice as if time had turned back the new manhood in his body to replace it with angelic prepubescence. His movements were light and airy, his smile a flood of light directed wherever it faced. Color returned to his skin and hairs stood up all over his body in static electric expansion to a new, larger form.

"What's happening to you?" Erica asked softly, in awe.

"I don't know exactly," he beamed, "but I feel strong, big. Somehow I am not just a body anymore, I'm more than that now. And purpose. I have purpose. I didn't have that before."

Second Pass

"Malanga," she said simply, "you have to go to Malanga. I think there is something wrong with you. Maybe there's internal bleeding, or something is wrong with your brain."

"No! Not Malanga. It isn't anything to do with my body or my brain. My spirit has become real in me, I am ready to begin my work." He floated away in a trance-like state, leaving Erica frightened and alone. She watched him leave as she slowly put on her jet pack and jetted to join him.

Chapter 4

The Overseers meetings always started with a reading of the Commitments and Agreements, followed by a chanted song prayer of Memory and then the Commander spoke. A regular meeting. On Adjur, at the end of the month of Balan, the Overseers took that 4.8 minutes of extra 'adjustment' time to announce some special new gift from them to the inhabitants of SIL. Balan, the thirteenth month of the SIL calendar, was considered a festive month, a month of giving thanks for the Eye and for the fact they were alive and free from Earth. Throughout Balan were festivals, ceremonies, and games. Many individuals received commendations for jobs well done.

This Balan had been different. The elevation of Andrew Stetler as Head of Security was turning out to be an unpopular issue with the Firsters, and Sylvana's death made matters worse.

As the Overseers traveled their various routes to the Finding Chamber, where Commander McVee floated his way to recovery from hemareflux, all were aware of the tension on the faces of most Silians. Normally the Balan meeting of Overseers turned SIL giddy with excitement as to what the Adjur gift would be. But the Overseers were not meeting in the Eye Chapel because of McVee's health, and it was as if the change in location changed the mood.

Dr. Malanga was thrilled the Overseer Meeting would be held in the Finding Chambers, for it gave her the rare opportunity to observe these oldest Silians as a group rather than individually. Her long-held expectation that these people would be dying of old age soon had been joyfully proved incorrect; the older they got the healthier they got. She hadn't talked about this to anyone except her Sponsors, because she wasn't quite sure if this phenomenon was a result of her newly discovered practices of Finding, or because of some unexpected benefit of living on SIL. She was hopeful this meeting, and her observation of it, would settle some of her questions, or bring out other ones which would lead her to understanding. With Commander McVee sick, it gave her the excuse she needed to attend the normally secret meeting, and to have her Sponsors present at his side as well. Each Sponsor had been given a very specific aspect of the group to study.

Second Pass

Commander McVee was held firmly in place in a healing perch, surrounded by deep orange and maroon drapes typical of the Finding practices for convalescence. Dr. Malanga had placed him in the large chamber just outside of her actual suite of offices and had the structural engineers build a circular rail at three levels with harness attachments for the Overseers. There was soft reflected light coming from behind the Commander's perch, and additional lighting for individual Overseers at each station on the rail. There had been some difficulty connecting the electrical supply lines for amplifying and recording the session, but all devices were in place and had been tested. Singly and in clusters Overseers arrived, jetting first to Commander McVee's side to ask after him and then to their stations.

The gathering was solemn, as always, but also sad. There were three hours until Adjur and they had not decided on a proper gift for this year. Many things had been discussed, and even a few had been placed into the category of final choice, but the death of Sylvana changed many things for, other than those who had died in the explosion set by the Commander thirty-three years ago, this was the first murder on SIL. Though the actual murderer had not been identified in the melee, there was an investigation to find the person and, rumor had it, the gift might be to grant amnesty as the Adjur offering to Silians.

A sad-eyed Commander looked over those gathered, recalling his past dealings with each. Alexander Machmood, Chief Elder, had been his enemy in the beginning. He and Machmood had been at the NASA Academy together and formed a fierce rivalry, as was promulgated by the program itself. Where Machmood had eagerly gone after every new technological fad, McVee had stuck to the slower route of waiting until things had been proved before jumping on the bandwagon. Soon their abilities pitted them directly against each other, vying for the slot of Commander of SIL. The battles between the men became famous, each trying to out perform the other in all tests of knowledge and skill. In the final assessment, McVee had won the position, Machmood being assigned the prestigious position of Flight Crew Coordinator, but McVee's departure for SIL on that early flight was delayed so he could receive the Nobel Prize. Machmood became "acting" Commander of SIL until McVee's arrival, and the two found the compromise amicable, until McVee defied the trends of the day and created a scandal when he received his Nobel Prize by giving his acceptance speech in writing, displayed on the autovision but not spoken to the public, as a protest to the increase in illiteracy rates at the time. Machmood watched from SIL with disgust, for he had been a strong supporter of automated learning, video books, teacher remote classrooms, and all other progressive movements in education. When McVee was suddenly sent to SIL earlier than originally planned to quiet the scandal on Earth, Machmood waited for him with renewed anger and readily accosted him upon his arrival.

The subsequent explosion of the spare oxygen tank, killing crew members and jolting SIL into its current eccentric orbit, happened at the height of their renewed conflict. When it became clear McVee had deliberately set the explosives to 'prove a scientific point,' Machmood organized the posse to find, and destroy, him. This, of course, began the rivalry between philosophies on SIL, ultimately resulting in the current political situation. Ever since, SIL's population was divided into vehemently opposed camps. McVee was restored to the good graces of the general population, more or less, by the discovery of the Eye and it's oxygen-producing potential, thus saving all of their lives. And it was his expertise alone needed to develop that discovery into a working oxygen-production plant. Over the years the men stayed as friendly opponents, but these last few weeks had started to make them friends. McVee wasn't fooled by their moment of peace, for he knew Machmood was first and last his rival, friendly or otherwise. If anything happened to McVee, Machmood would become Commander, an eventuality Machmood reminded him in jest, which wasn't really jest at all.

Kitty Quan was seventy-five years old and, as Resource Planning Chief, she was remarkable. Other than the fact that McVee had developed a way to manufacture oxygen, it was Kitty who really had kept them all alive. Her greatest asset was the fact she never questioned need, just how to provide for it. She found materials on SIL no one knew existed, created new materials through engineering and chemistry, and was able to grab things from space and turn them into useful, lifesaving resources. Only she could support life out of the components of a meteor, glow dust, gas clouds, and the mysterious residue from space that formed a perpetual tail on SIL's outer shell. She taught her skills to as many young people as possible, but they lacked both her attitude

Second Pass

and the sheer determination to create. Her nickname had been Magic when the crew was limited to its original ranks, but that had changed to Magi when some of the children misunderstood the fable "The Gift Of The Magi" to be about their beloved Kitty. Kitty had never said one political word in her entire time aboard SIL and never took sides in arguments. She established and maintained an atmosphere of wisdom at Overseer meetings far beyond the actual wisdom in the room.

Ernestine Wasserman floated in her perch like an emaciated parrot. At seventy-three she still had flame red hair cut to form an egg shape around her head instead of the usual circular cut most preferred. Why she kept her hair that way was unknown, and anyone who questioned it was met with the coldest indignant stare possible. She was secretive, collected small things—bits of this and that—and was argued bitterly with Kitty Quan when one of her bits was needed for Kitty's work. She had been a carpenter on the original crew, and while not spectacular in any aspect of her designs, she was reliable. She volunteered for every assignment involving danger and spoke only regarding her work. She had never been involved with any person in friendship, sex, or partnership of any kind, and simply refused to talk about herself. In political matters she tended to do whatever her Commander seemed to want, being loyal to the position rather than to the man. This made her appear contradictory in the large picture of her allegiances, yet once she decided what her stand would be there was no swaying her. McVee usually tried to get her thoughts first on important matters, to know exactly where she stood. Her stances, though based on an allegiance to the Commander, were seldom predictable to him.

As Chief of Design Henry Wan Lu was a bit of a prima donna. He ran his shop as an emperor and was a tyrannical teacher. His family on Earth had been a foster home, and though he had the clearly Chinese name of that family, he was strangely mixed between Turkish and Mandarin, giving him a Taras Bulba look. The Turk blood had gone to fat in his face, balanced by a rather large nose. He was strictly Firster in his politics, shunning any mention of Earth. He often incited rebellious feelings in the young with his terrible accounts of the ills of Earthly life. He sat ready to pounce, McVee knew, to convince everyone Sylvana's murder was an example of the horror SIL would surely become when new arrivals from Earth took position in Silian society. His shunning of Paul and BQ and their family was nearly violent, and he held McVee personally responsible for the Commander's son's friend being there at all. For a man of seventy-three years he was more fit than most men of forty, and seemed to be getting stronger every day.

Steven Upine and Crawford Lun had been a couple since the earliest days of SIL, even before McVee had joined the mission. Their relationship was not taken seriously at first, since Lun was much younger than Upine and had worked as a Battery Maintenance Engineer. These engineers were the least trained of the crew, with only a certificate of Electrical Proficiency necessary to get the job. Lun, who had been only twenty years old when he arrived on SIL, was extremely muscular, strikingly good looking, and had a penchant for wrestling with the other young guys on board. Upine, indirectly in a supervisory capacity as a Solar Engineer, had regularly assigned Lun to his work crews, and was erotically interested in the wrestling of young men. As the first homosexual couple on SIL, others treated them with exaggerated politeness. But when the explosion occurred, these two showed stronger loyalty to each other than any of the established couples at the time, and worked tirelessly to help the injured, repair the structure, and comfort the distraught. Dr. Malanga unofficially deputized them as assistants in the Medical Quad, and sent them to comfort and assist the ill for as long as anyone could remember. They were so respected by grateful fellow Silians that young guys would purposely wrestle with each other in their presence as a show of their acceptance of their particular sexual interest. Once they were so unconditionally accepted by the rest of the crew, all prejudice or intolerance of any particular sexual taste or romantic interest vanished. McVee was eternally grateful to them, and held Upine in high esteem as a friend, and fellow Elder, often turning to him for guidance.

Erica Pimmit, the same age as Steven Upine, was an Astronomer in the Star Mapping Division. She was a Celestial Cartographer of extraordinary ability. Her discovery of elements beyond gravitational pull, which play part in determining orbits of celestial bodies, won her the Nobel Prize in Science the same

Second Pass

year as McVee, though she was already on SIL when the prize was announced. Her acceptance was also unusual, for she determined that her $300,000 prize be put into a special fund to support life on SIL, and called for other wealthy people to do the same, resulting in a SIL fund of over $6 billion. Her leave from SIL, during which she was to sign all of the papers and create a governing board of the trust, never happened as result of the explosion. The money would have been lost, or gone back to the original donors, had she not sent properly executed documents preventing the fund from being tampered with by any one other than her or her attorney, Stanley Buckman. Stanley refused to relinquish the funds when the crew was declared dead by the government, thinking it would one day be put to use to conduct a better search. The changed climate regarding space exploration, as the result of the alleged tragedy on SIL, rendered him powerless to do so, but got him angry enough to refuse to cooperate. The other donors had given their donations on the same agreement, which Pimmit stipulated as a requirement for donations to be made in the first place. It was this fund that formed the basis of George McVee, Junior's current position. And Pimmit sat in her old age with a permanent smile on her face; she devilishly believed she was cleverer than anyone, and may well have been. She conducted herself with restraint and played her cards very close to her chest in Overseer matters. She was detested by Firsters for having created the funding now responsible for bringing new Earth-born inhabitants to their world, but feared by the Borns as a potential megalomaniac who might just call in her favors when they arrived and form a coalition to overthrow SIL. Neither of these positions made much sense to her, but she wasn't about to tell them that and end her fun.

Lee Ray Smoot, the youngest Elder at seventy years, was simply a computer geek with no social abilities whatever. His thick glasses, elongated neck and bulbous eyes won him the nickname "Turtle Man" from the children of SIL, and earned him constant mockery all of his life. Yet, on SIL, he had somehow captured the interest of Lula Stern, the only Programming Secretary in the first crew and one of the sexiest women on SIL. Speculation as to why led to legends about the size of his penis, and, generations later, the male sex organ was now called the 'smoot' on SIL. When the explosion first occurred and it was unclear if they would survive, Lula found herself pregnant with a little girl. They instantly called on the chaplain to marry them and when the child was born she was named Colla. The development of the Eye Chapel and subsequent ritual chanting of names of things from the Earth, the only time references to earthly things was allowed in the early days, formed the collective assumption her name was simply a reference to Coke Cola. But actually the name was short for Collateral, the appropriate expression for how the parents viewed their child. To these computer-absorbed lovers, the child represented their faith in being rescued. It turned out that Colla was as much a bombshell as her sexy mother, as were there other daughters: Perception, Conscience, and Defiance. Blind as a bat, Lee Ray Smoot squinted from his Velcro post across the chamber at Commander McVee, a man he thought he knew something about, but could rarely remember what exactly that was.

The group before the Commander represented survival, and survival was the main topic on his agenda for the meeting.
"Elders of SIL," he began as usual, "we are still alive!" A murmur, more than an acknowledgement, came from the group. "Okay," he conceded, "that doesn't seem so grand today as it did a few decades ago. Nevertheless, we remain the focus of Earth and will take on more vulnerability as a result."
"Commander McVee, Senior," an acid voice of Erica Pimmit interrupted, "funny that you are suddenly interested in Earth, not to mention the *dreaded* Earth presence here in your little maniac's heaven!" Groans and giggles came from several of the Elders, though most just looked with faint and expectant interest at the Commander. "Lucky for my fortunes to help provide housing here on SIL for those who want it. But I wonder, Commander, if your early fears will be materialized by the presence of these newcomers. Your indoctrination of paranoia is very alive in my memory, and I would love to see if you were justified or merely crazy in those days."
"Overseer Pimmit," McVee began, "save your sermons. How you judge me is not of great interest to me nor of relevance to this meeting. And a day without being reminded of your Earthly wealth would be a relief to us all." There was approval at this, and Henry Wan Lu even clapped. "We have serious business to discuss, and decisions to make about our Adjur gift. You know Chairholder Sylvana was an irritant to me, yet her memory must be honored and her place in our history preserved. There is sentiment that

Second Pass

we should grant immunity to her murderer as an Adjur gift, and sentiment to severely punish this act of treason. We must decide this within a short time so our gift can be presented in time. Commander's Vision, first given, is such:

"My own action in early days threatened the lives of all Silians and took the lives of eleven. You, Machmood, hunted me, wanting me dead for my offense, justifiably. The deliberate explosion of the spare oxygen storage tank was a large risk, not understandable to many even today, but a risk for science which produced positive results and new hope. That I am here today, alive and relatively well, is because I was granted amnesty for my offenses in view of the gains. Many argue I was only spared execution because my knowledge was vital to survival, and that I've held everyone hostage with this knowledge." Knowing looks were exchanged between many of the Elders, but tradition held their tongues; each was allowed to make statements uninterrupted.

"Sylvana Lauretta was not my friend, and was completely opposed to everything I stood for. She rebelled against my ideas about SIL as an Earth-free haven, yet, in time, I saw the fallacy she proclaimed to all, as she grew to adopt my early views politically. She has always opposed me, and in her opposition has always provided balance. Every system must balance to function. CV is she should be honored and her murderer, if caught, should be kept in holding for a period of 4 E-years and then tried in accordance with the views afforded by time distance from the murder."

CV, Commander Vision, set the tone for discussion and had very strong influence over the final outcome. Overseers were required to discuss with the intention to uphold a CV, bringing forth all arguments for and against, pointing out related secondary concerns. During this discussion, the Commander had to remain silent, adding nothing to his statement, neither defending nor rebutting any position. When the final vote was taken, the Commander did not vote, but considered the outcome and accepted it as the best way to uphold the CV or reject it. If rejected, the Commander could restate the CV and was allowed to add to it, and the process was repeated. That they were just hours from Adjur meant the discussion had to have an outcome. If it were rejected, the Adjur gift would have to be decided, and would most likely be the distribution of new fruits developed by the biobotanical team. This had been the planned Adjur gift before Sylvana's murder.

So the discussion proceeded, heated, cooled, argued, and shouted until a decision was crafted. Malanga and her Sponsors watched the Elders carefully, looking at stress reactions, skin coloration, outward signs of blood pressure, and epinephrine production. They noted little out of the norm for heated argument, but saw many strange psychological effects. Moods were inconsistent, alliances in argument were temporary and protean, a short temper could follow or precede a show of tolerance, and small victories were gloated over openly. They were surprised that the Overseers process was so human and interactive, though never having seen it before, anything at all would have been surprising to them. They noted everything, each watching their assigned Elders.

Machmood held the consensus papers and read from them. "Overseers find Commander's Vision inherently good and just, upholding principles of Silian law and life, respectful of Elder's rights to decide and properly flexible," he began with the prescribed statement he knew by heart. "Overseer Vision is to pursue investigation to apprehend the murderer and follow the course of Silian Law in granting holding for a period of 4 E-years and then tried in accordance with the views afforded by time distance from the murder. The Adjur gift thus being unrelated to this incident of the murder itself. Political reaction to this will be sharply divided along party lines and is anticipated to give little or no relief to the current tensions on SIL. Strongest will be the supporters of Sylvana Lauretta, angry that her death will not be brought to justice immediately. Borns will likely taunt these newly angered Firsters by gloating over their implicit victory, further exciting tensions between the groups. Adjur gift recommendation is the declaration of a commemoration to Chairholder Sylvana in form of permanent renaming of a portion of SIL in her memory, to be decided by Overseers should the OV be accepted by the Commander."

McVee was not surprised by this compromise. It did uphold his CV. He was impressed by the extent to which the individual Elders were able to look past personal political alliances and recognize the larger problem of morale on SIL. He accepted the OV and it was written into the Visions Chronicle, and then turned to the resulting question of the Adjur gift. He had to present a CV on it very soon, for it was only two hours until Adjur now. *Damn responsibility*, he fretted inwardly. This system was difficult for a Commander, for he had to think quickly and decide almost instantly things that would permanently alter the future. He was unsure how he would do this when Malanga jetted forward.

"Commander," she said softly, "you are showing signs of stress. We cannot allow your blood pressure to elevate further or hemareflux might recur. May I suggest a ten-minute recess? Is that allowable to the Overseers? I have no experience with your processes and do not mean to suggest the inappropriate."

"Dr. Malanga," Machmood said loudly, "I do not see any change in the Commander at all! What are these signs?" He scowled at her menacingly, and she started to hum.

"Look at the slight purpling under his jaw, the visible pulse of his jugular and the protrusion of his eyes."

"I see nothing," he said after jetting across to McVee, "nothing that wasn't there before."

"May I interrupt?" McVee asked, jumping at the chance to get more time to think. "The doctor is right, I am feeling slightly light headed. Let us recess for five minutes."

The odd thing about these meetings was there was no reaction to anything at all from the Elders, except when they spoke. The medical staff didn't know if this was usual or not, it certainly wasn't within the realm of normal psychology. They noted the response, or lack of it, in their subjects and looked at each other a bit confused. Malanga, however, didn't seem to even notice, though they recognized her humming as a pacification, not a sedation.

* * * * * *

"You can't do it Lizzie," insisted Erica, "if you tell we'll get restricted!"

"It sounds like that would be a very good idea! He could have died out there! He *did* die out there!"

"Since when did you become such a big shot adult, huh? You aren't any fun anymore. Ever since you started your Sponsorship with Doctor Malodorous you just don't see the fun in life." Erica pushed her fists together in exasperation as she always did. "Why do you have to act like such a... such a..."

Elizabeth looked at her twin sister and considered her options. What she had just heard about Jun-Jun was dangerous and ridiculous. Not only was the boy putting his life in danger, he was putting all of SIL in danger of a hull breach. She didn't know what that meant exactly, but it was bad. Hull breach was the first terror word any child learned in school; the term used for an oddball child as well. Malanga would certainly be interested in seeing him for an examination, to make sure he hadn't damaged his health balance. There were parts of the story much more interesting than illness, death, or the destruction of SIL.

"Look, Erica," she smiled while humming inaudibly, "I'll just tell her to have him in for an energization session. He'll love that, we'll have Toby do it, he's Jun-Jun's favorite anyway. And Toby will know the questions to ask and update the file on his health."

Erica looked suspiciously at her sister. "You won't tell what we did?"

"I won't tell," she promised.

"How will I know? What will you ransom me for guarantee?" Erica folded her arms across her chest and waited. Asking for a ransom as a guarantee was serious. Possessions were precious on SIL, and all the kids knew what each other kid had, so when they saw Erica with something of Lizzie's they would know Erica had the upper hand in something. The mystery would be good for her image, and she needed new friends now that Jun-Jun wouldn't talk to her anymore.

"Oh, alright! Damn you Erica! I'll ransom my..."

"Your new jet gloves!" she interrupted.

"My new... I can't do that. Everyone will know."

Erica's evil smile said it all, and Lizzie's humming was not affecting her twin, as usual.

"Shit. Okay, my new jet gloves," she said, throwing them at her.

Erica reached out and caught the gloves with little effort, her eyes never leaving her twin.

* * * * * * *

"I'll talk to you later, Elizabeth," Malanga said, "the Commander is about to resume and you need to be watching him," she reminded.

"Okay, but at least let me schedule an energization for Jun-Jun with Toby. I'll explain it all later."

"Of course that would be fine, Elizabeth," the doctor was confused. "You know you don't have to ask me to schedule an

Second Pass

energization." She looked at her best student and realized there was something serious the girl wanted to discuss. "We'll have a consult right after the notes on the Overseers are compiled," Elizabeth looked relieved. "But it will take you away from the Adjur Celebration, is it worth that?"

"Oh yes, it is," she said to her mentor, "it certainly is."

"Well, child, you are making a good impression on me and I realize this is very important. I've never known you to forgo Adjur. Very interesting, indeed," she said as she jetted to the Commander's side.

"Order," the Commander intoned as he pressed the play button on the sound machine. The low sound of the brass bell recording reverberated as the Elders took their positions again. He looked at them with the new enjoyment felt by all who cheated death and would now continue to reside on the ego side of the void. When they were in place, he continued.

"Commander's Vision, second given is such: Adjur Gift to the general population will be new fruits developed. First the succulents, which are ripe, harvested, and will be prepared into tarts as soon as word gets to the kitchen."

They all looked at each other, finding no objection to the Vision. It was a very good gift and they all wanted to taste the new fruits themselves.

"Just one minute!" the squeaky voice of Ernestine Wasserman made each of the Elders jump. Her raw caw was as disturbing as her hair.

"What could you possibly find to object to?" asked Kitty. "Why don't you just enjoy your pies like the rest of us?"

"Miss Quan," Ernestine puffed, "I believe I have the floor! Do I not have the floor? Don't I have the floor! I have the floor, you shut up!"

"Jesus, Ernestine," Henry Wan Lu chimed in, "you have the damned floor. God, how I hate these meetings."

"Well," said Ernestine in victory, "why don't you just die then and make room for some fresher ideas in here?"

The Commander was scarcely able to obey the silence rule. In his interpretation of the law, he was to remain silent while they found the best way to uphold his Vision, and this certainly didn't constitute discussion of the Vision. But he could feel Erica Pimmit's eyes burning a hole in his head, just waiting for him to make one sound. She lived to uphold rules, allowed scant room for interpretation, and took great glee in stumping Overseer Balan meetings. So he sat silent and let them bicker.

"So," Ernestine continued, "you have the kitchens ready, do you Commander? Isn't that a bit cocky, to assume we will automatically accept your Vision? Is this an indication of your sentiments against poor Sylvana, or just another supremacy ploy?" Even though she knew he wasn't allowed to answer her, she remained silent, as if waiting, for dramatic effect. The only sound was a groan from Dr. Wan Lu, not loud enough to enlist the fastidious Pimmit's objection, but clear enough to express his opinion. "Nothing to say for yourself, Commander? Figures!" She laughed. "Well, why do we have to waste energy on cooking? Let them cook for themselves."

"You know it takes more energy if everyone cooks for themselves than if the kitchens cook them, Ernestine," said Kitty. "You just want to be ornery. I move we vote."

"Supported!" yelled Wan Lu.

"In favor," said Erica Pimmit blandly.

Everyone made the affirmative gesture, including, to Wan Lu's disgust, Ernestine.

"Adjur gift granted," Pimmit yawned. "Tell the kitchen," she said to her assistant, who jetted out of the room.

"Good," the Commander said, knowing that along with the assistant, all spies, who would find out from the messenger en route, would be jetting all over SIL to spread the word of the Adjur gift. He planned this moment for his most serious discussion, a discussion that had to be kept private. "Dr. Malanga, I must insist your entire staff leave for a few moments. You alone may stay to observe me, but there are things of utmost urgency to discuss at this time, of a nature that is inappropriate for even you to hear."

"Of course, Commander," Malanga said. "All of you go to the lesson room until I call for you." As they left the room, the Elders waited in tense silence. It was very rare for this to happen at all. The strangeness of the new location for their meeting was disturbing as it was, but these words from the Commander meant there was something they didn't yet know about to consider, something important.

"We seem to be alone. May I remind you, Malanga, that you are under penalty of expulsion if you let what you hear be known

Second Pass

outside of these chambers. I believe you are trustworthy in this regard?"

"Commander, if you would like me to leave as well, I am happy to."

"That isn't necessary. Let us continue," he smiled at her briefly, and then turned to the others. "Let me make an Information Statement. We have a serious situation. Eleven Earth governments through the secure uplink, each have contacted me offering vast sums of new technology and a treasure of goods if we set up exclusive manufacture contracts with them. The Turkish are even promising the development of a new type of craft that will allow us to have Earth access for three years each pass instead of only four months. It is hard not to be swayed by these offers. As we approach Earth this pass we are in a situation unparalleled in history. We are a new nation, about to have our citizenry multiplied many fold. We have principles to live by here, principles that cannot be understood by the Earth-bound. I suspect there will be many leaks of information and many bribes. When the new arrivals are here we will have to keep a careful watch for those who carry these bribes. At this point in our development it would be most unfortunate to be compromised.

"Commanders Vision, third given is such: We are a sovereign nation, unique to all other nations. We are small but hold great promise and power to Earthly governments. It is time we recognize our strength and conduct ourselves accordingly. The murder of Sylvana is only an indication of the sort of threat we now must guard against. Our current two parties, Firsters and Borns, will soon be threatened by the incoming citizenry who will, most likely, want to form their own party. This party will, of course, far outnumber both of our small groups in a very short time. They will not understand what it means to live here; they will probably treat this as a vacation home to begin with.

"We have avoided the issuance of currency thus far, and, as we decided in our last meeting, new currency will be developed. With currency will come the potential for a class struggle between rich and poor. We must begin today to develop our new way of thinking, our new system of laws."

Every eye in the room, with the exception of Dr. Malanga, was on the Commander. Even Ernestine was looking steadily and soberly at the Commander. These words made real all of the ominous projections each had conceived; SIL would never be the same again.

"I have some laws to propose at this time. Proposed law A: New political parties can only be formed by citizens who have lived on SIL for one entire pass. Proposed law B: Any currency beyond that used to support a specific individual or family will be held in a bank for use at Adjur. Proposed law C: New businesses can only be owned by citizens who have lived on SIL for a minimum of an entire pass. Proposed law D: Marriage between new arrivals and long-standing citizens does not change the status of new citizens in these regards..."

He went on for nearly forty minutes. Elders were scribbling furiously. Things were serious indeed.

* * * * * * *

"Decline in physical tremors, so there was more coordination than noted a year ago," reported Toby, "even old Ernestine didn't..." The others snickered.

"I believe you mean Elder Wasserman?" Malanga corrected. "Sponsors can't afford to have personal reactions to others, Toby. You must remain in full connection to properly observe. And you others," she gestured to the room, "shouldn't fall for these little jokes when discussing those we observe." Her voice was calm and collected, without a hint of recrimination or judgment, yet the Sponsors felt the sting of reprimand as strongly as if she had slapped them.

"My apology, Doctor, her hair makes me think she is silly," Toby blushed at the admission. "My report is over now."

"Very good," Malanga said with a smile, "you have all observed well."

"But why do you make us watch the old ones so carefully Doctor?" asked Elizabeth.

"We don't know the effects of aging in space yet; these are the first to live to such an old age. The normal signs of Earth aging are not visible here. It is a mystery, but age must certainly have some effect."

"How would we know the signs of Earth aging?" asked Su Lee Kipperman, brushing her blue-black hair out of her eyes. "We've never been there." The way her full lips pronounced "been" with

British emphasis made the young men stare at her. Though she was older, except for Toby who was her exact age, they all found her to be the most exotic beauty on SIL.

"Of course you haven't," Malanga hummed, "but it is the only reference I have. You may access my notes on Earth aging - all of you may - so you can understand." She smiled, eyes distant.

The clicking sounds started somewhere deep in her throat, and others joined her. Most Silians frowned on the clicking, as they neither understood it nor could do it. But, as Malanga had taught her nine Sponsors, when you are completely relaxed the muscles of the throat can be used to make this sound. They were to do this each time they were finished with a procedure, signaling the return to calm from a focused state. This meant the session was over. The Sponsors had worked for hours, missed much of the Adjur celebration and now clicked with great relief. "Toby, Elizabeth," she said softly as the group began to leave, "meet with me now please." They stayed behind, Elizabeth nodding to Toby indicating she knew what this was about.

"Now, Elizabeth," she began, "what is this you needed to discuss?"

"Well," she stammered, unsure if she should tell the entire story Erica had confided, knowing it was her duty to report anything regarding health to the doctor, but afraid of her sister's wrath. "Uh,"

"We speak in confidence here, Elizabeth. You are new to the ways of Finding, but you must not hesitate to speak of that which we must know."

"The ways of Finding are in conflict with a confidence, Malanga. How do I do my duty and hold trust?" She was perplexed, angry with her sister, and scared for Jun-Jun, yet afraid to disobey her new mentor. "It is too heavy. I shouldn't be a Sponsor."

"Elizabeth," Malanga said sternly, "are you saying I have made a mistake in identifying your gift?"

"Oh no, Malanga, you do not make mistakes of perception," she said quickly. "You are Finder, she who knows without seeing."

"I do make mistakes," she smiled, "but not this time. With whom have you made this confidential agreement?"

"My sister, Erica," she hung her head.

"And if you do not tell me, is the health of a Silian in jeopardy?"

"Yes."

"Then your sister will understand in time that it was for the best, and until that time has passed she will not be aware of the breech of confidence."

"But, I..."

"You can tell her," Toby said, "you must tell her, whatever it is. We are a small group here, and matters effecting the health of one become the problem of many if not divulged." He put his arm around her shoulders, knowing from her face it was a grave matter. His lips glowed deep red in contrast to his black beard and hair. His glassy black eyes bore into her, knowing she wouldn't have brought this up if it weren't extremely important to tell, for to even come this far in face of a solemn promise between sisters told the whole of it without the details that make others understand the meaning.

Elizabeth's heart fluttered crazily; she knew she must tell. She clicked deep in her throat having calmed herself against her fears. She opened her large blue eyes and raised them to meet Malanga's; steady, calm, determined. "Jun-Jun and Erica have been conducting an experiment. Jun-Jun was hurt and almost died. He is now different, she says, changed by the experience and determined to continue. She was too scared to do it any more, and she is afraid he will die if he tries again."

"Elizabeth," Malanga said strongly, "you tell us end details without the beginning. You will explain the experiment. Start at the beginning and educate us with your words. Do not apologize for things you do not know, just inform us you don't know them so we will know you are telling everything." She hummed, holding Elizabeth in her eyes, mesmerized.

"I do not know how long it has gone on, when it began, nor how many times. They perform what they call 'freelocking' in the outbay portals. They dress warmly, smear grease on their faces and tether themselves to the inner hold, just outside of the shiplock side of the outbay. Once inside the outbay chamber with the airtight seal secure in the shiplock, the spacelock is opened by the one assisting. They keep it open for some time, until the air has completely escaped and the person freelocking looses consciousness." Malanga's eyes didn't change, but Toby was looking quite shocked. "They die, but come back. Or at least that's what Erica said. Then the one on the inside brings in the other and revives him. They record the results. Erica hasn't done it, only assisted. But the last time, Jun-Jun was dead for nearly 30 seconds and Erica almost couldn't revive him. When he did come back he was strange. He had seen something, or been somewhere, I don't know exactly, but he is now different. Erica was so terrified she refuses to do it again, but he is pressuring her." She resumed her clicking, calming her heart, slowing her breathing.

"Junior Bryant has done this several times?" Malanga asked.

Erica shook her head.

"Tobias," Malanga turned, "I want you to schedule a cycle of energization with Junior. The first two times you shall perform a Warming, two consecutive days, then commence with a full Energization cycle. Observe him closely. I want him to confide in you. Use only inclusive and embracive techniques of the hands. If it doesn't make him open, then use the same with the feet. Do not do any intrusive work on him."

"But," Toby said, "he has not requested this. Why shall I say I am doing it?"

"Find him and ask him if he wants Energization. You are his favorite one for it and have been his favorite since he was a small child. He will jump at the chance. You may use your lower humming to set the tone." She turned to Elizabeth, "Is there anything else?"

"No," she said quietly.

"You have done well, child, and your sister will not be the wiser. It was smart of you to think of the Energization. You are clever as well as talented." She smiled. "Now I must find the Commander." She jetted from the chamber leaving the Sponsors wondering what, if anything, she thought.

* * * * * * *

George walked quickly toward the doors to the ComRelay, interrupted from his work by the urgent call from his father on SIL. Through the doors to the large room beneath the satellite disk he ran across the highly waxed floor.

"Slow down there Georgie," called Woody, "I've waxed these floors like an ice rink and I don't want to have to clean your blood! Careful and you'll live longer." He waved gamely at George who whizzed past him.

George hadn't heard from his father since the board meeting, and news of the situation on SIL had suddenly stopped coming. With the preparations for the mass emigration to SIL heating up in his office, the information lacuna had gone unnoticed. There had been a sudden increase in the applications again, with one week bringing in over four thousand. Though they had to be reviewed individually to find the most deserving candidates for relocation, he already had tens of thousands more suitable applications than slots available and he wanted to simply not consider any of these new applications. Pressure from the board to increase the number of new occupants and vacationers was ridiculous and dangerous. If every vehicle were booked in both number of people transported and number of trips back and forth to the maximum, there would be no contingency for emergencies or unforeseen developments. And damn Stevens to hell for demanding a list of specific contingencies, asking George to foretell all possible problems so Stevens could judge which were worth worrying about. It didn't make sense to place lives in danger because he lacked the imagination or practicality to realize. The problem that will hobble the mission would be the one they cannot foresee.

It wasn't surprising to George that news from SIL had ceased flowing. The people of Associated were only interested in money and publicity, and any bad news might make travelers weary. But the call from his father was good, and his heart raced to hear his voice and see his video image. He turned the corner of the LOL ComRelay station with a screech of synthetic soles against floor polish as his father's face came into view. He waited for four seconds until his father would see his image in return. The Commander smiled, he'd seen his son.

"How are you?" George blurted.

"I'm fine son," his father replied, unruffled and calm, "hemareflux isn't as bad as they make it out to be. My limbs ache, but what do you expect at my age?" He chuckled to himself, thinking how much arthritis he would feel if he were Earth-bound, lucky to have only minor aches in his limbs. But there were far more important things to discuss that his health. "George," he began in a voice that made George's smile fade, "are you able to enforce a secure link with this transmission?"

George looked around. Woody was in the corner rubbing some spot with a cloth, there were the usual people in the mapping station intent on their work, and some interns plotting courses

Second Pass

in the navigation projection booth. Nobody had even noticed his presence, other than Woody, and all were too far away to hear. So he switched the setting to scramble the image and voiceprints, and turned on the blocking transmission signal so theirs couldn't be digitized and decoded. "There," he said, "all secure. What's so important?"

"What I am about to tell you, Georgie, is not to be mentioned to anyone. Not Paul, not Liz, no one. Do you understand?" His voice was firm and his eyes cold with seriousness.

Shocked, George said, "Of course. What is it?" He was curious and weary. If there was information this vital he didn't necessarily want to be the one who knew.

"Not even the President, George," his father continued, "no person alive."

"Dad," he said, "I'm not sure you want to tell me. I won't tell anyone, sure, but I don't know if I want to know, or need to know."

"You must know," he said, "and only you must."

"Okay then," he shrugged, dreading this new responsibility.

"I have received an offer from China to give private access to SIL in exchange for unlimited shuttle flights during this pass. They want to send an additional thousand people, all of the supplies for their quarters and materials and crews to build extensions to SIL. For this they will pay $3 trillion."

George didn't know what to say. He just looked at the screen shocked silent by the enormity of this offer. Stevens would kill to get more people on SIL, willing to risk many lives. If he found out about this offer he would go crazy to prevent these foreigners from taking slots from Americans. If they were allowed to go, then the remaining few American shuttles would have to be used to increase American citizenship on SIL, and there would be absolutely no contingency for mistakes.

"That's not all," the Commander continued, "I have received similar, but smaller, offers from eleven nations besides. With the original capacity of three thousand, we have the room, and the additional materials to build extensions could increase our capacity five hundred fold by the next pass. That would mean SIL would become a nation of over one million in two decades."

"But how could you allow it?" George asked. "I mean, wouldn't Congress have to approve it?"

"Yes," his dad said with a smirk, "OUR Congress, which is called the Assembly. Georgie, we are a sovereign nation. We don't have to answer to the United States. They may have built us, but they have no say." He could see his son's eyes grow larger with astonishment. "You have no idea what I think of this, Georgie, so don't be so quick to judge me. I haven't even told our Assembly, I don't know if I will."

"Don't you have to tell them?" George asked.

"Do I? It's a question I ask myself ever hour of the day. We are new as a nation, the Assembly is going through holy hell, and we have never tested our political system in this way before. As is, there's great opposition from the Firsters to allowing the new citizens anything but outsider status for eternity as far as I can see. What would they do with a multiplicity of languages and dramatic divergence in philosophical and religious beliefs?"

"So," George said trying not to assume anything, "what do you think? What do you think of this offer?"

"You remember how you hated me when you learned what I had done here? You remember how disgusted you were that I, a mere Commander of a NASA mission, had staged an explosion to launch SIL into an elliptical solar orbit just to avoid the bureaucracies at NASA and with Congress? I was wrong, son. I was wrong to do that, to decide for others, to enforce my self-appointed superiority on others. But," he paused, staring blankly to the right of the screen, "it may be best that I do it again. The Assembly isn't prepared for this kind of decision, and the Elders are too old to care. I don't know what to do. Do you understand?"

"Are you asking me to decide for you?" George refused to believe this, but asked anyway.

"Not exactly, son, not exactly," his father said, turning back to face him now. "What I am asking is for you to understand that you may be put in a position of threats, or bribes, or worse."

"Why would they threaten me? And if they have already contacted you, why haven't they contacted me yet?"

"Well, think about it Georgie," he said seriously, "they have made their first request, first inquiry if you will, with me. I haven't yet replied, and with all of the trouble we've been having here it has been some time since they first contacted me, time without a reply. Now, I've gotten another message from them recently, showing their earnestness and a bit of their impatience.

Second Pass

They have even expanded the offer to include small percentages of other nationals to balance it."

"But, how would it effect me?"

"If I say no, or if they think I am going to, then perhaps they'll think a threat to you might make me change my mind. We are famous, you know." When he said that he realized he shouldn't have. Of course his son remembered they were famous, and their fame had been the source of abuse to him from birth. "I'm sorry son, I shouldn't have said that."

"It's okay, dad," he said, not sure if he meant it.

There was a silence. Both of these men stared at each other from millions of miles away, an illusion of togetherness created by technology and mimicked by words. "I don't want anything to happen to you. Yet, you are involved without wanting to be, and I'm stuck."

"I accept all of this dad," he said, now honestly, "what can I do to help?"

"Just watch out for yourself. If there is anything funny going on, or anybody following you, call the police. And if you are approached or offered anything, well, just be prepared. I hope to God this doesn't get out. There will be hell to pay if it does."

George remembered the attempts on his life, the need for a security guard. Suddenly there were reasons where before there was only suspicion. Liz wasn't so paranoid after all, and George knew now why it was necessary to get protection. "It has already started, dad," he sighed, "and I'm afraid it is the 'worse' part of what you said." He committed to actually hire guards that afternoon.

Commander McVee reacted with a startled, concerned look on his face eight seconds later when the words arrived on SIL and his reaction relayed back. "What do you mean? Has something happened?"

"God," George said, "how do I begin?" He told his father about the threats to his life, the pressure from Liz to hire security, and his reluctance to do so. "And then, when we found out Liz was pregnant, I started to interview people for the job. I don't want..." he stopped short at the look on his father's face.

"What do you mean, pregnant? You are having a baby?"

George realized he hadn't had communication with his father about that at all. "Geez, I'm sorry dad," he became a teenage boy, "I haven't been able to tell you. Yes, we are having a baby. Liz and me!"

"Well," he chuckled, "I'm glad China and some thugs were able to bring this news to me. I am delighted, son!"

They talked about the baby, the possibility of having Liz and her child come to SIL, even if just for a visit, for it would be the only time he could see the baby. Then they talked seriously about the security, and George promised he would hire someone by week's end. When they finished George felt one hundred years older.

"Dad," he said in parting, "could you have Dr. Malanga come to the ComRelay. I need to speak with her."

"What? You want to find out if I'm healthy? I tell you I am, why do you need to talk to her?" He was agitated.

"Dad," George slumped his shoulders some, "I just want to get the details. Is that all right with you, or do you want me to stay in the dark? You don't tell a very complete story when it comes to your health, you know. I love you. Naturally I'm concerned and want to hear everything there is to know. Will you let me talk to her?"

"Of course, son, just wait a few minutes," said the white and gray face on the color screen as it receded into the fuzzed background. George waited, thinking about China and three trillion dollars. *And all of those other countries. What was going on? Why the interest in SIL, in getting people there?* He couldn't play innocent with himself effectively. He knew exactly what was going on and didn't like it. Confusion is most often an unwillingness to admit what is understood. And he understood that SIL was a nation, not just a space mission. And nations, new nations, must learn their way around just like a new kid on the block. They will be tested, violated. Attempts to dominate and claim it will be made, constantly. The attempts will progress until the nation is forced to save itself, into acts of war, or self-defense. He remembered the stories of the formation of Israel, decades before his birth, and how it was not accepted as a nation. Those who rejected it tried to reclaim it, to break it apart. From its early history Israel was a warring nation, forced to defend its very existence. SIL would go through the same process until it was respected by doubters and feared by enemies. How sad it must be for his father to watch this process as his life ends, to watch his attempt at escaping the rivalries and corruption of Earth become the very requirements of survival.

The face of Malanga filled the screen and he smiled. Her floating bubble of hair was her halo and her softly wrinkled face was her grace. "Hello," she said. It was a complete statement and required no response at all. She welcomed him, honored him, accepted him. From across vast distances she brought him into being as a beloved being. He hadn't remembered this quality about her from when he was on SIL, but that was a time of intense anxiety and psychological adjustment for him.

"Hello doctor," he smiled, "you make me feel peaceful. Thank you."

"Peace is yours always, George Junior," she whispered and sang the words. "You must not allow it to be buried within you or eclipsed by the chaos of others." She looked at him, or seemed to, and he said nothing. Her words healed him. "You will want to know about your father's health. I'll tell you. He suffered hemareflux, a condition unique to prolonged weightlessness brought on by open bleeding. The blood flow is designed to be outward, but factors of gravity complete the cycle. Where there has been no gravity, the flow changes slightly. Blood pressure varies in different parts of the body and the contraction and flexing of the vessels becomes different. Muscles change. When a wound is opened, the blood flows both outward and inward, crawling up into the tissue surrounding the wound. It sometimes travels backward in the vessel or artery, and pools in the capillaries. Clotting occurs, but separation of plasma also occurs. It becomes a threat of thrombosis and infection, and when the body reacts it reacts erratically, causing threat of stroke, and if there is an aneurysm it might erupt at any moment. The problems are immense, but due to your invention of the rotating plant tray to create gravitational pull, we were able to reverse the reflux and prevent these threats from materializing."

She had said this as if singing a lullaby to a baby. Even her most disturbing words were soothing. George found himself smiling not only at the fact his father was out of danger, but more because of the spell she cast on him. He noticed humming in her speech, humming between words and within words. He began to hear not words but see images explaining the medical information. He was transfixed. Woody was looking at him from across the room and noticed the change in him. How strangely he was looking at the screen, the odd smile like a smile on a child's face when lulled to sleep by softly stroking its limbs. Woody was drawn to him, slowly walking toward him. His pace was not in stealth but in wonder.

"I must speak to you of matters of urgency," she said, her face becoming strong rather than soft, her voice pinging rather than humming. "We are in social upheaval with the anticipation of new arrivals. Factions are fighting factions and violence is in the voices of the people." Her face had become dark, angled. "Your father is at risk from the followers of his early beliefs, beliefs he has changed with experience and age. He may be killed. If he is, Machmood will take his place as Commander and the balance of power will be upset." He was feeling determination now, impetus to act. "Your father saved all lives of the first occupants of this station, but he also risked everything on a foolish gamble. Those who hate him for his sins are the ones who are using his early philosophies against him, against all of us."

"What can I do, doctor?" he asked, helpless but wanting to act now to change the situation.

"In love of him act for the highest good of the most people."

"How will I know what that is? And what if he dies of old age? It may not be a murder that takes him," he was surprised by his own cool analytical manner.

"He is not aging," the doctor said simply, "none of them are."

"Of course he is aging," George said with contempt, as if the doctor were stupid.

"No, George, they are not. None of the elders is aging here. Their bodies are growing white and gray, the muscles are shrinking and the skin is thinning, but they are not aging. It is a phenomenon we are watching closely."

"What are you saying, doctor?" George challenged argumentatively.

"On SIL the body is not fighting gravity. Aging is slowed beyond recognizable symptoms, at least by Earth standards. I have no doubt they will die some day, but it won't be soon. It is as if space offers an extended life, a kind of suspended mortality."

"If what you are saying is true, then everybody will want to go to SIL! If they know, the people, if they find out there will be..." he couldn't finish, his vision of potential future left him speechless. "You must report to me directly, on secure ComRelay every development," he said with force. "You must!"

Second Pass

"In love of your father I will. Remember, act for the highest good of the most people." The transmission was ended. George stared at the screen, and Woody stood dumbfounded behind him, and backed away as silently as he'd approached, this time consciously avoiding detection by George.

George stood for about ten minutes staring at the blank screen, then broke his spell and walked briskly from the room. He needed to hire security for his family right away. He nearly walked into Woody as he crossed to the doors, knocking him back on his heels. George didn't even notice.

Chapter 5

Warehouses stretched for blocks, beyond the Combat Zone, Boston's affectionately named red-light district, out toward the docks. There were no lights along the side of the road, or not many, and no traffic other than occasional tourists going to eat at No Names, but they were always lost and frightened, so they drove quickly past the warehouses. Even the cops didn't pay any attention when they drove past because nothing ever happened out here. And the one warehouse with the lights on inside was barely discernable from the outside, light leaked through ill fitting roof tin and bent doors, but it was too far from the road to really be noticeable. Besides, it was evening, sun just set so the light wouldn't even be seen. The older man felt much more comfortable here than at Associated, and was pleased that the early morning LOL transmissions had all but stopped with Sylvana's death. Jiimson had been distracted by his new duties so their only contact was a young man in the shuttle outbay portal area, but he was not kept informed of developments. He would become more important later, if they could get in, which was why they met now.

"We need to scare him again," said the older man, "the first scare doesn't seem to have had too much of an effect." He looked at the three men gathered, disgusted he had to work with such low-life scum, but delighted too because nobody would ever believe he, with his well fitted suits, effete circle of friends, and expensive car, would have anything to do with them. He was secure, but determined.

"Why wudn't da muddeh even call us?" asked the younger man. He was really quite handsome, but it would never be noticed accept by horny women and men on the make. His thick black hair clumped in waves as sensual as the curve of a woman's breast, as solid and rich as his strong muscled fingers, the tip of one wave just brushing the top of his eyebrow, black above clear blue eyes. His thick lips were both voluptuous and vulgar, one of the many characteristics inherited from his working class family, traits never to be confused with thin-lipped blue blood upper-class.

"Stop talking like that," the older man yelled. "I've spent a fortune to improve your speech. You may not be able to look

Second Pass

respectable, but you sure as hell will act it!" He was getting a headache, and took the silk hanky out of his breast pocket to wipe his forehead. There was no sweat there, but wiping it made him feel better.

"Oh suh," the thug said in mock British, "so sorry. It shan't happen again!" He and the other two laughed loudly. Elbowing each other like high school football teammates; they didn't notice the older man pulling a gun out of his inside breast pocket.

He grabbed the laughing goon by the shirt collar and slammed him against the tin wall with a resounding bong. With the point of the gun pushing into the younger man's upper gums, some blood began to appear on the lower lip. "You will do as I say or you will die, do you understand?" Veins stood out on his forehead.

"Hey," the younger man said as his two friends backed away, palms outstretched like they were smoothing a tablecloth in mid air, "I was just kidding with you. See? I can talk normal. Don't be so uptight, man."

"Do you realize what this is all about? You were scum when I found you and will always be scum. Either you do exactly what I say or you are dead! That goes for all of you!" Beads of sweat formed on his brow.

"Put the gun down, man," the younger said, "I'll do what you want. Geez! Why are you so uptight?"

The older man lowered the gun, but kept it pointed at him, and eased away. "I'm not uptight, things just aren't going right. We need to get the contract. We've got to make little Georgie move his butt..." a cell phone signaled from the young man's belt. "Check that!"

The young man fumbled with the pager and smiled, "Bingo!" he said. "It's him."

"Okay," the older man put his gun back in its holster. "Let's do this thing right." He snapped open the phone. "Your security is my business. May I help you?"

* * * * * * *

George entered Liz's home office where she worked furiously on the computer, surprising her. She swung around in her chair, hair flying in an arch.

"Oh, it's you!" she said and returned to her work.

"Glad I could brighten your day," George said sarcastically. "I've gotten better greetings from the clerk at the bank."

"Be glad I even turned around, George," Liz said unaffected by his comment, "I'm in the middle of writing my will. The way I figure it, you'll be dead soon from some assassin or murderer, I'll get all of your money, then I'll get finished by some thug before the baby's born and there'll be no one to inherit your money. Of course, if we had security I would be able to freely throw my arms around your neck, kiss you, and have a normal life!" She was laughing as she spoke.

George rolled his eyes. "Liz," he said, "I'm going to hire a company today, or at least start finding out what's available."

Liz stopped typing and turned to him. "Really?" she asked. "Should I take off my clothes or put something in the microwave?" George looked puzzled. "What makes you think I'll believe you this time, George? You've said that quite a bit, usually to get dinner or to get laid." She started unbuttoning her blouse.

"Stop it, Liz," George said, "I spoke to my father today. He wants us to all come to SIL. Whatever crazies are out there gunning for us, I want to be able to let him see his grandchild."

"I'm still doubtful," Liz said. "Let me see an action other than talking and I'll make you better food that Sienna and fuck you till morning."

"Impossible, Liz," he chuckled, "you're no match for her."

"You've slept with Sienna?" she made a face, "What was that like?"

"You know what I mean," he said as he pulled a yellow paper from his briefcase. "Where's the phone?" he asked.

She searched under a pile of papers and extracted the cordless phone and handed it to him, and then leaned back in her chair with her arms folded across her chest waiting. He dialed the number and waited. "Damn," he said, "voicemail." He dialed Liz's number and pressed the transmit key. "There," he said, "an action," and he crossed to Liz and kissed her. "What do I get for that?"

"You have my permission to sleep with Sienna!" she said, ending in a shriek as he tickled her sides. "Okay, I'll sleep with you," she said returning his kiss.

* * * * * * *

Second Pass

The phone on George's desk rang quietly twice, then the secretary picked it up. He just waited for her to send the call through. The light blinked, indicating the line was on hold, and his intercom buzzed. He pressed the bar. "Yes?"

"Sir," the young man's voice said hesitantly, "it's the President."

"President Woodly?"

"No, President McKenna! I mean, ex-President McKenna," his voice was quiet.

"Put the call through," George said. McKenna had applied for a place on SIL, and he'd been approved. The line clicked in and George said, "Hello Mr. President, how are you today?"

"You know Dr. McVee, Junior," he said in a booming voice, "why don't we just dispense with the formalities and you call me Paddi? I'm no longer President and, frankly, I'd like to forget I ever was."

"It will be difficult for me to call you that, sir," George said honestly, "but please call me George."

"I'll call you George if you call me..." he stopped to think, "how about Mac? That's what they called me at Yale and I have damned fine memories of those days."

"Well," George giggled, "how can I help you, Mac?"

"See, that wasn't so difficult was it?" He didn't leave room for a response. "I was wondering what had become of my application? It's been many years since I put it in, and many more years since I first told you I wanted to have a place on SIL. Do you have any decision on that yet?"

George was confused. The letter should have gone out months ago. "Well, sir, Mac, sir," he sighed, "you were approved months ago. You should've gotten the letter. Hold a minute while I check," he put the call on hold and buzzed the secretary. "Jim, did the letter to McKenna to out? It should have months ago; he says he didn't receive it. I'll keep him on the phone while you check, just buzz me when you find it." He switched to the other line, "You still there...uh... Mac?"

"Sure thing George," he said like he was playing a game.

"Jimmy's checking on it. Meanwhile, how's life out of office?"

"Well, life is great, my place in it is rather uninteresting by contrast."

"I can't imagine you are bored. I read about your speaking engagements all the time."

"I go, I run my mouth, I get a T-shirt or beer mug and I go back home. Most of what I say is hogwash anyhow," he had lowered his tone. "But, every now and then..."

The phone buzzed. "Sorry to interrupt," George said, "that must be Jimmy, hold on please," and he switched to the other line.

"It went out, but we never got the acceptance confirmation. It must have gotten lost in the mail. I'm sending another one right now," he said efficiently.

"Thanks, Jimmy." He switched to the other line. "Hello, Mac? It was sent out but we never got the acceptance confirmation. It must have gotten lost in the mail."

"Well that sure is good news, son," he said with a laugh, speaking once again in his public address tone. "I've been thinking, George, thinking it will be kind of lonely up there. Did you ever consider trying to send more people? Why the way it's planned it'll be like a small town college campus! Just thought we could take advantage of more of the space we built up there back when I was Vice President. We spent billions to make room for three thousand."

"Well," George found it curious to be asked this by the President, former or current, he was still the President, "I have the figures in front of me. I don't see how we could extend the transport vehicles more than they are already scheduled without putting lives in jeopardy if there is any kind of emergency."

"What if we had more vehicles?" he asked like a student with a very good idea.

"You know very well the current fleet, sir," damn the Mac shit anyway. George didn't like this at all. He wondered if he should tell the President about China and the other offers. He wondered if he already knew. "Where would we find more vehicles? We can't make them in time, you know."

"Hmmmm," the thoughtful voice at the other end said, "What about other countries? I hear some of them have real active programs? Perhaps I could talk to some of my old friends and get them to contribute some vehicle time. Hell," he said in a burst, "we could even offer them some citizenships on SIL, more than the international allotment currently agreed upon!"

Second Pass

Just like that, George thought, *they didn't bother me, but they intercepted the mail, found out he was going there and asked him to help with their effort.* "I will have to think about it," George said unenthusiastically.

"You do that, George," McKenna said seriously, "and I'll be back in touch in a few days. Don't want to meddle, of course, but this interests me more than my speeches. You decide what's best."

"Well," George said to refresh his mood, "I guess I'll have to think about this! No time like the present. I look forward to talking to you again soon," George said decisively.

"Well, thank you for your time George," he said.

"You're welcome, Mac," and hung up the phone.

George looked at the figures again. His way, SIL total population would be 1,678; Steven's way it would reach 1,990. The Chinese and other nations willing to provide more shuttles could bring the population up to SIL original capacity of 3,064 without having to build on to the structure. And there would be new births immediately, not to mention several hundred by next pass, so construction would have to start on new housing outer shells immediately.

This population explosion on SIL would present severe problems for the original occupants and threaten the ability to preserve a stable government. But what would the outcome be if the government became less stable than it currently was? There wouldn't be any place for detractors to go, and living in close quarters with enemies for 18 years would certainly bring out the worst behavior. *It isn't your problem,* he told himself, *dad must figure it out, not me.* But reason was useless. He was terribly worried about the future of SIL and concerned, too, about his own child.

He and Liz had interviewed several security companies and decided on Major Max as the best company. They had been round and round about all considerations, but it was Liz who finally made the decision based more on intuition than reason. It really didn't seem to matter. All of the companies were about equal in services offered, price, and reputation. So Major Max it was, and George was very glad the decision was made. But it didn't make his worrying less.

The pregnancy was well on the way now and Liz was plumped up like a little ball. She looked beautiful pregnant, while she was very good looking normally. The slight flush to her face and the robust new energy certainly suited her well. She had also developed much more appetite for sex, and this pleased him, though many nights he was too worn from worry and long hours to actually perform for her.

They had decided to go to SIL for four months, but to return to Earth. He realized this would be the last time he would see his father, but he felt strongly that Earth was the best environment for his child. His main concern had been education, oddly enough. As he looked over his own life he saw that education had given him the greatest gifts and brought the greatest satisfaction. Liz agreed, and they had already made several reservations with major universities for early consideration of their child.

He put the papers down and tapped on his intercom. "Steve," he said, "I'll be down in a few minutes, meet me in the front."

"You got it," was the jovial reply. Steven Masters was their head of family security. He was on duty during the basic working hours and weekends, with Mondays and Thursdays off. He was an impressive young man. He was well mannered, intelligent and had a great sense of humor. His family was from Philadelphia originally, and he had been brought up with Philadelphia society graces augmented by a flair of southern hospitality. Handsome, his thick blond hair accentuated his dark brows and blue eyes. He was as tall as George, but was a wall of muscle from rigorous exercise. George couldn't imagine when he had time to work out, but he kept fit and was very good company. George would chat with him on the drives to and from work, and he was actually quite perceptive about some of the issues around SIL. George trusted him and felt his life and his family were far better off with him in charge of their well being.

"Marty's going to take the night shift, boss," Steve said when George got into the car. "His kid's birthday party is Thursday, so I'm going to switch with him. You got any problem with that?"

"No problem here Steve," George said as they drove. "I didn't realize Marty had a kid."

"Yeah, a little girl," he said, "cute as a button."

Karen, Sam, Marty and Joe were the other security guards for them. Between the three they were covered around the clock. A sixth man, Justin, came in once and a while to spell them under certain circumstances, and would be joining full time when the baby got there. All of them were young and fit, hand-picked by

Second Pass

Steve. Every change in the routine was reported in advance to both George and Liz, and though they had never disapproved, they could have and things would be done to their wishes.

"Busy day?" he asked.

"The usual, but I'm beat."

"You got a ton more mail at home today," he reported, "probably more applications."

"What, no letter bombs?" George chuckled. He still thought this business of protection was over reacting. There hadn't been any indication of trouble from the Chinese or anyone else, and he wondered if there really had been an offer. The governments of the world were all supportive of the effort he was making. In fact, many of the countries had donated something for decorations or supplies on SIL. Good will seemed to abound around all mention of SIL, except with Stevens at Associated, but he was sour on everything, so he didn't count.

"You are safe with me, George," Steve said.

When they got home, Steve helped George sort the mail, and they ate together. He and Liz still kept their two homes, but Liz stayed with George more lately. She was getting big and liked the company, and the help, found at George's. He had offered to move in with her, but she clearly preferred coming to his place. George suspected it was Sienta's cooking and fussing more than his company. With Liz due home any time; there were good smells coming from the kitchen.

Sienta came to the living room with a tray of crackers and some beer. Her short frame was dressed in a brightly colored dress, mostly reds and purples, with a turquoise apron on. Somehow, with her middle-aged body, her apron was always hiked way up in the front, making her appear pregnant herself. Her black hair was twisted into a cinnamon bun on her head, and the white flair was its icing. She never had the pins pushed in quite all the way, though she spend much of her free time fixing them. She wore too much lipstick, too little deodorant, and was quite taken with the security guards. She always had a special smile for Steve, whom she said resembled her first husband. George had seen his picture and there was no resemblance whatever, but he didn't mention it to her.

"Buenos tardes," she sang as she entered the room.

"Hey there Sienta," Steve said with his eyes on the tray. "Whatcha got there? Smells good!"

"No, no, no," she said turning the tray away from him, "ju not gonna hab no nuthin till you gib Sienta big hallo!"

He threw his arms around her and said "Mama!" as he kissed her cheek. She giggled with delight and even blushed a little. Ever since the first time she saw him they had played this way.

"Sienta," George interrupted, "did you get my note about Tom and Shandor?"

"They gonna come eat; I gonna go home." She folded her arms defiantly in front of her ample bosom. She didn't like Shandor and thought he was just taking advantage of George. She treated him like a mouse in the pantry, always trying to catch him eating food or changing her way of arranging the kitchen. "Ju tell meester beeg moobie star he not gonna get nuthin from Senora Sienta if he no gib you respect! I no care if he man from moon base, he ain't got no mama and act like animal!"

"Now Sienta," George reasoned, "he is our guest and we will give him every respect we give any guest. Besides, you like Tom and if you treat Shandor badly, well, Tom might not take you out to the movies!" He knew he had her there.

"Tom good man; Shandor pig," she said in dismissal, "dat boy have no mama. Madre de Dios..." she muttered her way back into the kitchen.

"She'll make a great meal," George said.

Eventually Liz arrived, Steve went off duty and Sam Kaplan took position outside, then Tom and Shandor came. Sienta's dinner was spectacular, but George was distracted. The call from McKenna had unnerved him. Even Shandor's slapstick didn't engage him, Liz noticed, and the evening was wearing on him.

"So George," Tom said, "you've been an absolute pill this evening, and a bitter one at that! What's bugging you?"

All eyes were on him and though he hadn't made any attempt to hide his mood, he now felt intruded upon. What could he tell them? There was so much, too much, and each was a confidante, but he could say nothing. "I guess I have a lot on my mind," he said lamely.

"Nonsense," Tom said, "there is no more or less on your mind tonight than there ever is. Something has happened and you need to talk about it."

"Really, Tom," he said, "it is nothing." Gut feelings told him this wouldn't get him off the hook, and it didn't.

"Something has happened, something's troubling you," Tom said, "and one of us at this table can help with it. It may not be me, your truest friend and advisor, not to mention father figure until you found the Commander. It may not be the lovely mother of your child, who has the same level of clearance as you. Hell, it might not even be Shandor, who bows before the water you walk on. But something's up and we are gonna get it out of you if we have to sit on you!"

"Okay," he said, "there are parts I can talk about. But if you ask questions I can't answer, I won't answer them. There are things I can't share with any of you."

"Not even me?" Liz asked with mock hurt.

"Agreed," said Tom. Shandor was just silently watching all of this.

"Shandor," he started, "what do you think will happen when all of these people get to SIL? How do you think people there will react?"

"Uh," Shandor was surprised to have a question directed at him, "I don't know. I guess there will be some jealousy, some hurt feelings. But then it will be really exciting for the younger people. We were always fascinated to learn about Earth, to find out why knowledge of it was forbidden."

"Jealousy, you say? Why jealousy?"

"Well, because the older people didn't have a choice about returning home, and they didn't have a choice, really, about living their lives on SIL. These new people could do anything, and they choose SIL. The old ones will be jealous." He said this with a certainty that shocked even himself.

"He's right," Tom said, "there will be many noses out of joint."

"But," Liz added, "it will just be an adjustment period. Things will be unsettled for awhile, then balance to a new equilibrium."

"But what about the treatment Paul and BQ and their kids have gotten?" George asked. "They have been shunned, sabotaged, and held to an inhuman standard. Any little flaw in them is held as the reason to not allow others to come to SIL. This concerns me. There has now been a murder, and it was basically pardoned. Does this give permission to kill the ones you don't like?"

"Oh, it all sounds so dramatic," Liz scoffed, "you don't know what led to her murder any more than I do."

"But," Tom cautioned, "he does have a point. There are some pretty twisted psyches up there. Imagine the mental breakdown from being trapped in space sure to die, suddenly finding there was a way to live, but still trapped, then discovering it was intentional sabotage of the mission by the man who, no offense George, would become their tyrannical leader, and then discovering you could return to Earth and realizing you are severely damaged by the experience, enough to make you no longer fit in. I say there is some deviant psychology possible, and murder wouldn't have the same significance."

"The only thing," Shandor said seriously, "is the feeling of loneliness and how it makes all of them accept each other. I mean, I was the lowliest of the low, but I was certainly not expendable. When any crisis comes up, everyone is needed to face it. It isn't like here on Earth, where there are so many people you can afford to have whole groups of enemies. There is no prejudice on SIL, at least when I was there. We couldn't afford it."

"So Shandor," George turned to him, looking directly at him, "how many people will make it okay to murder, to hate? How many people will be enough that prejudice is affordable?"

"What are you asking, George," Liz said. "How can he know a number? How could anyone?"

"The capacity of visitors this pass is fixed," Tom said, "so we know exactly how many people there will be. From what I've seen of your projections, the community will remain well balanced, the age span will represent a fair cross section and the people who have been on SIL from the beginning will reap much benefit from the newcomers."

"So 1,248 new people is a good number?" George asked bitterly, "or if there are ten more will it be too many? And what about the next pass, and the one after that? And what if there is a population explosion pressing the limits of occupancy?"

"George, calm down," Liz said, "the total population after this pass won't even be half of the original occupancy allowance."

"Oh George," Tom said suddenly, "I see what's happening. How could..."

"I can't answer that question, Tom," George said, "or probably any more." He hung his head. Liz looked at Tom as she realized what George was considering.

Second Pass

"George," Liz said gently, "we are not dumb. If there are people pressing for full or close to full occupancy it isn't coming from our government. My God, they must be crazy!"

"What is going on?" Shandor asked loudly. "What are you all talking about? There couldn't be full occupancy this pass."

"Why not?" Liz asked pointedly.

"Well," Shandor thought about this crazy idea, "it just couldn't be!" He was almost yelling now, with fear in his voice. "It would ruin everything there! You can't bring in all of those people; fill up all of the spaces! What if there was some emergency? Where would the food come from? And those people won't know anything at all about life on SIL! They could make mistakes! They could kill everybody there!"

The others looked at Shandor in amazement. He was terribly animated, overwrought with anxiety. Liz patted his hand to calm him, but he pushed it away.

"You see the reaction?" said George. "And he isn't even up there, hasn't been for years. I don't know what to do."

"George," Tom had his professor voice, "just what are they pushing for?"

"I can't tell you," George said sadly, "though I want to. I don't know how to make these decisions. I can't decide for an entire population what it's future will be. How can any one man? And I am an American, they are Silians! They must decide for themselves, but it is up to me. How can I decide for other people?"

"Your father did," Liz said plainly.

"What's that supposed to mean?" George spat.

"Just that he did," Liz said, "and he did it because of something he believed in more than the value of a single human life."

"But I'm not him," he was angry now, "and you wouldn't dare say it runs in the family."

"That's not what I'm saying at all, George McVee, and you know it," she snapped. "I'm just saying he might be able to decide what to do. Your father George, he is the one who can help you with this. He not only has shown the capacity to decide for others, but he is Silian. He is the quintessential Silian, for God's sake. He is the one who can decide. We can't. We can only support you, and believe your decisions are the best. We could disagree, but that would be pointless because we can't know all the facts. Your dad is the only one you can turn to for help."

"She's right," said Tom.

"But he was willing to kill us all!" Shandor was standing now. "Willing to risk all of us for his damned experiment! The bastard!" He bellowed the last words to shocked faces. None had seen him this upset before, nor had he ever expressed any thoughts whatever on the origin of SIL's current dilemma.

"I didn't know you felt so strongly, son," Tom said with interest, "you've never mentioned it before."

Shandor looked at them like someone who was just brought back from fainting with cold water to the face or ammonia under his nose. He looked less wildly at them and seemed confused. "I didn't mean to call your dad a bastard," he said quietly, "I didn't even know I had an opinion. What happened to me?"

"It's okay," George said, "you know you don't have to worry about calling him a bastard, you probably learned it from me. I am surprised how deeply you feel about this, though."

"But," Shandor screwed his face into a perplexed twist, "I don't feel that strongly about it. I mean, I sort of do, but mostly don't. I don't know what happened."

"I think I do," Tom said, "and it will help us a great deal. You were raised by the community at large on SIL, without any consistent parents to guide you. You suffered under many views, which held you apart from the group, and tonight you've found a place for those views, a way to use them that makes some sense to you. And in doing so you've instructed us, or I should say, George, in what he can expect from some of those people. The good news is that most of them will not live very much longer, and gradually things will change."

George couldn't take any more. He alone knew the old people weren't aging as they do on Earth, but it was another part of the unbearable burden. "I'm tired," he said, "I can't keep this up any more. I've got to get some sleep."

"We understand George," Tom said. "Do you want us to leave?"

"Why don't we have desert," Liz said. "It'll calm nerves. Besides, Shandor will pout all night if he doesn't get desert."

"Stop treating me like a child," he whined with mock pouting, eliciting a laugh to break the tension.

"Do you plan to take Liz and the baby up to SIL?" Tom asked to change the subject slightly.

Second Pass

"We," Liz said quickly to stop George from saying anything, "are thinking about going for a visit, just the four months."

George took her hand as she passed his chair. "We think Earth is a better place for the kid in his first years. Besides, I wouldn't want to be held responsible for everything my father has done up there!" They chuckled.

"George has to go along with the diplomatic mission on the first shuttle," Liz explained, "and to oversee the smooth delivery of people and supplies to SIL. He is the mastermind, after all. Then we will go later and join him there. But we will return to Earth and live here." She left the room.

"That seems reasonable," said Tom.

"What about you? Both of you?" George asked.

"I can't make up my mind," Shandor said. "Most of the time I think it would be better to be there, but I love the way I'm treated here."

"Yeah," Tom said, "no more free meals for this celebrity up there!"

Liz and Sienta came from the kitchen each with a tray. On the trays were crystal bowls containing a pear and vanilla ice cream. Covering all of the pears was a thin coating of chocolate, but one was covered with a tan sauce.

"We habing a tube talk," announced Sienta, "all chocolate and one maple! Sienta to join ju, eef eez hokay?"

"But who gets the maple?" asked Tom.

"Sienta tell story," she announced brightly. "Een hannor ob new baby and hold friend."

Chapter 6

Junior Bryant giggled as he jetted toward the Finding Chambers, anticipating the Energization. He pushed through the main entry door and flew through the outer chamber, noticing there were no others waiting there for treatments. Checking his appointment notice, he turned to the left toward Chamber 5 and opened the door. The room had burnt orange walls and some attractive woven drapes, the kind showing up all over SIL now in preparation for the new arrivals in a couple of years. Predominant blues, reds and gold decorated the cozy space. In the center was the scoop shaped Energization chair, suspended from the ceiling by a black iron tube three inches in diameter. The chair was deep red, almost burgundy, with black Velcro straps floating idly in the weight free space without movement from air currents. Facing it was a smaller black chair, hanging from a similar iron tube. This tube was not connected directly to the ceiling as the other, but was looped over a circular track which allowed the chair to rotate anywhere around the main chair in a full circle. It had panels of jets on its outer surfaces, and jet control buttons on the arms.

Tobias Manndle perched on the smaller chair. At 27 he was mature looking, with rugged looks and heavy stubble, and though he shaved twice daily it maintained a permanent stain on his face. His eyes were light brown, nearly matching his hair, but were saved from obscurity by his thick, black eyebrows and startling black eye lashes. Well muscled by nature, he had bulges all over from his rigorous workouts in preparation for Earth at next pass. He pushed off of his chair gently and started floating toward Jun-Jun, smiling and looking through the boy. Even though Jun-Jun was well aware, and used to, this beginning of the Energization, he felt butterflies in his stomach and couldn't suppress a laugh.

"Laughing already?" Toby said darkly. "You'll never survive this session." He said this as he pushed Jun-Jun across the room to the large chair with pokes to his ribs and stomach. Jun-Jun giggled and fought the tickling jabs a bit, but knew better than to really fight.

Energization had been developed in the first years of the 13th century as a therapy widely accepted by the medical societies of the day. It was forgotten until the late 20th century when it was viewed as alternative medicine and not widely practiced. Studies

Second Pass

were done and it was found very effective, but the puritanical roots of Western society were strong enough that it was only practiced by special healers, and viewed as silly by the medical community. They couldn't argue with the results. Its ancient roots were all but forgotten, overshadowed by the miraculous effectiveness it demonstrated over ailments that had, up to that time, baffled scientists.

The theory was simple: when you laugh your body assumes you are happy, healthy and stress-free. Prolonged laughter boosts all of the body's systems to a healthy harmony based on this simple fact. Early experimenters with prolonged, forced laughter found the immune system to be greatly enhanced as a result, and if the state was repeated on a regular basis the body would begin to heal even the deadliest cancers and infections, naturally producing antigens and curative secretions no chemist could simulate.

The Finding practice of Energization was a complex set of techniques of tickling, both physical and psychological, which rendered the patient helpless with laughter, but not in pain and without creating feelings of danger or invasion. Energization began at the age of three for the children, and was done on a regular basis, eliminating most childhood diseases. It was applied to teenagers less frequently, but, when prescribed, a full cycle consisted of seven weeks of regular sessions. Adults scheduled cycles no less than twice per year, but were encouraged to seek out therapy if undue amounts of stress began to hamper them. In addition, there were no taboos on tickling between friends and families on SIL, but very carefully held boundaries about erotic tickling, limited to people actively in a relationship. Sex in general was promoted as healthy, a direct response to the repressed sexual mores of Earth societies and the horrible violence this had caused.

"Now Jun," Toby said as he began to fasten the Velcro straps to hold him in place against the soft curved chair, "you seem to be under some stress, so we'll take care of it! Do you think this is going to tickle?" As he fastened him to the chair, his fingers occasionally found a vulnerable spot and tickled for a moment. Jun-Jun was already laughing and squirming, tucking his chin down deep into his collarbone and trying to clamp his elbows tightly to his ticklish sides. He couldn't answer, but knew he wasn't expected to. "I think this is really going to tickle," Toby said, "even more than last time." He punctuated this last statement with a deep tickle under Jun-Jun's right arm, now firmly held in place. He let out a shriek.

The session had begun, and Toby went about his work. Jun-Jun was laughing and twisting, enjoying himself and glad he was back in his body after his free-lock experience. Toby, now in his chair, jetted it behind Jun's chair and reached around with both hands and tickled his stomach, flexing his fingers while keeping his palms pressed against the abdominal flesh. Laughter filled the chamber, laughter that would continue for the prescribed twenty minutes.

* * * * * * *

Jun-Jun flared his jet just enough to propel him slowly through the hallway, still peaceful from the energization. Floating inside and out, he passed the teaching hall and the nursery. Children grouped by age and tunic color were being instructed or supervised by adults in the matching tunics, some bored, some playing, but all paying attention to the adults. Jun-Jun was happy to be free of his early education, happy to be able to experiment. SIL was vast compared to one human, but was finite and held no geographic secrets or unexplored areas. Exploration of the mind was freedom, taking you to places unfamiliar and unimagined.

Jun-Jun still smiled, a giggle waiting just beneath the surface of his skin, ready to break into laughter with the slightest provocation. He changed direction and began to propel himself quicker past the metal workrooms. The use of torches always bothered him, threatening explosion with mishap or criminal action, but he had to go this way to the living quarters of his friends to keep his visit to them secret.

Since Erica's defection from the project she was spending most of her time with Elizabeth, working at the fiber dying works or in the Chapel. He knew this because he still tried to get her to rejoin his effort, and in the trying knew the excuses. When he was sent to find her he always found her where she said she would be. Whenever they were passing one another in this or that passage, she looked at him with sinister, resentful eyes accusing him of some terrible sin, threatening his disclosure. Her absence hadn't grieved him for long, though, and his determination to explore freelocking grew daily.

Second Pass

He couldn't continue the experiments alone, however, and while playing tether in the exercise room he'd gotten friendly with Marcus Isievitsch and Nikki Parrish. Today he would speak first to Marcus, then Nikki, about the experiments. Risk taking was part of experimentation. That was the principal drilled into them from earliest schooling; breaking the secrecy might just bring him new assistants. And better ones than Erica turned out to be.

Marcus was his size and weight, roughly, and had the same instinct for competition, playing hard to win any game offered or stumbled upon. They had taken turns checking the ship's outer joints, for example, talking the design engineer, Sortan Mohamad, into scheduling them on alternate shifts. Mohamad's suspicion became enthusiastic support as their spirit of competition produced meticulous inspection records. He was able to run statistical analyses of the data, and had been rewarded for the preventative maintenance the results produced.

Marcus was a disappointment to his parents though, who were both highly technical, and his studies were fairly poor. It wasn't for lack of ability; he simply wasn't being challenged by his work, and was easily distracted. "In a normal society," he informed his friends, "I would be a warrior, a hunter. That's in my blood, not tinkering with microbes or stresses on metal alloys!" His arms were strong, and he infuriated older and conservative Silians by tearing the sleeves out of his tunics, though the girls were thrilled. And his popularity with girls was surprising, since he had his father's hook nose and hirsute propensity. Undaunted by his dramatic features and the new furry landscape puberty had recently provided, he taunted boys his age into tests of strength which they always lost, while he kept getting stronger. It wasn't until he met Jun-Jun that he found a constant companion, which happened when they were both thirteen, and even though Marcus was always ahead of Jun-Jun in strength, stamina, sexual development and rebellion, Jun-Jun had stuck with him.

Nikki was a stark contrast to Marcus, blond hair almost transparent on her pink skin. But when his black eyes challenged her on a point of disagreement, her piercing blue eyes seemed to freeze his coal to shattering sub-temperatures and, by sheer force of will, she had won every argument the two had ever been in. Marcus never felt lust for her like he did for other girls, and this made him more curious to be around her. She was a feather floating through the air and he a burning asteroid; to see them together was comical. Her rebellion was expressed subtly, and outwardly only with her long fingernails, the only female who'd ever grown them long, and the effect turned her into an even more delicate feather with her elongated hands flowing elegantly off of her slim torso.

Jun-Jun found Nikki in the Eye Chamber one day, letting gossamer winged pollinating flies land on her nails by holding perfectly still among the plants. She looked at them with the same wonder with which most viewed the Eye itself. "Their wings are like little bits of the Eye," she said when questioned, "and that makes them the most important living creatures on SIL." Jun-Jun had never before thought of creatures on SIL, though he'd learned of the variety of evolving species in class, and had never met anyone who could find poetry in bugs. She fascinated him from that day, and her polar attraction to Marcus brought the three together.

SIL was built in layers from the outer shell. The first layer was structural and created an air filled envelope between alloy spheres held apart by angled tubular beams. After that were the storage rooms, supply and refuse chambers, raw material stockpiles along with rooms of recyclable junk, thermal balancing chambers, and waste collection chambers directly connected to first stage reconversion chambers. Inside of this layer on one side of SIL were navigational stations and facilities for all ship operation, with housing for individuals on the other. There were nine more layers of housing on that same side, balanced by all sorts of occupational offices and laboratories on the other side. In all, these twelve layers only represented one eighth of the radius of SIL.

The grand exceptions were the outbay portals at five locations on SIL. The original designed called for six, but only five remained operational. The sixth had been converted into the Eye Chamber, the Chapel, the Exercise Chamber, Finding Suites, large Assembly Meeting Hall, and an Art Gallery. The five outbay portals and its sixth multi-function counterpart all formed a large intersection at the center of SIL, known as the HUB. Most travel within SIL accessed the HUB, as it represented the shorter distance to travel between locations in many cases, and was lined with quicklifts and automated transport tubes.

Past the labs, classrooms, storage bins and technological development complexes was a long curved hallway opening onto

Second Pass

the Eye Chamber, Galleries and Chapel. Jun-Jun jetted by these with blurring speed toward the living area. On L4 he slowed himself, grabbed a corner post to swing his body around and let go, hurling himself down the rows of private living quarters.

The door marked 'Isievitch' was no different than other doors at first glance, though it was actually quite different. The difference was that two doors each side of it were unmarked, meaning that this family occupied five units. With only three children, this was out of the ordinary.

Marcus's father, Andrew, was one of the original bioengineering specialists on the ship. His first mission had been more involved with human biology, cloning, development of fetal disease prevention, and genetic altering. His transfer to botany came soon after the original explosion. Coming from outside of that specific specialty gave him a fresh approach, and soon his expertise proved itself as he quickly learned to develop hybrid plants, which became the main source of food on SIL.

To do this, however, he needed to have some laboratory space away from the Eye Chamber, because cross-pollination with experimental DNA implants could potentially kill off existing crops. So he was given two extra living units in which to conduct all experimental cross-pollination. The Isievitch home was larger than the others, from the outside, and many of the new generation who knew little of his history were jealous. Yet due to the doubled use of the space for work and living, with an active and growing family, it was in fact more cramped. The combination of jealousy from the outside, and close living quarters on the inside, made tensions mount and often explode between father and teenage son.

Marcus answered the door and let Jun-Jun in. As they jetted to his room, Marcus pelted him from behind with small bits of chewed paper.

"Cut it out," said Jun-Jun.

Marcus laughed out loud. "What's with the girly voice Jun? You sound like a cartoon!"

"What do you mean?"

Marcus couldn't contain himself. He just laughed and pointed. Jun-Jun was used to such antics from his partner in crime and chief rival. Marcus always poked fun at him to get a little wrestling match started. Jun-Jun didn't go for it.

"Is my voice really different?"

"Yeah," Marcus started, then changed to a high-pitched squeak "it sure is! What you been doing, eating estrogen supplements?"

Jun-Jun stopped for a second and thought silently. Marcus was waiting for a comeback, his eyebrows raised and a smirk on his face. But Jun-Jun looked at his friend with confusion and said, "My computer had me re-do voice recognition. It thought it was some software problem..." he drifted further into his thoughts, "...I guess dying changes you."

"Dying?" Marcus looked at his friend. "Did you say 'dying'? The only thing dead about you is your dinky little smoot!" He punctuated this with a pop shot to Jun-Jun's shoulder, which was stopped before hitting its mark by a hand clamped on his wrist.

"I'm serious," Jun-Jun said throwing the hand to the side, "I have died 7 times in the past month. But you can't tell anyone."

"Are you crazy? How could you die? I mean, die and come back?"

"I'll tell you if you promise not to tell anyone at all. Promise?"

"Yeh, I promise not to tell anyone you have lost your mind along with your male voice. You are weird Jun, really weird."

"Let's go over to the paper production lab, there's a place there we can talk."

"Why can't we talk here? Nikki is supposed to come over later and I don't want to miss her."

"Well, I don't know."

"What are you afraid of? Nobody will hear us here."

"I know, but what I'm about to tell you is, well, very secret. And it could be grounds for expulsion. And not only for what I've done, but for you too if you just know about it."

Marcus's eyes opened wide. Expulsion was the most severe punishment, to be let out to space, abandoned to explode in the void. "You're just trying to be dramatic. To make up for your leetle teeny voice!" He mocked Jun's voice with these last words. "To go with your teeny weeny smootie!"

"Look Marcus, if you're going to be an asshole about it, then forget it. I though you would be interested in..."

"In what? Okay, I'll cut the crap, even though you do have the small smoot syndrome. What's this crazy talk about you dying?"

"I've been doing an experiment lately, me and Erica."

"Oh yeah, what, you tried to make it with her and she killed you, right?"

"I'm serious Marcus."

"Go on, jeez."

"I was thinking about how the Commander was willing to risk his life and go outside the ship after the explosion. So I wondered what it was like." Marcus wrinkled his eyebrows. "So I figured out a way to go outside SIL."

"Are you talking about hull breech? You trying to blow up part of the hull? That's crazy!"

"Not hull breech, not the explosion part at least. I mean to go outside—without a suit." He let it sink in. "To enter the void without protection."

"Shit!" Marcus said quietly. "You went out, out – there?"

"I call it freelocking. You get warm thermal clothing, tether yourself to the outbay portals, then open the outer port."

"You're bullshitting me. You'd explode! And freeze!" He started laughing again. "You had me there for a minute. Good one Jun." He again tried a jousting jab at his friend, and again was stopped. This time Jun-Jun held onto his wrist and pulled him close.

"I'm serious." He held Marcus right in front of him, face to face, staring into his eyes.

"You couldn't be," Marcus stammered, as unsettled by the way he was being held as much as by what he was hearing. "You'd be all...exploded...and shit."

"You don't explode right away," Jun-Jun said, letting him go. "You pass out first, then die, and then you explode, like a couple minutes later. I have her bring me back in before I explode."

"Back up one second here, smoot breath. You tether yourself to the docking ports, put on warm clothes and go outside? Your skin would either freeze or get irradiated. You couldn't survive that."

"Very good, teacher's pet. I protect my skin and hair with a thick layer of grease from the machine shop. It is an insulator, blocks radiation, and can't freeze."

"So you're telling me you do this and then you die. If that's true, how could you be here now?"

"The longest I've done it is for 30 seconds. Erica pulls me back in after that and then resuscitates me."

"Why the hell would you do something like that? You're crazy! How does she resuscitate you?"

"She gives me mouth-to-mouth, to get me breathing again."

"What that girl will do just to get to kiss you. Kissing you dead!"

"Yeah, she was pretty upset the last time. She didn't think she would bring me back."

"Well, I'd be upset too. You were dead! Doesn't that bother you at all?"

"There is something that happens when you die. Something wonderful. I've seen things a normal person can't see. I saw IT! That thing that makes everything work, the thing that keeps us all, and guides us. And I could see forever – as far as I wanted."

Marcus looked at him for a long time. His parent's had been Jewish on Earth, but had not kept up their faith on SIL. They talked of God and duty. Death is the end; life the focus. He'd never thought about beyond. "What was it like? Dying?"

"The first moment is scary, but then everything is peaceful. There's this incredible shaft of warmth, all glowing and radiant. It's like light, but different than light. Like a tunnel. And you go down it, farther and farther away from here, from this. You are above everything, or outside of it, and you can see it all. But seeing is understanding too. I saw, and understood, everything! All the reasons! All the chances! It is all so—perfect!" Just talking about it gave him the feeling again, of being outside, looking back at life. He felt warm, connected, vital.

He knew his friend wouldn't be able to understand, and he knew, too, that he might have spoiled the chance to proceed by telling him about it. But even that seemed trivial as he was transported back to that feeling. Even if it all stopped that moment it would have been worth it.

"Did it hurt?"

"What is pain? What is fear? What is cold? They are all nothing, completely nothing. They are the reasons for things happening, but they are also not really there."

"I don't understand."

"You can't understand. Don't try."

"Why is your voice so different? Why do you sound like a girl?"

"This is the voice that knows no stress, no need, no struggle. I've been transformed."

"You should go see Dr. Malanga. You're not right."

"I did see her, from out there. And I know she is Truth. She gives us back what we should have that we take from ourselves."

Second Pass

"I don't mean see her from your mystery place out there in dead land. I mean you should take your body to her."

"I was called for an Energization. She arranged it."

"Lucky you! Bet it was fun, huh? Did you get Toby?"

"It was beyond fun. Toby is the best, but now that I know how to get out of my body, and how to see the energy from out there, it was easy to let it in. It was incredible." He grabbed him by the shoulders, fingers digging into his muscles. He was looking with an intensity Marcus had never seen in him before, but was also as relaxed and calm as if he were asleep. "Do you?"

"Do I what? You aren't making sense." Marcus pulled away from Jun-Jun, rubbing his shoulders.

"Do you want to see what I've seen? Go where I've gone? Do you want to see time from outside of time, and see Truth?"

"What do you mean?"

"Look, Marcus, Erica won't help with my experiments anymore. I need someone else to help now, so I can finish. You are my best friend, and I know you'll do anything I do, only better. Well, I need to do the experiment on others, not just on me. We need to really learn about this and chronicle it. There has to be at least someone else, like you."

"What would I have to do?"

"I have to do two more free-locks to make nine. At first I was going to do seven, but now I know it has to be nine. Then you will do nine. And we need to find a girl to do it too. If it's going to be a legitimate experiment, we have to document the effects on both genders."

"So I'd have to get in warm clothes, smear grease.....wait a minute! You want me to DIE! To hell with that!"

"Don't tell me you're too afraid to do it. I did it! I guess I'm the better then."

"The hell you are!"

"So, you'll do it?"

There was sound in the other room, then the door opened and Nikki floated in. "Hey you two! Jun, I didn't know you'd be here!"

"Don't be so eager to say hi to him, Nik. He wants you to die."

"Cut in out Marcus, that's not fair," said Jun-Jun.

"What? You want me to die?"

"Go ahead, Jun, tell her."

* * * * * * *

Nikki loved her new breasts, small by comparison to her mother's but huge to her because of their recent arrival. She loved how they moved under her tunic when she changed directions by twisting her spine from one side to the other quickly. She did the movement as often as she could, and tried to work it into her everyday activities without others noticing. Her nipples hardened and her belly glowed warm when she did it. It was her secret way to bring into the day's public moments her night-time bliss of fondling her breasts and vagina that sent shuddering waves of electricity through her body.

Flushed pink, her cheeks rode her victorious smile closer to her eyes when she noticed Alex Jiimson watching her. For other boys to have caught her would have been worse than expulsion into the void, but Sven's gaze made her feel like large warm hands were embracing her entire body--a sprite nymph held safe by the gentle giant of infatuation.

Alex tried to imitate her movement, but sent himself spiraling out of control through the eating pod. No others were present to see him flail across the chamber, and unlike other teens who would have found cause in his mishap for relentless persecution, Nikki thought it was cute rather than an embarrassment. She did a mini click of her jet and arrived perpendicular him, her feet at his side.

"Uh, I, uh..."

Her giggle sounded like a million stars sprinkling onto a soprano harp to him. "Lex, you almost kicked the holders off their rack. Are you hurt?"

He didn't answer, but with a now athletically adept arch of torso twisted to parallel and kissed her on the mouth. She pulled her head back, but with enough suction to pull his lips with her. His arms circled her waist and pulled her toward him as his tongue parted both sets of lips. Nikki felt something better than she could make herself feel, down there, but was so out of breath her scalp started to tingle.

"Oh my! You'll make me faint if you take my air like that."

"I was waiting for you Nik," he said with the relief that comes from successfully finishing a phrase without his voice sneaking

Second Pass

in an unwanted squeak in the higher register of his diminishing youth. "I want to be near you all the time. I can't help it."

"You silly, you wouldn't want to be with me in the dye vats! Or when I change my brother's poo-naps either! In fact..."

"Shhh! Nikki, I love you. Come into the new village construction with me. The workers are on rotation break for another thirty minutes."

"Well, if you promise you won't..."

"I'll promise anything to get you to go."

"And forget your promise when we get there?"

"I will not!" he said as she jetted away from him toward the main corridor.

"You'd better!" she said with a giggle as she swung herself around the corner beam and launched her trajectory down the central fall way toward the area for housing the new arrivals.

* * * * * * *

"Shhh!" Alex said, as he covered Nikki's mouth with his hand, "someone's coming."

Two workmen floated down the central corridor of the new arrivals' housing unit, talking in tense hushed voices. "McVee should have been the one who died, damn it."

"Well he didn't. I can't be blamed for that."

"Kitterage is getting worse since Sylvana's death. He won't let any of us alone for one second. Watches us like a fucking comm remote cam sensor."

"Then you'll have to be more careful, much more careful. We've still got some time, but not much."

"What do you mean, not much? It's still more than two years away. By then Kitterage will have forgotten or died."

"I wouldn't count on it. Here's my case."

"I told you you'd left it under the grasp ledge, dummy."

"You just figure out how we can maintain the direct link and don't worry about calling names. You aren't so bright yourself, idiot. If you'd been quicker Sylvanna would be alive, McVee dead and Kitterage silent." Their voices faded as they jetted away.

"Is there going to be some accident or something? Those guys were scarey." Nikki pulled herself closer to Alex.

"I couldn't get a good look at them, and didn't recognize the voices. Did you?" "I'm worried, Alex. What if they try to kill McVee?"

"He's old anyhow, so why worry about that? I'd just like to know who those guys are. I need to report them."

"Why do you always do that?"

"Do what?"

"Report people for things? I mean, we just broke a directive, but it isn't bad that we did it. Some rules are wrong."

"I don't report everything."

"It seems like you do."

"I just report the things that seem dangerous, the things that would put us in jeopardy. I want SIL to be safe. I want you to be safe."

"That's so sweet, you being worried about me. I..." Nikki suddenly thought of the freelocking experiment Jun-Jun had told her about and it's potential for hull breach and death. For the first time she realized she might be in real jeopardy, or put SIL in danger. Fear tightened her stomach with icy fingers, her mouth went dry.

"Are you sick?"

"No. I'm just worried that there might be danger, or something might happen to SIL some day."

"I will always protect you and SIL." His arms around her were warm. She received his kiss. But after a prolonged moment, pulled away.

"What is it Nik?"

"I just...I...Alex. I need to talk to you about something."

"Can't we kiss instead?"

"This is important. Did you ever wonder what it is like to die?"

Alex's eyebrows blended into a knot in the center above piercing eyes. "Die?"

"Yeah, like what happens, where you go. Things like that."

"Not really, I mean. I decided to be recycled instead of expelled."

"Not your body, silly. You! What happens to you! Did you ever wonder?"

"I am my body. What are you talking about? When you die it just stops."

"No it doesn't." The statement emerged with a finality she hadn't heard from herself before. But she knew for certain. "You don't just stop, there is more. You go to this place outside, or inside. This other place. You know things, see things."

"What are you talking about? You sound as crazy as Kitterage."

"I'm part of an experiment. An experiment about death, about going beyond your body." She watched his face for signs of disapproval, but saw none. Just confusion. Then he looked suddenly angry.

"Are you in danger? I'll kill anyone who experiments with you and hurts you."

"I can't tell you it isn't dangerous, but if I get hurt it is not someone else who is doing it to me. Believe me."

"It scares me to think you might get hurt. What is this experiment? I want to be there with you, to protect you."

"I've been freelocking. That's what we call it. It's when you go out on a tether without a suit, then get pulled back in."

"What! You can't survive that! You can't live outside of SIL! Who's doing this to you? It's crazy!"

"Just calm down."

"I can't calm down! You are crazy!"

Nikki was disappointed. She turned to go, but Alex grabbed her elbow and looked at her with pain and fear. His hand was tight and her little finger started to tingle. "Let go Alex, that hurts!" He loosened his grip. "I'm not going to tell you about it unless you promise you will listen, and that you'll trust me."

Seeing he was not going to get anywhere unless he did as she asked, he shook his head with resignation.

"I've only done it twice, but Jun and Marcus have done it loads of times and nothing has happened to any of us. We tether ourselves and go outside of SIL. It's beautiful! You see so much, know so much. I can't describe it. And once you know for sure you don't just end when you die, then everything seems different."

"You die?"

"Well, yes. But only for a short time, then they bring me back in and revive me."

"Nikki!"

"You promised to listen." She soothed him with her hand and he took a deep breath and tightened his lips. "Nothing has happened to any of us. The only thing that happened was that Erica freaked out about it and stopped doing the experiments.

But it is so incredible to see what you can see when you leave your body. And to know the things you can know. Oh Alex, I've never felt so complete, so happy in all my life. It's better than..."

"I don't want anything to happen to you Nik. Ever! I want to do it with you to make sure nothing goes wrong."

"I'll have to ask. But now we better go or we'll get caught here, which is much more dangerous than freelocking." As they left the main corridor a few of the crew were returning to work. They looked at the pair with suspicion, but said nothing. Everyone on SIL was eager to find out how they were progressing with the new living quarters in the construction site, and these were just kids; no harm in a little curiosity.

* * * * * * *

"You told Alex!" Marcus grabbed hold of the stabilization bars and shook himself back and forth in frustration. "He's the biggest mouth on SIL. And he's always reporting people for the stupidest things! He'll tell his dad and then we'll be on restriction or worse."

"He's right," Jun-Jun said calmly, "with his dad onto us it will just be days before we are in the detention unit. How could you do such a thing Nikki? It could mean the end of our experiment." His tone was even and calm, his eyes looked at her like a father looks on a newborn child, he even smiled slightly. "But it's not a problem."

"How could it not be a problem?" Marcus' voice was louder than before. He let go of the bars and took hold of Jun-Jun's shoulder. "What's with you anyhow? You admit the entire experiment might be ended, that we'll be in big trouble, but you smile like an Eye-chamber worker. Have you been breathing pure O_2 or what?"

"Listen guys, I'm sorry! Don't start calling each other names." Nikki was exasperated and lost. "I'll drop out of the experiment if you want me to. I guess I shouldn't have told him."

"No," Jun-Jun said softly, "It's perfect. Have him watch the next session."

"Are you crazy?" Marcus interjected.

Second Pass

"No, I'm not crazy. This is the best thing. The data we've collected is sufficient, and if we are found out we are the living proof that it isn't dangerous."

"He'll ruin everything!"

* * * * * * *

Svenbourg Jiimson spent much of his days brooding. Though he was new Chairholder, he was finding the position held little of the glory he'd imagined. *Oh, to be back on Earth where they had things like money to make people respect you,* he thought. He remembered the Earth lords who were exempt from laws and consequence because of their wealth. He remembered the fat, ugly men who got the young women. His memories were cut short by the hiss of the hydrolock opening. Alex floated past him toward his room.

"Young man, reverse your thrusters this instant," Sven intoned, "I've heard you have been in restricted areas."

Alex stopped, his heart fluttered between his throat and his chest. He had nothing to say to his father, so instead turned an insolent, smirk in that general direction.

"What were you doing in the new dwelling construction zone yesterday? And why were you with that little imbecile? I've told you not to associate with any of those children." By those children he meant Borns and their offspring. His every attempt to consolidate his power as a Firster was constantly undermined by the Borns. In his mind, SIL could be a perfect world, if not for the Borns and their unhealthy desire to include Earth's myths into Sillian education. The very greed he lusted for in his memories was just one of the things Firsters sought to prevent by limiting exposure to stories and ideas from Earth.

"I can hang out with anyone I want. You can't control me," Alex said defiantly. "I love Nikki and you can't do anything about it."

Sven's fist came suddenly, catching Alex under the chin and sending him spinning across the room. His body bounced against the ladder rungs that lead to the other level of their unit. Alex gathered himself and regained his breath, then jetted to his room leaving a trail of floating tears.

Chapter 7

Simplicity is often mistaken for plainness. George did not make this mistake as he entered the over-large meeting room appointed with stark Earth-toned furniture, massive empty walls, and coldly presented windows. The wall opposite him was pale ochre with a redwood colored lacquer frame around a picture of the current Chinese Prime Minister hanging in the center. Even though the figure in the picture was dwarfed by the surrounding wall, the fact it was the only adornment in the huge room made the importance of the position the man held be more apparent than the identity of the individual holding the position. Even the lowness of the chairs and sofas added to the impression that an individual simply was not important, though the position they held was.

Sihn Su Hwan waited patiently as tea was brought. The tea cups were small, as were the tea pot and tray in the set. The tea was a gesture, not nourishment. The drab gray colors of the server's uniform matched her dull eyes and expressionless face. She took her time, endlessly placing cups on saucers, spoons at their side, arranging everything before pouring the tea. Even the tea was a gray-green color with strangely little odor as it slowly filled the cups. The dry-looking biscuits would make the tea a God send, but George could live without either easily.

She finished her service and quietly left the room. Hwan got an amused smile on his face as he looked over his large belly at the dry biscuits before him. "Please," he gestured with his fat-dimpled hand, "you must enjoy some refreshment from my homeland. We get so little of our culture here. If it weren't for the cookies I might get homesick." His smile vanished and his eyes bore into George's. "With your permission, I would like to talk seriously about SIL."

"Of course," said George, picking up his tea cup, "that is why I'm here." He smiled and sipped the bland tea.

"I must reiterate our interest in helping SIL develop. There is great interest in the development of sustainable habitat in space from the Chairman himself. And," he lifted his chin with patronizing arrogance, "as the oldest civilization on Earth we feel it our responsibility to assist the newest."

Second Pass

George did not like Hwan, nor did he trust him or the Chairman, who had come to power suddenly overnight in China, with apparently no resistance. "As representative of SIL, I thank you for your kind words and generous intension. I regret that we had to say no to your earlier ideas regarding population expansion on SIL this pass. But you have not yet explained to me the new offer you referred to in your invitation." George wanted to get on with things. He had so much to do and no time to waste on this minion.

"You are most direct," Hwan said with an amused grunt. "But haste often negates the larger purpose. When we value our time as most precious it is inevitable that we will one day leave the room before the larger purpose itself appears. How stark life would be if it were limited to only that which we plan." He took a moment to bask in self-appreciation and a clear state of superiority to the hurried American. Then his face broke into a broad smile. "We understand your resistance to our earlier offer. It must have seemed so sudden and extravagant to you, as your own system takes so much convincing to result in allocation of adequate funds. So many different political parties to convince, so many personalities. For us it is a much easier process to do what is right."

"You have a very good understanding of the process our system puts us through." George looked at this arrogant man who was every bit as much a bureaucrat as anyone in Washington. "But it wasn't the suddenness or generosity of your offer that made it unacceptable to us. With limited time to prepare for transport, and limited space on SIL, we simply weren't in a position to accept."

"Here is our new offer," he said grandly. "We already have a fleet of 26 large shuttles built," he watched the surprise on George's face with satisfaction, "and will have a full 70 by the time SIL arrives. Our shuttle design allows it to travel further, extending the window from 4 to 6 months during which SIL will be within reach. We are willing to allocate 50 for missions to populate and supply SIL during those 6 months." George was stunned by this information. None of the intelligence gathered had indicated anything of this scope. "Before you respond, let me finish. Our engineers have devised a concept for greatly expanding SIL's capacity for occupancy as well. The new design adds layers to the outside of SIL between the entrances to docking bays and away from the Eye. The first additional layer would take 3 years to complete, but would, in 4 months, provide living quarters for an additional 3,000 people in a crude form. With each layer, too, there would be a doubling in size of plant bays and farming terrariums."

"Are you sure..." George began.

"I'm not finished," Hwan said with a polite bow of his head, "if you please." George sat back. "We are prepared to give all materials, prepared for delivery onto SIL by the beginning of the coming pass, for the construction of the new outer layer to SIL, plus the work force with which to build it. We also propose to provide transportation for an additional 3,074 new inhabitants."

"There is no way SIL will stand for that many new people, much less, uh..." George was stuck. He didn't want to show that American interests were having undue influence on SIL's development, but he knew Associated will make every move to have Congress block such an influx of Chinese.

"Chinese," declared Hwan. "It is no secret that there is an intention to keep SIL a western nation, if not an American satellite. We take no offense, as we would attempt the same if it had originated from our technology. We are prepared to allot 50% of these new inhabitants to be from American or western states. Our proposal includes 30% American and 20% of other nationalities, to be selected, of course, by you. In fact, your office would also select the Chinese who would travel to SIL. In the end, this would make a total population of 5064 until the next pass. A full 58% of these will be Americans, 12% from a variety of countries, and a mere 30% Chinese occupants. We believe this is a fair recognition of our donation to this new nation. The Chinese would also become full citizens of SIL, not retaining their Chinese citizenship."

"I don't know what to say," George began. "It does not seem feasible, even possible, to accomplish in the short time before SIL arrives. Besides that, I am not authorized to make such a decision. It would have to be decided by my father and the Assembly on SIL."

Hwan cleared his throat, and moved closer to George. He looked at him in silence for quite a while, as if waiting to see something. After some minutes he cocked his head slightly and squinted his eyes, as if trying to listen to a distant sound. He reached out his hand and placed it on George's forearm as he let out a long, weary sigh. "I know that you are distressed about the desire at Associated to maximize the occupancy on SIL, and the schedule they are trying to force will not allow for any shuttles to be free for contingencies. I also know that the Assembly on SIL is in chaos since the death of Chairholder Sylvana Lauretta, and that your father has been ill for some time, and then was wounded. I know that the chief of security has been replaced by his son, who is not proving to be very strong a presence. In consideration of all of this, you would be well advised to take council with your father. Try to talk him into accepting our proposal. It would mean his dreams would be that much closer to coming true."

George was shocked to silence. The Chinese were not known to have any intelligence gathering forces on SIL, nor were they particularly involved with the exploration of space. He had never considered boosting the population of SIL beyond its intended maximum limits, nor had he taken seriously any of the chatter about expanding SIL due to the fact that the window of access was a mere 4 months every 18 years.

"We will provide materials, transport, citizenship, workers, and money." He said with smug complacency.

"But what happens to the new arrivals?" George asked suddenly. "How will so many people ever be prepared to adjust to the extremely different environment on SIL? And what of the tremendous resistance to having new arrivals join the population from those already there? I'm afraid I cannot propose this to my father. I don't think there is any chance it will be seriously considered at this late date."

"We have very different assumptions of the future, Dr. McVee," he said. "You seem to have little belief in the adaptability of people. Our great nation has seen, in our many thousands of years of existence, that quite the opposite is true."

"Adaptability to naturally occurring changes is different than a society being hit suddenly with things that are not natural. And by natural I include the changes in political atmosphere and workings of government. An influx of people like this into a new nation has never before happened." George couldn't imagine that the indulgent man before him was sane. And was more convinced of his lunacy when he smiled and chuckled at his last statement.

"Suppose," Hwan began, composing himself, "you and your family do go to SIL and something should happen to one of the shuttles and there was no transport back to Earth after a visit of

4 months? With our shuttles, you would not have to worry. You would be prepared to face any situation that might unfold."

The huge meeting room seemed suddenly crowded, devoid of breathable air. Hwan's knowledge about the most private details of his recent conversations with Liz made him feel violated. In this vulnerability he realized that SIL was much more interesting to the rest of the world than he had imagined. There were too many unanswered questions, suddenly, about Chinese interests. He had to stop this conference and speak with his father. He couldn't talk to anyone else about it, not even Liz.

"Chairman Hwan," George said politely as he stood, "my schedule calls me. I will consider your proposal, but must warn you not to expect much. I will discuss it with my father, I give you that." He extended his hand.

Hwan stood and took his hand in both of his own. "When can I expect to hear from you next? These matters are pressing if we are to be ready in time."

"I will be in touch by the end of the month. I should have figured out something by then."

"Well," Hwan said, "it would be preferable to hear back earlier than two weeks as you propose, but if that is the soonest, it will have to do. I do not want you to rush into a decision, but I hope to be given the chance to fully prepare on my end should you accept our offer."

"Good day," said George.

"Good day to you, son," said Hwan, making George want to vomit. The thought of this man as a father was more than he could stomach. He turned and walked from the room.

"I'll have some more biscuits please," Hwan said as the door closed behind George.

* * * * * * *

Woody stood outside of the door to the Comm uplink watching George through the soundproof window portal in the main door to the chamber. He saw his face contort with anger and worry in the hazy blue light coming from the screen. He could not imagine what he was discussing, nor was he curious. He had great respect for George and his father.

"Well," said the commander, "so they got to you good it seems, son."

"Are you kidding? How can you laugh?" said George indignantly. "They want to take over all of SIL. We certainly don't want to hand them a new colony."

"Not so fast, George," he said, "they have some very good points. It would be much better for there to be a larger group of people on SIL, and mixing cultures proves enriching when people can accept each other. On SIL we have a common bond of survival in space. Whatever our differences, we work them out."

"Like killing Sylvana?" George shot back.

"Like killing Sylvana," Commander McVee said calmly. "She had gotten many people terribly upset, and was trying to create a political coup d'état and turn SIL into a dictatorship. It was very neatly taken care of, you must admit. And we will be much better off without her."

George looked at his father in wonder. He realized he didn't know this man at all, and would never understand him. "So you want the Chinese to bring thousands of people, and provide supplies to expand SIL's size?"

"No, not at all, it's a stupid idea," said McVee. "Don't look so surprised. I never said I would say yes, I just said there were some things about the idea that were attractive. Perhaps next pass after this one, but not now."

"What will I tell the Chinese Chairman? I said I'd talk to him within the next two weeks."

"You don't have to tell him anything, George," his father said calmly, "I'll tell him myself. Now," he said with a friendly smile, "do you feel more relaxed? I can't have my grandson growing up with a father who is obsessed with his work, can I? That's what I did to you and I don't want that to become a family tradition."

"I feel much better, dad. And I didn't turn out so bad, did I?" George asked. "It was hard, I'll admit, but it turned out just fine."

"You are amazing, son. You can be much more forgiving that I can."

"It's easy when you are the one to forgive. I was so angry, until I understood the good in you, and how you really were dedicated to your vision."

"Well, let's not harp on it. How is Liz?"

"She's fine," said George. "Since we hired the security company she is much more relaxed. We are a very unconventional family, I'm afraid, but it seems to suit her well."

"Are you happy, George?"

"I am quite happy," he said, smiling. "Things will work out, they always do. But now I have to get back to my office."

"Okay, son. I do understand. Good bye," he said as his hand reached for the termination button.

"Good bye, dad," said George. "You're a great father."

"I hope you'll forgive me one day son," he said and the screen went slowly black.

* * * * * * *

As the ComRelay screen flickered, three men floated nervously around the woman in front of it. She was impatient and nervous. There were a few minutes before the transmission block would be automatically detected by the computer system and be overridden. She knew this because she had been the one who wrote the security code; she was the only one who could temporarily override it. "Come on. Come on!" she hissed. Then the screen suddenly filled with the neat, handsome face she expected. "You took your goddamn time getting to the link, you bastard. Where the hell were you? You know we only have three minutes."

"I'll do what I want, when I want. If you get caught it's nothing to me deary. I can see Andrews face now—you, the one responsible for computer security the very same to breach your own system. How quaint. He will have another real case on his hands. Murder, conspiracy and now security breech. I suspect he's wishing his father was still in charge. But we waste time. What is happening on SIL? Who is taking command?"

She looked strangely at the screen. They did not know the Commander survived. "It is unsure at the moment," she lied. "There is no word from the Finding station yet."

"Not who is taking charge of SIL, you bitch," he realized she was trying to lie to him. "I know McVee survived the hemareflux. No more games! Who is going to be in charge of shuttle dockings?"

"It isn't clear. I'll let you know as soon as we know."

Second Pass

"You'd better not be lying to me, bitch. And you'd better see things are working as planned or you will be the first to have an accident once our people arrive...or before."

There was a subtle change to the screen. "Transmission over," she said and abruptly cut the connection. The computer screens in the room suddenly lit up, but she had managed to break the link before the breech was detected.

The three men floated down toward her as she loosened her feet from the Velcro straps and floated away from the ComRelay. All four quietly jetted out of the room.

* * * * * * *

Nikki woke in the morning looking forward to the fresh fruits being distributed. She loved fresh fruit more than anything, except Alex, that is. As she placed the newest hybrid into an eating sack, she felt hands around her waist. She knew Alex's touch, and leaned into it, making the two of them rotate slowly into a spin.

"You are the most beautiful woman I've ever seen," he whispered into her ear.

She giggled at being called a woman. "I'm just a girl, Alex," she said, "and you are the boy I love." She turned her head to kiss him lightly on the jaw, then turned back to her fruit. She bit the skin open and sucked the juice into her mouth, then turned and placed her lips on his and kissed him as the nectar flowed between them. The combined sensation of kissing and the sweet fruit was intoxicating, and they both got lost in the moment.

"Nik," Alex said when he pulled out of the sweet kiss, "I need a favor."

"Anything," she said, "I'd do anything for you. You know that. What is it?"

"I want to free-lock."

She pulled her head back, as fear filled her with adrenalin. She'd finally found someone to love, someone to make her feel like she belonged, and she didn't want to lose that. She was afraid of freelocking. She had assisted Jun-Jun and Marcus several times, and found herself having panic attacks when they were dead. It made her so nervous that she would forget things, forget the instructions for reviving them. She had never assisted on her own, and always tried to impress Jun-Jun or Marcus, whichever wasn't in the free-lock, as if she knew exactly what to do. But it was always afterward as they reviewed the experiment, when she could remember what to do. So far they hadn't noticed the several minutes she was quietly hysterical inside while standing helplessly by watching the other one revive the experimenter.

"Nikki?" Alex said, bringing her back. "Will you help me?"

She laughed nervously. "I don't think you should have me help you," she said casually. "I'd get so into the mouth to mouth that I'd forget to breathe into you and you'd die while I was kissing you passionately." She actually believed what she was saying.

"You are so silly. I know you'll help. I can't ask Jun or Marcus because they don't trust me. But if I do it, actually do it, then they will accept me. I know I can be an asset to the experiment you are all doing."

"Don't ask me to do that, Alex. Ask anything else, I'll do anything, just not that," she felt like she was going to cry. The panic was starting in her just from thinking about it.

"You have to help me," he said frantically. "It is the one thing you can really help with. Why won't you do it for me? You know it's what I want."

Nikki started to cry. She felt space open around her as if there were no protective craft containing, protecting her. Her hands tensed without her awareness and the fruit slipped out of the sack and floated into the air beside her, spinning, with droplets of juice spraying off in slow motion, mixing with the tears floating off of her cheeks. She inadvertently squeezed her left hand and hit a jet button, which twirled her suddenly, making her scream, then sob.

Alex caught her and brought her close to him. His own body picked up the torque of her spin, while hers caught the drag of his and they returned to the slow, mobile-like spin of their earlier kiss.

"Don't cry, Nik, please," he implored. "I'm sorry if you are upset, but I don't understand. You free-lock with Jun and Marcus, why not me?"

"I...I...can't..." she stuttered between diminishing sobs.

"Yes you can. You love me; I love you. It will make it better," he reasoned.

She looked at him and stopped crying. She fully intended to confide the secret of her deficiency in him, unaware of how strong

Second Pass

her own need to please Jun-Jun and Marcus was. But that need to live up to their expectations, to not be weak, to have excellent skills, was so invisibly powerful that with her firm resolve to share a very sacred, intimate place with her lover, she finally spoke. "I'll do it. I'll do it for you."

"I love you," he said, kissing her.

The sensation of the kiss interrupted her disbelief at what had actually come out of her mouth. Adolescent hormones and the calm that comes after a panic attack dissolved her horror. Or perhaps it was just more comfortable to run, finding refuge in sexual excitement, and the haunting familiarity in being made to do what she really didn't want to do.

"Let's do it now," Alex said, jubilant with excitement. He grabbed her by the hand and jetted swiftly toward the exercise chamber. "I'll go get ready. I've got everything stored in my locker."

The process of getting ready became something to focus on. Nikki helped him get dressed, and applied the grease to him. She found it to be much quicker to help apply the grease instead of the usual habit of the experiment subject applying his or her own, and she made a mental note to tell the others how this makes it go so much faster. She also loved the way his face felt through the grease and massaged it sensually into his skin, across his eyelids, and behind his ears.

When he was ready, she reached to open the inner chamber door as he hugged her with his legs around her upper thighs, making sure she felt his erection in the process. She turned her head to smile at him knowingly, and her body also turned. She grabbed behind herself stabilizing the torque this created to prevent going into a spin. He let go of her and then looked seriously into her eyes as she clamped the tether to his belt hook. Then he bent his head down and put himself into a tight ball, as she eased him into the tube. His neck was a bit stiff, so he reached his left hand to his head and pulled it to his chest to tighten his position more. The claustrophobia of this position made him realize he was about to die, and he jerked open his eyes and turned to catch sight of Nikki. Some grease from his face got on his forearm in the process and he thought he'd better take his suit directly to the laundry and direct them to remove the stain. If his mother saw his newest suit stained by black grease she'd have a fit, and he really didn't want that to happen, mostly because she might force him to tell her how it got there, exposing their secret.

Once inside of the chamber, Nikki locked the inner door. She couldn't look at him in there. The panic didn't come, though, as it often did. She felt a new confidence, believing this might actually be the way for her to overcome it. If she could, then she would never have to be exposed to the others as a weak link in their experiment. She reached to buttons and opened the outer bay door. As the air rushed out into the vacuum of space, there was a whistling sound she'd never heard before. Suddenly the corner of her tunic was sucked toward the rubber seal around the inner bay door. She looked in horror in an endless millisecond seeing the dark brown stain of her handprint, suddenly remembering when she had turned before and steadied herself with her hand. She had gotten grease on the seal. She had compromised the integrity of the hull.

Instantly she hit the button to close the outer bay door. When it was closed she then pressed the button to open the inner door, vaguely aware of the sounds of alarms around her. As she grabbed the tether to pull Alex in, she realized he was not moving on his own. His face was blue. She was surprised he was unconscious because she thought she would have pulled him in before he'd even passed out, much less before the effects of freelocking had killed him. The panic started then. Alarms were going off, a rotating red light was activated above the docking door, and she was screaming.

She pulled Alex toward her, thinking she had closed the inner door, but hadn't. His body had a sudden spasm and one leg kicked outward, entering the chamber between the doors and kicking the outer door. A small crack appeared in the window, vibrated slightly and then the entire window buckled in the middle, was broken into several pieces and sucked into space. She pulled him into the interior and hit the button to close the inner door. As it slammed shut she heard the strange whining, whistling sound again and realized the inner door was also breached. The emergency breach control gate starting to close, as programmed to do when there is a hull breach, to close off that section of the ship so that the entire station wouldn't implode. She grabbed Alex's limp body and jetted them through it just before they would have been trapped to permanent death in space.

Second Pass

Inside of the breach control gate's heavy steel contours she once again turned her attention to Alex. His lips were gray, his skin was now gray, not blue and his eyes had drifted open in an unfocussed stare. She put her mouth to his and tried to blow as hard as she could. Her panic was mounting. She pulled away to take in a new breath, but screamed instead. In her screaming she was trying to take in a breath and suddenly stars of light started to swim around her head. Then there was nothing.

* * * * * * *

Malanga entered the sitting room and looked at Jun-Jun. His eyes were red from crying. Nikki sat next to him looking down in shame, and Marcus was twisting his hands nervously. Alex's life had been saved, but there was a possibility of brain damage. She hadn't spoken to his parents about that, and didn't know what was the best course of action to take. She would decide later. She hummed.

"Jun-Jun, your experiment has nearly killed Alex. Don't you think it's time to tell me about it?" She looked at him calmly. She knew she needn't add her sternness to make her point. Jun-Jun was generating more stern recrimination inside of himself than she could ever inflict on another human being, and it would be plenty. Likewise, she needn't do anything more than comfort Nikki whom she would watch in the next years for signs of depression, knowing the girl was blaming herself for the entire episode. What's more, Malanga knew Nikki may never find it comfortable to love from this point forward; and this was worse than death. A loveless life reached its cold fingers far and sucked joy out of many. It was something passed on to any children that person might produce, as if it were the most dominant gene in existence. She had to prevent this.

"I have taken it upon myself to have Erika explain everything to me. I know all about freelocking, and am aware of the effects to the body." Jun-Jun and Marcus stole glances to each other, and Nikki started to cry.

"I'm sorry," she wailed, "I know I can be expelled for causing hull breach. Don't make me die! Don't let them kill me! Please!"

Malanga flew to her side and wrapped her arms around the girl. "They will never do that, Nikki, you are too valuable to them. You have done something that has given us all perhaps the most important advancement of our time."

Jun-Jun and Marcus looked at Malanga, dismayed. "What..." was all Jun-Jun could say.

"What you three and Erika have done is amazing," she began, with Nikki silenced and staring at her now. "You have opened a frontier for understanding that no scientist or Finder had ever thought possible to consider. You have opened the door to understanding death itself. You have made a priceless contribution to all living creatures."

"We nearly killed everybody on SIL!" shouted Marcus. "How the hell can that be a good thing? We have committed the gravest criminal offense anyone can! We're worse than, than...even what Commander McVee did to make everyone stranded in space was an attempt at improving something. We are..."

"If you need to be condemned, Marcus, you'll have to do something else," Malanga said simply. "Do you need condemnation for some reason?" Her question was serious.

Marcus looked at her and started to cry, causing Jun-Jun to turn to face him in confusion. Nikki went to Marcus and held him, becoming comforter. Malanga watched and smiled. *Just one more to go*, she thought. She watched Jun-Jun, wondering how she would break him.

"I need your help Jun-Jun. I need all of your notes on the experiments."

"What?" Jun-Jun turned so quickly he had to spin in a complete circle to face her again. "I can't give you those."

"Why not? I won't turn you in. But if you keep them, they will be found, and you will be the one prosecuted for hull breach." She let this sink in. "You are the criminal here, not these others. You are the one who thought of this silly idea. You were the one who wanted so badly to be like the man who leads us. But you choose to emulate his worst characteristics, his most destructive side."

Jun-Jun turned to her, fierce with battle in his eyes. "You said we had opened a frontier! You said we could help by what we did." He looked at her, at his friends, back to her, at the room. "Were you lying! I demand to know!"

Second Pass

Finally, Malanga thought, *finally*. "I see your new softness has disappeared. Your voice is lower. So much for the elevated state you had achieved."

This mockery stopped him. He looked at her with complete stillness in him. Suddenly he didn't know anything at all. He remembered thinking he understood everything in the universe, even God.

"I need you to do something for me," Malanga said, "something only you can do. It will make all of this turn into the great gift I think it might be. I did not lie to you. I've just expressed two different ways of looking at this."

"What do you want me to do?" asked Jun-Jun. "I can't even think now. You stopped my mind."

"I want you to become a Finder Sponsor. I want you to dedicate every moment of the rest of your life to the healing of others, the understanding of all that can be understood, and the maximization of your gifts. I want you to join our group." He was listening. His eyes were clear, his mind was focused. "If you will, I will claim responsibility for all of this. I will say it was an experiment I was having you conduct and that I am responsible. They will never punish me for hull breach, mainly because they cannot remain healthy without me. There are too few Sponsors trained to carry on, so I'm safe. Otherwise, you will be put to death. Do you want to live Jun-Jun?"

There was a long silence in the room. Every one of them realized the importance of his decision. In a quiet, humble voice he said, "yes, I want to live. I will become a Finder Sponsor."

Chapter 8

Steven Masters, the paper said in bold block letters across the top, Security Engineer. Liz read the resume with interest. The first time she saw him she recognized he was fit, handsome, and had many signs of breeding. Philadelphia families placed the mark of their money and stature on their young from the moment of birth. All of this didn't phase Liz one bit. She was looking at his resume again, looking for a reason he was so insistent on treating her like a pregnant woman, rather than a scientist. In Liz's mind, there was always something in one's past which creates the characteristics of the present. She figured if she could find what it was that started his pattern of ignoring the accomplishments of women, allowing them to be forever eclipsed by their biological state, then she would be able to appeal to him in that context and perhaps win the respect she felt her scientific accomplishments were due.

He was quite aware of George's accomplishments, and those of his father. He was able to speak about many of the prominent women who had helped build the space program at NASA from the earliest days, understanding the context into which each accomplishment fit. His respect for these women was every bit equal to the respect he showed for the men. In fact, as she pondered this she began to see that the thing he had respect for, and apparently great interest in, was the science itself, and what it had meant for the history of the space program and for mankind. She knew he had done extensive homework to bring his understanding to this level, so how could he have missed the mapping coordinate system for deep space she had invented?

As she looked over the resume, it became clear as well that involvement with astronomy, science, astrophysics and other related topics must have been entirely in preparation for his position as Chief of Security for their family, as none of his earlier positions had been in any environment related to science or space. He had headed security for a bank, a United Nations group traveling into a war zone, a championship soccer team when the World Cup had been threatened by terrorist groups, for a female Archbishop in Central Chile, as private security for the cryogenic storage of Cher's body, and on the location of the filming of 'Brutal', the hugely successful autobiographical film about the life of a gay hustler in London. There was a mix of politics, religion, pop culture and sports. If misogyny had been the root, he wouldn't have needed to acknowledge the accomplishments of women.

She found nothing. Again. She waddled down the hallway toward her study to lie down and rest her aching back on her couch, feeling silly and slightly guilty. Since her pregnancy, and the new intensity of media focus on George as the rendezvous with SIL approached, she felt left out, and clung to her main accomplishment, the deep space coordinate mapping system she had developed. She passed it off to hormones. *Why are we women so complicated?* she wondered, petting Slava. "And why does Mr. Masters find you so annoying, Slava? Huh? I think you and I are making his life very difficult by virtue of our very existence," she said to the purring ball of contentment beside her.

She looked at the clock and realized it was time to wake George for work. They had been sleeping in the same house every day since Masters had arrived and organized the security of their lives. She offered to wake George up each morning since she was always awake first and it gave her something to do. She grunted and had an involuntary fart when she moved into a sitting position. She giggled. *Maybe he doesn't respect me because I fart and burp all the time,* she thought with amusement. She giggled again as she walked into the master bedroom.

"George," she said as she stroked his cheek with her hand, "time to be judge, jury and hangman dear. All those people waiting to see if you are going to allow them to float away their lives in outer space."

"Hnnng?" George said, rolling his head toward her with his eyes closed. He always looked so young when he was first waking up. It was as if he took his maturity off with his suit and tie at night before bed. He was an angel, even in his early middle age.

"You must arise and face the..." He suddenly grabbed her hand and pulled her on top of him.

"Judge, jury and what?" he said as he tickled the top of her buttocks, quite sensitive in her late stage of pregnancy. She struggled to get away, but was laughing too hard to manage anything other than twitching and getting stuck under her enormous belly.

"George McVee Junior, unhand me!" she said in her most ominous voice. "If you don't I'll invite Shandor to live with us and wake you up every morning!"

That got his attention. He stopped immediately. "You wouldn't," he said, wary that she might.

"I might," she shrugged as she gathered herself together. "And I'm going to try to get up, now that you've pulled me down, and every time I've moved all day I've farted so if you know what's good for you, you'll get out of this bed which is about to be consumed with foul air." With that she pulled herself onto her elbows and did, in fact, fart.

George jumped out of the bed, and ran to the bathroom shouting, "Quick! Circle the wagons! Women and children take cover! The end of the world is near!"

Suddenly Steven Masters ran into the room with his gun drawn. He had one shoe on, and no suit jacket, obviously having been caught by surprise by the yelling. He looked at George, who was naked and showing morning wood from having to pee, and Liz who was on her hands and knees with her butt to the door as she was crawling backwards toward the edge of the bed with her hair completely in disarray. She had twisted her head around and was looking almost under her arm in a very awkward position.

George started to laugh, and then Masters joined in. Liz tried to remain serious and stern, but was unable and also started to laugh.

"Well, little lady," Masters said, "I seem to be jumping the gun a bit today, no pun intended." He winked at Liz and grabbed a towel from the back of a chair and tossed it to George. "Good God, man, cover your indecent self!"

George took the towel and walked quickly into the bathroom, shutting the door.

"Any news from the expecting mother? Did you sleep comfortably?" Masters asked Liz.

"You know I can't sleep, why do you bother to ask," she said angrily.

"I know it must be hard, Liz," he said with an appeasing tone, "is there anything I can get you?"

Liz was very annoyed now. "No," she said bluntly. "Just go downstairs and do your job. You might need two shoes today." He held his hands up in a truce gesture and backed out of the

Second Pass

room, looking so understandingly at her that she wanted to throw something at him.

As he left she let herself into the bathroom. Over the sound of the shower, George said with a half shout, "did you say something to me?"

"No, I did not!" she yelled back. "I was just explaining to Mr. Masters that he needn't shoot us for laughing in the morning."

"Common Liz," said George, "why are you so hard on him? We should be glad he's so attentive."

"Oh Jesus, George, you are so ridiculous," she was yelling even though he'd turned off the water and opened the shower curtain. "That man shows me no respect, and now we can't have any privacy at all. A man and woman should be able to have some laughs in the morning without being intruded upon."

George sighed and leaned back on the sink. "Someone could have broken into the room, or thrown something in through the window. We don't know what they will try next if they seriously want to harm us. He needs to respond to anything unusual."

"Since when is it so unusual for us to laugh? I suppose the next thing will be that he'll come running into the room when I have an orgasm if I'm not too quiet." She was really worked up. She watched herself from within as if she were a different person. She was acting much more upset than she really felt, but was unable to stop herself. This lack of control made her mad at herself and at nature for giving her so may damned hormones. *How can a child be born with any kind of normal psyche if a mother must go through such ridiculous moods in pregnancy?* She wondered to herself, still unable to shake the mood.

George, dried now, pulled her into his arms and kissed her forehead. "Liz," he said softly, "I love you. Masters is very good at his job and I'm thrilled about that. And it was funny, you must admit." He kissed her again, and pulled her chin up with the side of his forefinger. "Why can't you forgive him? He's as tense as we are."

"It's just that you get to work, he gets to work, Sienta gets to work, Tom gets to work. Everybody gets to work except me! When women worked in the fields they got to keep their jobs, take a break to squat and give birth, then continue working. Why can't I work!" she was crying now, amazed at herself and unable to stop.

George held her and swayed slowly back and forth like a teenage suitor at a prom trying to put all of his emotion into a slow dance. He just held her. "Your work is very important, Liz, very important. But you don't live back then. You are going to be a mother soon, and we are all trying to carry on without you so you can do that. Many things at Associated would go much more smoothly if you were there, believe me. If it would help, why don't you go over there today and talk to your friends. Visit them. I'm sure your ideas will help them." He smiled at her; she was calmer now. "Maybe you could poke around some and see if you can figure out who is giving away our secrets to the Chinese. You have a very good sense about that."

"You know, Dr. McVee," she said as she wiped her eyes with his towel, "you may just have something there. I can go incognito: astrophysicist under cover as pregnant tub of lard." She laughed. "Thank you George, what would I do without you?"

"Well, just as long as you don't fire Masters 'without me' today I think we'll manage. He's just trying to support you and doesn't know how. I'll take one of the other agents with me today. Why don't you ask him to drive you to Associated? I want you to be protected by the best man, and he's that man."

"I know," she said.

* * * * * * *

The card ran through the slot for the tenth time and the double red lights appeared from behind the blackness of the square scanner beside the door. "I've only been gone for three months," said Liz to a secretary with a cart full of inter-office deliveries.

"I don't know, Ma'am," he said looking helpless and a bit wary. "I can call the front desk for you if you want me to."

"It's okay," she said, "I'll wait here. Just get June Sartin and have her come out here. I'll have her work it out. I know it isn't anything to do with you."

Relieved he didn't have to call security, he smiled nervously and slipped himself and his cart through the door quicker than Liz had ever seen that happen before. She was rubbing her back and thought she might have to turn around and go home if it was going into another cramp. The last time it cramped she was confined to the bed for three days because of pain rather than doctor's orders. She waited for about five minutes until June came to the door.

"I'm so sorry Liz," June said breathlessly, "I got a call from tracking, there's another irregularity. God I wish you were still here. Those bozos don't know how to read the screens or the printouts," she was babbling, oblivious to Liz's state. June had never had children and had never had any partner, man or woman, that Liz knew of. She had beige hair that used to be some color—maybe blonde or red, or even brown. It simply was such a featureless color it didn't even lead to speculation.

"June!" Liz said, exasperated, "I need to sit down. My back is cramping and I've been standing here forever trying to get in. Who in hell took me off of the security system?"

"Oh my God, I'm sorry Liz," she said as she opened the door and let her through. As they walked she continued, "There have been so many changes lately, you wouldn't believe it. Stevens has been having an absolute field day lately." They got to her office and Liz plopped into a chair, knowing she'd never get up on her own, but not giving a damn either.

"What do you mean, field day?" she asked.

"Well," she said as she moved file folders from stack to stack on her desk, "he's a bit of an organizational menace...damn it!" she said when a few folders slid off the desk and emptied their contents into one pile on the floor. "I'll never get these things sorted if they keep getting messed up," she said looking at Liz.

Liz knew not to take offense. She had a long history of misunderstanding with June Sartin, who had started her work at Associated as a senior editor for their documentation division. Her interest in working at Associated was due to the science fiction novel she was writing, so that her work was actually research for her novel. This is an inventive way of managing research and development support for a writer, but was taxing on the others who worked with her.

As senior editor, she had to interview all of the engineers about the technical input they were providing for the various documents produced at Associated. But in her interviews she would say things that upset the engineers terribly, or mix data up as if to intentionally provoke them. As complaints came in to Liz, she started watching June. At first she reviewed her work, and found it impeccable. There was never a mistake, not a detail out of place. And many of the things she reportedly had said to the different people seemed not to exist at all. Eventually Liz had to call June in and confront her. In that meeting June had guiltily explained that she needed to see how people in engineering reacted in emotional situations having to do with their work being contaminated or destroyed so the characters in her book would be based on actual human behavior.

This was fascinating to Liz. June shared her view that everything in life could be a controlled experiment if you set things up properly and were able to maintain your emotional distance. Instead of firing her, Liz moved her into the satellite dish control center. Every day there was some mishap with the data being collected, and often important details went unnoticed because everyone was so completely clinical in their world view. By putting June in the middle of that, there were ample real situations that did not need to be invented, providing her with more research material than she could possible use. But also, by having June there watching people from a more emotional and experiential point of view, she began noticing small aberrations in data, inconsistencies between what was observed and what was recorded, and a view of emerging patterns. This new approach helped Liz figure out the deep space coordinate mapping system.

"Maybe I should leave you to your work," Liz said to June's hunched back. "Or I could take those and separate them back into their original folders for you if you'd like."

June turned around and looked at Liz as if seeing her for the first time. "What is your current clearance level?" she asked.

"Well," Liz said tersely, "I am director of this department, if you've forgotten, and am the one who decides on your clearance level and your need to know. I imagine I can look at anything in your office with or without your permission Sartin."

June's shoulders sagged and she turned her eyes to the ceiling without moving her head in that direction. She let out a heavy sigh. "I know your position, but what is your current clearance? Stevens has started this system he calls 'provisional clearance' which basically means that anytime you want to see anything you don't already have in your possession, you must apply through his office."

"What?" Liz was shocked. "When did that start? That is clearly against all procedural guidelines and against the federal regulatory rules on clearance!"

Second Pass

"It started several months ago," she suddenly looked confused, "I don't really remember when."

Just after the Chairholder was murdered, Liz noted. "You know, June," Liz said, "I am not feeling at all well and think I should go back home and take a nap."

"I thought you were going to organize these files for me," she said like a child who was about to have a tantrum. "You did offer."

"And you questioned my clearance, my 'provisional' clearance. At any rate, I might get them messed up. You'd be better off doing it yourself. I'll let myself out."

Liz was aware of the security officer chatting with someone in the hall and knew she was actually watching Liz. *Of course they sent a female one,* Liz thought, *that way she can follow me into the bathroom if need be.* Liz then turned a corner and ran into Woody.

"Little Lady!" Woody said with a smile that made Liz feel much better. "You don't know how lonely it has been with you gone." He looked at her abdomen. "And from the looks of you, we should be preparing for at least triplets! Oh Lizzie, how I've missed you." He grabbed her in a warm embrace. "Where are you going?"

"Well," she said glancing with her eyes in the direction of the security guard, "no place I'm not supposed to, apparently."

Woody chuckled, "Don't worry about her, Liz. I asked her to keep an eye on you. I wanted to make sure I got to see you before you left."

"I would never..." he held up his hand.

"You would never leave without seeing me, but others might not respect your time and use you all up so I'd just get a tired pregnant woman needing to soak her feet in cool water! Are you comfortable walking with me a bit outside? It's such a fine day and I could use fresh air."

He took her elbow and they left the building. They turned left out of the main entrance and headed toward Intelligence Avenue. This had been a pattern from many years before when Liz was young. Woody always walked with her to the frozen yogurt shop a block away. Her stomach gurgled with anticipation.

"Liz," he said seriously once they were out of view of the building's windows, "there are some things you need to be aware of. I thought you could talk with George about them as well, if it's not asking too much."

"What is it?" Liz asked.

"There have been some very brief comm. uplinks lately. They are erased from the log, but I can see them in the internal calibration manifest. I've been keeping a daily record privately."

Liz was completely focused now, remembering what George had asked her to do. "Is there any pattern? Isn't there any operator code entry? There must be, because you cannot operate the Comm-link without one."

"Well, that's the problem," he said as he stopped and sat on a bench along the avenue. "There is no pattern, and all of the operator code entries are a private one George and I created for his private talks with people on SIL, off the record, as it were."

"Well then is it George?"

"I don't think so. George always tells me before he's coming in, and always lets me know after he actually did come. Someone has found out our private code and is using it."

"Well, it should be easy to track. When it is there in the internal calibration manifest, just check the video printing record, or the security tapes of the room. If it isn't George, then you'll see who it is." It seemed so simple to her.

"You know thought of that," he was slightly hurt that she had suggested this, "and every time, the tape has been erased, or has static on it. Which means that the people doing this know this facility very well. And there is danger for George," he said.

"How so?" she asked.

"By using his secret code, they are telling him that he's been found out and that perhaps his own transmissions aren't that secret. Besides, if we expose them, they will then be able to expose George, and then GAO will get involved and there will be a big mess, probably a Congressional investigation of George, no one else."

"I..." she stopped short as warm liquid gushed down her legs from beneath her skirt. "Oh my God!" she yelled.

Woody didn't know what had happened and looked around, but saw nothing. "What is it Liz?" he asked.

"My water just broke. I need to get to the hospital. I'm having a baby, Woody!"

Chapter 9

Jun-Jun jetted in a lazy, zigzag from the outer plant trays that held the huge leafy oxygen producers, past the fruit trees, through the medicinal herbs and cooking plants, all the way to the spongy mosses and miniscule flowers on the trays closest to the Eye. The click and hiss pattern of the tray mobilizers sounded like a very slow clock sighing after each tick. The insect population was wildly busy and quite noisy, providing an unstructured overlay of sound to the regular metronome of the mechanized trays.

The Eye Chamber had been expanded over the years, and now reached nearly a mile from the outer hull of the ship where the Eye was imbedded about two-thirds of the way to the Hub. It had also been expanded side to side by an additional half mile in each direction. While the original chamber had only been as large as a stadium dome, the new size provided so much more oxygen and food that there was little concern for survival as there had been in earlier days. There were many who had started already to hoard food because they sincerely believed the new arrivals would create a crisis, but they were the ones who had always been certain they were about to die. They were generally the same group who refused to enter the Eye Chamber or Chapel for fear the Eye would somehow become dislodged and suck them into space. This was irrational, of course, because if that were to happen the entire structure would fail and everyone would die. But by staying shy of the Eye Chamber they kept in eternally blissful ignorance about the vast supplies available to sustain the population, and by refusing to enter the Chapel they precluded the extremely comforting sense of community and inner peace a meditation in the Chapel produced.

Jun-Jun had been assigned to watch them, get to know them, as a Finder Sponsor. He realized this was to make him understand the severe terror his freelocking experiments had caused these people, and the need for absolute secrecy as Malanga had instructed them to continue the experiments for the past eighteen months under much more controlled conditions, and with a much larger number of people to free-lock. In fact, all Finder Sponsors had to free-lock at least once, and most elected to volunteer to become test subjects and perform the exercise seven times minimum. The only Finder Sponsors who did not have to do this, in fact were not allowed to do it, were the ones who had completed at least half of their Sponsor apprenticeship when Jun-Jun took his vows. What he did not know was that each of those, and the Finders in full service, were keeping close watch on all of the others as they went through their freelocking trial period and then afterward.

Jun-Jun was dizzy with oxygen saturation by the time he came close to the eye. His tunic was drenched with sweat from the heat and humidity that near the amplified rays of the distant sun, and he had removed his socks so his feet were free and cooler. He prepared himself for the grand moment—when he turned around with the Eye behind him to look through the mist at all of the rainbows as the vast, dwarfing array of plant trays danced their kaleidoscopic rotation dance as far as his eyes could focus. He turned with his eyes closed, aligning himself with his other senses, sharpening them, so that when he opened his eyes he would have maximum effect.

When he opened his eyes he nearly screamed, for one of the plant workers had followed him silently and was staring at him from about two feet away.

"Hey!" the old woman shouted at him. "Get out of the way! You are blocking the Eye and the plants are not getting their proper sunlight!" She tried to push him to the side.

He started to hum and she immediately calmed down. As she grabbed his shoulders to move him, he jetted in a half circle, turning her to face the cavernous Eye Chamber. "Look at it," he said through his humming, "look at the great beauty. Those plants are life; just as the rainbows and insects are. I come here to appreciate that we are all alive, to appreciate the miracle the Eye Chamber is."

She looked at him, then looked quizzically over his shoulder with cynicism. She huffed and pulled free of him. "You are the one who tried to murder us, aren't you? You tried to kill my son, Alex."

"Mrs. Marsdon-Jiimson, I didn't mean..." but he didn't finish. How could he? She was right, on all counts. His moment didn't happen, and another one did, one more real. She was well known to be bitter and resentful of children. Her last child had been stillborn due to her advanced age, and she took it out on all young people. Even though she had five children by her husband, it apparently had been the one who died, the sixth, who was to

Second Pass

make her life worthwhile. He didn't argue, but just jetted to the side exit and left.

He thought about going to the Chapel before the Sponsors' meeting, but realized he had exited on the opposite side of the Eye Chamber from the Chapel and didn't have time to go all the way around to it. He thought for a moment about going back in the side door and cutting through, but saw the woman's face pressed against the door's portal to see that he left as she wanted him to do.

He arrived about twenty minutes early to the Finders Chamber outer room and found Malanga there.

"Hello Jun," she said kindly, "you are early?"

"Yes Finder Malanga," he said politely using the long form of address to show his respect, "I was going to go to the Chapel, but didn't have time, so I came early."

"How do you like your studies so far?" she asked.

He thought about this. The apprenticeship had been a requirement, almost a punishment for having started the freelocking in the first place. He, along with Alex, Nikki and Marcus had all been made to become Sponsors. At first he had responded as anyone would to being punished. But when he began to learn the Finding ways, he realized that it was probably the most interesting thing he'd ever done. And later, when Malanga said she wanted him to continue his experiments secretly, but to teach the others, he began to love everything about being a Finder Sponsor. It was about the most prestigious position a young person could have on SIL.

"I love it, I really do," he said sincerely.

"You are a very special young man," she said. "How many times have you free-locked now?"

"Twenty-one," he lied, wondering what she was doing. She wasn't humming, but he felt as if she were. He had actually done it more than that, but had hidden it from the record so he wouldn't exceed the schedule she had set forth for the experiments.

"You know what that number represents, three sevens? Spirituality in abundance. Do you know what that means in relation to the freelocking?" She asked, clearly in role of teacher.

He hadn't realized that the numbers bore meaning in relation to things outside of Finding. He shook his head.

"It means," she said, "that you are no longer experimenting when you do it. And that means that you will do it nine more times only, not more than that. At thirty repetitions you will have come to the fulfillment of the Spiritual purpose of the practice in your life. After that you may only do it for the sole purpose of being of service to others."

He didn't know what to do now. He realized that he had just free-locked for the thirtieth time two days earlier. Suddenly he knew he had to tell her the truth. There was no other way. Otherwise she would expect him to report his experiences and there would be no reporting. And he knew better than to try to fake it any longer. He swallowed with difficulty and prepared to speak.

"I have a confession," he said, "I've already done it thirty times."

"You have," she said simply. He couldn't tell if it was a question, a statement to reiterate what he had said or if she was telling him she knew. He just looked at her, not knowing what to do or say. "Then you must only do it from now on for the sole purpose of service to others."

"What kind of service can freelocking be?" he wondered out loud.

"We don't know yet," she said, "but I have a request. Will you help me?"

"Yes, Master Malanga," he said looking at her in wonder, appreciating her gentle kindness in a new light, "anything."

"I would like to have private sessions with you, recorded for my Finders Log, but not for anyone else. I need to understand everything about the experience. Now that you've told me the truth without my asking for it, you can tell me everything about the experience."

"I would be happy to do that," he said, almost crying with gratitude for this remarkable woman.

"Good, then," she said, "we will start in the morning. Now," she said as she stretched into the cat awakening posture, "let us prepare for the meeting."

* * * * * * *

The warehouse was so quiet that the sound of the florescent lights lighting seemed intrusive. When the man in charge slammed his briefcase down on the aluminum table, everyone in the room

Second Pass

jumped. There were six men and two women in the room. Three of the men and both of the women would be going to SIL, the others would join them later. The man in charge, one of the ones to join later, had set up a large sketchpad and began to write on it.

"Here is the schedule for the shuttle traffic. You two," he said indicating two of the men, "and the women will leave in the fifth shuttle, posing as married couples. When you get to SIL..." He was interrupted by one of the women.

"Why do we have to pretend to be married? I've never understood that. She and I have been together for a long time now and we intend to stay together. There are lesbians on SIL for Christ's sake."

The man in charge slammed his hands down on the table in front of him. "You'll do as I say and you'll like it, you dyke whore," he said, "and you will go as married couples."

"You act so sure," said the other woman, "but where the fuck will you be when we get there? Fuck! We can do anything we want to do. Screw you."

"Hey twat face," said the man sitting closest to her, "if I'm your husband and you two are getting it on, then I get to watch."

"Yeah," said the other man of the two going on the fifth shuttle, "I like that action."

"You look in our direction and I'll cut your balls off, you asshole," said the first woman.

"Or maybe we'll make you two fuck for us," said her partner, "we wouldn't like that for the sex, but we'd love it just to make you squirm."

One of the other men said quietly, "From what I've heard he'd like that just fine."

"What the fuck did you say to me?" said the man in reference.

"Shut up!" yelled the man in charge. "If you don't stop, you aren't going."

"You can't do that now, jerko," said the first man, "we're already registered."

At this the man in charge smiled. "You are, huh? Well, then, where is your shuttle pass? Have you seen it yet?" He looked around and watched as they all looked questioningly at each other. "That's right," he said triumphantly, "I haven't issued them yet, and I don't need to until the last minute. Power has its privileges. If they only knew." He smirked to himself.

"You fucking son of a bitch," said the other man who had been quiet until this time. "You fucking conniving, lying asshole."

"So," said the man in charge smugly, "let's get on with our meeting. You four will go on the fifth shuttle. I will go on the seventeenth large shuttle flight with the ambassadors and visitors, only to stay for a few weeks of course. The two of you," indicating the two sitting in the back, "will go with the forth supply shipment as loaders, and wait for the eighth transport shuttle, which will be our target ship, piloted by our friendly flight captain here."

"Where do we hide out," asked one of the men in the back, "while we wait for you? If we do anything suspicious, we'll be held and questioned."

"Our contact on SIL in the outbay portal said he will contact you and get you to a safe place. You will be posing as plant tenders for three days until the other shuttle arrives."

"Wow," said the taller of the two women, "look at Mr. Horticulture there. I think you and your boyfriend are perfect for doing flower arrangements while you wait."

The man on the left in the back jumped over the chair in front of him and grabbed her by the neck, "I might be gay but I'm no lightweight, muff eater," he said as she was choking. She managed to drive her knee into his crotch and he let go and yelled. "You fucking bitch!"

"Silence!" said the man in charge. "I can still replace you, all of you!" He looked around the room. "And I can expose this entire plot at any time, saving the day. So keep on fighting. You'll get nothing."

"He's right," said a voice from the back of the room. "And I assure you, even if you pull this off. If you don't do exactly as he says, there will be no re-entry for you. I'll have your shuttle shot out of the sky when you return to Earth with the goods. I can always retrieve it as part of the salvage investigation later. You forget that I have the entire Navy at my command. So shape up now!"

Chapter 10

George sat at his desk looking at the picture of his son: light brown hair thick and curly, cheeks round and red, caramel eyes. He stared at the eyes, which he rarely saw open at home due to his current schedule. At two years of age Georgie was a strange combination of precocious and uncontrollable. His will was strong, unbreakable one minute, then soft as clay the next. George had taken him to the hill to watch the stars at night ever since he was an infant. First the trips were to calm the sleepless baby with the cool air and monotone recitation of the names of constellations and stars. Later these nighttime trips were increasingly conversational as his son's speech evolved, beginning with the toddler imitating the sounds of the names his father said, and later becoming a competition to be the first to find, and name, such landmarks as the North Star and the Ursa Major. And there was the game 'Where's SIL?' in which George taught his son to point to the place in the sky where it will first appear.

Liz, too, took Georgie to the hill. Lately she was the only one who took him there, as George's schedule kept him away at night until after the tot was asleep. "Daddy at SIL?" he would ask Liz every night, because he wasn't able to distinguish between 'getting ready for SIL' and being there. The first shuttle would leave in just three months, and the orbiting nation was now visible through most amateur telescopes. Georgie loved looking through the telescope they kept on the hill, but Liz had no idea if he'd been able to distinguish SIL from other stars and planets.

"Time for bed now," Liz said to Georgie as his chubby hands grasped the telescope firmly.

"Where daddy?" he asked. "Daddy at SIL? SIL in sky? Georgie go daddy, SIL!"

"Excuse me," Steve Masters said as he approached Liz from behind, "there's a call for you on your business phone. Shall I take a message?"

Liz looked at her watch. She couldn't imagine who would be calling her at 8:30 in the evening on the business line. She knew if she was distracted Georgie would miss his bedtime and be hard to deal with the next day. "Take a message, would you?" she asked.

Masters turned to the phone and said, "I'm sorry, she's unavailable right now. May I take a message?" He listened to the phone and looked at her with a comical face-mouth screwed to one side and eyes rolling up to his eyebrows indicating the other person was taking their time, saying something. Then his face changed and he stood straighter. "One minute please, sir," he said curtly and hit the mute button. "He said he's calling from Beijing from the Chairman's office. The Chairman wants to talk to you." He held his free hand up asking what she wanted to do.

Liz felt fear grip her. She had known since before Georgie's birth that the Chinese had tried to get George to expand the living quarters on SIL and allow an influx of Chinese inhabitants. George had initially said no, but then, when Commander McVee told him he was not opposed, a dialog had begun between the United States government, the Chinese leadership and SIL. George had been largely cut out of the loop. The end result was a compromise in which some supplies would be taken to SIL and a few additional large shuttles would transport more inhabitants. George had lost the battle to reserve three shuttles for contingency transports should anything go wrong, with Stevens pushing the revenue issue with big business backers of the inhabitation of SIL. But, until now, there had been no mention of the Chinese for months.

"Would you get Georgie into the house?" she asked, "He's going to be hard to handle, but I guess I really should take this. If it takes much time, have Sienta get him ready for bed."

"No problem, ma'am," Masters said, having completely changed his approach once the baby had been born. "I'd be happy to help." He turned his attention to Georgie as Liz took the phone.

"Come on little man," Masters said, swooping Georgie into the air causing him to squeal with delight.

"Hello," said Liz as she moved away from the racket and put a finger in her free ear, "This is Liz, with whom am I speaking?"

"One moment, please," said the heavily accented voice. "The Chairman of the People's Republic of China is on the line. Go ahead."

"Hello, Elizabeth?" the chairman said in a booming voice. "We are many miles apart, no?"

"Hello Mr. Chairman, sir," Liz said ignoring the question, assuming it was rhetorical. "How can I help you? Dr. McVee is not here if you want to speak with him."

Second Pass

"Oh no, not wishing to speak with Dr. McVee, but wishing to speak with you. We are many miles apart, no?"

Now that he'd repeated the question she hesitated. Of course they were many miles apart. "Well, yes, many thousands of miles. Can I help you?"

"Many hundreds of thousands of miles, just under one million now, and ever growing closer." He said this with finality; she was confused, though now realized he was talking about the distance between Earth and SIL. Then he continued, "And many families wishing to see their relatives, many governments wanting to create ties with SIL. Many people more than those who can go are wanting to live there, too. Can you accept that?"

She had never before spoken to this man, nor heard him speak. All of the news clips were video only with audio translation broadcast as the sound. She realized that there was always an extremely awkward pace of translation, with the kind of hesitation that seemed to be the result of the translator not fully understanding what was being said, and having to grasp for translation. She had always assumed it was a difficulty in language, but now she realized that this man spoke in riddles without apology and it was very difficult to know what he was talking about, or where it was leading. "Yes, it is very far. Yes, there is much interest. Yes, there are many who want to go who cannot at this time. I do not find any of those things difficult to accept," she said slowly, "do you?"

Now there was silence on the phone. She had turned his game back at him and he was slowing his pace, thinking of the next response. She wished George were there. "So, acceptance has a wide range. Between you and me there may be great distance in understanding. But I think that your human heart beats just as mine. We are close in our hearts."

"Mr. Chairman," she said, tiring of this game, "my son must get to bed and I have many things to do. I am honored that you call me, but I must ask you to allow me to help you if I can. Is there something I can do for you?"

"Ah, the American way of hurrying. Your son will grow healthy and strong no matter when he goes to bed tonight." He said this in a softer voice, a voice restraining anger. "In your country there is opportunity for all, equal in the eyes of your God. In fact, your government is making its business to assure other countries believe the same, and treat their citizens as such. But your nation is only a few hundred years old; it is an adolescent. China is many thousands of years old, and we remember many things, lessons. As your country proceeds on its own path of imperialism, calling it Democracy, you may forget that China is your big brother, for more experience. We value our citizens, but they must remember they have a place within a larger picture that they have no control over."

"Can I do something for you, sir?" Liz was now angry, "If so, please tell me what that would be. Otherwise, I am sorry to say I do not have time for a history lesson. How can I help you?" she asked with finality in her voice.

"You can only help me if you help your country accept our wisdom, otherwise," he said with a slight cough, "we cannot be of much use to each other. Good evening, Elizabeth, it was very pleasant speaking with you." The line clicked silent.

Liz stared at the phone for a few minutes, then looked up into the sky. Life by itself required very simple things—food, clothing, shelter, love. But life among people demanded very complex things. The complexity always baffled her. Why, when things can be accomplished efficiently and simply, would anyone add such a baffling complexity of intrigue? She would have to discuss this with George, but she didn't even know what she was discussing. The Chairman hadn't said anything of substance at all, and yet she knew it was some sort of threat.

When she got to the house she heard laughter coming from the bathroom, with Sienta babbling in Spanish with Georgie who was giggling and splashing water. Masters was standing in the hallway so he could easily turn toward the bathroom or to the outside where Liz had been. Seeing Liz enter through the back porch sliding doors, he then retreated into the living room where he would be able to monitor the situation by sound and not interfere.

Liz got Georgie to bed, said good bye to Sienta for the evening, and went and sat in her study. When George got in, around 10:00, she was deeply engrossed in her calculations. His arms around her waist and the soft kiss below her right ear were a welcome excuse to take a break.

"My love, my love," he said, "how is our family today?"

"You know I hate that kind of talk, George McVee," she said with irritation. "Particularly when we have much more important things to discuss."

"Okay," said George amicably, "and what is more important than our family, may I ask?"

She sighed and smiled. "Oh you," she said, "how can I resist your appreciation like I do? Our family is fine. I'm so business all the time. I'm sorry. How was your day?"

"Well, that can wait," he said dismissing it, "until you have told me what is on your mind. What is it? I know there is something."

"I got a call tonight from the Chairman," she said.

"Stevens?" George asked, surprised, "is he getting demanding again?"

"Not the Chairman of Associated," she said, "the Chairman of the People's Republic of China."

"What?" George said completely focused now. "He called you, here?"

"Yes, indeed he did. He felt the need to tell me a few things that every child knows are true, and then add some vague facts of the ancient history of China compared with the juvenile delinquency of America. Or words to that effect."

George looked at her, expecting at any moment for her to laugh and admit the ruse. But she didn't change her expression. "I think you'd better tell me all about this phone call," he said seriously, "let me get a beer and kick off my shoes. I have a feeling this will be a long one."

After an hour of discussion about the call, neither one could figure out anything more to say, other than it was indeed a mystery. He was going to speak with his father and the President about it the next day, and see what developed. So George changed the topic. "I've been working on the shuttle scheduling today."

"Of course you have, dear," Liz said, mocking him. "And the sun rose to the east this morning. I'm so glad we can have these deep talks."

"God, that does sound lame, doesn't it? What I meant was, I'm working on our schedules. It is very hard to work everything out with no backup shuttles. But I came up with an idea." He got some papers out of his briefcase. "I thought about possibly going to SIL on separate shuttles, so I could be there a bit earlier. And then returning on the last shuttle together."

"What difference would it make if we travel to SIL together or separately?" she asked. "I'll do whatever works out the best."

"The main difference is the time differential. It would mean you would be on SIL one month less than I would be. But that would make it so I could be there to monitor the shuttle schedule better."

"Well," she considered, "I could use the extra time to get ready. And Sienta would be much happier about that. She still thinks that she has to prepare food for us to eat for four months, you know."

"I'll talk to her again," George said wearily, "but if you are willing to go separately, it makes it possible for Steve's family to go sooner."

"Does that mean...", she asked with excitement.

"David, can look after me while Steve stays behind to watch over you," he said.

"So you are granting them visitor status?" Liz was excited about this. Steve Masters had asked about passage for his brother and his wife, Becka, right after little Georgie was born, and George had put him off. This made Liz happy because she really liked Dave and Becka, much more than Steve in fact. They had never taken a honeymoon when they'd gotten married and now, childless, they valued their travel vacations more than anything.

"It's the right thing to do," George said, "and this way they can spend more time up there."

"George McVee," she said going over to sit in his lap, "you deserve a big kiss for that." She kissed him. "It will mean so much to them. Did you tell them yet?"

"I thought I'd let you call Becka and tell her yourself," he said with a smile. "But you're sure you don't mind?"

"Mind? Are you kidding? Wait until Becka and I get up there. We will have an adventure like you men can't even imagine."

"What are you talking about?" he asked, wary.

"Never mind," she said as she went for the phone. "There are things we women do that men just shouldn't ever find out about. You don't have the ability to comprehend." And she began pressing buttons to call Becka.

* * * * * * *

Commander McVee had Malanga assist him to the ComRelay room, with the stipulation that everything she heard be treated as highest security. He needed her keen powers of observation both for himself and for the man he would be talking with. Since his bout with hemareflux he hadn't really ever gotten back the dexterity in his limbs he thought he should have.

But he also had become a complete advocate of the ways of the Finders. He had noticed that the older crew members weren't aging properly, nor was he. He knew there were many observers from among the Finders who were assigned to each elder in the council, and he knew Malanga was learning a vast amount about the human body in a weightless environment. He had also heard about the freelocking from her in a confidential meeting, and was as fascinated by it as she had been. Their constant secret meetings had become a foundation between them that went unsuspected, yet the fact remained that they were closer to each other than either had ever been to another human. And while not a romantic relationship, it was more intimate and permanent than most marriages.

He needed Malanga to observe him, as she often did, and then read back to him later the progression of energy fluctuations his non-material body had gone through. He found this method of feedback was entirely enlightening and led him to many discoveries about what was actually happening in meetings.

He remembered the first time they had conferred about his energy-map progression (EMP as they referred to it) after the Overseers meeting in the Finders Station. Once everyone had left the meeting, Malanga came to him to check if he needed anything. He had asked her what she had noticed during the meeting, and she had said she needed to review the data before she would know exactly what had been noticed. He thought this was a complete dodge on her part to avoid telling him anything at all, but she corrected him by showing him the results of her observations, which were a long list of characters inscribed at different markers on a timeline on her notepad. He insisted that she explain what each mark was, and as she did, he began to get an understanding of what she was watching.

He thought she was observing the normal medical things like blood pressure, pulse, breathing rate, etc. But she was watching fluctuations in the aura, the proximity of energy orbs that orbit the each body, and other things not normally seen by the human eye. As she described, he was able to draw some startling conclusions, which even she had not figured out. As a result, they created the basic concept behind the EMP, which she had refined to an art in the years since. From an EMP you could see who was in harmonic relation to whom, what the vibrational impact of an idea was on the various body systems, how the mind embraced different aspects of information, the subtle invisible communications based on intention between people, and the manipulations on a psychic level that were in the room. He needed this today to find out what his vibrational harmony was to the things he was going to be discussing.

The screen flickered to life and a rather fat, Asian face filled the screen. Malanga immediately began to jot characters in a row next to the timeline on her pad.

"Hello Commander McVee," Hwan said, "I don't know whether to say good morning, good evening, or good day. But greetings none the less." The face beamed with jocular friendliness. Malanga looked back and forth between the screen and her pad several times as if perplexed. But when the Commander looked quizzically at her, she motioned for him to continue. "And I don't mind at all that you have someone there watching this. I just hope they are able to meet your security requirements if we are to converse freely."

"My greetings to you, Mr. Hwan," McVee said easily, "my assistants are as trusted to me as yours are to you. Do continue."

"I see you waste no time on idle chat or social convention," said Hwan tersely, "so let's get down to business. I understand that you have given two opposite responses to our offer, and we are confused. You said you were in favor of our offer of more inhabitants, more shuttles, and more materials for the future expansion of SIL, yet you deny us access outside of the four-month parameter available to the American technology. How are both things possible?"

Malanga kept her clinical face on, but was quite surprised all ready. Nothing had been said about any negotiations for additional inhabitants on SIL, expansion of the physical station, or any relationship between Silian government officials and the Chinese, if that was indeed what Mr. Hwan was representing. She wanted to interrupt and tell the Commander that he was in breach of trust of all Silians, but she knew these were the highest classified matters and remained silent, expecting that there was a very good reason for them.

"You are only partly right about my responses, and completely wrong about their contradictions. We will accept 750 new inhabitants, half of whom may be Chinese, but the other half must be from a variety of cultural, racial, political and religious sources."

"But our QY vehicles have much greater capacity than that. One QY can carry 250 passengers, and they have a nine-day round trip turn-around including refueling and restocking. We have 70 QYs in our fleet! In the six months we can reach you we can do so much more!" Veins were stressed on his temples, and his skin tone had darkened considerably. Malanga held up her hand where only McVee could see it as an indication to slow down, to release stress from the situation.

"Our current circumstances will only allow you to travel to us for one month," McVee said. "You will be coming to reach us only after the Americans have finished their four month access."

"I understand that you don't want them to know what you are doing," said Hwan with a thin smile, "but it will not be possible for us to go undetected."

"Ah," said McVee with victory in his voice, "but they won't be able to do anything about it at that point, as all of their vehicles have too short a range."

Hwan looked directly at his camera, keeping his eyes open and directly focused even while he thought. With a quick blink of his eyelids he indicated his thinking was complete and he resumed his speech. "We have 70 QYs, and to deliver 750 people will only require one of them to make three trips, which is the maximum in a 30-day period. What will we do with the other 69 vehicles? Did we build them just to waste money and time?" he asked pointedly.

"I propose that you use the remaining 69 vehicles, which represent the potential for as many as 207 trips, to deliver materials for the building of extensions to SIL." McVee let this sink in. Surely Hwan would realize that this meant there would be room for an additional several thousands of occupants by the next pass, and McVee knew the Chinese were patient people.

"What do we get for this great wealth of materials we will supply you with? There's only so much alien fruit even my people will eat," he said in a feeble attempt at humor. "What can you offer us?"

"I would like to introduce you to someone very special, Mr. Hwan," said McVee, "my off-screen assistant you were so worried about before." He motioned for Malanga to enter the frame of the camera on the ComRelay. She looked at him with no expression for a full minute, assessing the situation. She had no idea what he was doing, but assumed he was buying time while he thought of a response. She freed her feet from their straps and floated into view. "This is Dr. Malanga, or, as we say here on SIL, Finder Malanga."

"Glad to meet you Madam Finder," said Hwan as if he greeted people with this title every day.

"The honor is mine," she hummed.

"Finder Malanga has discovered an entirely new method of health care. With her methods, called Finding, applied on Earth, your people will become the healthiest in the world. The American medical establishment is too myopic to accept even the most simple and easily proved innovations Malanga has discovered. In China, where ill-health threatens much of your population since the earthquakes nearly 40 years ago, Finding will reverse the trend of your population's demise and place you once more on the path to world majority."

Malanga realized she would have to give up her discoveries, and that Commander McVee had done this without even discussing it with her. He did indeed feel that he owned everything and everyone on SIL, she realized, and his arrogance had not lessened at all. But she also knew that this was her chance to change the trends on Earth in ways she had only dreamed of as an idealistic medical student decades in the past. It was a gift; it was intellectual rape. She had no idea what she felt about it.

"Can you do what he says?" asked Hwan.

"Yes," she said humbly, "and with the Chinese people to work with, we can accomplish so much more. Here on SIL we can develop medicines that can be used on Earth," she hesitated, took a deep breath and said, "In China, and we can eventually teach those coming to join us on SIL the ways of Finding. By next pass..." he interrupted her.

"Not next pass!" he said. "You will send some people back to train us here."

McVee had anticipated this, and was ready. "Hwan," he said evenly, "we have discovered something in the past few years that

Second Pass

needs much more study. Without an understanding of it the ways of Finding cannot be adapted for Earth."

"What could make it impossible to have immediate benefit? I demand to know!" he shouted.

"On SIL," McVee said quietly, "we do not age."

Chapter 11

Finder Malanga looked around her living quarters. She liked the warm earthen tones of the central room, and loved the way the bright coral cushions she had attached to the walls near the Velcro stabilization mounts looked. The cushions were placed so that a small group could settle in, attach themselves with the Velcro, and have an intimate chat. This evening was critical and every aspect had to be such that trust and comfort were never in question.

Laws of balance were coming into a new light for her. She had been so shocked that the Commander was negotiating with the Chinese in total secrecy, and that he had told them their findings about aging when the information was merely an observation and not understood at all, that all she could do at the time was hum internally. After the link had been terminated she busied herself with tending to the Commander's health, such a natural thing for her to do it made her invisible. But that event had shown her that the Commander was as arrogant as ever, and proceeded with his work as if he were shuffling papers instead of lives. She knew she needed to create a perfect counterbalance, equally secret, built on trust rather than deceit, forward looking, and with equal arrogance. She planned to put this into action tonight, immediately. She prayed she had chosen the correct people.

There would be no alcohol, no music, no special lighting, and no atmospheric scent. What transpired tonight had to be absolutely natural and not reliant on any outside stimulus or artificial feeling of trust or well-being. She had chosen her guests carefully, and wondered how it was that three couples happened to be those guests. Could it be that people found each other in pairs that were perfectly balanced? Or was it that people who were trustworthy and intelligent would only find like-minded people attractive? She did not know, but upon reflection determined once again that these six were the correct ones for her to work with.

Her guests arrived within ten minutes of each other, with the Dunns last to arrive. Tobias Manndle and Danny Lieberman had arrived first, mostly because Toby, who had just completed his apprenticeship as a Finder five months ago, came early to see if he and his partner could help get ready. Instead of having him help, Malanga had shocked him by having him wait in the main room while Danny helped her. When Sylvia and Bill Bryant arrived he was able to make idle conversation with them until the whole group settled.

"Welcome," said Malanga. "I am not humming, there is no music, I have done nothing to create any kind of artificial atmosphere to make us feel united. I have invited you each here on your personal merits, and the fact that you are couples only speaks to the quality of each of you in this room." She looked around and saw, to her contentment, that she had managed to get their entire attention, and by removing what amenities would normally be expected at a social gathering had indicated this was no regular social gathering. "I have asked each one of you here because of one quality I find each of you to have—trust."

Toby looked at Sallie Dunn, still the most beautiful creature on SIL, gossamer-winged insects from the Eye Chamber included. He had never thought of her as trusting or trustworthy particularly, but as reliable and unbiased. The quality she and her husband displayed more than any other was patience. They had been outwardly hated and sabotaged by nearly everyone on SIL from their first arrival. They had never retaliated or lost their patience, no matter how obviously provoked. They had their moments, like all couples, where they picked at each other, and were, in that regard, quite normal. They simply had chosen SIL as their home and the home for their twin girls and learned to live with whatever that brought.

As for Sylvia Bryant, in Toby's eyes she was the most trusted person on all of SIL. She had access to all records, all communiqués through every means on SIL and never showed any indication of the knowledge about people that she must have. She had never treated anyone badly, no matter what she knew of them in the secret world of secure communications. Even when the various scandals emerged over the years, scandals she had to have known about in great detail before everyone else found out, she had never given the slightest indication of what was to come. For this, she was trusted.

Her husband, Bill, was 1st Officer of SIL. This placed him second in command of the navigation, engineering and all technical aspects of SIL. His position was his occupation, appointed by Commander McVee and considered part of the NASA team when SIL was an American sponsored space mission. There was some discussion lately in the Assembly about making it an elected position, but the Overseers had squashed that proposal, pointing out that the skills necessary to hold the position of 1st Officer had to be determined completely by demonstrated abilities, and not by the ability to win the popular vote. In the course of the debates, which reached into every corner of SIL, a doctrine of separation of technology and politics had emerged. But the fact that the debate had occurred at all indicated that sometime in the future it would come up again, and eventually the nature of the position might drastically change. Throughout the entire process, Bill Bryant was clearly the person who would be elected if it came to that, and on his ability everyone agreed—regardless of political party, generation or social position. The fact was that everybody on SIL trusted him.

He turned to look at Danny. Trust. He and Danny had become a couple because of a deep trust. Both had been raised by parents whose profession was psychology; Danny by his mother, Toby by his father. They had been selected for the initial crew of SIL so they could observe the effects on human psyche of prolonged isolation in space, and had been denied development of any normal building of friendships or social interactions with their fellows. They studied everyone, all the time.

When SIL had been propelled into its current eccentric orbit by Commander McVee's sabotage, they were handed the Holy Grail of psychology, each in a different way. Danny's father had been killed in the explosion, leaving Millie, his mother, to fend for herself. She had been selected for the mission by Toby's father, Director of Mental Health in the original SIL crew structure, and was an expert in stress and induced psychosis. Finding herself in a position of extreme stress, both from losing her husband and thinking she was doomed to die a slow death through oxygen starvation, she understood from her professional view that these environmental elements might well constitute induced psychosis, as she was witnessing in many of her fellow scientists at the time. She found refuge in studying others as they developed the same symptoms she herself displayed. But when her own stress became too much for her to bear, she sought out Dr. Malanga, Medical Director of SIL, to ask for a work up on her own condition. Malanga, in discussing mental health issues with Lieberman, saw that this woman was extraordinary, and had a completely unique view of their situation.

Second Pass

She and Malanga turned their therapeutic relationship into a partnership, and together they developed the art of Finding. When Millie found herself pregnant to Stanley Gillis, Resource Officer, she decided that all children she would bear would be given the family name Lieberman to honor the love she had for her late husband. She chose to live alone with her children, even though she and Stanley kept their relationship going. They collaborated on how to manufacture equipment and different substances used in treating illnesses from the refuse of SIL and minerals collected in space.

Everything in their world was discovery, and as the children became part of the picture, they were encouraged by their mother to pay attention to everything they could observe, to find a use for every object or substance they found, and to practice full disclosure of their mind's inner workings at all times. Daniel and his siblings had known no privacy of any kind growing up, so they had learned to construct a very private inner world into which no entry from the outside world was granted. Only Toby had found his way into that private sanctuary.

Toby's father, Dr. Victor Manndle, had set up all of the mental health paradigms based on psychology as it was practiced on Earth. He used a healthy combination of chemical and therapeutic treatments to address every psychological symptom anyone displayed. Part of his rationale for insisting on such intrusive meddling in people's moods was to afford Lieberman and his other staff maximum opportunity to observe. As the entire community on SIL was comprised of scientists, they had no problem complying.

Manndle's wife had been design librarian, and was a fastidious record keeper. She liked to think of the human mind as a complex structure, and fancied that between her organizational and analytical skills, and her husband's thorough tracking of every shift of mood or personality on SIL, they would one day map the human psyche. When the explosion happened all of their records, which had been kept in the spare oxygen tank's storage area, had been destroyed. Mrs. Manndle never took work home with her, so every last bit of collected data was lost. She was much more depressed by the loss of her life's work than by the potential loss of her life. And when she had children, she vowed to keep everything in duplicate. So Toby and his siblings also had had no privacy.

When Daniel and Toby met there was something so comfortable they spent every possible moment together. Each showed no interest in any detail of the other's life that wasn't offered. Each felt that they weren't being constantly observed and charted, as they felt at home. Soon they fell in love. The irony was that the lack of any sort of intrusion led to each of them allowing the other into their most private heart. Trust had built their relationship.

"Trust is vital," began Malanga. "I am witness to information that I cannot share with you. When you discover what it is, which you will soon enough, you may be furious with me for not disclosing it earlier, but I cannot. You will have to trust me."

"What do you need?" asked Sallie. "I will do anything you ask. Anything."

"You know we will too," added Bill Bryant on behalf of himself and his wife, "though I cannot imagine you know things that we don't know." He and everyone else laughed.

"I want to form a unity," she continued, "a unity of trust, directed by me. I need information of different sorts. Constant information."

"I'm uncomfortable observing others and reporting to anyone. I will not do that," Daniel said bluntly. "It isn't a matter of trust. It is a matter of privacy. Every human being has a right to absolute privacy, even in a place like SIL."

"Especially in a place like SIL," added Toby. "But I am willing to do as you say, Master Finder."

"Toby," Malanga sighed, "you must call me Finder Malanga now that your apprenticeship is over. Or better yet," she said as she looked at all present, "I would like all of you to call me Solange in private. The nature of what I'm asking is more personal than any titles would indicate."

"Danny," said Sylvia, "are you willing to at least learn what Solange is asking?"

"I am so willing," he said as if an oath. Toby giggled at him; the others smiled.

"I need something specific from each of you. Sylvia, I need to know if there is any way to tell every single time the ComRelay is used. Bill, I need to have a complete dossier on every new inhabitant of SIL in the coming pass. Sallie, I need to know everything that has been done to you and your family as means of ostracism or the shunning you have endured, and any new ways that might occur, particularly for the new arrivals. Paul, I need

Second Pass

to know everything George tells you, his mood changes and the dates they change. Toby, I need to have you compile all of the experiences the Finder Sponsors have themselves and that they observe in others, just like we have done for the Overseers but for everyone on SIL and all the new arrivals. And Daniel, I need you to learn to speak and read Chinese."

They all looked at each other with wrinkled brows at the last statement, then collectively looked at Daniel as if for an answer.

"What?" said Daniel, "Why are you all looking at me? I'll learn Chinese, that I can do."

"And there are two more things I need from everyone," Malanga said gravely, "one is to not ask me what this is about. I will tell you all as soon as I can. Until them you must trust me. And the other is that we will keep our meetings completely secret, each one happening in a different place on a different day at a different time. There must be no pattern. I will meet with you individually on a regular basis within the framework of our normal patterns of social and professional interface. I will alert one from each couple when we will meet as a group."

"We are happy to help," said Bill carefully, "but I trust if SIL or its population is in danger you will alert me."

"Of course I will, Bill," Malanga said. "I'm so sorry to have to do this in this way. I appreciate your trust and hope to prove worthy of it. Just remember, the time will come when you will want to hate me for not letting you be more prepared, but in time I will explain why I will not be able to do that. If I defy that trust, I will expel myself."

* * * * * * *

Willa Marsdon married Sven Jiimson on Earth before going to SIL. She was a progressive thinker, siding against science, which had led to the overpopulation of the world with older people, and, therefore, completely opposed to having children. She loved plants, not people. On Earth she had inherited a family farm and, as soon as it was in her possession, she had kicked the tenant farmers off of the land and taken over herself. She sold most of the livestock and many of the tools and farm equipment. She built huge greenhouses, each with a different controlled climate, so she could have plants from every habitat on Earth.

In her quest of self-reliance, she had done all of the research and design for the greenhouses, and made several inventions regarding controlled habitats that she had patented. The government contacted her when they were developing SIL, having learned her name from the patent office in connection with some of her innovations they needed to use on SIL. Thrilled to be offered work as a mechanical engineer and draftsman, she joined the work force for SIL. Her anti-science views had put her in direct conflict with every other person on the staff, and lunch breaks were usually accompanied by the sound of her getting into a verbal battle with someone over some scientific topic.

Svenbourg Jiimson was drawn to her because of her strong will and unconventional views. He was completely devoted to science, but enjoyed nothing more than irritating his fellow scientists. Willa Marsdon was his dream woman. They first met over debates he intentionally provoked. After some weeks of his provocations, it became expected that the two of them would be facing off over lunch, coffee and even in the lobby of Associated after work was finished. They provided a soap opera vitality to the methodical work at Associated. One day, in the middle of one of their fights, he grabbed her and kissed her. She fought for a full three minutes before she gave in to his kiss, and they were married one month later.

When she learned that Sven was going to SIL, she insisted on going along, and was granted a position as a mechanical draftsman for SIL. Once there she discovered that there was one topic they had not discussed before marriage that was much more important than anything they had fought about: children. She found herself pregnant and, as her logic would flow, contacted Malanga for an abortion. Malanga mentioned this to Sven, expecting the couple had decided this course of action mutually, and Sven exploded. He and Willa started a month of constant battle on the subject of children, confining their arguments mainly to theoretical issues of population and society. The time was just long enough for Willa to feel the first movements of her little child inside of her, and, after that, she couldn't imagine killing the living thing.

Corey was born just months after SIL exploded. Four years later Willa found herself pregnant again and Suzanne was born. Willa tended her children as she would tend plants, and Sven had no time to bother with them other than to discipline them when Willa asked him to. She felt that just as pruning plants to help them grow was essential, so was it integral for development that children be denied things they needed so they would find ways to provide these things for themselves. She was a mean mother, and unbending in restrictions she placed on her children. When they became angry and started to rebel, she felt she had succeeded in turning out sufficiently independent and strong willed individuals. It never occurred to her they needed love.

Suzanne died of a bladder infection that went into her kidneys at age 11 because she was hydro-anorexic, denying herself fluids to the point of constant dehydration. The dehydration caused constipation, and so she drank oil to induce diarrhea, which further dehydrated her. After many years of this, she developed the infection that killed her. Willa and her husband blamed Commander McVee for her death, thinking it was the fact she was forever confined to space for her disorder, never thinking it was their own strange relationship with their offspring that had so broken her.

She vowed to never have children again. She dedicated herself to the development of the Eye Chamber and directed the farming effort there, designing the rotating tray system and giving constant lists of needs to the bioengineers whose responsibility it was to create a complete ecosystem of plant life that would be self-perpetuating. Willa knew what soils needed, which plants absorbed which minerals and which left deposits of which. When the Eye Chamber was fully functioning, and the development phase gave way to maintenance, she kept herself occupied all day, every day, in the Eye Chamber.

After several years of this, she suddenly had the idea to have more children. So, at the age of 41 she had Ingrid, at 42 she had Alex, and then, at age 43 she gave birth to a little girl, Isiins, who was stillborn. Malanga had told her she was too old to have children when she was pregnant with Ingrid, but the healthy birth convinced her that Malanga was just spouting medical rhetoric. With the still birth, she finally got the message and stopped getting pregnant.

With the expansion of the Eye Chamber and coming of the new arrivals on SIL, she again focused on her plants, mechanical drawings and plans for the expanded facility. She rarely had anything to do with her children or her husband. The children on SIL knew her as Plant Lady. Every learning expedition to the Eye Chamber during their schooling years had placed tension on the children for whenever they were there, Willa might at any moment grab one of them and start to quiz them about the names and functions of different plants. She was terrifying to the children and often suggested punishments to their teachers for insufficient knowledge. The teachers never punished the children as directed, but the children were terrified none the less.

Willa looked over the workers installing new tuber trays. "What are you doing, you nitwit," she screamed, "you cannot put more lime in the soil until next month! You'll kill those plants, then what will we eat when the locusts arrive to destroy our lives? Go trim the fruit trees, a job an idiot can understand." She jetted by the bewildered worker and slapped her on the top of the head as she sped by, causing the worker to tumble head over foot until she crashed into a tray of leafy oxygen generation plants. "And watch where you're going, you clumsy fool."

"Excuse me, Mrs. Marsdon-Jiimson," said a young boy, clearly terrified to speak to her, "but there is something strange on this juniper here," he said pointing to a shrub with dusty teal berries.

"What is strange?" she snapped. "There are no abnormalities," she stated while she inspected the plant and its berries.

"No," he said, his hands trembling with fear, "underneath. Look underneath. There is something different about the roots of this one plant." His shaking finger pointed under the grid through which the roots grew into the thick slime soil.

She gave an exasperated grunt and jetted to the other side of the tray. He held up the plant and its section of grid so the roots came out of the goo, and there, among the normal pattern of roots was what looked like bright orange radishes growing among the roots.

Willa pushed him aside and grabbed the plant herself. She looked at the abnormality. This was indeed something new and very different. She looked at the tag on the plant to see if it was one of the new experiments with bioengineering with hopes to develop new species, but it was not. She reached into her bib pocket and pulled out a snip attached by string to her garment. She cut off one of the orange growths and placed it in a little container, then Velcroed it into her storage pocket.

As she started to put the plant back into the goo the little boy tapped her on the shoulder. "You should let me do that, Mrs.

Second Pass

Marsdon-Jiimson," he say humbly, "it is not your place to have to work in the soil. That is our job."

"You will not tell me what my place..." she stopped short. "What did you say?"

The boy, visibly frightened but not backing away like most children did said, "It is our job, not yours. You are the one who made this all possible. We wouldn't be alive without your plants; there would be no food to eat or air to breathe. Let me do that."

"What is your name, young man?" she asked abruptly.

"Ali Wong, ma'am," he said shyly.

"How old are you son?"

"I'm eight," he said, "or, well, I'll be eight next week."

"Ali," she said, holding his shoulder with her hand, "I want you to take this sample to the biotech lab. And when you come back, come see me in my station near the berries." She jetted off, yelling directions to others as she went.

Ali took the container and fastened it into his belt pack and jetted to the laboratory. His hands were shaking from excitement, not fear.

* * * * * * *

"This is Jiimson," Sven said to the screen. "Without going into much complexity, am I to understand that you are offering this money," he looked at his papers, purposefully shuffling through the stack to find the one containing the information he sought, "$4 billion to SIL for 'humanitarian services' as you call them?"

"Yes, Chairholder Jiimson," said the representative from Saudi Arabia, "that is exactly what we are offering. Do you have any questions?"

"Just one thing," he said with a smile, "what might we want with money? It is useless on SIL, and we are approaching the pass in just a few weeks, so there is no time to purchase anything and get it ready for transport before the time of this pass is over. So I really don't see what your offer has for us that is useful."

He switched to another channel before they could reply. *They'll learn that dealing with me is a bit different. I don't need them or their money.*

"Good day, Chairholder Jiimson," said the sing-song voice of the ambassador from Thailand, who's long black hair shined with blue highlights.

"Good day, Ambassador Songnakorn," he said, "how can I help you?"

"The question is not how you can help us, but rather how we can help you."

"What is your proposal?" he said impatiently, "I have many foreign envoys to deal with at this time. Please get to the point."

"We wish to embrace the culture of SIL by developing an educational exchange program. We want to offer living quarters for anyone who is coming to stay on Earth from SIL, and a teaching position in the Bankok University."

He thought about this. They weren't trying to buy him. This interested him. "Tell me more. Your offer is kind, and we will consider it for anyone who is staying and keeping their Silian citizenship. And while this is kind of you, it gives nothing directly to SIL. How can SIL benefit from this?"

"We have four Thai citizens who wish to come to SIL and stay, along with twelve who will visit for the four months. For those who visit, we are willing to have them deliver some of our cultural heritage treasures for permanent exhibit in your gallery on SIL. For those who stay, we ask that you allow them to teach about our culture and literature to your citizens. It is by learning about each other that we grow in understanding of all human beings, and by sharing our cultures that we remain rich as a race."

"That is insufficient. We will accept that, along with seed samples of your best rice and tuber species. In addition, you will sanction trade agreements with SIL, providing us with your best silk fabrics, chemical supplies to maintain our supply of antibiotics, and an open market in the future."

She paused at this. He knew she would not be in a position to guarantee any such assurances, for she must get it passed by her minister of trade and through their Parliament, and ultimately agreed to by the King himself. "Your price is not too high," she said. "We must pursue the process, but His Majesty the King has told the Ministers that we are to agree with any terms SIL requires. We wish to honor the newest nation with our support."

He laughed arrogantly. He loved receiving such deference, and got sexually excited when he felt the power of his position.

Second Pass

"This conference is complete then," he said dismissively, "until you have the assurances of your government, there will be no further discussion."

He switched the CommRelay off and turned to his assistant. "I'm finished for the day. Erase the records of this transmission." He jetted from the room.

* * * * * * *

"Here's another one," Sylvia Bryant said to Malanga. "The transmission began at 4th hour and lasted for 35 minutes. During the course of the transmission there were five different channels accessed. Each relay came through the Low Orbital Lens from a different point on the Earth surface."

"Do you know who made the link from our end?" asked Malanga. "Were there any video disk recordings from the surveillance camera?"

"No," said Sylvia, "but Bill worked with Toby to rig another camera, an old web cam from the early days of Internet communication on Earth. He built it into the old mounting hook for the Velcro stabilization straps when SIL first lost gravity, before we were sun-centric in our orbit. From that we were able to record the conversations, with a clear view of Chairholder Jiimson as he made them."

"But why would he go to the trouble of erasing his transmission? He has every right to use the CommRelay for whatever he needs." Malanga was mystified.

"He was speaking to representatives of the heads of governments from all over the world," Sylvia said.

"But that is to be expected," said Malanga.

"Perhaps it is in the content of the discussions. I will have the transcript prepared and delivered to you."

"No," said Malanga, "you must not have it delivered. You must bring it yourself."

"Of course, Finder Malanga," she said. "I will not make the mistake again."

* * * * * * *

George was very tired. He got little sleep these final days before going to SIL, and thought some days he would never be ready. So much depended on him now. And he was worried about the Chinese. They had pushed and pushed for much greater involvement than they were being granted, and in the process he had given up any chance to use their space program vehicles to help in case of an emergency. The talks with the Chinese had leaked to Stevens, and the entire board was outraged. As a result, they were able to push for their maximum shuttle use schedule, to maximize profits. There was no room for error now.

The phone rang and he picked it up. "McVee here," he said distracted.

"And that would be Mac here," said the former president. "You left a message for me. Sorry I didn't get back earlier, but I've been packing!"

"I guess I'll be seeing you very soon. But that's not why I called," George said.

"I didn't think it would have been. What can I do for you?"

"I would like to meet with you tonight at 9:30. I am scheduled to have a private CommRelay link with Paul and I would like to have you in on it. The link is scheduled for 10:00, so that will give us a half hour to talk beforehand. Could you possibly do that?"

"Done," said McKenna with his usual jocularity. "I'll be there at 9:30."

"Thank you sir," George said.

"George, you know I hate it when you call me that." And the president hung up the phone.

* * * * * * *

"BQ," said Paul, shaking his wife, "you've got to wake up. We are to speak with George in ten minutes."

"Okay," Sallie said groggily, "let me get my tunic, it's cold in here." She opened her sleep sack and floated over to her jetpack. She pulled on a tunic and strapped the jetpack over it. "Let's go," she said.

As they jetted through the Hub, they chatted about the times they had snuck into various secluded places on SIL to make love when they were first here. The memories were pleasant,

Second Pass

and when they got to the CommRelay they took time for a long embrace. Then Paul switched on the screen.

After a four-minute delay, the image of George came into the screen. Next to him was the former President of the United States. Paul and Sallie were shocked.

"Mr. President, sir!" said Paul.

"Please, Paul," he said with a knowing grin to George, "call me Mac. And you too, BQ. I'm just an ordinary citizen now."

"It will be very hard for me to do that, sir," said Paul.

"Hey Paul," George said, "I know what you mean. But look at it this way, you either have to call him Mac or Paddi, and I think Mac is much easier." They all laughed.

"What is on your mind?" asked Sallie. "I'm as curious to know as I am eager to see you up here. Five weeks isn't it?"

"Yes, five weeks," said George. "We need to talk about the Chinese."

"That's odd," said Paul, "why the Chinese?"

"Several years ago," started McKenna, "the Chinese began an intense effort to bring a couple thousand people to SIL. They have technology for space craft that can prolong the window of access to 6 months, and were going to transport materials to build out the outer shell of SIL so that there could be an additional 5,000 living units. Their workers were going to sleep on the large shuttles while constructing the new quarters and then move in, all in six months."

"Well, that would put them here in one week," said Paul, "but we've heard nothing about it. Under the current plan we are going to approach the maximum occupancy as I understand it. Plus I don't think there would be adequate food or water to sustain the population at that level."

"Well," George said, "they stopped pushing about a year ago."

"Well then," said Sallie, "it looks like we don't have to worry about the Chinese then."

"I beg to differ," George said. "They stopped pushing, and have remained completely silent, giving the US a bit of the cold shoulder as a matter of fact. But our satellite surveillance shows that they have continued to build space craft, and seem to be starting preparations for launch."

"They couldn't just crash SIL could they?" asked Sallie.

"What kind of defenses do you have?" asked McKenna.

"You mean, like military defense?" asked Paul, his heart racing. "Do you think they would attack us?"

"It is not like them," said McKenna, "but there is always that possibility. They didn't seem like they would take no for an answer, then suddenly stopped talking. Completely!"

There was a sound behind them and Paul and Sallie turned to see Bill standing there, open-mouthed. "Hey gang," he said. "Feel like some light saber exercises?" He smiled at his joke, but his smile was without any sincerity.

"Mr. President," said Paul, "may I introduce our 1st Officer, Captain William Bryant."

"Pleased to meet you, Captain," said McKenna.

"Pleased to meet you too, sir," he said. Neither he nor the former president offered to use a more familiar name. Sallie got chills in spite of her added tunic, realizing for the first time that they were a nation, an actual nation, and as such had to face everything a nation must face. She had not been granted a vote in the matter, it having been decided by those who had lived on SIL from before the first pass, and those who were SIL-born. But had she voted, she never would have considered this level of gravity.

"Captain," said McKenna, "how much of our conversation did you hear?"

"Sir. I heard the Chinese have stopped pursuit of SIL with their plans a year ago, but have continued to build their space craft and appear to be preparing for a launch. Do you think we will need to prepare a defense against invasion?"

"It is always wise to be prepared," said McKenna, "but never wise to provoke panic among the population."

"What type of defense would you suggest?" he asked.

Paul turned to Sallie and then to Bill. "Are we serious here?" he asked. "Are we really having this conversation?"

"Yes," everyone else said at the same time. He was silent.

"I have a suggestion," said McKenna. "Win the war, but don't fight a battle. There is a solution."

"I am all ears Sir," said Bill. "We have few resources that can be redirected for a defense, I'm afraid. To be honest, I never thought we would have to wage war."

"Forget the war," said McKenna. "I'm an old Irish Catholic, and an Irish-Catholic schoolboy at heart, I'm afraid. You know, the damnedest thing about that is I still have fantasies about

Second Pass

Catherine Isley to this day. But they will remain fantasies because she never let me even talk to her, much less lift her skirt."

"I've had my trouble with advances in the past too," Bill admitted. "I see what you mean," he laughed, "the 'aspirin defense' is what you are suggesting I believe."

"You are entirely right Captain," said McKenna.

"Please call me Bill, sir," he said.

"Only if you call me Mac," said McKenna.

"Done," said Bill. He switched off the CommRelay screen. Paul and Sallie looked at him in shock.

"You just hung up on the President of the United States!" said Paul.

"What the hell were you two arrested development boys talking about," said Sallie, "aspirin defense my ass."

"Yeah," said Paul, "I'm Irish, Catholic, and went to a Catholic school and don't have the faintest idea what you two were talking about."

"You never knew Catherine Isley," said Bill with a chuckle. "The girls were given an aspirin by their mother's and told to hold it between their knees the entire time they were with the boys. It was the first birth control pill."

"So," said Sallie, "we're talking denied access."

"Precisely," said Bill. "I've got to get to the metal shop." And he jetted off.

Chapter 12

Solomon Gould and Tom Robinson sat together on a concrete bench near the fixed chess boards in Intelligence Park. They came here for several reasons, but primarily because it was equal distance between Associated and MIT. Two old men, sitting together. There was nothing remarkable about this, other than the fact they were only two. All over the city of Boston there were groups of elderly huddled together. Some laughed, some argued, some fed bread crumbs to birds, but most of them just sat and stared. The world had come to that. Technology advanced to the point that life expectancy was much expanded, but there were fewer younger people and so the balance had shifted. The elderly were a powerful presence, and their political clout, a result of sheer numbers, resulted in increased visibility—more parks, more senior transport vehicles, more senior recreation activities. But there wasn't much more for the old people to do.

Solomon Gould was the power behind Associated, a founder and financier mostly out to pasture now. Tom Robinson had been a janitor at MIT as a means of cover his grief. He almost accomplished erasing his days on SIL from his memory, though not really, until he found out he had produced a son, Shandor Iracs, who had been orphaned when his mother was killed in the explosion on SIL after Tom had returned to Earth. The discovery of his son, stowed away in the shuttle cargo bay when that first shuttle to SIL had returned to Earth, forced him to wake up. And Shandor's instant fame on Earth brought Tom out of hiding. MIT had made him full professor emeritus when they discovered that their library custodian was indeed an astronaut with expertise in electromagnetism and wave transmissions.

Each man had a bag by his feet. Gould's contained toiletries, a huge supply of medications and his private records. Robinson's held photos of his son, George, Liz, Gould and others with whom he'd spent the last twenty years, and original texts of Plato's Republic, Aristotle's Poetry and Rhetoric, Eudora Welty short stories, Anne Sexton's complete works, and a few other essential building blocks of modern society on Earth.

They were leaving that evening on a flight to Florida, and were scheduled to leave for SIL on the first shuttle flight two days later. And they were waiting for Shandor and George to arrive.

Second Pass

Gould turned to Robinson about to speak, when he was stopped by a raised hand. "Let's not talk," said Tom.

"Well, okay," said Sol, "but you aren't going to make much of a traveling companion if you are going to snub me."

Tom laughed loudly; making the less hungry birds fly off. "Snub you! Huh!" he laughed, "I'm just afraid that you'll be the only one for me to talk to once we're up there. I don't want to wear out your supply of old war stories before we get started. Nothing worse than reruns of the stories we old farts tell."

They chuckled for a few minutes, and then settled into silence.

I'll die on SIL, thought Tom, *just like Scari did.* He looked across the boulevard at the baseball field filled with little leaguers and their white haired coaches frolicking noiselessly in the distance. He didn't want to leave Shandor behind, and had tried talking him into coming with him to SIL. But his son had known abandonment and abuse on SIL, and fame on Earth. There was no contest in the boy's mind, Tom knew. And Tom suspected that perhaps he ought to have stayed to be with his son, and that going was, in effect, abandoning him again. But he wanted to die on SIL with Scari's ghost.

Gould thought about everything he'd known and seen. Everything that made up a picture of living that was so bound to the earthly he couldn't imagine what life in space would be like. He was apprehensive of meeting Commander McVee, convinced he would hate him, then get to know him and discover they were alike in their less than admirable attributes. *He's such a bastard,* Sol thought with a wince, *but then many would argue so am I! Ha! That would serve me right, proving all my enemies right like that. But I've worked most of my life to make SIL happen and to justify the very things that drove that madman to do what he did, so I belong there.* He was driven to understand what made the Commander tick. And he had his own secret mission to carry out. And it was so very important to him that he didn't care it meant he would die in space on SIL. *There's simply no other place for me to be. I will catch those bastards!*

"Well, well," said Tom.

"I thought you said no talking."

"Very funny. But look who's coming!" He waved to Shandor and George as they got out of the car. George motioned them to come to the car, so they creaked to a standing position and did their best to hurry to the curb.

"Hey you two old farts," said Liz from inside of the car.

"Mommy said fart!" said Georgie in the back seat, laughing loudly.

"Are you ready to see your husband off to space?" asked Gould.

"I am so ready," said Liz in her nagging wife impression, "I can't wait to use any razor I want to shave my legs!"

"I guess I'm in the dog house for protecting my rights as a hairy mammal," said George.

"Hairy mama! Hee hehe..." little Georgie went into another cascade of giggles.

"Look you guys," said Liz, "have a good trip. I'll be there in five weeks. But if I don't move this car I'll be escorted by the police. Georgie, say good bye to daddy."

"Good bye daddy. Daddy on SIL?"

"Not yet little man," said George as he lifted the suitcases out of the back, "but soon. Tomorrow night you'll see me on the television."

They waved as Liz drove off, then turned in unison to walk toward the T-station. They made their way back to the bench and Shandor picked up the bags of his father and Gould with one arm, and arranged two others in the other hand.

"Where are your other bags?" asked Shandor. "You are each allowed to carry two with you."

"But you assume," said Gould, "that we have enough possessions to fill two bags for the trip. Son," he said putting his arm around his shoulders, "I have little of importance to carry with me. The important things are already in Florida."

"And I," said Tom, "have everything I need to start new civilizations on distant planets!"

It was meant to be a joke, but there was tension. He didn't know how to say good bye to his son, knowing that he would not see him again. Airports and public transportation weren't designed for final departures. They were sterile, impersonal, overcrowded, and anything but tranquil. There was no worse place for a parent to lose a child. *Some day*, he thought, *there will be a final scene in an opera that takes place in an airport*. He chuckled to himself, realizing this thought was probably why he hadn't found fame as a theatrical director.

"Dad," said Shandor, "may I talk to you privately?"

"Of course you can," said Gould, eager to go off with George to share the new information he had, and more eager to get away from the awkwardness of the moment. "Come George! We have dragons to slay!"

Tom felt bad that Shandor had had to ask for this privacy. In his view of himself he did nothing but make mistakes. He found himself to be the worst father in history, and felt terribly guilty about that.

"I'm sorry son," he began, "that I didn't arrange a better place for us to say good-bye. To be honest, I didn't know how to do it so..."

"You don't have to worry," interrupted Shandor, "about saying good-bye. It is irrelevant."

Tom stopped and looked at his son. He was so handsome, and had so much of his looks from his mother. Tears welled in his eyes as he thought of all he felt for his son, and all he wished he'd known how to give. *It makes sense for him to reject me, I've acted like I've rejected him now for the second time in his life. I guess that does make me irrelevant for him.*

"Dad," said Shandor, "are you there? What happened?"

"I was just thinking, son. You know I love you don't you? You know it tears me to pieces to leave you here, knowing I'll die on SIL, that this is our final good-bye." He started to cry, for the first time in many years.

"Well," Shandor said wrinkling his face comically. "Even though we are having this tragic little scene here, I brought you a present." He held out the two suitcases he had in his other hand.

"What is this for?" asked Tom, not sure if he should take them.

"It's for your birthday," he said.

"But it isn't my birthday until December," said Tom.

"Well, it is actually for your birthday in December, but I had to give them to you now. You are leaving you know."

"I know," he said, sniffing and feeling more awkward than he'd ever felt before. "It is lovely luggage. But I've no time to repack."

"They are already packed. Look inside." He handed one of the suitcases to his father, and helped hold it while Tom opened the clasps. He opened the case and looked inside and became confused.

"These aren't my things," Tom said. "I mean these shoes are three sizes too large for me." *I'm rejecting his gift!* Tom realized with horror. "Son, I am so grateful, really."

"Dad," Shandor said rolling his eyes, "those are my shoes."

"Oh!" Tom laughed, taking them out and handing them to Shandor. "They must have gotten in here by mistake then."

"It's no mistake, Dad. I'm going with you. I'm coming to SIL. Happy Birthday."

Tom dropped the suitcase spilling all of its contents. Sol saw this and started to come over to help collect the things, but George motioned him to stay where he was. Sol looked confused, and George just motioned with his head for him to watch what was happening. Tom looked at his son and started to cry outwardly. He grabbed him and hugged him as he wept, standing on the clothes that had spilled.

"Son," he said with elation, "this is what I've always wanted. Always! To be with you is all I want. I couldn't figure out how to be with you and Scari at the same time. I felt I owed it to her to go to SIL, but owed it to you to stay here. I didn't know what to do, or how to do anything at all. I was so confused, so torn. You can't imagine..."

"Dad," Shandor said. "Slow down Dad. I wanted it to be a surprise. I wanted to tell you a couple of years ago that I was going back, but if I had you wouldn't have known it was because I love you and want to be with you. If I had just gone alone, you wouldn't have gotten that message. This way you know. You know how much it means to me to be with you." Now Shandor started to cry. "Now we can be together. And having you on SIL will make me belong like I didn't before."

"Enough of these theatrics," said Gould intruding. "We have a shuttle to catch." George and Shandor stooped to gather the things together and repack the suitcase quickly as Gould pulled Tom aside. "You," he said sternly, "aren't going to get out of listening to my war stories that easily. Bringing your son along so I don't get so much of your time. Well, let's see, where to begin. Did I tell you about the first girl I dated? It was in Vermont, many years ago...."

Second Pass

* * * * * * *

The world watched on autovision, simulvision, and in person, as the first of the shuttles to join SIL on its second pass lifted off. McKenna was seen off by the current President, along with the Secretary General of the United Nations. The rocket shattered the serene morning with the loudest roar man has yet made. The group inside was strapped in, the crew in their places and all of the luggage in place. Many people had said goodbye for the last time to friends and families. George checked off the names in his mind from the master list of all who would be traveling to SIL.

The cargo bay was already three-quarters full before the people's luggage was added. The rest of the bay was filled with provisions, equipment, and machinery. But in one end were eleven identical crates, each holding a large ring-shaped metallic structure to be added to the outside of the docking ports on SIL's hub. The rings held the highest security clearance, with only two people knowing exactly what they were for, and why they were needed. Bill Bryant had contacted Solomon Gould and secretly sent designs for the attachments. Gould and Bryant had figured a way to make docking on SIL possible only for certain vehicles equipped with an attachment. Every technician who worked on the development and attachment of these parts was told a slightly different story as to their need and use. All of the stories were so mundane that they weren't discussed. But what they had accomplished was vital—only those who were wanted could dock on SIL, and the adjustments to existing craft had to be made partly on Earth before liftoff, and partly in space just before docking.

Chapter 13

Willa Marsdon-Jiimson put on her favorite peach tunic and added a turquoise belt for accent. She had gathered her children for a meal together, the first time in many e-years, and they were impatiently waiting for her to emerge. She heard their calls, and remembered why she preferred the Eye Chamber so much. "I'm coming in a moment," she yelled from her dressing sphere." She was frustrated with her ear bobs, which kept floating away just as she was about to snap their backs on. "Alex," she yelled, "Corey! Take the sacks from the heater will you. I should be there in a second. Ingrid, come here to help."

"Boy," said Ingrid sarcastically, "I get to help the plant lady. How lucky is that?"

"Go help your mother," said Corey authoritatively, "and be appreciative."

"Oh, I'm sooo appreciative," she said, "but who are you to tell me what to do shrivel smoot?"

"Ha, ha, ha—shrivel smoot! Good one Ing," said Alex. Then turning to his older brother said, "She's right you know."

"Ingrid!" her mother yelled.

"Just a jet away," she yelled back.

As she turned herself so the burst of hot air from her jet would hit Corey in the face as she jetted, the personal comm unit sounded. "Why don't you get that?" she said over her shoulder as she left.

Corey was busy with the food sacks so Alex picked up the ear piece. "Hello, Plant Lady's Lyre, Alexander speaking."

"Oh Alex, she must come quickly!" the excited voice said at the other end, "The large leaf tray assorter has come off track and dirt is spilling everywhere!"

"Hey mom," Alex yelled, "some one is having a fit because of something about the elephant ear plants!"

"Tell them to leave a message," she yelled as Ingrid got the first of the ear bobs fastened.

"No!" said the voice on the comm, "she must come now! There is smoke coming from the generator!"

"Is their flame?" asked Alex, knowing that a fire in the Eye Chamber could potentially explode SIL. "Mom! There's a fire in the Chamber!"

Second Pass

"There is no flame, only some smoke. But she must come!" The personal comm went dead. Alex couldn't tell if it was because it was disconnected or if something else happened to sever the communications. He slapped his brother on the back and jetted out the door toward the Eye Chamber, speaking on his wrist comm to Jun-Jun.

"Fire?" his mother said, alarmed. "Did you say fire? Hurry up Ingrid."

"Stop moving," said Ingrid, "I can't fasten this if you keep moving your head."

"Hurry, you idiot," Willa said, "SIL could explode and you want me to keep still."

"SIL might explode and you want to have matching ear bobs on," she said with a sneer.

Willa pushed her out of the way and jetted past her with only one ear decorated. She yelled for Corey to put the sacks back in the heating unit except for his and Ingrid's as she sped past.

* * * * * * *

George sat behind the navigator of the large shuttle control center checking their approach to SIL. By his calculation they would need to start their adjustment blasts of the steering jets in about thirty minutes and there were still technicians on a space walk to correct a solar panel.

"How much more time will they need?" he asked. "We will need to trim our approach in about 30 minutes."

The pilot looked at a flip chart of instructions and then said, "Confirm that Dr.," he said switching to his mouthpiece microphone, "Bud. How much longer?"

"We're just fixing the final bolt," he said, "and should be done in about..."

There was a clicking sound, then a loud snap followed by static on the comm channel. The captain quickly switched off the speaker connection to the rest of the cabin, but the entire flight crew had heard what happened. With calm he then began to whisper into his microphone.

George realized something was wrong. His fear was confirmed when the passenger crew master's voice came over the speaker in the cabin. "Captain Winslow," his voice sounded hushed like he was himself whispering into his phone, "I think I just saw one of your crew spiral away from the shuttle. Is there a problem? He looked unconscious."

Again the Captain flipped a switch on the consol and continued his rapid whispering. George could see his hands moving much faster than usual and began to worry. "Is there something wrong, Captain?" he asked.

"Just a minute, Dr.," said the Captain, "we have a slight incident."

The navigator looked at George with his face twisted into a worried expression. George looked back and nodded, as if to say everything was fine, but had no idea why he did that.

"Mac," said the Captain under his voice into his microphone to the other mechanic working outside of the ship, "is Bud there? He isn't responding. Hello?"

"The coup....singe...er....ut....isted....ear."

"Repeat," said the Captain, "your last transmission is not coming through."

He listened but heard no words, just clicking and various forms of static. He kept switching from channel to channel to try to pick up the signal better. Suddenly he found a channel with groaning on it. "Bud, is that you? Hello, Bud. Come in."

But the channel was lost. Again he switched to the main external shuttle communications channel. "Mac," he said, "Please repeat last transmission."

This went on for a few minutes. The crew master was reporting that one of the mechanics was spinning away from the shuttle, apparently lifeless. He then saw his hands jerking in the distance and reported this. The Captain was now able to get longer phrases of intelligent speech from Mac and was starting to piece the puzzle together.

George had not understood why it would be necessary or even advisable to do the repair

on a solar panel when they were about to make their final approach to SIL. Once docked they would be on SIL's power grid and there would be plenty of time to make an adjustment. The outbay portals on SIL were on an interior cavity, so if anything happened to separate a technician from a repair or resupply exercise they would float only so far before running into another part of SIL across the outbay portals vast open bubble.

Second Pass

He had discussed this with the navigator, but was not able to really get any information from her, as the crew had not been briefed on the sudden repair, and really had no information to give. She had called to engineering, but they were evasive, as they always were. It seemed that the engineering division was always embarrassed when there was anything wrong with the physical shuttle, as if a flaw in design or a malfunction reflected directly on them. A silly notion since they had nothing to do with the design or construction, and their entire job was a perpetual fixing of things that were broken, badly designed, or improperly manufactured.

Suddenly the Captain made a sharp movement with his arms that caught George's eyes. He was unstrapping himself from his seat and loosening his socked feet from the Velcro stabilization strips. He spoke in low tone to the ship's first officer and then jetted back past George and out of the connecting door.

"What's up?" asked George as he passed, but the Captain just waved and smiled nicely as he sped by.

"That's odd," said the navigator, "he's usually more conversant than that."

* * * * * * *

Willa entered the Eye Chamber and found smoke filling the air. Three of the large leaf plant trays were disconnected from their tracking devices and floating freely through the vast space, bumping into other trays. Dirt was floating everywhere and there were many dead insects floating with the dirt clumps.

"What happened here?" she demanded.

A very nervous man looked up at her. He had been the manager on duty and had been distracted when it happened. "We don't know," he said, "all of a sudden there was an alarm and when we looked, one of the large leaf trays had gotten off its track. Then we noticed that the others behind it were smashing into it, so we tried to stop the array rotator and when we did the smoke started."

There was a tap on Willa's thigh. "Excuse me, Mrs. Marsdon-Jiimson," said the small voice, "but I think the trouble is not with the trays or the rotator."

Willa swung her head down and saw Ali Wong looking up at her.

"Ali, run along," said the man. "You don't know anything about it."

"Silence," Willa said to the man. "I will hear what Mr. Wong has to say."

The man was puzzled, but knew better than to oppose her.

Ali reached up his hand and took Willa's lovingly in his own. "Follow me," he said and jetted toward the loose trays. There were about a dozen people around each tray trying to stabilize it, but their jets weren't synchronized and one of the trays had started to spin. "Watch out!" yelled the boy with authority that surprised them all.

As they approached the furthest tray, he moved them around to the underside of it. At one end, where the stabilizing cables were attached, there was a root structure twisted around it. Willa looked to see which plant it was coming from and realized that it had grown nearly ten meters from a random plant in the middle of the tray. She started in that direction, but was stopped by Ali.

"No," he said strongly, "first we must look at the top." With that he jetted quickly around the end of the tray and followed the cable from where the root had grabbed it toward the other end. The cable had snapped and recoiled from the release of tension. It was lying among the plants. When they got back to the same plant who's roots had interfered with the cable underneath the tray, they saw that the cable was also trapped in a tight coil from a shoot which had grown from the plant outward. None of the other plants, which were identical, had such a shoot.

"What's this?" she said.

"Watch," said Ali. He jetted down into the leaves of the plant and grabbed the cable. He then turned his back to the tray and jetted. The man reached out to stop him, and the hot reverse blast from the jet was forbidden to point toward any plant, but Willa stopped him. They watched as he traveled further and further from the tray. The shoot kept stretching, as if pulled from an endless spool of cable. They kept looking at the plant end of it and saw it was coming from out of an enlarged bulge in the plant central trunk like shaft. There was some sort of moist sap or secretion from the plant lubricating it as it rubbed on the side of the opening. Willa reached out and found the liquid to be extremely sticky and quickly gave up trying to remove it from

Second Pass

her fingers, holding her hand away from everything else. Ali flew upward to the point the cable would have been in if it were still attached to the rotator mechanism.

"Now," yelled Ali from about 20 meters, "watch this. But you better back away from the plant."

With that he let go of the shoot and it quickly, but not violently, recoiled and was taken into the bulbous growth on the plant's core. If it had just been a retraction from stretched tension, it would have recoiled much more quickly. But it seemed that the plant was retracting it at a steady speed, like an arm gathering in something it had collected.

"What the hell?" said the manager.

Ali had flown beside it as it went and ended next to them. "I saw the root begin to grow out of its normal pattern two weeks ago," he said. "I followed its growth every day, and kept checking the plant from above. The bump in the center just grew slowly. It was exciting to watch. Then yesterday a small split started to appear in the side of the plant shaft, so I reported it to the office."

Willa turned to the manager. "Get me the report." He looked at her in surprise, but turned to get it. "Go on," she said.

"Well, I was watching the slit at the top and suddenly a little shoot came out. It was cute, and had a very skinny end. I went around to see what the root was doing and saw it had grabbed on to the underside of the cable. I didn't know if that would harm the tray's movement, so I went to the top, where the cables connect and watched it."

"When was this?" demanded Willa.

"It was this morning," he said. "I'm sorry I didn't say anything, but it started growing fast and I was just watching it." He looked down, as if ashamed.

Willa lifted his chin with her hand. "Tell us what you saw, Ali," she said quietly, "you did nothing wrong."

The workers who had gathered looked in dismay at each other. Willa had never shown such a soft side, particularly not to children whom she treated much more harshly than adults.

"Well, I looked back at the plant tray below and saw that the shoot was growing so fast, it was reaching up in the air and coming straight at me. I got out of the way, and it's a good thing too." He looked at Willa and giggled. "It spit at me!" he said. "Or at least I thought it did. But what it really did was spit that sticky stuff at the cable just below its connection and then that guided the rest of the shoot to that place. The shoot grew and grew and then wrapped around the cable and pulled it. Then the cable snapped. It started to go toward the tray. When it got there," he coughed and a little drop of blood came out of his lips. One of the women moved toward him, but Willa stopped her. The boy hadn't seen the drop of blood. "I tried to pull it back, to put the cable where it belonged, but it was so sticky I had to let go. Then the cable swung around. I'm sorry," he said, "my chest hurts. Anyway,.."

"Where were you when it snapped?" asked Willa, looking carefully at him.

"I was a little too close," he said shyly. "But I watched the plant pull the cable to itself."

"Ali," said Willa, "did the cable hit you? Were you hurt?"

With this the boy started to cry. He pulled up his tunic and there was a deep gash on his abdomen that made everyone gasp, including Willa. There was a thick clear gel film over the gash, however, so there was no blood.

Willa pulled the boy to her and stroked his head gently. "We will get you taken care of, but please tell me what happened."

The boy hesitated. He didn't want to get in trouble, and he didn't want to distract everyone from the situation. "I was in the way, and the cable cut me. I pulled up my tunic and then the plant spit at me, right where I was cut, and then the blood went away and it stopped. I could see inside of me." He sobbed at this point. His fear was released with his story. "I didn't want to hurt..." he hesitated.

"We don't want you hurt either," said Willa.

"No," he said, "I didn't want to hurt the plant. It spit at me because I thought it was doing something bad." His eyes looked up at Willa with fear and hope. "I think I made the plant break the cable. I was watching it and it didn't want me to."

Willa smiled at the boy. "Get him to the Finders immediately," she said with anger. "You didn't do anything wrong, Ali," she said softly to him. "In fact, I am very glad you did everything you did. Now, go get attention to that cut."

She jetted away so suddenly some of those gathered twitched is surprise. She went straight to the machine door and entered the room. She found the engineers in the smoke and explained that there had been an unusual drag on a cable and it snapped and the torque on the motor caused it to seize. They looked at

Second Pass

her with surprise, because they had just found one of the large machines seized. They had just called for a new engine to be delivered.

"So, get the machine shop to deliver it right away. Do not allow them to delay until after the shuttle has docked. And get all of the ventilators turned to maximum filter so the air is cleared. I will not have the new arrival's first view of the Eye Chamber be one of smoke and dirt!" She spun round and jetted away.

* * * * * * *

Sylvia Bryant looked at her husband as they listened to the communication from the shuttle. One man had died during installation in space of the adaptor ring to prepare the shuttle for docking, but they had gotten it attached and would arrive in visible range in about twenty minutes. They would be fully docked within three hours. The second pass had begun.

Chapter 14

Thinking does not prepare for being. What can be planned is an event, procedures and processes, timing, and other things that are the structures of experience. The return to SIL had been entirely thought out, planned, and now the execution was imminent. Every shuttle trip, payload and passenger list was itemized far beyond need. The food, supplies, and materials for expanding SIL for the eighteen years it would follow its eccentric solar orbit were all collected and divided into trips. Construction designs to the greatest detail were developed and recorded. Increases in projected population growth were accounted for. New medicines and new diseases from Earth were counted into the mix, including partial development of new drugs to fight disease more effectively when finished were siphoned off and a sample was going to Dr. Malanga for parallel development. Fuel for the shuttles, along with water and food supplies, were stored, and every molecule of oxygen that would be inhaled by the travelers and crews was accounted for.

George had felt prepared in his own work as well. Every person who would be visiting, all of those who would be emigrating to SIL permanently, and those who would be coming to Earth from SIL, many of whom were born on SIL, had been arranged for. Every seat was full. George would be gone for four months, and, while not exactly a vacation because he would be working tirelessly on SIL to manage all of the arrivals and departures, he was considering it as vacation. But when SIL was first visible, and as that shining speck grew into the outline of the place so long ago he had reunited with his father, he was not at all prepared for his feelings.

The whole process of discovering SIL had been a series of accidents. His rebellion against societal belief that science was bad, and space exploration entirely foolish and wasteful, had made his life lonely, but pure. He knew what he believed, and was willing to live with any and all results of that knowledge. His lifelong annoyance with his mother for telling him his father was dead when he knew in his heart he was not had led to a strange, sterile kind of relationship between mother and son. His youthful devotion to the development of the Low Orbital Lens, or LOL as it was now called, was the most perfect symbol of his entire outlook.

Second Pass

That the governments and people of Earth had decided science just wasted precious resources, that advances in medicine just made people live too long, and that space travel was complete lunacy, had given the perfect setting for his rage and bitterness to manifest. He wanted to develop LOL not to explore deep space, but, rather, to keep alive a long family tradition of thumbing his nose at popular trends and government controls. It was another well-planned thing that delivered him to a reality he simply was not prepared for.

SIL now sat before him, just beyond the window near his seat, and he suddenly felt enormous dread, not the elation he expected and had actually experienced up to this point. He looked down at his son's photograph in his hand, just a few years old, and wondered if his son would continue to love him as he grew up. He wondered if this generation's little Georgie would be so rebellious and filled with the bile of being cocooned by fame from an early age. He wondered if his son would love his mother, Liz, and respect the choices she would make in her future. Nearly everyone who had young children was married; he and Liz hadn't gotten married. Would this be a choice that, somehow, with some unknowable future twist of fate, would turn little Georgie against him, against Liz? Or, would it be some other choice, some other turn in the road of life that would make little Georgie feel deprived of normalcy, estranged from the average?

George was shocked that these were the thoughts in his mind as they made final preparations to dock. He wasn't thinking of his father, or Paul and BQ and their twins, or of the thousands of lives that were about to change forever. He tucked the photograph into his pocket and eased out of his stabilizing restraints. After pushing off from his chair he traveled across the small post-cockpit area and into the doorway to the main passenger seating area.

He pulled the microphone toward his mouth and looked at the one hundred and three passengers in front of him. Most of them were craning their necks to see out of a window. Their murmurs had become a pitched frenzy. The resulting din was punctuated with cries of delight and awe as they began to feel how enormous SIL really was. But its enormity had grown from their first view, a little sparkling speck of dust in eternity, so vulnerable and insignificant, as they made steady progress toward their new home. Many were crying with joy, he imagined, though some may have had regrets or second thoughts fueling their tears.

"Welcome to SIL," he said into the microphone. "We will be docked in four hours. The procedure is very delicate, as the slightest movement can make our approach misaligned." Everyone was listening to him, and the silence was completely opposite the earlier cacophony. "We will be entering the inner courtyard through that horizontal slit you see just below us. From there we will travel approximately 1.8 kilometers to the docking port hub. SIL was designed to have all docking take place in its center so that the process would be housed in a basically enclosed space. I'm sure there will be as much excitement on SIL as there is in this shuttle. Are there any questions?"

He looked around the group and thought no one was going to ask anything at all, until one young woman pointed excitedly and said, "What is that tail we saw when we were further away? It was on the opposite side from the burn mark."

George had seen the debris that was following the structure and wondered too. From far away SIL looked a bit like a comet, but when he was first on SIL eighteen years ago, the tail hadn't been nearly as big or dense. He guessed it was just a gradual buildup as SIL traveled and its gravitational pull collected whatever was in space to collect. "First, that 'burn mark' is the Eye, which is the central element, as you know, that makes SIL a non-Earth-reliant habitat. To keep the Eye always pointing to the sun makes the planet's mass attract space dust on the opposite side, just like any comet. The trail is much larger and denser than on my first trip last pass, and I expect that is normal. We've never before been able to watch the development of a comet from its beginnings."

There were a few other questions, but nothing with much depth, as people wanted to see, not learn. He put the microphone back and felt a bit awkward, having been prepared to answer many more questions than came. He realized that, to these people, he was the one they had tried to impress, or in some cases bribe, to secure their passage on SIL. Once their place was achieved, his importance to them waned. He went back to his berthing to prepare for docking.

At last he started to feel excited. Seeing how excited the others were made him remember the wonder of this man-made planet, and what it represents. He was also suddenly quite eager to see his father, BQ and his best friend Paul. *Can you still be best friends when you haven't seen someone for eighteen years?* He wondered.

Second Pass

The atmosphere in the shuttle seemed to change subtly as they entered into the central courtyard of SIL. The lights illuminating the interior seemed quite blue compared to the clean white of the sun and its stark contrast to the velvet blackness of space. Inside of the courtyard there was now relativity in terms of size and distance they hadn't ever seen from inside of the shuttle. This made it seem real. They had arrived.

* * * * * * *

Willa looked down at Ali, asleep, but breathing with difficulty. Finder Malanga had assured her his condition would not worsen if she went to the welcoming, but had also been most frank with her that his chances of survival were slim. He had damage to his liver and spleen, as well as signs of internal bleeding, though her scans could not verify where. He was weak; Malanga thought he would most likely die within a few days.

Willa had never liked children, particularly her own. She had little use for people, in fact. But this child was different. When she first saw him a strange feeling had overcome her. She saw a glow around him, and when he spoke she was transfixed, as if the sound of his voice held power over her. She had dismissed this as lack of sleep, or too many hours in oxygen saturation in the Eye Chamber. Now that he had been mortally wounded, she felt unfinished. There was something this boy was to do in her life, and until it was done she couldn't be satisfied.

"You are sure nothing will happen to him if I leave," she said harshly to Malanga.

"I'm quite sure," Malanga said sweetly. "He will sleep now for several hours. If he dies, it will be from loss of blood, but the internal bleeding has slowed, even as we stand here." She looked again at the clear, hard resin covering the small torso, and wondered what it could possibly be made of. "I must study him more, Willa," she said, placing her hand on Willa's shoulder, "and I have to ask you to leave. Go, welcome the new arrivals. Welcome them in my place. I cannot leave him now; you must."

"I will," said Willa hesitantly, "but will return the moment formalities are completed." She jetted out of the room and down the long central hallway.

Malanga watched her go, and, once Willa was out of sight, allowed the grave concern she felt overtake her face. She looked down again at the small boy's face, in awe as she always was at how peaceful a person can be when they are in mortal difficulty. His small features were so soft, so innocent. His eye lashes were so perfectly shaped and spaced, and his lips the softest color of purple rose. His breathing seemed better, and there was more color in his cheeks.

Turning her attention to the wound, seen clearly through the hard coating the plant had deposited, was different, she noticed. The flesh at the opening was starting to get little white patches, normally not appearing for several days, of newly forming skin. She brought the light over closer to make sure of what she was seeing. Not only were there white patches of new skin, but there were tiny capillaries growing into the open space where the flesh stopped. Again she adjusted the light for a clearer view. She tried to lift the hard, shell-like coating from his skin. Where she managed to lift it a few drops of clear liquid filled the space.

She quickly gathered it onto a slide and put it under the microscope. What she saw astonished her. The liquid, where exposed to air, became a solid mass, hardening instantly. But what was inside remained liquid and was filled with cell-like structures, swimming in the liquid. The cells were very close in structure to stem cells. She penetrated the outer shell with a microscopic needle and drew a miniscule amount of the liquid into it, then deposited it in a solution to allow it no access to air. Stowing it in a container, she turned back to Ali, who was watching her. She gasped.

"Where am I?" he asked sleepily.

"You are in the Finders Chambers, Ali," she said with a smile, "I am Finder Malanga. You have been injured. Do you want some water?" She felt silly offering him water, but it was the first thing that came to her mind. She looked at the gauges on the machines and his entire system was now reading as normal for a child.

"No," he said simply, and kept staring at her.

An awkward moment passed slowly. She looked down at his torso and found the would much smaller now and nearly completely grown over with new skin. "Does it hurt?" she asked.

"No," he smiled, "it feels really good. And I'm hungry now. They said I could ask for food."

"Who said?" she asked.

"I don't know, the voice from the plant I guess," he replied as he itched around the edge of the clear shell.

"The voice from the plant." Malanga looked at him with renewed interest. "What else has the plant told you?"

"Oh," he scrunched his face to think, "just that I am going to be fine, and that I will always be fine. Stuff like that. Nice stuff. Stuff to make me feel better."

"Do you always hear voices from plants?"

"Only the ones whose roots are changing. They all talk to me," again he adjusted his position and itched more.

"Does it itch?" she asked.

"No," he said, "but they said I need to scratch to start peeling the shell off. It will be done soon, and then they say it will need air."

Malanga thought about this. The boy had obviously developed a psychic connection with the plants, but she wondered if the plants were the initiator or the boy.

"You know," she said, humming beneath her words, "I often speak to plants in my mind too. Ever since I was young. They have such darling little voices, don't they?"

Ali again scrunched up his face to think. He was becoming more animated and his breathing was now normal. The wound was now just a magenta mark on his skin. "I don't know about plants," he said, "the only one that talks to me is the one that hurt me."

"But you said 'they' about the voice. Is it more than one voice?"

"Well," he said with authority, "it is one plant, but it has a double voice. When it talks it's like a whole lot of people are talking. It kind of sounds like an echo, but at the same time."

He twisted his head a bit to one side, then looked down at his torso with a scowl. "They just said I can take off the shell, but I'm afraid it will hurt. I don't know how to talk back to them."

Malanga came over to him. "May I look?" she asked.

"Sure," he said, leaning back so she could better get to his wound.

She reached out toward him and touched her finger tips to the edge of the shell. She was going to lift the shell carefully from the edge, but as soon as she touched it, it became powder in her hand. She then brushed over the center of it and it just wiped off like nothing more than chalk powder. In seconds it was clear, and only a light pink streak remained of the once life-threatening gash. She was amazed.

"I guess you didn't need to worry about this hurting you," she said to Ali.

"Nope," he replied, "that didn't hurt at all. I guess I can go now, huh?"

Malanga wanted to study him, and learn everything there was about this new plant. She saw a look of disappointment in his face and realized he would want to be at the welcoming ceremony for the newcomers. "Of course you can go to meet the newcomers," she said, "but will you take me to meet this plant, and let me examine you more closely later?"

"You mean I can go to the welcoming ceremony?" he asked with excitement.

"If you want to, of course you can."

He got up and jetted past her, then hit his reversers and turned around. "Yes," he said.

"Yes?" she asked.

"Yes, I will show you the plant and let you examine me." Then he was out the door.

* * * * * * *

As George entered the cavernous docking bay he became instantly disoriented. They had docked in the same bay he'd been in several times before, but couldn't recognize anything. The entire area was brightly colored, including the tunics everyone wore. It was clear they had developed fabric dyes, and they certainly had developed clothing and hair styles. But there was an atmosphere everywhere of the human imprint. Before the surfaces were monotonously colored, unadorned by any markings other than directional signs and technical indicators. Now there was artwork everywhere, and small personal touches, like initials of lovers and doodles. What was lacking was the disharmony of graffiti, the chaos of unplanned or uncoordinated decorations.

He saw Paul and BQ, and recognized their children from images sent through the years. He also recognized his father, who hovered apart from the rest to the left. With him were a group of older people who, George assumed, were the elders. There was a large group of children singing in a choir, and several other groups.

Second Pass

Each group appeared to be organized by age or occupation, their clothing reflecting their group. There was one group, however, that interested him more than the others. They floated apart from everyone else to the far right, and were of every size, shape, age, ethnicity and type. A very short woman was suspended in front of and above them as if a leader. She stared directly at George. He felt a surge of recognition then a deep sense of dread. He turned to his father and fumbled a bit with his jet pack controls, then jetted a bit too quickly in his direction. There were giggles from the children at his clumsiness.

"George," his father said as he gathered him in his arms. "I've waited a long time for this hug."

"I am so glad to be here. I can't wait for you to meet your grandson," said George. He started to tear up. "Little Georgie is the sweetest child on earth."

"I'm afraid you are wrong about that son," he said.

"Wrong?" George laughed.

"Wrong, because you were the sweetest child on earth, or in space. I love you son." His father then pulled him close again and the two wept silently.

The moment was broken by the wailing of a woman' voice. When George turned and saw an old woman holding a young boy at arms length before her, the wail diminishing to a whimper. She was the woman whom he had seen earlier. The diverse group around her were now clustered around the boy, who was holding up his shirt while the others were looking at his torso with excitement and joy, some of them poking the boy with their fingers making him laugh.

"What's with the kid?" George asked the Commander. "His tummy looks pretty average to me."

Commander McVee patted his son on the shoulder and jetted past him. He met mid-air with the older woman and they spoke for a few moments, then both jetted to the boy. George watched as the woman was talking quickly while pointing to the boy's stomach, then toward the hallway. Commander McVee finally shook his head in understanding and returned to George.

"It seems we have witnessed two miracles today, son. Your arrival and a plant that can harm and heal." He looked at George, who was puzzled. "There was an accident in the Eye Chamber yesterday when one of the plants apparently reached out and grabbed a guide cable, pulling its tray off track."

"Don't they trim the plants often enough?" George asked, remembering how meticulously the farming area had been maintained before.

"Well," said the commander with a shrug, "it seems the shoot grew quickly, as if it was an arm reaching." He looked at his son's confused face and chuckled. "There are many odd things that happen here, son. This is the latest. When the cable snapped the boy was injured, they thought fatally. But the plant secreted a liquid onto his wound and somehow it healed him in less than twenty-four hours."

"Extraordinary," said George. "Does Paul know about this? He will be…"

"We will tell him directly," said the Commander, "but the oddest thing is that it was the boy who knew which plant it was, and who has been noticing strange changes in many of the plants lately."

They returned to their place in the docking bay, and the welcoming ceremony continued. George met the leaders of SIL, reconnected with the different elders he had met before and then listened to the children's choir sing SIL's anthem. Afterward they all ate a delicious meal, and had tube talk, with the boy, Ali, telling the story of what happened with the plant.

Chapter 15

"Life is different here now, Liz," George said to the CommLink image of his lover in front of him. "What was such a simple life is now extremely complex."

"How so?" asked Liz. "Is it because there are more people? Nearly all of them have arrived now, it has got to change things."

"Well, certainly," agreed George, "but it was different before I got here. There are established structures, unwritten rules, conventions and very old grudges. The murder of the Chairholder has people very upset still, and that was years ago. Paul and BQ have never been accepted either. It is as if they intruded just yesterday. And forget about the new arrivals, they are not going to have an easy time of it at all."

"Well, you have to help them all adjust."

"Common, Liz, I have no say here. I'm just another new arrival, and having my father be the Commander puts me in the middle of more difficulties and disagreements than I can count."

"Then don't count," she said with authority.

"What do you mean, don't count?" He was aggravated by her comment. She always had the solution, always stated it simply, and he never understood.

"What I mean is don't get involved with things other than what you understand. They are trying to intimidate everyone new by having all of this undercurrent nobody can know except insiders. When I was in Paris it was the same thing, everybody spoke their neighborhood's particular language, just to intimidate outsiders."

"But I have to take it all seriously," he nearly shouted. "I have responsibility to these people who have come here. I feel like I lied to them. I had no idea it was so hostile here."

"Paul has been telling you that for nearly twenty years, how did you miss it?"

He was mad now. She was trying to make him mad, he knew it, which made him madder still. He would get angry, she would keep pushing, he would blow up, then he would understand something that was right in front of him all along. He hated the way she did this, the way she knew before he did what was going on.

"Just tell me what it is I'm missing, Liz, for Christ's sake!"

"George," she said with a sigh, "I have nothing to tell you. Well, that's not exactly true. I have two things to tell you. First, you are the person leading these people, and you must help bring things out into the open. Use the President, he's brilliant at this kind of thing. He can help you."

"What is the other thing?" he realized he was asking her to understand things that he himself didn't understand.

"That I love you. I'll see you in less than a week."

"I take it this conversation is over?"

"Isn't I love you a fine way to end it?"

"I need you here. I really do. I love you too."

The screen went blank, he was alone again.

* * * * * * *

"That's just how it works here," said Paul. "I've been fighting it for years. Well, not exactly fighting, more like rolling over and playing dead. But now there are some real problems. I see what you are facing," he said with a smile, "it kind of makes me nostalgic."

"You are sick," said BQ with a laugh. "To think of those early days with any kind of longing is totally insane." She turned to George. "As for you," she patted his forearm, "you just need to decide what you are going to try to do here. All of the shuttles have come and gone except for the one bringing Liz, and that leaves to get them later today. In fact, they will be arriving here in two weeks. So I suggest," she looked at the two men as if for permission, "that you use those two weeks to our advantage, not your own."

"I beg your pardon," said George with surprise, "your advantage?"

"Yes," she said strongly, "our advantage, for me and Paul and our children."

"What possibly can you mean?" asked Paul. "George has much on his mind and must get ready for Liz."

"I beg to differ," she said, "and if you will let me talk, you will understand." She looked as if reconsidering this last comment. "Well," she began again, "you might understand." She rummaged through a sack on the wall and produced an electronic pad. Her fingers flew around the surface bring to the screen what she was

Second Pass

looking for. "I've been making some notes in the past months; notes about the way different people have been acting since the new arrivals got here. In particular, I've noticed some of the Elders have been working very hard to get to know them. And, interestingly enough, they are all members of the Borns." She looked at Paul, who was about to speak, but held up her hand to prevent his interruption. "And your friend Machmood is also courting them, which seems out of context. Other than his place as Chief Overseer, which makes it mandatory for him to work with them."

"I don't see how that is anything out of the ordinary," said Paul. "Machmood has to meet with them and if the Borns are the only ones taking their place of leadership seriously around here, so what?"

"There's more," she said, continuing to poke at the surface of her electronic pad, bringing up more information to the screen. "It's also none other than Alex Jiimson!" She looked at the two blank faces staring back at her. "Don't you see?" she asked with frustration. "The new arrivals are making even the most closed minded people reach out to enlist support from these newcomers. And there is no irony lost that the most ardent enemies of these people for the last ten years are the first to change their stripes."

Paul cleared his throat as if pulling on his armor. "I don't know," he said sarcastically, "I think they are just making appearances and will find out everything they can from these people and use it against them soon enough."

"You seem to believe that the only reason to befriend someone is to later betray them," she said sharply. "I'd hate to be a new friend of yours."

"Please," George said, "you are falling into exactly what my father didn't want to ever happen here." They both turned their heads quickly and Paul, who hadn't anticipated the movement and wasn't holding on tightly, flew away from his perch on the wall and almost ran into BQ. "Watch it, you might end up getting friendly with each other if you get too close."

BQ gave Paul a playful shove which sent him ramming into George, who pushed him back. The two played catch with Paul, who was laughing a silly, insincere laugh, until he grabbed onto George with his arms and legs. "Now who better watch out!" he said as he started to tickle George's ribs.

Suddenly a siren sounded. Paul and BQ looked at each other with alarm. Paul pushed backward from George and stabilized himself with his jet pack. BQ loosened her Velcro straps and jetted with Paul toward the door.

"What is that?" George asked. "Where are you going?"

"It is the emergency call to gather in the main assembly room," said BQ. "It preempts everything we are doing. Every person on SIL must go there."

"But how will the newcomers know?" asked George as he started up his jet pack. But as he approached the door he heard an announcement over speakers hidden throughout the station explaining where everyone was to go.

As George entered the main hallway he saw hundreds of people. Most of the newcomers were not well skilled with their jetpacks, and there were collisions everywhere and angry voices. Some of the new people had brought suitcases with them, George didn't know what for, and nearly all of them carried some sort of camera bag, satchel or purse. They were also easily distinguished by their clothing and the fact that some of them wore shoes, which nobody on SIL had ever worn. One lady lost a high heeled shoe in a small mishap which sent her crashing into a main support beam. She had tried to avoid bumping into someone, and applied too much thrust with her jet. She had hit the beam very hard and she started to bleed little beads of blood into the atmosphere. Her right shoe, with a long sharp heel went spinning across the hallway, and lodged itself into the wall material with a *thunk*.

At one point, BQ made a motion to Paul, who nodded in agreement as she turned in a different direction. George watched her and saw that she was in conversation with someone through the microphone on her shoulder strap. He caught up with Paul.

"Where's she going?" George asked. "I thought we all had to go to the main assembly chamber."

"She got a message from Sylvia and has to go meet her in the Comm Center." Paul immediately jetted a bit ahead and George got the strong impression that the discussion had ended. He also sensed that there was something that made him uneasy about this development which he was not going to talk about.

As the approached the final turn to the main assembly room they were stopped by the packed crowd. Far more people were trying to enter than normal, and with the navigational mishaps of the new comers there was a log jam in the hallway. "Just like rush hour traffic," said George. "It reminds me of when I was young and the old people were still driving. Way too many people."

Paul held up his hand to silence George. His head was cocked strangely and George realized he was listening to the conversations of others. George then tuned in, too, and began to hear the words shuttle, hijack, explosion and other distressing things. Rumors were flying, as they will, but they all seemed to have to do with a developing impression that a shuttle had been stolen and had exploded.

As the rumor grew, the noise in the hallway got louder. People were crying, and some were shouting in argument with others. Paul had never seen this kind of animation in a crowd since the day Chairholder Sylvanna had been murdered. He was about to say something to George as the crowd suddenly surged forward.

They entered the room and saw that his father was at the podium station at the far end, deep in conversation with Bill Bryant, Finder Malanga, Alexander Machmood and Andrew Stetler. Paul saw at once that this was serious. Commander McVee saw his son and waved him and Paul to come to him.

"George," his father said, "do you remember everyone? You remember Bill Bryant, of course, our First Officer, and Finder Malanga..."

"Hello Solange," George said.

"George," she said "we are in need of your help. And we will also have to call on you Paul. It seems you will be working together again as you did at MIT." As she spoke George felt himself begin to relax, and glow with warmth and a sense of wellbeing. Paul grabbed him gently by the elbow and squeezed once, then let go.

"And this is Alexander Machmood, Chief Overseer." George remembered years of complaints about the passive-aggressive sabotage Machmood had done to Paul. Then he turned to the only other person in the group.

"I don't believe we've met," said George. "I'm George McVee, Junior."

"Andrew Stetler," the young man said, extending his hand.

"Andy is our head of Security," his father explained, "and took over that position from his father several years ago." He allowed the two men to exchange a few polite words, then interrupted. "Now that the formalities are over, I expect you all to work together as if you have known each other for a long time. George,

Paul," McVee said seriously, "there has been a horrible tragedy. We don't have all the information yet, but several shuttles in the fleet have been blown up, some were carrying visitors back from SIL, others were bringing supplies to SIL. And one shuttle has been stolen from the SIL outbay portal."

George was in shock. "What do you mean? How can that be?"

"It seems that there was some cooperation with people here. In fact, under the laws of SIL, we cannot proceed to address the population without the Chairholder present."

"Where is Jiimson?" asked Paul. "He's always the first one around when there's a chance to get attention."

"That's part of the problem," said Stetler. "He helped steal the shuttle."

"What do you mean, 'helped'," asked George. "Were there many?"

Malanga moved to his side and entwined her fingers in his, with her other hand gently resting on the crook of his elbow. George suddenly felt the uncomfortable gaze of the entire group.

"There was only one other," said his father, "Dave Masters and Jiimson stole the shuttle." George was confused. David Masters and his wife, Becka, had come with him on the shuttle. He had granted them visitor status as a favor to Steve, who as head of his personal security team had helped him so much.

"Did Becka go with them?" George asked.

"We can't find Becka," said Stetler, "and the tapes of the docking bay show that only Masters and Jiimson left with the shuttle. She is still here somewhere, but so far we can't find her."

"There's more," said Machmood. "There were four small shuttles and three large ones in transit today, along with one more small shuttle scheduled for departure tomorrow." George was well aware of the shuttle schedule, and was also aware that his wife and child were to be on the shuttle the next day. "All seven of them were destroyed by explosions simultaneously," he said, "and the one on the ground in Texas was stolen. It took off in the chaos of the explosions."

"Over seven hundred people died," Bill Bryant said. "And millions of tons of supplies that were on their way here were lost."

Second Pass

"How is that possible?" asked Paul. "It takes hundreds of people to launch a shuttle. How could it be stolen? There is no way it could..."

"It seems there is a way," said Bryant. "During the chaos, a group of people from Washington arrived and had everything in order, with clearance from the White House, to send a security team up here to help us. Since the shuttle was scheduled to launch only 11 hours later, the preliminaries had all been done, and it was simply a matter of starting the launch sequence."

"Are you saying the President of the United States is somehow involved?" The booming, and familiar, voice of former President McKenna came from behind them. All turned toward him and saw him standing there with Tom, Shandor and Willa Marsdon.

"Finder Malanga," said Willa. "Please excuse me, but we have a problem. One of our technicians has been knifed in the Eye Chamber. I had others put him on a board and start to bring him to your chambers, but when they tried to exit the door, the healing plant grabbed him and has put him in a cocoon."

Malanga began to hum. "Was he hurt badly?" she asked.

"His throat was cut. I think he was dead. We acted as quickly as we could." She bowed her head in gesture of humility and grief.

"With your leave," Malanga said to the Commander, "I must go to the Eye Chamber. Will you excuse me?"

"Go," the Commander said. Then he turned to Paul, "Will you have your daughter join the Finder in the Eye Chamber. Once she has relieved the Finder, I will need her to return to us here."

"I understand," said Malanga as Paul spoke into his shoulder strap, "I will return as soon as I can. If the worker is dead, I will return quickly." She joined hands with Willa and jetted across the chamber, which was now nearly full.

"Is my wife safe?" George asked.

The group looked at each other uncomfortably. Then the Commander spoke. "She is safe," he said, "but she has no security. Steve Masters is also among the missing."

"I repeat my question. Is the President suspected of being involved in this tragedy?"

"No," Bryant said, "his team was authorized to take the shuttle early."

"But you said it was stolen," said Paul.

"After the shuttle took off, two of his crew were murdered. There was a group who had stowed away on the shuttle and then, after it was in orbit, were seen cutting their throats. Shortly after that the cameras and audio went dead. We don't know where the shuttle is or who is on it."

"The only thing that is certain," said Commander McVee, placing his hand on his son's shoulder," is that we have no shuttle fleet. There will be no more shuttle runs this pass."

George looked at his father and realized what was being said. He was stuck here for 18 years. Liz and their son would not be coming.

Chapter 16

Woody woke from his nap and looked around. Something was strange. At first he was puzzled that there was a locker in the room, but as sleep cleared from his mind he remembered he had decided to sleep in his office, rather than go home the night before. There had been an emergency board meeting called by Stevens at 11 pm the previous night. He wouldn't have known about it except that Liz had asked him to check messages, as she had already left for Houston. There were the usual messages, and one from Solomon Gould's secretary.

"Hello Liz, this is Trina from Gould's office," the message began. "I'm sorry to bother you but something has come up and I have no access to the CommLink and I thought you might want to hear this and relay it to George. Stevens has called an emergency meeting of the board tonight, and the security memo came automatically to Gould's computer. I wouldn't think anything of it except that Stevens has ordered the building shut down and all employees to vacate during this meeting. With George, Tom and Gould all on SIL, and continuous CommLink activity and LOL surveillance, I found it a bit odd that this secret meeting would take place and that everyone would be forced to leave the building, leaving vital functions of communication and navigation unmanned on this end. Would you have George tell Gould and Tom and have them look into this. Gotta run. Have a great trip! I know you and little Georgie will love SIL. Anyhow, I have to vacate my office as well. See you soon."

When Woody heard this message it was 9pm. He suspected something was up, and knew that he could relay the information to George via CommLink at about 4 am. So he made a show of leaving the building for the night, stopping by Stevens' office and asking if there was anything he could do for the director. Then he left, went around to the rear of building two, let himself in with his security card, followed the 4th floor tunnel and went back down to his office, where he got onto the security system and erased his entry from the log, which only he had the capability to do.

After that he had turned off all lights in his office and went to sleep, with his alarm set for 3:50 am. He figured that the meeting would be over by then and the building would be clear. But he never woke up. He looked at his clock. Adrenaline rushed through his veins as he saw it was noon. He sat up quickly and was hit by nausea that caused him to vomit spontaneously. Rubbing his head, and slowing his movement, he looked again at the clock and realized it was flashing noon, which meant the electricity had been interrupted. This gave a reason that he had missed his alarm, but caused another alarm. He recognized the feeling in his body, and realized he had been drugged. He went to the sink on shaky legs and splashed cold water in his face and drank a good amount. The nausea was short lived, but he was moving slowly.

He turned on his computer and found that it was 10 am. Sensing something terribly wrong, he opened his door slowly. Nothing. The hall was empty, which was normal for that part of the building. But there were none of the usual sounds. He walked down the hall and checked into the different offices. Nobody was there. He went into the CommLink chamber and stood there. The display screens were blank. The night time lighting was in effect. There were no technicians at all. He waited and listened. Nothing. Silence. Then he realized that the oddest part of the silence was that from the time he woke up until now, there hadn't been any rumble of the gargantuan satellite dish movement, which normally occurred every two to six minutes, depending on the point of Earth rotation of the northern hemisphere. Something was very wrong.

He proceeded down the hallway, and there wasn't any person in any office. Bathrooms were empty. In the office of Security, where the television monitors were in a bank on the far wall, they were all blank, there weren't any of the usual video images of the entire complex. He went to the computer and hit the space bar to activate the display. There was an emergency warning screen saying that there had been a gas leak and the building was quarantined. This perhaps explained his nausea, but logically, if the gas had filled the building it would have killed him in his sleep. Plus that did not explain why there was no electricity, except for the computers. Lights also worked. He knew that the computers and lights were on the same basic electrical line as the surveillance monitors.

He crossed the room and checked behind the bank of monitors and found that the main power cord was plugged in to the wall. He followed it a short distance, and from the very awkward position his body was not in he saw that it had been cut. Again he experienced the jelly knees of an adrenaline rush. As he crawled

Second Pass

backward to get out from behind the bank of monitors, his hand felt something stick to it. He lifted his hand and saw a dark green toothpick, half chewed. He pondered this. A vague memory came to him, but without enough substance to know what that was. He placed the toothpick in his pocket and made a mental note to sit and think about it, figure out why it bothered him. Where had he seen such a toothpick before?

He decided he would go to the board room and see if the meeting was still going on. Confident now that there was nobody in the building at all, he walked without the caution he previously had displayed. He got to the boardroom doors and noticed that they were locked. He knocked lightly, but heard nothing, so he got out his master key and unlocked the door. It was pushing against something heavy on the other side and he couldn't get it to open. He gave up and went down to the end of the hall and took the right turn to the front door to Steven's office, which had a direct connecting door to the boardroom on the other side.

Again he found the door locked, and had to use his key to open the door. This time the door opened easily. He stared in disbelief at the scene before him. There was blood everywhere. Bodies with their throats cut were all around the room. Chairs were broken and there was a pile of bodies three deep against the far door. The entire board of directors had been slaughtered.

* * * * * * *

"I got here as soon as I could," said BQ. "We're going to have to have more training for the new comers and their jet packs." While she was talking, Sylvia was completely distracted, and, from all appearances, very nervous. "What is it, Sylvia? I've never seen you like this."

Sylvia turned to BQ and let out a big sigh. "We are in the middle of a massive terrorist attack, both on earth and here on SIL. I asked you to come because I can trust you, and you have strong ties to influential people on Earth, if you are willing to use them."

"Of course I am," said BQ, "you needn't ask. What is going on?"

"The entire shuttle fleet is either destroyed or hijacked. Everyone on SIL is stuck here, there will be no more supplies, hundreds of people have been killed, and nobody else will be coming here, at least until the next pass."

BQ jetted over to Sylvia and hooked her feet into the floor straps next to hers in front of the CommLink screen. "Is Liz okay? Did her shuttle blow up?"

"No, thank God," Sylvia said. "Her shuttle was commandeered after it took off early from Houston with a Presidential team of investigators and security. They were coming here to help us, but two of them were killed, right on the monitor, then the video link went dead and all radio communication stopped."

"Good God!" BQ thought for an instant, trying to piece it all together. "Are they coming here? Do you think we will be under attack? SIL has no defenses, at least not sophisticated ones. We were waiting for the supply..." she stopped talking as she realized that with the supply ships out of commission the military defense supplies being delivered would never get there.

"Exactly," said Sylvia. "But we don't know where they are. Either one."

"What do you mean, either one?"

"The shuttle that was docked here was stolen a few hours ago."

BQ closed her eyes and prayed. "What can I do?" she asked quietly.

"I'm not sure," said Sylvia, "but I'm going to deputize you, secretly, to be my second officer of communications, and am revoking all of the passwords and access codes from my entire staff. Are you willing to do that?"

"Of course I am," BQ said.

"This is a top secret position," Sylvia went on as if she didn't need to hear the answer to her previous question. "You cannot discuss anything you hear with anyone other than me and Bill."

"I see," BQ said. She and Paul shared everything with each other. The reason they had survived their years on SIL was chiefly due to open communication with each other, built, of course, on their love. "I normally share everything with Paul," she said.

Sylvia stopped what she was doing and turned to look directly at BQ. "I know you do. I'm working that out." She stopped and rubbed her temples. She had no reason to preclude Paul from access to the information. It was clear to her that Paul and BQ were the only people on SIL she entirely trusted, with the exception of Solange Malanga. She intended to use Solange as an advisor on all of this, and grant her access to all information.

What she hesitated on was the tension between Paul and Machmood. As Chief Overseer, Machmood had access to all information; it was in the constitution of SIL. But Machmood had proved himself to be highly political and a bit untrustworthy, not always able to separate his personal grudges and motives from his work as Overseer. Because the population of SIL had been so small until now, there wasn't the sense of objective distance to the post of Chief Overseer as there would be in a large nation. Granted, all politicians were corrupted by their power, and it would be pure folly to expect anyone to hold a position of power without being motivated by their own personal vision on the direction of their governing.

The problem came in because Machmood had made it clear he would do nearly anything to foul Paul's work and authority. Sylvia knew that Paul's input would be very helpful, but if it ever came to light that Paul was granted access to the information while Machmood, who was constitutionally guaranteed that information, was denied access to it, she could be decommissioned.

"It's complicated," Sylvia said. "If I allowed it, which would be very helpful, but it was ever found out, I could be decommissioned. I don't know if I'm willing to take that risk."

"Well," said BQ with a smile, 'perhaps there is a way to get his input through me without him having access to the information in a formal way. I'm ashamed to admit it but sometimes I talk in my sleep."

Sylvia laughed out loud. "Are you suggesting that we employ feminine complicity? I mean, that is strictly against my ethics, even though it lies clearly within my capabilities."

The two women looked at each other. BQ knew how to do this perfectly so Sylvia's position wouldn't be jeopardized, and Sylvia knew she could trust her fellow woman. "I would never suggest such a thing, Sylvia. You can count on me. I will not give this information to any other person."

"Okay then," Sylvia said as she turned on a recorder, "Sallie Hempman Dunn, you are now deputized under top secret classification as First Assistant Communications Officer. You will report directly to me, Sylvia Bryant, Chief Communications Officer, on the matter of the breach of security and theft of a transport shuttle from SIL on this date, and directly ordered not to give any information regarding, related to, coming from or used in the carrying out of security and communications to any other person. All top secret conferences will be recorded and encrypted so as to secure them for future reference without making them available to any source during the entirety of this mission." Sylvia turned off the recorder. "Let's get started," she said.

She turned on the CommLink security recording system, set up all of the proper filters and frequency specifications, then opened the link directly to the Low Orbital Lens. They began to pick up various frequencies as the system rapidly scanned space in their quadrant for any radio communications. This resulted in nothing but static from interstellar electromagnetic interference. She then adjusted some of the parameters. Instantly they picked up all communications on SIL, which sounded like a crowd during intermission at a theatrical event, each being recorded separately for perusal later. She sent that to run in the background and then started scanning their quadrant for any electronic communications.

For several minutes there was nothing. Then a crackling sound came intermittently to their speakers, and a random seeming spike showed on the visual graphing screen. She further focused the scan, and was still getting nothing but blips of sound, milliseconds of transmission that ended as abruptly as they appeared.

"Excuse me," said BQ, "but I seem to remember something like this from what Paul told me about the first time they received transmissions through LOL. I don't know how the technology has developed since, and it has been nearly twenty years, but what they found they could do was to take a transmission and break it up into micro-bursts which both condensed the transmission and broke the condensed stream into very small parts. These could then be sent out on a variety of frequencies."

"I remember reading about that," said Sylvia. "I believe you might be on to something." She turned to the system control and entered a series of parameters. She scanned several frequencies at once and found that the transmission micro-bursts were occurring on five different frequencies. She then recorded all five simultaneously and took the sequential stream of these bursts and put them together on a single recording. After that she was able to expand the bursts and send them through a filter to a single speaker.

"Copy," said a voice they didn't recognize.

Second Pass

"Rendezvous at 23 hundred hours at coordinates..." The conversation went on with mostly technical phrases. The two voices signed off and there was silence for a few minutes. Sylvia kept the channel open and the recording going as she and BQ took the data and plotted it on the space map. What they found was that two ships, presumably the two shuttles, were heading for the old space station from the early 21st century. It had been out of commission for nearly 50 years, since the first of the earthquakes that reorganized the continents of the Earth.

"They won't find much there," said Sylvia. "That old tub is empty and deteriorating.

"That won't matter, really," said BQ. "They have their own life support systems on the two shuttles. The space station will allow them a place to stow things, and to be able to pass from one shuttle to the other without having to go EVA. It is really quite brilliant. What I can't imagine is what they would want to stow. Perhaps they will just use it to change shuttle crews."

"Oh, I think they will have plenty to stow," said Sylvia. "They took tons of supplies with them, and an entire range of highly sophisticated tools."

"What do you think they are planning?"

"I don't know," Sylvia said, "but I intend to find out."

There was suddenly some activity on the speaker. "Q2 this is Q1, come in please. Over."

BQ recognized the voice, but she couldn't place it. "I know that voice," she said.

"Q1 to ahead, this is Q2. Over."

"Q2, we have a flight path developed to Target. Are you ready to receive? Over."

"Roger that Q1, transmit when ready. Using predetermined frequencies in microstream. Over."

"Roger Q2. Transmission commencing. Over."

Sylvia's hands flew across the CommLink controls, readying it to receive the transmitted data stream. She had never done it before, not in micro-bursts on an array of frequencies, but she figured it would be the same setup as receiving their voices, just set for data instead of voice.

A loud squeal started to emit from the speakers, so she quickly turned the volume down. The squeal lasted about 20 seconds then abruptly ended. She reached and switched back to voice reception and turned the speakers back up.

"Reception complete," said Q2. "Communication complete if you are finished. Over."

"Just one thing," Q1 said. "I haven't heard any reports from the surprise we left at Associated. Have you picked up anything on your monitoring of news broadcasts? Over."

"Not a single, fucking word Mr. Chairman. Over."

"Do NOT break handle reference Q2! I will come and do to you what I did to those dullards on the board if you do that again. Over."

"Oh, yeah. I read you boss. I guess it's hard to break old habits. You did require us to call you that. Over."

"Just don't do it again. They can't catch us, even if they know who we are. But security is imperative. Over."

"Roger that Q1. My ears are dead if yours are. Over."

"Rendezvous at 23 hundred hours. Radio blackout until twenty-two hundred thirty unless emergency situation arises. Over and out, Q2."

The graphic display of the communication on those five frequencies flattened, and the speaker fell silent. Sylvia took the disk that had recorded the data transmission and pushed off the console to the other side of the room, inserting the disk deftly into the other computer.

"I love it when you do that," said BQ. "I've never had the dexterity."

"Do that move as many times as I have and you'll become an expert acrobat. Now let's see what they transmitted."

Sylvia and BQ watched the screen. The system scanned the disk and was unable to find any software program with which to read the data. Sylvia then displayed an index of the files on the disk and found that the thousands of files had a wide variety of extensions. She scratched her head. Changed some setting and the files came up in a different order. "Shit again! I can't make this out," she said. "The file types are so inconsistent that they must have come from different programs. Damn it!"

"Wait," said BQ. "How do you have them sorted?"

"First, by time of transmission. I figured that way they are in sequential order. But then I changed it to sort by extension."

"But what if they were not transmitted in order? Or the extensions were somehow encrypted?" BQ said. "Try sorting them alphabetically."

Second Pass

Sylvia changed the sort parameter again and the files appeared in alphabetical order. "Now that's interesting," she said.

BQ looked at the screen and saw that there were many files by the same primary name, and each file name had 30 different extensions, consistently. The disk contents appeared in groups of 30 files with the same names.

"I think you've cracked their code," said Sylvia. "They broke each file into 30 parts and then organized them by extension. The extensions aren't generated from a program, but were put there by the user."

"What kind of information do you think it would be?" BQ asked.

"It could be nearly anything. Documents, sound files, images. I mean, there's no limit."

"Yes, but if you and I had just stolen two shuttles and were going to rendezvous, what would we need to have before the rendezvous? Obviously they already know where they are going to rendezvous and when. What else would they need to know?"

Sylvia searched the database for data on the old space station. "What do we know about the old space station?" she asked. "You know, it really doesn't make sense to use it as a personnel transfer, because with the adapters we had to put on the docking port they won't fit the space station ports. And if they want to transfer themselves or their cargo they will have to go EVA."

"Then they aren't going to do any of those things," said BQ. "They are going to do something different. But what?" She took her feet out of the straps and jetted across the room. "Is there a survivable atmosphere capability on the station? Could they somehow take up residence?"

"I don't really know. It would have to be airtight. I know of no damage to the hull. I believe it was abandoned because SIL was built. No other reason. I suppose they could live there, but remember it is totally Earth reliant, and they eliminated the entire shuttle fleet."

"What did they take with them?" BQ asked.

"The docking commander was knocked unconscious and is just now regaining consciousness. I've asked Malanga to let me know when I can speak to him."

Sylvia kept fooling with the files. They weren't text files, nor were they data files. If she added an image file extension she got them to open, but they were mostly black with some flecks of white. "BQ," she said, "come over here and look at this. What does it look like to you?"

BQ looked at the black square. There was a white line coming from the bottom left corner and curving slightly upward toward the center of the screen. Then there was a spot of white in the upper right corner that looked like a speck of dust. "Hmm," she said, "doesn't look like much to me, what is the next one?"

"It's the same thing," Sylvia said. She added the image extension and the identical image flashed onto the screen. "See?"

"Well, they aren't exactly the same," said BQ. "Can you switch between the two? Back and forth so we can see the exact difference?"

"Sure," said Sylvia. She put the two next to each other, but that showed nothing. So she did as BQ suggested. "There. Do you see any difference?"

"Do it back and forth real fast," said BQ. "It looks like the line is slightly longer, just a few pixels, but longer."

Sylvia flashed them over top of each other as fast as she could, and there was a slight lengthening of the line between the first and second pictures.

"Do the same with one later in the list. Like a few hundred files ahead." BQ was getting excited. When Sylvia chose a random file much further in the list of file names the picture was substantially different. The black square was the same, but the speck was now a bit larger and the line was shorter but thicker.

"Nothing," said Sylvia. "Nothing at all."

"No, wait," said BQ. "It looks like the line is perhaps double now, or about to become double. See how the edges are brighter and the center between them is slightly darker?"

"You are right," said Sylvia, "but what does that mean?"

"It's video!" said BQ. "There are 30 frames per second in video and these are individual frames meant to stream together. How many files are there, total?"

Sylvia put them in a folder and then got the properties of the folder. "9900 files."

"Let's see," said BQ, "at thirty frames per second and sixty seconds per minute that makes," she used the calculator on another computer. "5.5 minutes of video."

"Let me create a cascade of the images and then we can watch some video," said Sylvia.

Second Pass

* * * * * * *

"Attention!" shouted Machmood to the gathered elders. "We cannot afford to follow every tangent and every opinion to the point we have no central focus."

"What is your central focus?" demanded Erica Pimmit. "You seem to think that your ideas are our ideas."

"Erica, I think nothing of the sort. Yet if we all talk at the same time," he said looking around the room, "we will never accomplish anything at all." He paused. There was silence in the chamber for the first time in two hours. "That's better. News keeps coming in, and the situation keeps changing. We must not be premature in our reactions."

"The situation will continue to unfold," said Kitty Quan with a calm voice, "and we will wait until such time and decide what to do then. In the mean time, there are many things we do know that we can begin working on."

"That makes absolutely no sense," cried Ernestine Wasserman. "You say we should wait and you say we should start working. Which is it?" She peered at Quan with one eye slightly squinted and the other eyebrow raised.

"I have just received more news," McVee said evenly. "The situation continues to become more grave by the minute. The entire fleet of shuttles, large and small, are now out of commission. There will be no more transport to or from Earth this pass." He let this sink in. "Everyone here on SIL will remain on SIL until next pass. This means we are overpopulated at our current capacity.

"We aren't going to have enough living spaces for everyone here?" squawked Wasserman. "We must start to build more immediately! I volunteer to direct the construction and the EVAs to do it myself! And Kitty will figure out how to make the materials."

A chuckle rumbled through the group. The idea of Ernestine Wasserman hauling steel beams through space was too ridiculous to ponder. The Commander raised his hand, and Machmood rolled his eyes.

"Not so fast," McVee said. "There is more. Over 700 people have now died in the explosions of the vehicles, and we have a murderer on the ship. We don't know who, but we must find out before more people are lost."

"Who was murdered?" thundered Machmood. "It was probably done by one of the new Earth beings."

"No one has died, but one of the technicians in the Eye Chamber had his throat cut. And yes," said McVee deliberately looking at Machmood, "it may well have been committed by one of the new arrivals, but it may well have been one of us. Remember that the Chairholder was murdered many years before any new arrivals from Earth lived on SIL."

"I beg to differ," said Henry Lu, "when she was murdered there were new arrivals from Earth. The Dunns were..."

"Would you please be reasonable," said Steven Upine, "The Dunns had nothing whatever to do with that murder. She was murdered by one of the original members of the SIL crew or one of their offspring. In fact, the murderer may be one of us. To insinuate that the Dunns had anything at all to do with it is ludicrous."

Again Machmood slammed his gavel. "Come to order! Do you hear yourselves? You are no more of the demeanor of a group of elders and Overseers than a bunch of school children. We must let the Commander speak."

"This is our current situation, then," he said with a nod of gratitude to Machmood. "We have nothing to do but accept it, so please let me finish. The entire shuttle fleet has been destroyed, and everyone on SIL will remain on SIL. We must find the person who attempted murder..."

"Excuse the interruption," said Lee Ray Smoot, "but you said a technician had his throat cut but then said 'attempted murder.' How can both be true? One cannot survive having their throat cut."

"Please do not interrupt..." Machmood began, but was cut off by the Commander.

"It's okay, Alexander," said McVee, "it is a logical question." Machmood glowered in his station, but said nothing more. "The technician, Mandrick Katuko, had his throat cut and should by all rights be dead. But he was in the Eye Chamber and apparently, as the others attempted to help him a plant emitted a gel-like substance at Mandrick and he was covered by it."

"If you suffocate or bleed to death, you are still dead! I say he was murdered!" Ernestine croaked from her perch. "We must apprehend the murderer! I'll lead the expedition to find him!"

The commander looked at Machmood with a wink, unleashing him. "Elder Wasserman," he screamed, "one more outburst from you and I'll have you expelled from this chamber and from these proceedings!"

The room fell silent. Machmood had never threatened expulsion before, which they didn't know if it was even possible for him to do.

"Katuko is not dead," said McVee. "The substance the plant covered him with seems to be saving his life."

"Just like Ali Wong," said Upine half to himself. Erica Pimmit smiled at him and imperceptibly nodded her head once.

"At any rate," the Commander continued, "we must find the murderer. The situation on SIL is part of a much larger picture that encompasses all of the earth, and has serious implications for our future as well of that of the Earth. We will have to reorganize SIL to accommodate everyone on board. At current count there are 375 people on SIL who were only planning to be here temporarily or were preparing to move back to the Earth. All of them were to be transported back to the Earth in the next six weeks, and we were to receive 115 more to move to SIL permanently. This means we have 260 people without housing, and we must start immediately to build this housing."

"We can easily find the room for these people to be housed. There are many empty spaces not yet occupied or developed on SIL. It will be no problem in terms of space. As for the materials, however, we will have problems in that regard. We were expecting four more large shuttle shipments of materials which will not be arriving. However, we have the ability to create all that is necessary in our midst as it is." She seemed at peace, relaxed and confident. As long as there was some need for her to take care of, she was fulfilled.

Commander McVee waited for a reaction, but none came. It seemed as if everyone of the Elders was now realizing that this situation was not merely another reason to debate—it was real, and was not going away. "The history of SIL has been one of overcoming great odds. We have survived and flourished in every situation we've faced. And we will do the same in this one.

"Now, what we must first do is make a statement to everyone on SIL..."

There was a commotion in the room as the door flew open and Bill Bryant jetted in. "Excuse me, Commander," he said, acknowledging the other Overseers with a brisk nod. "There is an urgent message for you. This just came in through the CommLink from the White House." He handed a paper to the Commander, who took it and read the paper. His face went white and his hands started to tremble slightly. He read it again, and a single tear drop floated up from his left eye.

"The entire board of directors at Associated has been murdered," he said, "and Ronald Stevens, who had called the emergency meeting, is missing. He is suspected of murder, and conspiracy."

* * * * * * *

Woody returned to his office and sat on the side of his desk. He had called the police and waited in the board room until they came. He answered numerous questions and gave them access to every part of the complex they had requested, and promised he would not leave, explaining where his office was and how they could find him there.

As he walked back through the empty building he had formed a plan of sorts. First, he would reactivate the CommLink and find out what was happening on SIL. Then he would contact Liz in Houston. Contacting Liz before he knew what was going on would be a mistake. But before any of that, he walked directly to his file cabinet and opened the bottom drawer and pulled out an envelope which had been given to him many years ago with the instructions he was to open it only if the future of Associated was in jeopardy.

He tore open the brown paper and found it contained another white envelope. On the front were the words: "Woodward Higgins: On the event that the future of Associated Laboratories, Cambridge, Massachusetts, is in danger of failing as a business, or any other situation that puts continuing operations in question or is a threat to the future of said Associated Laboratories. Copies of this document are registered with the State of Massachusetts,

Second Pass

Office of the Governor, and with Copley, Henderson and Brighton Attorneys at Law."

Across the back of the envelope were the signatures of Solomon Gould, Thomas Robinson, George McVee, Jr., and Wallace McKenna, President of the United States. He took in a deep breath and tore open the envelope. There were several documents inside, which included the original bylaws, articles of incorporation, succession of directorships of the Board of Directors from the very beginning of the corporation, the lease of the land where the current building was built, the patent papers for the invention of the gyroscope, which had been the initial discovery upon which the company had been built 150 years earlier, and a legal document that made Woody have power of attorney over all of Associated Laboratories and its subsidiaries, and made him ad hoc chairman of the board of directors.

His hands trembled slightly as he placed the papers carefully back in their envelopes and then into the drawer of the file cabinet. He considered burning them and just going home, walking away from the whole terrible responsibility. He knew, however, that the Copley, Henderson, as the firm was called, would immediately be on top of their copy of these papers, and the Governor's office would be duly notified to examine their copy by the firm the moment word of the trouble at Associated was common knowledge.

He went into the CommLink chamber and flipped the alternate power source on behind the main console. Then went to do the same behind all of the banks of gargantuan monitors around the huge space map room. When he was flipping the last switch he felt the familiar rumble of the large satellite dish as it repositioned itself to pick up the direct link to LOL.

Back at the CommLink he adjusted the settings and went through the security codes for restart. Eventually the main menu showed on the screen. He started the sequence for connection with SIL and waited. There would be a three minute lag between sending the signal and it being received and retransmitted back to him. His hands shook terribly now, and he shoved them briskly into his pockets to steady them.

A wince of pain came as his finger hit the end of the green toothpick. He stopped cold. Now he remembered. He had found the other toothpick on the floor at this very location, nearly 4 years earlier. He ran into his office and opened a container he kept on his desk. There it was, the original one. He took it out and compared them. They were identical. He picked up the phone on his desk and called the number of the FBI investigator who had given him his card an hour earlier. When the man answered the phone he explained to him that he had some possible evidence that might render some DNA. He hung up the phone, put the original toothpick into the envelop in the bottom drawer of the filing cabinet, and placed the one he'd found that morning in a small plastic bag and carried it with him back to the CommLink.

When he returned, he saw the beautiful face of BQ looking quizzically at the screen. She was talking over her shoulder to someone else, and soon the face of Sylvia Bryant came into view and was seen adjusting settings. Tom hit the video on switch, which he had forgotten and as his image appeared on their screen 90 seconds later they both looked up.

"Hello BQ, Sylvia," he said. "We have a very serious situation here. Are you on the most secure transmission?"

"Yes sir," said Sylvia, out of character. Tom knew if she was calling him sir there was tension on her end as well. "We, BQ and I, are the only two who will know of the content of our conversations. I am only authorized to give information to Bill Bryant, my husband and first officer of SIL, and the Commander."

"And I," said BQ, "am authorized to pass information on to no other person. We are at highest security here on SIL. Have you been informed of our situation?"

"I have not, and I have quite a situation here as well," said Tom.

"We have heard of the shuttle explosions and the commandeering of the last Earth-based shuttle on it's Presidential mission to aid us," said Sylvia. "Is that what you are referring to?"

Tom looked with dazed eyes at the screen. The hairs on the back of his neck and arms stood up as adrenaline hit his legs and made his knees weak. "I had no idea," he said quietly. "Why are you in need of a mission of aid?"

"My God," said Sylvia. "You have no idea of what is going on." She stared at him from the screen for a few moments. Then a puzzled look turned quickly to one of alarm. "What was your reason for transmission? You requested the highest security. What is your situation?"

Second Pass

"Last night, at eleven pm, an emergency meeting of the entire Board of Directors of Associated was called by Stevens. A false evacuation of the building was called. I disobeyed and snuck back in and slept in my office. This morning I woke and found I had been drugged, and when I went to the board room I found every member of the board with their throats cut and Stevens missing. All main power to the complex had been compromised."

Just then he heard a door open at the far end of the room, and he flipped the screen off, hit the mute button for transmissions, and pretended he was dusting the console. A deputy came over to him, presented his FBI credentials, and Tom handed him the plastic bag with the toothpick in it. He explained where he'd found it and sent the man on his way. When he turned the screen back on, again he found the women adjusting their screen settings. He flipped his switches back on.

"Sorry about that," he said, "a guy from the FBI was just here. He's gone now."

"Are they the only ones who know about what happened at Associated?" BQ asked.

"Yes, they are, and we have created a complete media blackout. But from the sounds of things, the media will have their hands full. What is your situation though? You said the President was sending an aid mission."

"The shuttle stationed here was stolen," said Sylvia in a bland, official voice. "The Chairholder of the Assembly of SIL has left with the shuttle, and it is on a rendezvous course with the stolen shuttle from Houston. They are the last two shuttles in the fleet. All others were destroyed. More than 700 people are dead."

Tom thought about this for a moment. He realized that Stevens must have something to do with this as well. "What time did the shuttle leave Houston?"

"We are told it left at 8:00 in the morning. Three hours ago," said BQ.

"Then Stevens is on it," Tom said. He knew Stevens had plenty of time to get to Houston and be on that shuttle, plus he had the clearance to walk right past security guards and stow away.

"With the entire board of Associated gone," said BQ, "who is in charge? Gould is here with us, as is George Jr."

"What I am about to tell you goes no further than the two of you," Tom said sternly. "I must have your word on that. Not even the Commander or your husband, Sylvia, may know it. Do you understand?"

The two women looked at each other, hesitant. Each knew that this meant they would alone know the whole situation for the moment. "I don't know if we can promise that," said Sylvia. "There will be many decisions to make and we are not authorized to make those decisions. I fear at such a time it will be necessary for whoever is in charge to know everything."

"What I am about to tell you is already known," said Tom. "Gould and George, Jr. know it, but they won't realize it until they know what has happened here. By the time the decisions are made, it will be known by those in charge. You must never indicate that you knew any of this. Right now, you two, the FBI and myself are the only ones who know what happened here last night." He looked at the women, first Sylvia, then BQ. "Will you keep this to yourselves?"

"We have to tell them the Associated board were all killed," Sylvia said, almost defiantly. "And I don't know what you are about to tell us, so I cannot promise silence. I'm not trying to be difficult, but I'm charged with the security of SIL, and as a sovereign nation I cannot do anything less than fully discharge my duties."

"Well enough," said Tom, "I am confident that what I am about to tell you will be such that, once understood by you, you will see it is of no consequence and that the powers that be will know soon enough. And you will quickly understand why it is better if you never knew it."

BQ now spoke, "Woody," she said, "I know you are the most trustworthy person at Associated. My mother said you were the only man I was to fully trust in my life, and I live by everything she taught me."

"Well, then," said Woody with a smile, knowing more was about to be disclosed than he'd initially intended, "I will trust you in return." He went on to explain the contents of the envelope and the fact that he was now in charge of Associated. As he explained, the women then realized that upon telling the command of SIL the news of Associated, they would then tell George, Tom and Gould, who would know immediately that Woody was now in charge. Even Sylvia saw how it would be better if they only relayed the information about Associated's board, and keep the knowledge about Woody to themselves.

Second Pass

"And so," Woody continued, "I have made some decisions. I will put the CommLink on stasis for now. If you need to transmit, send warning and I will have it transferred to my personal CommPad and will uplink at the next earliest convenience. I will be staying here at Associated, and having nothing at all to do with the press. I don't know what is going on, but I'm determined to find out."

"We have something you can perhaps help us with," said Sylvia. "We have unscrambled some data that was transmitted between the two shuttles. Could you receive it and pass it on to Liz? I know she's in Houston and is destitute that she won't be able to see George for 18 years, but she is a scientist and will want to help. She can figure it out if anyone can."

"I'll do one better. I'm about to call her," said Woody, "and I'll have her fly back immediately on the Associated jet, which I'm sure is in Houston as we speak. She can look at it here." He monitored the data transmission, then said. "Got it. Ladies? Take care. Oh, BQ," he said, "your mother was my sister. You are my niece."

Chapter 17

"How do we know this guy knows how to operate this thing?" asked Steven Masters, jerking his head at a rough angle toward the shuttle commander.

"Will you take that bloody toothpick out of your mouth when you speak to me?" Stevens snapped. "You act as if I didn't teach you anything at all about manners." He looked at Masters with a demeaning snort. "Of course he can operate this 'thing' as you so eloquently put it. He happens to be the person who trains the astronauts how to fly the shuttle. And what does it matter to you anyhow?"

"You know," said Masters with a laugh, "they are going to pin those murders on you. So you can just take your attitude of superiority into the big house with you when you've got some big black daddy's dick up your ass."

Ronald Stevens had great contempt for Steven Masters, and did not trust him. He'd chosen him to train as a security officer because he was dumb, and therefore controllable. He also knew everything about his past, and held many trump cards over his head. What he hadn't anticipated was that Masters had patience, and was very clever. He had managed to work his way into the lives of Liz and George Jr. much more effectively than planned. He had also been chosen for his good looks, with the twin motives that he might be able to seduce Liz, or that George would become jealous of him, whether Liz was seduced or not. But apparently Liz and George were completely invulnerable on the sexuality front. Liz joked and flirted openly with Masters as if he were her best gay friend, and George seemed incapable of any kind of jealousy.

"Oh, don't you worry, Masters," he said with obvious anger, "I will make sure the authorities know you are the assassin if I ever get caught. But that's not going to happen, though." There was a crackle inside of his right ear that made him jump.

"Stevens, this is Jiimson, come in."

"What the hell is the matter with you?" he yelled. "I said complete radio contact until we are on our final approach to docking with the station."

"Relax," said Jiimson, "the scrambling device I put on our radios cannot be broken. You don't need to worry. In fact," he

Second Pass

said in a boastful voice, "what are they going to chase us in? A jumbo jet?" He laughed uproariously at his own joke.

"What the hell do you want?"

"I just thought it would be a good idea to go over the plan again. I'm not sure if there is enough oxygen and water to sustain us. Did you bring everything I put on the list."

Stevens rolled his eyes. "Yes, dumbo. I put everything on the list and more. We here on earth happen to have the system of space travel down to a science."

"But what if we run into unforeseen circumstances? What if we..."

"Are you fucking freaking out here? Are you going to blow it for us all?" Stevens was irritated now, mostly because he had the same fears. "We will rendezvous at the old space station, use our twin booster power to approach our target, snatch the prize, hit SIL and then zip back to Earth. Just like that. No worries, man."

"But what if we run out of air?" he sounded extremely tense.

"Then I'll kill you and the rest of us will have all we need."

"Very funny," said Jiimson nervously.

"What makes you think I'm joking?" asked Stevens. "Our boy Masters here is very good at eliminating people," he said with a wink at Masters who was following the conversation in his own headset, "and he recently got lots of practice. Now get off of this radio and keep off of it!"

* * * * * * *

Ali Wong tried to keep away from people, other than Willa. Malanga had him come in nearly every day for many months after his accident, and all of the Finder apprentices poked and prodded him endlessly during that time. Others on SIL thought of him as a celebrity and wanted to find out from him what Malanga was learning from his mishap. There was a rumor that the gel reversed aging, and they supposed he would be able to give them some secret information.

Then the attention died down—until the day of the shuttle theft, when his friend, Hermes Whipple, got his throat cut and was also covered with the clear gel. Hermes had also survived due to the plant's intervention, and that renewed interest in him.

Willa Marsdon was the only person he liked to be around. She treated him no differently than before the accident, other than the fact that she was a bit nicer to him than to the other workers. She demanded that he do his work, kept him to his schedule, and became furious at anyone who interrupted him to ask questions about the clear gel.

Ali was looking under the plant trays in the upper-most regions of the Eye Chamber when he heard a strange sound. He slowly eased his way to the edge of the tray and saw someone dressed completely in dark green working through the trays. Curious, but with a sense that danger was in the air, he kept watching from where he couldn't be seen. The dark green intruder crept between the trays and was paying very close attention to something that was out of Ali's range of visibility. Suddenly there was a loud cracking sound amid yelling and then a shriek that ended in a gurgle. He watched as the intruder briefly sped past his view and out the door.

He jetted from behind the plant tray and saw Willa hanging mid-air with a huge balloon of blood growing from her chest. Her arms were flailing spastically, but without cognitive organization. He knew she would soon be dead if not already. He grabbed her by the waist and jetted to the far side where the plant was that had healed him and Hermes. When he got close enough the plant tentacle snatched her from his grip and lobbed a bubble of clear liquid at her. Simultaneously another long tendril shot out to where she had been. As it grew a tight clump of small yellow flowers formed on the end. They were trumpet shaped, but where the flowers would normally open outward toward the ends of their conical petals, they had a domed cap that covered three-quarters of the opening, with a sharp beak-like point that reached back down into the funnel of each blossom. There must have been about 70 of the blossoms in a tight cylinder. As the tendril approached the blood, which had now broken into thousands of independent beads and pools, it twisted around and gathered the blood into the interiors of the trumpet-shaped blossoms. When most of the blood had been collected, the plant retracted its shoot and plunged the flowers into the bubble.

The clear gel absorbed the blood into millions of tiny canals, much like the blood network that surrounds the nucleus of a fertilized egg to nourish the fetus. The network of canals broke into ever finer versions of themselves, and eventually he couldn't

Second Pass

see Willa through them. He turned away and jetted to the intercom at the side of the Chamber. He punched in the code for security, but quickly disconnected, and punched in the code for the Finders instead.

"Finder Malanga's quarters," said the voice.

"Help! This is Ali Wong in the Eye Chamber. There has been another murder, or attempted murder," he got all flustered, "come quickly! It is Madam! Madam Jiimson-Marsdon! She may be dead."

"Has she been...is she..."

"Yes, the plant has put her in a covering, and took her blood. Hurry!"

"Have you contacted security?"

"Just come!" he yelled. Then he sped back to the plant.

Willa wasn't there. He looked all over and she just wasn't there. He panicked. As he sped around tray after tray, he went behind the large-leaved oxygen producers and ran face to face with the dark green intruder.

Ali stopped and stared into the eyes, which were visible through small slits cut into the cloth head covering. He started to jet backward, but an arm shot out and grabbed him by his left elbow, and pulled him in, turning him around. He felt his jetpack bump into the person's chest and then felt a knife blade against his throat.

"I would kill you," a woman's voice said, "but that damn plant won't let me. I would have killed that witch if you hadn't saved her."

"Kill me then," Ali said bravely, "if you have to kill someone. I don't need to live."

"Oh, you do need to live," she sneered, "you need to live because you give me power."

She took a scarf out of her pocket and tied it around his mouth, then placed him under her arm like she was carrying a book and jetted out of the nearest doorway.

Seconds later Elizabeth Dunn, Toby Manndle, Solange Malanga and Su Lee Kipperman jetted into the Eye Chamber and went straight to the phone station Ali had called from and only found the phone floating in the air, still engaged. They saw the clear orb filled with a web of blood at the end of the plant, but not Ali.

"This must be Willa," said Su, "but where is Ali?"
"I don't know," said Elizabeth. He must be hiding. He was terrified and probably hid."

Toby was half listening to them, and half meditating on the essence of Ali. Malanga had taught them how to identify the energetic essence of a person while working on them for the purpose of being able to identify them without seeing them. It was the first step in advanced healing. In circumstances when someone was unconscious, absent, in surgery, or on the verge of death, one or more finders were stationed in the room to feel the energetic essence and hold it. She found this resulted in far fewer deaths and much quicker recovery from anesthetic and coma. Toby, she discovered, developed the strongest connection of any of the finders, herself included, and she attributed that to the intense connection he established with individuals when he did energization cycles with them. As Jun-Jun's experiments with freelocking continued, Toby was always present to hold their essence, and to guide them back.

What normally happened when he did this was a kaleidoscope of scenes from their childhood and other fanciful images flooded his awareness. Taken together these gave a very clear impression of the person. But as he did this with Ali's essence, he saw nothing but blackness, with a trail of yellow smoke. He tried again. When Ali had been unconscious from the laceration to his torso, Toby had gotten a very clear picture of the boy's elemental being. There were all sorts of small animals furrowed into the ground, nestled into hollow knots in trunks of trees and single clouds in the sky, floating alone, apart from the others. He also had gotten images of a bright star or sun, one that you could look at directly without any sense of being harmed by direct exposure, and from the light there were large arms reaching out. He tried to get any of these, or anything similar, but there was nothing. He tried again, fearing that somehow this image meant he was dead. Again he saw the yellow smoke.

"He is going deep," said Malanga, holding up her hands to keep the others from interfering with his meditation. "Go further," she said quietly into his ear, "follow the essence, find the core."

Then his view changed. As if there were some huge magnet pulling him into the smoke, he got closer and closer until he was seeing almost a microscopic view of the smoke. The vapor trail became particles, and the particles came closer, got larger. He recognized them from his study of the medical text books from his student days, but couldn't remember what they were. He knew every cell in the body, and every bacterium, virus and germ spore. It was none of these. He let out a deep breath and spoke without opening his eyes.

"What is yellow, round and fuzzy, microscopic, but with little bumps all over it like an old fashioned underwater mine?" he asked the women.

"What?" they asked simultaneously, having been concentrated on other things.

"I'm seeing something that worries me," he said, "it's like yellow smoke. When I go close up on it I see it microscopically, as I described. I remember it from our text book, but it isn't one of the cells of the body, or a germ, microbe, spore, bacterium, or virus."

"You are so wrong," said Su Lee, "it is a spore."

"What type?" asked Elizabeth.

"It's pollen," Su Lee replied. "Simple flower pollen."

"How could pollen be of his energetic essence?" asked Elizabeth. "He has no allergies at all, remember. It was quite remarkable."

Toby thought about this. They had even talked about the fact that he was completely allergy free, and his body never produced a single histamine when exposed to any type of plant life. They had even wondered if that aspect of his makeup had anything to do with his extreme rapid healing when in contact with the plant sap.

"It is," said Su Lee, eyes closed and obviously doing an energetic essence survey of her own, "not his energetic essence we are seeing. It is a direct communication from the plant that saved him and Hermes, and is trying to save Willa now." Her eyes snapped open, and she gave a little nervous giggle.

They all approached the plant. They looked at it from all sides, including under the tray where its roots were exposed. They saw no pollen, and no source of pollen like a blossom or bud, so they returned to their examination of the membrane surrounding Willa. The blood was beginning to disappear and she was again visible. Her eyes blinked open and she opened her mouth to speak but quickly shut it with a surprised look on her face. She put her hand up to her mouth and stopped half way, working her fingers as one would if testing the viscosity of oil.

"She's trying to say something," said Elizabeth.

Willa pointed to her throat, to the gash that looked like a deep maroon abyss into her throat. She waved the palm of her hand toward them, shaking her head.

"What, Willa?" Toby asked. "What are you trying to say?"

Willa looked down for a moment, as if she were deeply sad. Her shoulders trembled and shook. She was crying. When she looked back up her eyes were filled with near hopelessness. Again she waved the palm of her hand toward them, but this time she was making little movements with her fingers. Her hand went in a meandering path, but the path was going over to her right, getting always further away.

They looked at her, leaning in as if getting closer would make them understand better.

"We don't understand," said Malanga. "Forgive us, Willa. Can you do it again? You mustn't give up, we will understand."

Willa's shoulders rose and then fell. With resignation she did it again. This time, however, she brought up both hands, joined at the heels of her palms with fingers reaching upward and outward. Then she began to wiggle the fingers of one hand like she had before. This movement gave way to that hand, palm toward them, meandering as it had before, fingers wiggling, going ever more to her right. This time she ended the movement by pointing into the distance with her index finger.

"Quickly," said Toby, "follow me. I know what she is trying to tell us." He jetted to the plant's main foliage, leading with his nose. Suddenly he sneezed. "There it is," he said rubbing his nose, "I've found the pollen. We need to follow the pollen. The plant has created a path of pollen that will lead us to Ali."

* * * * * * *

Commander McVee was floating behind the main podium, with the Overseers in a semi-circle behind him. Before them were the entire population of SIL, except for the Finders and the missing. He raised his hands for silence, which came instantly.

"Sven Jiimson has left SIL with the stolen shuttle." There was a shocked murmur in the crowd that quickly dissolved into silence. "We have learned from Earth that all of the shuttle fleet has been sabotaged and destroyed, except for one shuttle that was about to leave to bring the final group to SIL and begin the departures of our short-term guests, and the one docked here at SIL, which were both hijacked." He let this news be absorbed. He needed people to follow what he was going to be telling them, all the while realizing they would be dealing with many emotions as they realized the full meaning of the situation. "We do not know where the two shuttles are going, but they seem to be on a path toward each other. We do not know why they were stolen, or why so many people lost their lives."

"Are we safe?" yelled one voice in the crowd.

"Please," the Commander said, "there is much more to tell you. Allow me to finish and then I will answer any questions you may have." He waited for a moment. "With the entire fleet of shuttles either destroyed or stolen, there will be no more shuttle runs to or from SIL on this pass."

Suddenly there was extreme commotion in the crowd. People were yelling, crying, some were in shock and a few started to panic. Those who thought they were here for a visit of a few weeks suddenly realized they would be here for 18 years. Others who had lived on SIL realized that there were far more people than they had planned on hosting, and the reserves of food, water, oxygen and clothing would be severely threatened by the extra people.

The Commander allowed them to experience and express their emotions for a few moments. He knew there was no legitimate reason to prevent them from their reactions. He looked at the frightened and angry faces with a deep remorse. All of his life he had wanted to create a perfect place, a place where men didn't need to kill each other, or feel aggressive competition, or be repressed by society. He intended SIL to be the perfect place, the utopia wise men had always dreamed of but never dared to build. He saw that no matter where people were there would be all of the elements of humanity. His guilt was extreme, his remorse immense.

Tom Robinson looked at Shandor, who had come to SIL to be with his father, but preferred to live on earth. Shandor had experienced extreme abuse on SIL as an orphaned child. As he looked at Shandor, his son turned toward him. For a moment Tom couldn't tell what the emotion in Shandor's eyes was. Would he hate him for bringing him back? Would he forgive him?

Shandor looked at his father and realized they would be here on SIL until the next pass, but in that time his father would surely die and he would, once more, be orphaned, but this time it would be for real and forever. He thought about the Earth and how he loved it there. How he had at first been terrified to be exposed to continuous space and open air, only to grow to love it and yearn for it. His weeks back on SIL had challenged him with feelings of claustrophobia so strong that he visualized being back in Boston so he could sleep at night.

All around the room people were awakening to the new reality, and with that awakening came fear, anger, frustration and a feeling of hopelessness. Throughout all of the ages of civilization there had always been tyrants who held their subjects in fear, despots who used abuse to keep people in line. But never had there been a change in circumstances like this; the entire world had just changed for the next 18 years and nobody could do anything at all about it.

George fought back tears. Liz and his son would not be coming. He wouldn't see his son until he was a man. Just like his own father hadn't seen him for the same amount of time. He hung in the air stunned. He forgot to breathe. The room around him started to fade, and little lights began to sparkle all around him as he fainted.

"We are going to have to adjust to this as best we can," the Commander continued. "We will be able to produce enough oxygen, water and food to sustain everyone, I am told by the various department heads of SIL. But everyone will have to perform a task to keep SIL running. We will need to build more living quarters, manufacture more clothing, and increase production of everything here. In the next weeks we will begin training programs for all of the skills necessary to live on SIL. Lists will be posted for everyone to read. On these lists will be all of the different jobs required for maximum efficiency and sustainability. Please find jobs you are interested in." A buzz was now going around the room. People, who were packed very tightly, were all talking to others near them.

The Commander held up his hands, but this time it took some minutes before he had attention from the crowd. "We have another problem that is more pressing," he said. "There is someone on SIL who is trying to commit murders. So far the attempted murders have all taken place in the Eye Chamber. We

Second Pass

will be increasing security there and everywhere on SIL. "This is Andrew Stetler, Head of Security." He turned to his left and waved Stetler forward to join him. "I'll immediately need as many men and women who can join our security force to report to Andrew Stetler."

Stetler waved quickly, embarrassed and angry at the situation. He addressed the crowd. "We will be setting up this assembly room for registration to become part of the Security force immediately, and within the week we will also have registration for training here as well. Please consider if you are interested in joining our security team. It will take us a few days to process applications and determine who is qualified for this job." He turned and took his place back behind the Commander.

People were now talking again. Many wondered what the qualifications would be for this security position. Alexander Machmood glared at the throng before him. He had argued forcefully with the Commander and Stetler against having any of the new arrivals on the Security Team. His position was not the majority, however, as the other Overseers and Assembly Members thought it was better to integrate the force so that people were equally represented by those who enforced laws. He had conceded because he had to, but did not like it at all.

First Officer Bryant worked his way through the crowd. He approached the Commander and they whispered to the side. The Overseers were keenly aware of this conversation, and were craning their necks from their Velcro perches to try to hear what was being said. Bryant was explaining something to the Commander who was listening very carefully to every word, occasionally asking a quick question, receiving the answer and then signaling for Bryant to continue. As the spoke, his wife and BQ joined him.

Machmood detached from the wall perch and jetted over to them. "We can't have secrecy in face of this situation," he started angrily, "and the Overseers and Assembly must be aware of all developments if decisions are to be made."

The group looked at him with surprise. "Chief Overseer Machmood," said Bryant, "we have managed to intercept communications from the shuttle that was stolen from SIL. We must keep the Commander informed."

Machmood started to protest, but the Commander interrupted. "Machmood," he snapped, "would you please return to your place. You will be informed of all information, you have no reason to doubt it. I am the Commander and must be briefed!"

"You cannot withhold information from..."

"If you do not return to your post I will have you arrested," the Commander said sharply. "We will continue our discussion and you will be informed in due time." He looked directly in Machmood's eyes. "What will it be?"

Machmood fumed, but kept silent as he returned to his perch. When he got there each of the Overseers he passed tried to ask him what had just happened, but he ignored them and took his place, staring hatefully at the Commander.

Bryant then approached the podium. "Ladies and gentlemen of SIL," he said, "we have just learned that there are many new attacks around the United States related to today's events. As this news becomes available you will be informed of any and all information that is not subject to security clearance. In addition, we must discuss all new developments with the governing bodies of SIL before we share much of the information with you. That said," he sighed, "we can inform you that among those who left Earth on the stolen shuttle was the head of the Board of Associated Laboratories, and a couple of others whose identity has not yet been determined. We do not believe they will be coming to SIL, but if anyone is it would be they, for they are in control of the only existing shuttles. We must enact a state of high alert in the event of an attempt to return to SIL."

"The Overseers and the Assembly have been in session since the first sign of trouble. They have appointed an interim Chairholder of the Assembly to fill the position vacated by Jiimson, who stole the shuttle. The interim Chairholder will only preside over the meetings and represent the decisions of the Assembly and Overseers to you. A new Assembly Chairholder will be elected by the total population of SIL in four months. Until that time, I would like to introduce your interim Chairholder, former President of the United States, Patrick McKenna."

He strained his eyes around the crowd. "I do not see my son, Jun-Jun. Are you there son? We need you up here."

People looked all around and eventually there was a slight parting of the crowd and Jun-Jun approached his father at the podium. Bryant took his son to the side as the Commander returned to the podium.

Chapter 18

Sylvia and Bill Bryant jetted into a small chamber off to the side of the large Assembly hall with their son, Jun-Jun. Sylvia and BQ had been following all of the developments and were highly concerned about the one murder in the docking bay and the other attempted killings on SIL. It was hard to establish any profile of the murderer, particularly where motive was concerned.

There were hundreds of new people on SIL about whom little was known, in spite of the extensive background research on each applicant. This lacuna of information grew out of the fact that in many people's minds SIL remained the utopian experiment Commander McVee had originally intended. It clearly wasn't a utopia, but when people thought of SIL they thought in terms of a near perfect place devoid of many of the stresses and corruptions of Earth's human societies.

Applicants for permanent relocation to SIL were judged on things like suitability to sustaining life in a weight-free and enclosed environment, ability to cope with the type of occupational demands for survival on SIL, political adaptability, and demonstrated need – such as various problems of aging and different chronic ailments that benefit from the environment on SIL. There was particular attention paid to those with interest in plants, creative arts, and education. They tried to stay clear of people with strong, fundamentalist religious connections, or rigid political leanings. In the mental health profile they checked for such things as claustrophobia, anti-social peculiarities, and demonstrated need for psychotropic drugs that weren't readily available on SIL. They did not check for history of being abused, problems related to unresolved anger, or dissociative disorders.

For visitors to SIL much less was known. In the struggle between George Jr. and Stevens, many were permitted to visit simply because they had the money to do so, and passed a cursory background clearance, but nothing elaborate. Now that they were trapped, against their will, for the entire 18-year pass, revenge of sorts could play a major role. In addition, all of the new arrivals had already experienced a cold shoulder from Borns and Firsters alike. For new inhabitants, there were any number of passive-aggressive ploys to show them they were not welcome, ranging from comments designed to be overheard to artificially produced problems with food, hygiene and housing. Visitors were dealt with in a much more overt and angry way, as Silians sought to show them they were completely unwelcome both because of their drain on available resources and the perceived philosophical contamination they brought. Some went as far as an outright shunning of them and obtuse and insulting acts of protecting their children from coming into contact with them as if they carried some dread disease. These severe circumstances would make any healthy person want to fight back, and an unhealthy one might find murder to be the most viable option in a troubled mind.

As for the residents from before, many of them believed their lives were directly threatened by the presence of newcomers, whether for relocation or vacation. The Overseers and Assembly were split nearly in half on issues of citizenship, access to the Silian economy, provision of health care and applicability of laws and probation periods. Paul and BQ had never been accepted by a large percentage of the people, and both political parties had rationales about why they were unwelcome.

Chairholder Sylvana's murderer had never been apprehended or brought to justice, and those hungry for revenge remained unplacated. Chairholder Jiimson had been a major rabble rouser for the cause of finding the murderer and exacting severe justice and would not let the issue die. Now that he had been exposed as a traitor to SIL, it diffused his authority in large part, yet it had also created a small group of dissidents who made him their ideological martyr. Those people were keeping to themselves and holding clandestine meetings that were taking on the attributes of fanaticism which could well lead to terrorist acts.

Once Bill determined they were out of earshot of anyone and that there were no electronic listening devices around, he nodded to Sylvia, who hugged their son.

"Jun," she began, "there are some very serious things going on, and we need your help."

Jun-Jun looked from his mother to his father and back with questioning eyes. He began the near inaudible humming of the Finders way. "What do you mean?" he asked. "How can I help?"

"Son," Bill began, "there has been another attempted murder just a few hours ago. Nobody on SIL knows because it happened when everyone was in the Assembly hall. Willa Marsdon-Jiimson has had her throat slit in the Eye Chamber." He took a breath, wondering how the news of Willa's attack would affect him.

Second Pass

Jun-Jun stopped humming abruptly, his eyes wide open and darting back and forth between his parents. "Is she dead?"

"No," Sylvia said, "at least we don't think so. Ali was there and witnessed the attack and was able to get her to the healing plant. She has been enveloped in the gel and," she looked at her husband for moral support, "from inside of a full body cocoon of gel she is able to make eye contact and communicate through gestures."

"You know she was very mean to all of us," Jun-Jun said. "We always make fun of her. But since I began studying to be a Finder, I've realized that she is the one who has taught us to take life on SIL seriously more than anyone else. I was always mean to her," he started to develop balloons of tears from his eyes, "and I haven't changed my behavior to match my new respect." He started to cry audibly. His parents were surprised by this, for as a young man and rebel he rarely showed emotion, other than his highly excited rantings against existing laws and social codes.

"Why does this upset you so?" his father asked. "It is unlike you to be so emotionally connected to people."

With this the tears ended suddenly and his eyes flashed confusion. "You don't know me much, do you?" he threw at his father. "Ever since I developed freelocking you have lost touch with me. But let me tell you one thing," he was now nearly shouting at his stunned parents, "I am a different, more sensitive person because of freelocking!"

He stopped short, realizing how ridiculous what he just his was, given the tone of voice. He laughed out loud. *I am absurd! I have lost my mind just like the Commander.*

Sylvia and Bill looked at each other and then at their son, joining in his laughter. "You certainly are calm," said Sylvia.

"And so tranquil," his father added.

"I'm sorry," Jun-Jun said, "I care about Willa more than I thought. And I'm frightened. What is happening?"

"There's more," said Sylvia. "Ali has been kidnapped by the murderer and can't be found anywhere."

"We need you ask you some questions about freelocking," Bill said to his startled son. "What exactly happens when you are out there?"

"There are rumors," Sylvia said, "that you have an expanded vision, a hyper awareness. We need to know about that."

Jun-Jun looked at his parents in wonder. They had been so vehemently opposed to his experiments that his father had even threatened to place him behind prison bars to prevent him from continuing his experiments. They had placed restrictions on who he could have as friends, and tracked his every movement. It was only the interest of Solange Malanga in his experiments, and her intervention by taking him in as a Finder apprentice, that had prevented his parents from enacting their harshest confinement.

"There is expanded vision," he began. "When I am out there, and I die," his mother gasped quietly, but he continued, "I can see things differently."

"What do you see?" his father asked. "Is it like seeing your life pass before your eyes, as many in near death report?"

"You only see that the first time," Jun-Jun said, a new energy overtaking him. "And what you see is like a combination of actual vision and dreaming. Suddenly you are no longer trapped in time and space, and you can see other worlds, other levels. You know quite a bit about anything you direct your attention to. But then you go to the feeling place."

"Jun," Sylvia said looking at her husband, "we can't understand what you mean. What is the feeling place? What kind of other dimensions do you see?"

"The feeling place is like watching the ripples travel outward in concentric circles when you throw a pebble into a still pool. But you are seeing feelings other people have had about you, feelings you've caused them to have by your actions..."

"Before that," Bill said with a hint of impatience, "what about the seeing? Do you see, or *can* you see this reality?"

"Well, sure, you can see this reality," Jun-Jun said with a confused look on his face, "but that isn't the interesting stuff at all, except for..." he broke off his sentence and looked down, blushing.

"Go on, son," Bill said. "Tell us what you can see."

"Well, sometimes, I mean, once or twice, I swear," he looked nervously at his mother, who cocked her head and gave a soft snort of amusement and confusion, "I don't want to hurt you mom. Could I just tell dad?"

"Son," his father said sternly, "you must tell us both. I doubt you can say anything that would seriously insult your mother. And if you do," he said with a grin, "I will protect you from her." Sylvia gave him a good-humored slap on the shoulder which sent them

Second Pass

both spinning in opposite directions until they righted themselves with their jetpacks.

"Well," Jun-Jun began again, "I did go look in on some of the girls when they were undressing." He ducked his head and made a face like a huge, false smile, his eyes looking sideways at his mother.

"That is excellent!" Bill shouted.

"Yes," agreed Sylvia, "that is exactly what we hoped was possible!"

Jun-Jun looked at his parents like they were both crazy. "You wanted me to be a voyeur and watch girls get naked?"

"No," Bill laughed at the misunderstanding, "I should punish you for that. But what we hoped you'd be able to do is to look at SIL, or around SIL."

"What we need to do," Sylvia said, "is find Ali and whoever has abducted him. Could you do that if you free-locked?"

"You mean, free-lock and while I'm dead look around SIL for Ali?" Jun-Jun asked.

"Exactly," both parents said simultaneously.

"Well," Jun-Jun was thinking. "I guess I could. I'd have to do it quickly though. I can't sustain longer than about three minutes of death."

"Three minutes!" Sylvia shrieked. "I don't want you dead for one second. I think this is a bad idea."

"Not so fast," interjected Bill. He turned to Jun-Jun. "What do you need to do it quickly? You said you were outside of time and space. How can we solve the time problem?"

"Well," Jun-Jun answered, speaking slowly as he was seriously considering the problem. "If I knew the general area where he was somehow. Or if I could find his other being person..."

"Other being person?" asked Bill. "What is that?"

"Well, each of us is the body part and another part that can exist separate from the body. It isn't the electromagnetic biosphere, it is like the core person. In Finding we call it the essential being. It's like the essence of the person, but not their physical form." He sighed, showing disappointment. "I'm not very good at that. It is hard for me to find it. Malanga hasn't let me assist in any surgeries yet because I'm not good enough at it."

"Well, who is good at it?" asked Sylvia.

"Toby is the best," he answered, "and Elizabeth after him. And, of course, Finder Malanga is the master."

"Could one of them be involved, maybe? Could they assist you?" his father asked.

"Or could *they* do the freelocking instead of you?" Sylvia asked excitedly.

"They couldn't do the freelocking," Jun-Jun said, "I'm the only one with enough experience to really do what you are asking." He thought for a short time. Then began again, hesitantly. "I would need to establish a psychic link to someone, or open to their vision, like doing a remote viewing of their psychic vision of the essential being rather than their eyesight. And I don't know if that is even possible."

"How can we find out," his father said in earnest. "You are the only hope we have, son."

"We must find the murderer and try to save Ali's life. He isn't in the Eye Chamber, so he can't be protected by the plant."

"We will have to ask Malanga," said Jun-Jun. "She would know if it is possible."

"Then," Bill said, "we will ask her. Do you know where she is Sylvia?"

"She's in the Eye Chamber."

"Let's go then," said Bill as the three jetted off to the main axis corridor toward the Eye side of SIL.

* * * * * * *

Tom, Gould, Paul and Patrick McKenna had all gone with BQ to the CommLink room when the general assembly was finished. Commander McVee had given permission for them to work together to try to decipher the intercepted transmission from the stolen shuttle. When they arrived in the CommLink room BQ first checked on any transmissions or communications that had occurred in her absence.

There were over 300 communications sent to SIL from NASA, and one from the shuttle—the conversation between the two shuttles. They began with that one, and were shocked to learn that the head of Astronaut Training from NASA was among those who were on the shuttle. McKenna knew him personally, and explained to the others that he was a former intelligence officer in the CIA who had been an Air Force pilot in his younger days. Houston Rhinegold, the man in question, had been passed over for acceptance into the Astronaut Training program because of a history of broken marriages, which, at the time, disqualified anyone from becoming an astronaut.

McKenna had become aware of him during his years as a Senator from Massachusetts, long before he became President. Rhinegold had climbed the ranks within the CIA quickly and was particularly gifted at analysis of public messages delivered by heads of state and their spokespersons. When China had begun its moves to broaden its powerbase, McKenna was the Chairman of the Intelligence Committee in the Senate. Rhinegold had given almost daily briefings to McKenna on developments in China and had been instrumental in detecting a pattern of references to Korea in public statements made by China. The result was that Rhinegold had surmised that China was positioning itself to forcibly take over Korea and annex them to their growing empire. His arguments were so convincing that the report from McKenna's committee resulted in the United States sending a ground force into North Korea, which backfired and created great animosity for the United States in that region. Forced to withdraw the troops by the United Nations and public opinion around the globe, the power vacuum that resulted gave China the leverage to form an alliance pact with Korea.

In the end, there was an investigation of Rhinegold and it was found that he had misunderstood, with good intentions, the actions of China. The CIA needed to drop him to save face, and McKenna had arranged for him to move into the NASA position, which was not a public position at all. He thought Rhinegold had done his best, hadn't intentionally worked against the interests of the United States, and deserved a soft reprimand rather than a public flogging. As Director of Astronaut Training he had proved to be quite valuable, and his ability to understand the psychological profiles of those in training made for a flow of effective and talented astronauts.

Apparently, however, Rhinegold had not overcome his resentment toward the United States, and was using his inside knowledge of NASA to assist in the disabling of the shuttle fleet and the theft of the shuttle. What McKenna also knew was that Rhinegold didn't have the navigational expertise to lead a shuttle flight, though there was nobody more experienced to pilot the shuttles. After discussing this, the group decided to have McKenna communicate directly with the current President, and head of

NASA, to find out exactly who else was missing on that shuttle, and what highly classified information the President could pass to him about developments.

As he was on the CommLink, the others reviewed the communiqués from NASA and learned little they didn't already know. They then turned their attention to the intercepted video sequence.

"Here is where it seems to split," said BQ, enhancing the enlargement of one frame of the video sequence, "then the split disappears." They all looked as she took them through the sequence.

"Wait!" shouted Gould. "Go back..." BQ started to go back frame by frame until Gould stopped her. "There it is again, the split and rejoining."

"It's a helix," said Tom quietly, "it is a slowly rotating double band of light that only appears to split and rejoin. In actuality it is two parallel lines that are twisting around each other slowly."

Paul had BQ zoom out again and play the entire sequence. He checked the telemetry data that was included in the NASA communiqués and saw that the trajectory of one of the lines was that of the shuttle that had been stolen from Earth. He assumed the other line represented the other shuttle, which had been stolen from SIL, and the point where they came together was the old space station. He had Tom and Gould take the relative position of that point of rendezvous and project it to the location of the space station to determine the exact moment in time the station would be located at that point.

"If this is what you think it is," said Gould, "then they will rendezvous with the space station in four hours, thirteen minutes and six seconds."

"You always were scary with your exactness," Tom said to Gould. "But for the first time I appreciate your more anal side."

"Why thank you, Tom," Gould said with a flutter of the eyelids, making everyone laugh.

"What we are seeing, then," said Paul, "is that the two shuttles will rendezvous and then dock on opposite sides of the space station, but in a common orientation, and then use their combined thrust to take the station into a different orbit." He tapped his fingers rapidly on the desk top. "BQ," he said suddenly, "can you track this trajectory in space while Gould tracks it in time?"

Second Pass

"Yes, we can synchronize," she said. "Can't we Sol?"

"Sure can," he said with a clipped voice.

"Tom," Paul continued, "can you find anything out there that would intercept with this trajectory at the times it will be in those locations? They are going somewhere and we need to know where it is."

"Sure thing," Tom said.

For the next hour they all worked feverishly, but with no results. Frustrated, they looked again and again at the video image. Paul meanwhile was going over the NASA communiqués with McKenna who was now waiting to hear back from NASA and the President as to any other missing personnel.

"Is it perhaps intentional what equipment and supplies were on the shuttle that was stolen," asked McKenna, "or mere coincidence?"

"I firmly believe there are no coincidences in this matter," said Paul. "It seems to have been planned perfectly. It is clear they worked on a surgically precise timetable."

"Well, let's look at the manifest for the shuttle," McKenna said. "Perhaps it will tell us something."

* * * * * * *

Toby led the others through the hallways outside of the Eye Chamber. True to their expectation the plant had created a trail of potent pollen, invisible to the eye, but keenly sensed by anyone with pollen allergies, as Toby was. How this plant had done this, along with all of its other amazing attributes, was ignored now. It only mattered that they find Ali.

They were just turning down the hallway that went to the fabric dying bins when they were joined by the Bryant family. Malanga stayed behind with the Bryants to discuss their plan to find Ali using the combination of Jun-Jun's freelocking and Toby's essence awareness. Meanwhile, Toby and the others continued to follow the pollen. The sniffling and sneezing that had been Toby's initial reaction to the pollen had transformed to an enhanced sense of smell, and Elizabeth and Su Lee had also developed this sense as well. The three sniffed their way down the hall, and then found that the trail turned into the vast network of rooms where fabrics were developed. The complex had over 200 different rooms, and each room had multiple exits and entrances, interlocking in a labyrinth.

The scent was obscured by the odor of the different dying vats and fiber preparation solutions. They could follow it no further. When Malanga and the Bryants caught up with them, and learned they had come to a dead end, she turned her focus to the proposed freelocking and organized the group. Sylvia called Stetler and had him position guards at every exit from the cluster of networked rooms, preventing the murderer from escaping. Meanwhile, Malanga and her group went to the docking ports to prepare for the free-lock.

Chapter 19

The Overseers hung from their perches feeling more weight than if gravity had been present, the Finders and apprentices only half watching them as the distraction of heightened alert bested even their most determined attempts to focus, and the Assembly Members floated in a tight gaggle devoid of their usual partisan chatter. For this meeting there were special guests, including George Junior, Bill and Sylvia Bryant, Paul and BQ Dunn, Solomon Gould, Tom and Shandor Richardson and Former President McKenna. All waited for Commander McVee to arrive; no one could breathe easily.

SIL had been many things in its history. For those who were on the station from its original mission it had gone from coveted job assignment, to death trap, to miraculous life-sustaining environment. For those who came at the first pass, when George, Jr. discovered it through the Low Orbital Lens, it was a compelling and intensely interesting environment which offered an alternative option to living on earth. At that time, for the original inhabitants, they had to adjust their thinking from knowing they would live out their natural lives there, to the possibility of returning to Earth either for a visit or to live again on a planet. For those who had just arrived it was a prestigious appointment. The big controversies were philosophical and political, never questions of mortality, and where you stood philosophically wasn't particularly threatening outside of one's own mind. But for everyone on SIL, the current events had turned it into a dangerous and threatening place.

Hull breach previously had been the only mortal worry on SIL. There was the occasional accident that took a life, and there were deaths from old age, disease and thwarted birth processes. But now there was an anonymous killer on SIL, and that killer was part of a plot that rendered those on SIL captive, and for many against their will. The announcements in the large Assembly Hall had been met by outrage, fear, recriminations, finger-pointing and threats. Most of that was an immediate reaction, and the few hours that had passed found much of that reaction diffused. People had been assigned to tasks, and the most immediate task was to identify quarters for everyone—to create acceptable intermediary living arrangements until a more permanent solution could be found.

Silence was the most ominous element in the current tension. This group of people had never gathered without lively discussion or argument. But mortal threat made them equals; as Stendhal said, "Sleep, like its big brother death, makes equals of us all." For those gathered, to refrain from controversy spoke of the monumental dilemma they all faced. And unlike an audience being kept waiting too long by a capricious star, there was no rustling of clothing, no random coughs of annoyance, and no nervous chatter.

The doors at the back of the room hissed open and Commander McVee jetted in. His long white beard flowed behind him like backward squid tentacles as he flew through the atmosphere. He wore a dark purple robe with magenta socks, and was carrying some papers. His face seemed much older than just a few hours before, and the difference between his white hair and his skin was subtle at best.

Finder Malanga spoke quietly to Elizabeth Dunn, who quietly left the room by a side door. Nobody saw the exchange or the departure. All were intently focused on their Commander.

He stopped at the front of the room, nodded to the Overseers, acknowledged the others who stood near them and then turned to the group in the center of the room. The Assembly was a group he was particularly proud of. In numbers and strength, it represented that he had accomplished one of his goals: a non-earth-reliant, life-sustaining environment in space. It also represented the utter failure of his secondary mission: to eradicate the ills of earth, the politics and the fighting. A tear floated up from his left eye and caught on a tuft of his white hair.

"Citizens of SIL," he began, "our situation remains unchanged, though there are many developments related to it I must report. I ask your agreement to treat everything said in this room as confidential and of critical importance, to be kept in the highest security. Are there any who cannot maintain silence?" He looked over the crowd, and then turned to the Overseers and gathered leaders behind him as well. There wasn't any movement. But he waited. The door at the side of the room opened and Elizabeth came in carrying a small leather medical bag. He waited for her to join Malanga before he continued.

Second Pass

"The entire shuttle fleet has been destroyed or hijacked, as you know or have heard. Hundreds have died in that process, including, for those shuttles in flight, the saboteurs. The shuttle stolen from earth was taken by Mr. Stevens, President of the Board of Directors of Associated laboratories, along with head of astronaut training at NASA, the head of security for my son's family, and two others who have not as yet been identified. As far as can be determined, the one stolen from SIL was taken by my son's security guard and one of the docking bay technicians—none other.

"We also learned that the entire governing board of Associated was slaughtered late last night in Cambridge, and all Associated personnel were locked out of the facility. LOL communications were shut down temporarily as well.

"The government of the United States and the Secretary General of the United Nations has joined with the Head of NATO and of the EU to form an investigative task force. Other than that, we have determined that the two stolen shuttles are intending to meet at the old Space Station that was put out of commission when SIL began operations. We do not know what they are planning from there. It is possible that they may try to return to SIL and try to take over. But if they do, they must within six days or we will be too far from their range to be reached. Therefore, we must, in the next six days, be prepared to defend ourselves."

Finally there was a murmur in the crowd, but it was slight and didn't last long. A few questions were obvious—was there any way to defend SIL, did we need to form a military unit, what measures could be taken—but they, too, quieted quickly. The Commander continued.

"As a security measure, the docking ports of SIL were altered and a special adapter was added to all shuttles to prevent anyone coming on board that was not invited. A new adapter will be developed on very short demand so that the shuttles cannot dock with their new adapters or in their original state. Other than that, First Officer Bryant will work with our Security team to develop plans for defense. I ask you all to cooperate with them in any way asked of you."

He then turned to the Overseers. There was a slight quiver in his robe, unnoticed by all except Malanga and her group of Finders. Malanga grabbed the case from Elizabeth and opened it, withdrawing an injection cylinder, and jetted to his side. Paul noticed and flew with her toward his father.

Commander McVee's arms flew up and his papers scattered around the room. It seemed as if he were fighting Malanga and Paul off. Others started toward them, not understanding what they were seeing. Paul finally got the flaying arms of the Commander under control and Malanga injected his neck. He went limp.

"Quickly!" yelled Malanga, "get him to the Finders area immediately! Clear the way!"

George had been only half listening to his father's speech, thinking of Liz and their new child, when the commotion brought his full awareness. He started toward his father, but was knocked off of his trajectory by Paul who flew into him from behind and to his left. Paul's motion had been so forceful that he basically stayed on course, while George flew awkwardly into the feet of some of the Overseers. He righted himself and went back toward where his father had been standing, but saw only the backs of several people ushering him out of the room. He followed them.

McKenna then spoke loudly to the crowd. "Please stay here all of you," he said in a firm voice that surprised those who had not known him as President. "There is work to do. The Commander is in the care of our head Finder and will be aided in every way. He has been under considerable stress, and is obviously suffering from extreme fatigue." People started to settle down and all eyes were on him. "So, we must begin to organize ourselves in such a way that we can meet the new challenges and prevail. SIL is our home and we must not only defend her, but work to unify a deeply divided populous..."

* * * * * * *

When the yellow dust filled his lungs, Ali wasn't frightened any more. He knew the plant was with him, and would protect him. He stopped struggling to free himself from the straps that held him immobile against the beam. His captor had dragged him deep into areas of the fabric manufacturing sector he'd never before seen.

The large dye containers interested him. With the yellow mist around his head, each thing encountered was shown to him as part of a web. The vats were translucent white plastic enclosed tubs mostly filled with dark liquids. As he passed the first one he saw the indigo vat with his eyes, but also saw the fabrics it produced, the people who worked on it, the clothing that was made in that color and those who wore them. His vision was inside of his head, reaching outward to connect with nearly every part of SIL. As the next one came into his visual range he saw the orange colored fabrics it produced and everything related to those.

Wondering why this was happening, he turned to look at his captor and was amazed at what he saw. First he was startled to intuitively know it was a woman. He saw her without her face mask, even though it was still covering her face. He saw that she was a new arrival, that she had come on the same shuttle as the Commander's son, and that she was related to his body guard. He saw the struggle in the outbay portal and the theft of the shuttle. When he watched as she slit the throat of the man who was at the command station of that docking bay he winced and almost cried out to stop her, but checked the response when he realized it was already in the past.

They passed through the fabric preparation area and went into a closet. Thinking this would be where he was to be hidden, and perhaps killed, he tried to remain calm. She pushed him deep into the closet until his back was pressed hard against the back wall. She pushed harder, slamming him against the wall. Prepared for pain he braced himself, but instead of pain there was a whoosh of cold air and the wall gave way behind him. Suddenly they were outside of the dying area completely and in a maze of tubular beams that went as far as he could see. The beams formed little angled clusters in a repeated pattern between what would have been the outer wall of the dying area and another dark gray wall that was very strong metal. It was much colder there than inside SIL. He could see the geometric shapes formed over and over that seemed to curve far away from their location. Each direction he turned his head he saw the same thing, and looking as far as he could see in the dimly lit area it seemed that the inner wall and outer wall joined in the distance as they curved away from him.

He didn't realize that he was just inside of the outer hull of SIL until he allowed the yellow dust to give him his extra vision and he saw the Commander as a much younger man hiding there, with people looking for him but not finding him. He saw that the older men who were called 'Engineers' came here to check the joints for strength on some kind of maintenance routine, swinging from one to the next, propelling themselves with their strong arms from clustered joint to clustered joint. Then he saw that beyond the outer wall was open space. And it was here that she pulled Velcro straps from her bag and bound him to one of the beams.

"It is useless for you to cry out," she said menacingly in his ear, the first words she had spoken during this ordeal, "you are far away from all people. You will remain here until I..." she suddenly sneezed and flew away from him. "Damn!" she said when her head cracked into one of the beams. She then jetted toward him and slapped him hard across the face, as if her sneeze had been his fault. He just stared at her with large eyes, afraid but calm. "You will stay here and perhaps die. I don't care. I will be back." And she sped away from him, leaving him very alone in the darkened place.

He was about to cry, but the yellow powder gave him vision of Finder Malanga and Jun-Jun. There were several others around them, and Jun-Jun was being wrapped in warm clothing and grease put on his face.

* * * * * * *

Jun-Jun took a deep breath inside of the chamber, bracing himself for the ice air that would come when the outer docking portal door opened. He was pulled violently outside of the tube as the pressurized air escaped into the vacuum of space. His umbilical pulled taught and he felt the life leave his body.

He experienced the release from his body and watched for a second as his eyes rolled back in their sockets. He was outside of his body. Little flecks of light danced all around him and he fought the euphoria of death, and purposely turned away from the tunnel of light the flecks became. He zoomed across time and space through SIL. He willed himself to see into the fabric dying area he had been told the plant pollen had shown the others as the location of Ali and his captor. He found no-one in that area. He panicked. His formless essence flew in every direction, splitting into hundreds of shards of conscience. Then the yellow trail found him, and dragged him swiftly along its path. He went through the walls and flew outside of SIL, then back into the dead space between the outer skin and the inner walls. There he saw

Second Pass

Ali bound to a support beam. He was able to look into his eyes, and it seemed as if Ali was seeing him. The child's eyes were wide and happy to see him.

Suddenly Jun-Jun was given understanding of everything that had happened, heard all of the words the captor had said, saw her face and then was propelled around the inside of the shell up to the point just beside the Eye itself where she was hiding. He saw she was preparing something, and his conscience froze when he saw she was planting explosives that would dislodge the Eye, breech the hull and collapse SIL. His non-physical mouth formed a scream. "Noooooooo!"

* * * * * * *

The first shuttle arrived at the ghostly space station and docked. The clanking inside of the shuttle was exaggerated to an ear-shattering crash against the silence. The second shuttle was visible as they had approached, but when they turned into their final position they were facing the opposite direction. It seemed like hours before the other loud crash came, sending shudders through the shuttle. Then they flew into action.

Every man was wearing an EVA suit and each began his assigned task. One went into the old station dragging long coils of cable. He found the nuclear fuel module and connected the cable ends to its outlets. Another ran the diagnostics for the main computers on each of the shuttles to operate as one, while another man ran connecting wires to the onboard computers of the station.

When all of the connections were in place, the entire cluster of space vehicles lit up. Where there had been silence there was now cacophony. The integrating systems brought everything to life and all computer screens showed the same spiraling helix configuration BQ and Sylvia had seen earlier, only this time there was a red blinking light that indicated the exact location on that trajectory of the composite craft.

"We are on our way," said Stevens into the microphone. "We will be within range of the satellite in 42 hours. Gentlemen, get some sleep. We need you to be very alert when we arrive."

* * * * * * *

Malanga struggled with the Commander. His breathing was erratic and his muscles were still in spasm as he went through seizure after seizure. Elizabeth monitored his heart and brain functions. "Finder," she said quietly, "his brain function is partially blacked out."

"I knew this might have happened," said Malanga sadly. "The hemareflux he suffered several years ago left clots. He has had an aneurism in his left frontal lobe," she said. "He will not survive."

She turned her head as tears rose from her eyes. She had loved this man, had understood his vision and his need for it. She realized that everything she had discovered about the art of Finding was a result of his work, and, as controversial as his methods may have been, he alone had contributed more to mankind than any ten other men. Due to Commander McVee science was not lost, non-Earth-reliant environments had become a reality, bioengineering of plants had developed into remarkable superfoods and nutrients, Finding had been developed, and much more. She wept openly, knowing that the heart needs its moment to speak exactly when it feels, not later. This, too, was a direct result of this man who now clung to life. It is the heart, not the brain, that is the principle organ of existence, and if that organ is denied its expression at the moment of emotion, it broke down the brain function later.

"Shall I go get his son?" asked Elizabeth.

Malanga looked at her and shook her head. "Yes, my dear, and get Paul. This day is a complete day of loss for George. Get them and bring them here. Tell the others nothing."

As Elizabeth flew from the room, the party with Jun-Jun entered from the other side. Jun-Jun was limp and pale. Malanga kept watching the Commander as she ordered them to place Jun-Jun in the next resting bay, but to leave the barrier between them retracted as she needed to tend to both simultaneously.

Jun-Jun was being brought back to life by Toby, who had held his essence during the long freelock. Just as Jun-Jun started to stir, George, Jr. entered with Elizabeth. Paul was behind them.

He looked down at his father, and then turned to Malanga. "Is he dead?"

"No, George," she said over her humming, "he is alive, but he will be dead soon."

"What happened? Why was he fighting?"

"He wasn't fighting, his brain was not functioning properly. He was in seizure. It was the hemareflux from years ago. It formed clots and they have traveled to his brain."

George looked at his father, numb and still inside. "Will he speak? Can I talk to him?"

"He can hear everything we're saying," she hummed, "and perhaps he will talk." She looked at him sadly, knowing the awful burden this day was for him. "Do you want us to leave you alone?"

"No," said George, "he needs your help. He trusts you more than he has ever trusted any other person, Finder Malanga, please stay with us." He reached out his hands and took his father by the shoulders, leaning into him and weeping on his shoulder. His father's right hand came up shakily and caressed his hair. George pulled his head back, and looked at his father, who began to speak slowly.

"SIL is yours, George," he said softly. "I was wrong to try to make it into something separate from Earth. Any place people are is a good place. Help them get along." He stopped with his mouth open. George, thinking he was dead, let out a cry. But the Commander's face moved in jerky movements and the eyes blinked back to knowing. "George," he said, "Be true to Liz and your son. You will see them again, thanks to the Golden Sun. Await their arrival." The Commander then looked at Malanga, then back to George. "I've loved you both." He was gone.

Suddenly Jun-Jun cried out, "Stop her! She is bombing the Eye!"

Everyone turned to look at him in shock. "Who?" asked Malanga.

"The one who took Ali. She is outside of the Eye, in the outer shell. Go quickly and stop her. She is planting a bomb..." and he fainted.

"Does anyone know where he's talking about? Call the engineers!" shouted Malanga.

"No," said George. "I know where she is. Let me go."

Everyone stopped. "George," Elizabeth said, "just tell us. You should be here with your father." Paul held up his hand, and put his other hand on George's back.

"My father is gone. She is exactly where he was years ago. He showed me where. I can go and stop her. I will be with him there, doing what he would have done."

He jetted toward the main door. "Please go tell BQ and Sylvia where we are going." As he sped from the room, he wondered what his father had meant about the Golden Sun.

Chapter 20

Stevens looked at his gathered crew. They hadn't been told the exact truth about their mission, and each had been told something different. He had them assemble in the cargo bay of the shuttle to brief them on their mission. Even in the briefing he would not be disclosing the exact truth, but just enough for them to get their jobs done. Houston Rheingold knew more than any of the others, but even he did not know the complete picture. Stevens alone knew the exact truth.

Steven Masters and his brother, Dave, positioned themselves on either side of Stevens and, by their postures, made it clear they were his body guards. The three faced the rest of the crew. Houston Rhinegold looked smug, and considered himself invaluable to the mission, regardless of the attitude of expendability Stevens showed to him and every other member of the crew. He had brought Lew Mackelroy with him from NASA. Mackelroy was an excellent navigator and had been the coordinator between NASA and Associated when the Low Orbital Lens was first deployed. He had worked directly with Liz to adopt her deep space mapping system and guide its implementation throughout all sectors of NASA.

Next to him was the entire rest of the security team that had been trained by Masters to guard George, Jr. and his family. This group was a small army, trained in hand-to-hand combat, though each had another skill necessary for this mission. Karen Smith was originally from the hills of Kentucky and was one of eleven children. While her brothers and sisters were all uneducated, she had attended Vassar, thanks to the help she got from her school guidance counselor in exchange for sexual favors. She approached him the day she arrived at the Middle School and told him she wanted out of Kentucky, out of poverty and out of her family's abuse. He told her the only way out was for her to go to college. They struck a deal and, at the age of thirteen, she began a nearly daily routine of studying hard, and providing him with sex. He positioned her to become Valedictorian of her senior class, and recipient of a full scholarship to Vassar. She promised to marry him when she graduated from Vassar, but as soon as she arrived on campus and became friends with Vassar's Dean of Students, she wrote him a letter of dismissal. Her skill level was impressive across the boards – she graduated Suma Cum Laude from Vassar with a degree in engineering, was a brilliant gemologist, was a master manipulator, excelled in sports, was politically savvy, and she gave excellent head.

Sam Kaplan, on the other hand, was rather dull, or so he appeared. He was very strong, but not bright at all. He had no hair on his body, the result of a nervous condition that had its onset when he was sixteen and discovered he was gay. He came from a fundamentalist Christian family and had been sexually abused by his minister father from the time of his earliest memories. He could have become dangerously bitter, but instead had shut out the world with his mind. He had become an electrician's assistant and he was able to read almost any instruction manual and follow it to the letter. He had a near photographic memory for diagrams and mechanical drawings, and once he set himself to a task could not be distracted by anything.

Marty Wellington was saved from being beautiful by his large nose. Otherwise, he was perhaps the sexiest man alive. He had a kind of magnetism that drove everyone to distraction, and when he entered a room every eye stayed on him. Unfortunately, the moment he spoke, his arrogance was an instant turn-off. His value on the team was his strength. He worked out constantly, in one way or another.

Joe Martin had been for years the chief mechanic at the most successful automobile repair shop in Boston, but had left that to run his own private computer hardware repair company. The combination of skills between the two businesses made him so intuitive about any mechanical or electrical device that he was by far one of the best skilled in the country. His link to Masters came when he opened his computer business with a loan from Masters. The conditions on the loan were the typical underworld conditions, which basically meant that Masters owned Martin. This situation created huge resentment in Martin, for it would be years before he was going to be able to work off the extremely high interest of the loan. When Masters approached him with a way to make good on the loan, and turn a profit for himself, he jumped at the chance. He would do anything to be free, and the prospect of achieving that freedom along with a handsome profit was irresistible to the simple minded man.

Justin Kirkland, the final member of the team, was a pilot who had been expelled from the NASA astronaut program by Rhinegold years before. He was a drinker and lady's man, not to mention arrogant. His father had been abusive to his mother, and had beaten her to the point of brain damage. When she was in a mental institution as a result of the damage his father had sued for, and won, full custody of the boy. Thus began a steady stream of different women in the household, all of whom left in short order when they found out the abuse that came with the bold confidence of his dashing father. His father had blamed all of his problems on lack of education, and ingrained in his son the need to have maximum education to assure all they were entitled to by birth was delivered. This idea of entitlement became a constant demand once he graduated from MIT with honors. He entered flight school at Goddard as an enlisted Air Force corpsman, and worked his way through the rigors of the Top Gun training and landed in the NASA program quicker than anyone had previously.

But that same year his father had been shot and killed by one of the women he was fond of abusing, which made him furious. He set out on a path of revenge drinking and drugging, with multiple sex partners every day and night. Whenever he wasn't doing his training he was indulging himself, seeking to feel he was getting all he was entitled to. But the more he drank the thirstier he got; the more he drugged the more he felt trapped in reality's uncomfortable binds; and the more he fucked the lonelier he felt. All the while he was not sleeping much, and rarely ate balanced meals outside of the food provided by NASA. Rhinegold kept covering for him, and sometimes substituted his own test results for Kirkland's, just to keep him in the program. Rhinegold started coming to visit him on days off, and even went whoring with him in an attempt to real him back in.

Then Rheingold's problems started, and others took control of the training program when he was testifying in front of Congressional panels in Washington. That was the end of Kirkland's stint as an astronaut trainee. He was expelled quicker than anyone before, just as he had been accepted. Soon after he was expelled, so was Rhinegold, and the two took to each other's company with days on end of drink, drug and sex, interspersed with constant self-pity and oaths of vengeance. When Stevens approached them, they were hooked before he even finished his pitch. Stevens had been prepared to enlist Masters' help in convincing them, and was startled when they signed on without much effort on his part. Later Stevens realized that this was great good fortune, for it gave him direct control independent of Masters' influence which, in a power struggle that seemed inevitable between Stevens and Masters, he needed all the leverage he could get.

Stevens considered his crew—nine men, one woman, all highly skilled in one aspect of their mission, each with a deep grudge against authority, and all, in one way or another, beholden to him.

"We have two targets in this mission, each one yielding over $10 billion in aerospace and gemstone value, and we have a buyer already lined up. As promised, each of you will receive $1 billion at the end of this mission, placed in an untraceable Swiss account. Upon our return to Earth you will each undergo complete surgical reconstruction of your features and fingerprints and other identifying biological characteristics, including your eyes. You will be free to travel the world just two years after that. But for now, our focus has to be on the tasks at hand, not the reward at the end."

He looked over the crew gathered before him and saw how ugly greed was. Most notable was the look of almost orgasmic bliss on the face of Kirkland, who felt he was finally going to get what he deserved out of life. Stevens was completely disgusted by them.

"Who is the buyer?" asked Masters bluntly. "How do we know you have one for sure?"

Stevens laughed. "You silly ass," he spat with contempt, "how could we have possibly come this far without a powerful supporter? How could I have gotten the details on the investigation team or gained entry to all of the shuttles in the fleet?" He just laughed. Masters glowered and mumbled under his breath. Stevens' laughter stopped abruptly, one neatly plucked eyebrow raised. "You know, Masters, we can continue without you. And by that I mean," he cleared his voice in a patronizingly British sort of way, "you will cooperate in action, thought and attitude. Anything less will indicate to me you have chosen to return to your pitiful impoverished state before I trained the gutter stench out of you." He allowed the threat to sink in, then added. "And death, of course."

With this Masters composed himself; his eyes froze to ice betraying the smile on his face. "I'm sorry Ronald," using the familiarity of a first name as both friendship and insult, "I am

Second Pass

totally with you. I just wanted to know who our beneficent patron is."

"And that," Stevens replied, "you cannot know. So," he looked around the group, "any other interruptions?" The bay was silent outside of the clamor of space vehicle noises. "As soon as we have synchronized the two shuttle guidance systems and recalibrated for our additional load, and rerouted the nuclear and solar energy to our vehicles, we will be off to our first point of rendezvous. Those of you who will be performing the EVA on site will be on a regimen of sleep, food and exercise for the next two days until we arrive. That would be the Masters brothers and Marty. Rhinegold is pilot of A-Shuttle, and Kirkland pilot of B-Shuttle. Mackelroy will be navigator, and will be located in A-Shuttle. I will ride in B-Shuttle with you Kirkland. Meanwhile, Kaplan will assist Martin in putting together the gem cutting station on the old shuttle. But first," he looked at Kaplan to make sure he was getting this. He received a blink in reply, and assumed that was an affirmative. "You must reactivate the O2 generator in the far Space Station Module. We must have a livable, workable environment. Once he has the module ready then, you, Martin, will install and activate all of the equipment Smith needs, under her supervision." There were a few sucking sounds and low laughs from the men acknowledging Smith's oral abilities. Most of them were coming from Kirkland, and she backhanded him sending them both spinning in opposite directions. "Enough!" yelled Stevens. "I will not tolerate that childish behavior. I have given Smith a stun gun to silence any of you who get out of line. She is the only woman here and will be treated equally." He turned to her, and she smiled shyly in reply. "You have my permission to use that stun gun as much and as often as you need." He then looked to the rest of them. "We have just over 40 hours until we arrive at our destination. I suggest you get to work. I will not tolerate misbehavior of any kind."

* * * * * * *

BQ had sent the intercepted video clip to Woody at Associated to see if he could get any of their engineers to make sense of it. He had called in only those of the engineering staff he felt he could trust, excluding anyone who had shown particularly strong ties to Stevens. But they had not been able to do much with it.

Meanwhile he was continuing to communicate via the LOL at the CommLink with SIL, relaying all information to Liz. She was showing signs of stress only in her terse manner of speech, and the fact that whenever anyone brought up the subject of being separated from George for an entire 18-year pass, or questions about how she planned to manage little Georgie, she quickly turned the topic to work or something clinical. Woody knew she was deeply disturbed, and made sure to speak with her several times a day regarding work-related things.

He was sitting at his desk, preparing notes for his next CommLink conversation with BQ when there was a knock at his door. He looked up and, before he could say anything, the door flew open and little Georgie ran in. "Uncle Woody! Uncle Woody! Give me a ride!" The boy flew to his lap and crashed head first into his gut as Woody began to rise from his chair. Liz just stood at the door with just a trace of a smile on her lips.

"My God, woman!" Woody shouted. "When did you return from Florida! And you, little man," grabbed Georgie and tickled a squeal out of him, "are in for the ride of your life!" He flung Georgie over his shoulder and pirouetted across the room to Liz. The two hugged for a long time, and Woody was suddenly aware that she had buried her face in his chest and was crying. "Ah, my sweet little Liz," he said, caressing her hair with his free hand, "finally we see the human heart in ya. How lucky a man I am to be on the receiving end of it. Let it all out, Lass, let it all out before it eats you from the inside." He pushed the door shut with his foot behind her, and let Georgie slide down to the floor. He put both arms around Liz and Woody and hugged both of their knees, looking up with big, wide eyes at his crying mother.

"Don't cry, mommy. Don't cry," he said.

"Ah, laddie," Woody said, winking at Georgie, "when a lady cries it makes the world a better place. Tears belong on the outside, lad, not trapped in your heart."

"What about when a man cries? Or, even, a boy?" he asked with melodramatic seriousness.

"'Tis the same. All tears belong on the outside. Tears are the soul taking a shower, that's all."

Second Pass

Liz pulled back her head and kissed Woody on the cheek. "Thank you Woody," she said, "thank you for being there; for understanding."

He smiled. "But I don't understand Liz, I cannot. No person can know what this feels like but you. And whatever that feeling is, it is the right one. You poor thing." There was a beeping from the CommLink, indicating there was a transmission coming through. The floor started to rumble as the satellite dish adjusted its angle to meet the arriving signal. "Well, what have we here?" Woody said as he opened the door and the three walked over to the CommLink.

He entered the necessary codes to open the link and flipped on the screen. BQ's face filled the screen. "Uncle Woody," she said, "Commander McVee is dead." She started to cry, just staring straight ahead, neither hiding her pain nor wiping her tears. "The hemareflux left clots and he had a cranial embolism."

Liz picked up little Georgie and held him to her. Tears filled her eyes, and he squirmed to be free. She thought only of George. "My God, BQ," she said, "how is George? What a terrible loss he's suffered these past days."

BQ looked with shock from the screen. "Oh, Liz," she said and continued to cry. "George is coping better than the rest of us, I'm afraid. We have a fugitive murderer on SIL, as you know from recent reports, and George has gone to apprehend her. Everything is such a mess. When did you get to Cambridge?"

"I just arrived. I came to work on that video clip. I can't stand those people in Florida, and the ones from the White House are even worse. Oh, poor George." She just stood there. Woody didn't know what to say. Little Georgie wriggled free and ran into the center of the room, looking up at the satellite hub in the ceiling with his arms outstretched, twirling in lazy circles. "I can't stand not working on something. I can't stand being unable to help George."

"Well," Woody finally found his voice again, "we must then get to work. The Commander would have it no other way. BQ," he said to her, "is there anything else?"

"No," she replied, "unfortunately not. I wanted to give you the news. And one more thing. We are not letting his death be known. Both for the sake of stability here on SIL and for other reasons. I trust you two to keep this confidential."

"Well then," Woody said, "let us all put our efforts into figuring out this mess and finding the criminals. I'll leave the CommLink activated but on stand-by."

"I love you all," said BQ as she switched off her transmission.

Liz then turned to Woody. "I've been looking at that video over and over. I think I know what it is, and where it is going. Come over here," she motioned to him as she walked to the 3-D display table for star mapping. She reached in the bag she was carrying and produced a large plastic salad bowl and turned it upside down and placed it over the Earth marker in the center of the mapping table. She then opened up her small personal computer and displayed the video sequence. "When I first looked at this I thought it might be a flight path, simply because it has a fairly consistent arc, but the arc ratio changes in three places, once right at the beginning where it seems to hook, then again about a quarter of its length, and then again right at the end of the arc." She played the video sequence a few times. "See how it starts? It is just like a flight path that starts from an earth orbit, pulling away from gravity, then, once free of it, accelerating and correcting the course. But then here," she points to a bend in the arc, "it seems to do a quarter circle, then go off in a different direction." Indeed, the line did look like a demented hairpin with curves at each end and one part way along.

"Everyone was trying to zoom in on it," she continued, "and when they did they found the line was actually a double line that twists around a central axis. Some of the guys in Florida thought it was perhaps some DNA strain, but the twists of the helix are too inconsistent for that, and it is much too long in terms of distance between strands relative to its overall length." Woody smiled at this remarkable woman. He knew this surge of expert brain work was her way of coping with recent news. She continued, unaware of the fondness in Woody's gaze. "So I zoomed out, way out. I considered that if it were a flight path, the big bend at the quarter length mark must have been using the gravitational pull of another celestial body to propel it further out into space. But doing that would involve orbiting fully around the body, not just getting near it. So I ran some graphing software and found that in the middle point of the curve there is a distinct notch," she zoomed back in, "here. And right at the point of the notch," she zoomed in further to show the parallel white lines, "there is an extremely tight twisting of the two lines."

Second Pass

She went back and forth between the close-up view and the distant view, tracking it, calculating out loud what every point in the process might mean. "Liz," interrupted Woody, "I don't need to be convinced that your idea holds merit. I don't really understand much of this anyway. I am a janitor, after all." She stopped mid-sentence and blushed. "Just tell me what you think it means, and where you think it's going."

"Well," she was clearly flustered. She wanted to show she was still capable, and she was trying to convince the security guard that had dogged her every move for the past three years that she was more, much more, than the wife of an important man, and the mother of a child. "I guess you don't need to know all of that. I was just trying to make sure I was being thorough."

"Now that is something I understand," he smiled. "But I'm just sitting on the edge of my seat here wanting to know where it all leads!"

"And so you shall," she said, nudging him affectionately with her head. "The big bend has got to be the moon, and the notch is simply the entry into orbit and the exit from orbit. Instead of showing the whole orbit, they showed only the parts of the flight path that were forward progress. I think it was part of the masking, encryption process. They really didn't want anyone to understand what they were showing."

"So," Woody reasoned, "if that is the moon, and I don't doubt it at all, then where does it all lead?" "Georgie!" she yelled as he started to try to push buttons on the CommLink panel, which, thankfully was just out of his reach. "Don't play with the buttons honey. Here," she dug in her purse, "I have your toys here." He ran over to her and snatched the toy she was holding out to him, then ran to the center of the room, plopped onto his cushioned bottom and focused intently on the object.

"What on earth is that?" Woody said.

"Oh," Liz shrugged, "it's his favorite toy—a half-bear, half-dog. He thinks things like that exist on SIL, so I sewed two toys together to make it for him. Anyhow," she turned to the bowl, "I calculated the distance from Earth orbit to the moon and came up with a location. At first I thought they were going back to SIL, but it is not in the right location for the distances. So I ran different scenarios and realized that they were meeting at the old Space Station." She changed the mapping display so that the old Space Station was at the center point under the bowl. "I knew that if they docked opposite each other on the same end of the Station, they could use both engines and create a powerful thrust. And so I calculated the distance to the Moon from the station, figured out the fuel and speeds and found that they could indeed get to the Moon, orbit a few times to build up speed, and then go off into space." Sure enough, the moon lay exactly on one edge of the bowl's surface.

She then changed the display so that the dome of the bowl was now the distance of the full length of the arc from the Station. The Moon shrank and was now just about one quarter of the way from the center point under the bowl lip and the end of the trajectory was on the surface of the bowl. "There is one problem, however. With the fuel in both of the shuttles, and they took shuttles with extra fuel tanks and excess oxygen, they couldn't go that far, even with several orbits of the moon to boomerang them outward. So I called up some of my old team's engineers from Associated. I spoke to some of the guys who were really old and remembered more details of the Station. It seems that the old Space Station had a nuclear power source that could be used in many ways. Ingenious really, because it was intended to power the booster rockets to keep it in orbit and prevent orbital decay, but could also be diverted to the different life-sustaining systems on board. And", she adjusted some settings, "it also could be tapped into by other ships. The power generated by that can be plugged into the shuttle engines and give them tremendous power without using any of the shuttle fuel. That's when it all made sense! The power of those engines with the nuclear power source, considering that there would be the engines of both shuttles, can reach speeds of up to 80,000 miles per hour. They could go over 3,000,000 miles in less than two days! That puts the total distance into a relative achievability to match the trajectory in the video clip!"

Woody looked at her and laughed out loud. "I don't know exactly what you just said, but if you are that excited, then I'm happy too. But what does it mean about where they are going? What are they planning to do?"

"Well, I looked at all of the possible locations, of all of the different places they might go to and found an old satellite from the earliest days of unmanned space exploration. It seems that they are going to that old satellite. Why? That I can't tell you."

Woody looked back at her personal computer display and saw that the video was playing backwards. "Did you rewind that?"

Second Pass

"What?" Liz looked over at the display, puzzled. "It never did that before," she said. "It always stopped...wait..." she reached across to the display. She hit the rewind feature that keeps displaying the image. When she had rewound it to the end of the first display she pushed the play forward tab. The first image ended and the screen went black, and stayed black. "I always turned it off at that point," she said. "I just assumed it was the end." About a minute and a half later the original image started to display backward. "This must be their planned return trajectory." They watched as it uncurled from the end point, went back down, hit the moon bending the path and then took a turn. Liz froze the image on the screen, and went over to another table for a moment, bringing back a transparency, which she slid under the mapping table replacing her original display, then hit slow play. As the image unfolded on the screen, she was mapping the path with her finger on the table.

There was a strange loop, at which point she froze the image again. With renewed energy, she became animated and almost automatic. She went from mapping station to mapping station around the room. Saying numbers out loud to remember them until she got to the next station. Like a pinball finding its way down the incline, she worked from table to table, completely absorbed.

Inside of her, memories began to stir. She was back in the early days when she'd first met George and Paul. She remembered the excitement when they put together LOL and she developed the deep space mapping quadrant system in anticipation of applying the theory George had developed at MIT. Everything was electric. Everything was new. The adrenaline surged throughout her system, raising bumps on her skin and making her nostrils flair. She knew if she could match the exact moment they were going to begin their journey she could find out what they were looping around on the way home.

There were only two possibilities, however. One was Hubble IV, the other was SIL. She had to know what they were after, and when they started. She ran to the CommLink panel. "May I initiate transmission?" she asked.

"Let me," Woody said, nearly tripping over little Georgie as he jogged across the vast room to the CommLink. "I erased everyone's ID except my own," he said apologetically, "sorry."

"Didn't George tell you?" she asked. "Never be angry at a security guard asking for an ID."

Woody laughed, remembering when George had told him that. He initiated transmission. "Where to?" he asked. "SIL?"

"You got it," she said.

It took a few moments and the screen flickered to life. There was a blur of activity in the background of the CommLink on SIL. Different people were obviously working on a variety of stations, and without gravity, people and their various body parts floated around in a haphazard way. Suddenly the face of Solomon Gould floated by upside down, but snapped toward the screen as he righted himself.

"Liz," he said, "I'm so sorry about the Commander. And George, Jr."

"Sol," Liz said, "you are sweet, but we've got more important things going on. Is Sylvia there?"

He looked around, then held up a finger and pushed himself away from the screen. A few moments later, Sylvia's face came into view. "Yes Liz," she said, all business.

"Have you received or intercepted anything from the shuttles?"

"Actually, yes. They met up at the old Space Station about 7 hours ago. Bill and I were going over our security with Sol, BQ and Tom. We were creating a checklist. Anyway, Tom remembered something from the original specs of SIL about archiving all of the old Space Station systems. Well, I won't go into details now, but he had old remote controllers for the onboard video and audio systems and security cameras for the old Station. He and Bill found them and reactivated them and we've been able to monitor everything they are doing and saying. They are planning to retrieve the synthetic diamond lenses from two satellites. They have a buyer on Earth who will be paying $20 billion. They are going to return to Earth and get plastic surgery. Each member of the team gets $1 billion, leaving nearly $10 billion for Stevens. They fired their engines about ten minutes ago."

"Exact time?" asked Liz.

"Nine fourteen and twenty seconds GMT."

Liz ran to the mapping table, did some quick calculations and froze. The blood drained from her face. She returned, walking slowly. "I've determined the first satellite. It is an old one from the late twentieth century, more of a probe than a satellite. It

Second Pass

has a diamond of approximately 2400 carats. After that," she was speaking so quietly, so slowly, that she could barely be heard, "they are coming to take the Eye. They are going to destroy SIL."

There was silence in both CommLink stations. Absolute silence. The Eye was over 60,000 carats. Cut into individual stones it was worth perhaps even more than $20 billion. But without the Eye, SIL, and all of her inhabitants, were dead.

Tom Robinson came into view. "I have an idea," he said, "that will save us. I assume this channel is secure?"

"Yes," said Sylvia and Woody simultaneously.

"I believe I can disable the nuclear power connection to their shuttle engines. It is a matter of when to do it."

Bill Bryant was now beside him. "We need the shuttles back, so we can't do it until they are in fuel range of at least SIL."

"But when will they be coming back toward SIL?" asked BQ. "We only have eleven more days before SIL is out of range of Earth until next pass."

"And it takes three days to service a shuttle for re-entry flight," said Sylvia, "which really leaves eight days."

"They will be at SIL in six days," said Liz. "But if they suspect anything at all is wrong, they will abort their mission."

"It will take quite a bit to deter them from their $20 billion prize," said Woody. "I know it would me."

"And," said Sol, "who is their buyer? I suspect there is more to this picture than we are currently seeing. Even if they get to SIL in six days, they would have to somehow render SIL and all of us here harmless to them. The work to extract the Eye from the outer structure of SIL will take more than two days, it will take more like two weeks. And at that point there would be no possible way for them to return to Earth. And, with SIL disabled and the Eye gone, they wouldn't be able to sustain their own lives long enough to survive until the next pass. Something doesn't match."

Liz slumped in her chair. She was no longer bereaved, she was furious and frustrated. "Many of you know me, some of you do not," she began, "but I believe, with your permission and trust, that I can help figure this out. I must ask for complete trust and confidence—if that is possible." She let them sit with this for a moment. "I need to speak in complete privacy to George. If you will allow this, and if you all agree I am to be trusted, I will do my best to figure out this puzzle."

BQ was the first to speak. "Liz, you have my complete trust. I know you will do everything in your power to save George and all of us. Sylvia and Bill Bryant have never met you, but are familiar with some of your past work on LOL and with the deep space quadrant mapping systems. It will have to be up to them."

"Liz," Bill said, "since the Commander has died, Alexander Machmood is now in the position of Commander. He is the one you will have to convince. He does not like or trust BQ and Paul, is opposed to George being here, and has often argued with me, First Officer of SIL. The situation here is quite chaotic and extremely delicate politically."

"I propose," Liz said evenly, "that what I will do might be done without his knowledge. None of it will happen on SIL for the most part, and will be done more in the interest of saving the shuttles than saving SIL, at least on paper if it comes to that. Whatsmore," she added, "I will take full responsibility if I fail."

There was a long silence. If she were to fail it would mean the possible death of everyone on SIL, which truly does impact them. But there seemed to be no other idea on the table.

"Liz," Bill said, "I will arrange for a completely secret and private uplink between you and George. Right now he is apprehending the fugitive on SIL. As soon as he is available, I will bring him here."

"There is much I can do right away," Liz said. "And in the event George should not be able to communicate with me, I'll need one of you to work with me in his capacity."

"What are you saying," said BQ in alarm. "What do you mean?"

"I mean that George is going after a murderer. His father has just died. He has just been cut off from his family for the next eighteen years, and his abilities may not be as sharp as they normally are. He may well be killed in his pursuit. I know this. You don't have to worry about my reaction to that. We must have a secondary plan in effect."

Bill Bryant let out a low, astonished whistle. "You are one hell of a lady," he said. "Remind me to never be on your bad side. If you can say what you just said, given the events of the past few days, then you have my complete trust. If something should happen to George, I will be your counterpart in this."

Everyone was now waiting for Liz to speak. She, in these few minutes, had become the undeniable leader. She seemed to step

Second Pass

into the role with ease. "Go help George!" was all she said, then terminated the transmission.

She turned to Woody as soon as the CommLink was shut down and burst into tears, collapsing into his arms.

Chapter 21

Liz called Sienta from Associated and met her at home. Sienta knew instantly that much was wrong, but did not say a word to Liz about it. She had heard all of the news about the shuttles, the murders at Associated, the people stranded on SIL. She watched the story about George, Liz and little George with amused infuriation, knowing that her employing family was nothing at all like the individuals profiled by the media. But her years of service had taught her one thing, if nothing else, and that was to leave them alone until they were ready to talk.

Which is just what she did, greeting Liz with a warm, motherly hug and embracing little Georgie like her long lost soul mate, lost for centuries of hopeless despair only to have been reunited. Georgie loved the melodrama and attention. Sienta played her role to perfection, and managed to get him to bed early. She then tidied up the kitchen, sat alone at the kitchen table over a cup of tea, then a glass of wine. She made a final swipe of the sink after her mug and glass were cleaned, dried and put away, and hung her apron on the hook next to the broom closet. She calmly straightened her hair using the glass window in the door of the upper oven as a mirror, and marched resolutely to the study where Liz had been most of the evening.

"I know ju are being upset y muy, muy worried about the Mister George. I know ju are, seester Leez. But if you no gonna cry, jor heart gonna break more." Sienta plopped herself in the chair across the desk from Liz. She folded her arms on top of her bosom and waited.

Liz tried to pretend she didn't hear Sienta come in. She tried to pretend she didn't hear a word. She tried to pretend nothing was wrong. She tried. Tears started spilling on her papers and she looked up into the most sternly understanding eyes in the universe and started to sob. Sienta nearly ran around the desk and cradled Liz's head in her arms, muttering in Spanish. Here they stayed for nearly ten minutes.

Liz then started talking and crying. She told Sienta everything, including that Commander McVee had died. Sienta cried too, even though she had never met the man. Then she took control of the situation. She started asking Liz questions about the stolen shuttles, about the plot to take the synthetic diamonds, about

Second Pass

missing George, and about what Liz thought was going on. Liz allowed her this intrusion, for she was, more than any other, her mother. As she talked, her tears dried and became determined confidence. Her scientific mind came alive, and she started outlining everything.

"But who eez the one with so mucho dinero to want diamonds? Eez too big for ear rings and necklace. Madre de Dios! What could they gonna do with so many stones?"

"Okay, Sienta, here goes." She moved a stack of papers back in front of her, now that they were no longer in danger of being doused with tears. "It is clear that the stones aren't going to be sold on the jewelry market. The amount of money being paid would place the cost per carat at over $300,000, so they clearly aren't being used in that way. I've researched uses for diamonds other than selling them on the open market—military uses in particular. I found that the development of such large synthetic diamonds is an extremely costly affair, but without them large satellites cannot function and, more specifically, space based laser weapons cannot work."

Sienta was looking with very large eyes. She didn't understand all of the words Liz was saying, but understood enough to know that this was very serious business indeed. She nudged her chin forward to encourage Liz to continue.

"There are many countries wanting to develop their own surveillance and communications satellites, but few who can afford it. And space-based weapons are rather moot in today's world, unless they are planning to go after SIL. But the most puzzling thing is that even if they did succeed in getting these gemstones, they couldn't bring them back to earth until 18 years from now, and the people who did this will have to live with the people of SIL for all of that time. It just doesn't make sense." She was looking down at her notes when the phone rang.

"Hello?" Liz said in her usual business voice.

"Hello, Elizabeth," a booming voice said on the other end of the line.

"Who is this please?" she asked curtly.

"Is your son in bed? If I remember correctly, you are very concerned that he get his sleep so he can grow strong," the voice said. She felt apprehension. She recognized the voice, but couldn't place it. Son. Her son in bed. She tried to think. It was so familiar.

"Please state your name and your business or I will be forced to terminate this call," Liz said.

"My name is something your people have too much trouble pronouncing. Ah, but my business, you say? That I can state. It is many trillions of dollars, that is my business."

Liz suddenly remembered that George had told her about the Chinese offer of money for SIL, which he turned down. She remembered the conversation she'd had with this man before. "Mister Chairman," she said, "why are you afraid to speak directly to me?"

He laughed aloud. "You are so direct, so busy, in such a hurry," he said, "but in the end we all die. What does hurrying toward that achieve?" She waited in silence, furious to know she could not out wit this clever man. "We had a contract with your husband's father, a secret contract, that is. But he has hurried to his death and now we do not know what to do. So we turn to you."

Secret contract? What secret contract? "Why not speak directly to SIL?" she asked. "I am afraid that I cannot help you. I do not speak for SIL, and have no influence on those who do."

"Ah, but you are wrong," the Chairman said. "The woman is the handle that pushes the broom. You are the only one who can speak privately, in confidence, without security listening in on your transmissions."

"How..." she thought back. How could they have intercepted the conversation she'd had just hours before with SIL? Or was he just assuming that with the situation as it was she would have some privileges. "I'm afraid I don't know what you mean," she said evenly.

"Let me spell it out for you as directly as you seem to like things," the Chairman said with a new tone of coldness to his voice. "The Commander made arrangements with us, secret arrangements as I said before. We want to make sure these arrangements will still be honored, but apparently he told no one about them. We have gone to great trouble to develop our end of the bargain, and we intend to go through with it."

Liz realized that the Chinese would have the money to pay billions, and already had many satellites in space. They had been developing their own manned space exploration since 2003, and had continued to push forward with it. Now, many decades later, even when the United States had suspended their own space program. The general knowledge about their program was that they had suspended work on military space applications, and were looking to space as a place to house some of their citizens. *But*, she reasoned, *since the discovery of SIL 18 years ago they would be able to jump far ahead with their plans if they could send inhabitants to SIL.* She knew that some slots had been given to the Chinese, but not nearly the number they wanted. But if they could use military force to take over SIL, they could... her heart froze. She realized that the Chinese were the buyer of the diamonds, and they intended to use them as weapons. In fact, they didn't need to bring them back to earth at all. For all she knew they already had military satellites in space, perhaps some super laser devices that only needed the diamonds to bring them online. It had long been suspected that they had developed shuttle crafts that could out-perform the current US fleet. If they had managed to develop some with a significantly longer range, then the window of approach to SIL would extend beyond the 4 month window. Her mouth went dry.

"Mister Chairman," she said slowly, "how can I help you?" She reached over and pushed the button of the phone recorder, a device Masters had installed so any threatening calls could be recorded. Sienta's eyes widened with mischief as she wagged her finger in a scolding way at Liz, then turned it and tapped her temple with a wink, showing her approval of the cleverness of Liz's move.

"Actually, Madame Elizabeth, I thought I could perhaps help you."

"I'm listening." She silently took a piece of paper and wrote a note instructing Sienta to call Woody on his direct line and have him come to her immediately. Sienta took the note, and then removed her shoes before walking quietly out of the room to make the call. Liz judged it would take Woody about ten minutes to arrive and needed to keep the Chairman on the phone until he did. "Do continue," she said sweetly.

"How would you like to pay a visit to your husband? You could even bring your son along."

"I believe there are only a few days left before the window of access is gone."

"China is a big country," he said, playing with her, "and we tend to think in larger terms than you do, by necessity of course. If you were our size you would do the same. But then you aren't." He stopped and she could hear liquid pouring. She suspected it was tea, though it may have been liquor of some sort. "Our shuttles are built larger than yours, of course, and have a longer range." He paused, taking a drink that she could hear. "You are a clever woman…"

"Please, don't attempt flattery. It does not serve as a good companion to manipulation in this case. And," she let some anger into her voice, "one might resent the fact that you are taking advantage of a woman and child who have just lost the chance to see their beloved family for 18 years. Your thoughts might be large, but your heart is not."

"Quite so," he said, "quite so. I do have my people in mind, and sincerely want the best for them. But my offer to you was meant to reflect my sincere compassion for the situation you find yourself in. I believe family is the second most important thing in life. Second to the state, of course. I know how recent events must have affected you, and I feel very badly for you."

"Are you in some way responsible for these recent events?" she asked pointedly.

"We couldn't have caused the death of the Commander," he said sounding hurt, "surely you don't think we did."

"No, I think nothing of the sort. It is the loss of our shuttle fleet to which I was referring."

"What possible interest would we have in the destruction of your inferior fleet of a mere handful of toys?"

She decided to let it be for now. She didn't want to risk angering him and forcing a premature end to the conversation. "Forgive me, Mister Chairman," she said humbly, "I am very tired and very upset. We all feel extremely vulnerable since the attack on our fleet and such widespread loss of life." She took a breath. She had to find out more of what he had in mind. "Please continue what you were saying about your superior shuttles. I would very much like to have my family reunited."

"Of course you would," he said with a sigh. "But space travel is very expensive. Do you have any idea how much it costs?"

"Why trillions, if what you say is accurate," she said. "I am a scientist, not an accountant," she added.

"You make me smile, Lady Elizabeth. You are an exceptional scientist to whom we owe a great debt. Your deep space quadrant mapping system has brought the entire human race far forward in our evolution."

Second Pass

"Well, perhaps the debt you owe, as you claim, could be repaid by donating the use of your shuttles not only to reunite my family, but bring those who had not planned to remain on SIL until the next pass back as well."

"You see," he said, "this is where there is a problem. In our agreement, our secret agreement, with Commander McVee, we were going to deliver materials to build more layers of housing on the outside of SIL. We had also contracted, secretly, to deliver a few hundred workers to help with construction, as well as a fine sum of money to pay Silians for their hospitality."

She couldn't believe what she was hearing. Commander McVee may well have made some arrangements with the Chinese, but the way the Chairman kept harping on the 'secret' nature of the agreement, she knew there would be no proof as to what, if anything, had been agreed upon between them. "Even so," she said, "the shuttles that carry supplies and workers to SIL could return carrying those who wish to return to Earth."

"I'm afraid that is out of the question," his tone got suddenly harsh, as if he was impatient with a slow child. "Our shuttles will not be available afterward for such transport."

"But you offered that I might have my family reunited," she reminded him, taking comfort in his harsh tone. She liked the idea that she might have upset him.

"I meant to offer you and your son transport to SIL only," he said flatly.

"You still haven't told me what I can do for you. You remember? The high cost of space travel?"

She heard the front door to the house open and the hushed voices of Sienta and Woody in the foyer. A few instants later they entered, Woody carrying his shoes. She motioned Woody to come next to her at her side of the desk.

"Our intelligence people tell me that SIL created an adapter seal to the docking ports. If you provide us with the design specifications, we will take you and your son to SIL."

She had written the name of the Chairman on a slip of paper and handed it to Woody. He whistled silently with raised eyebrows when he read it.

"I will have to think about that, Mister Chairman. Is there anything else?"

"Well, actually there is," he said with his voice lower and more forceful. "If we find that you go to the authorities with any mention of this request, I'm afraid we may all be saddened at the fact that we have such little control of the safety of those on SIL."

The threat was clear. She knew he was serious. "I understand," she said. "But earlier you said that I alone had the capability to speak on a secure channel to George. If I'm not to discuss this with him, what possible good does my unique ability do?"

"You are so very clever, but I will forgive you. Please feel free to discuss anything at all with him, except our request for the design of the adapter rings. We want him to become the new person for us to negotiate with."

"But he is not in a position of power on SIL. Alexander Machmood is now Commander, and First Officer Bill Bryant is the next in command. George has no say at all in the government of SIL."

"I believe you underestimate your mate. I believe once he knows we are involved the balance of power may well change. But even if it does not, he is the only person who can speak to every individual on SIL. We have left a transmission disk in a magnetized compartment under your car chassis. We want you to establish a secure uplink and play the disk for him. It is a special disk, of course. It can only be played once. If played a second time, the laser beam that reads the disk will detonate it, for it is made of high density explosive material that has the power to eliminate all of Associated and most of the business district in Cambridge. Any attempt to play it first will have a disastrous result."

"But if it is played once and copied as it is played," she said, "the copy can be played and your disk destroyed easily by the explosives unit at another location."

"Well, to that I have only one reply," he said with gravity, "tell Woodward, or Woody as you like to call him, that it is really silly for him and your maid to have removed their shoes. Good bye, Lady Elizabeth." The line went dead.

Chapter 22

George knew the route well. His father had shown him the passages between the outer hull of SIL and the walls just inside of it. The intricate patterns of repetition were dizzying as the angled support beams formed their web structure which held the orbiting body together. He remembered the tour his father had taken him on, introducing him to every place he had hidden during his flight from the others on SIL right after he had caused the explosion in the second spare oxygen tank. They had wanted his father to pay for rendering them helpless and doomed in space. But the Commander had outsmarted his stalkers and, by traveling inside of the confinement between walls and hull, he had discovered that the result of the explosion had been the Eye itself, the huge man-made diamond which had proved to be the answer to sustaining life in space.

As George got closer to the location of the Eye he slowed, checking his progress so that he would not make any sound to foretell his arrival. He stopped using his jet pack and began to travel arm over arm like a monkey through this jungle of beams. As he approached the Eye area he saw that there were still signs of the intense heat that had been caused by the explosion. He saw also that nothing had changed in nearly 20 years since he had last been here. What he didn't see was any sign of a person.

He moved closer, until he was just a few meters from the edge of the Eye, where the outer hull was bent in at an extreme angle to meet the inner walls. No one was there. He examined the area expecting to find a bomb, but there was no bomb. He couldn't understand. He didn't see anything at all.

Being here, by the Eye, made him remember his father. He had longed for his father all of his young life. Even though his mother and step father had assured him SIL was lost in the accident and everyone had been killed, he believed the hope his heart gave him that his father was indeed alive. He hated his mother for abandoning hope, and his stepfather for intruding, invading his life and inserting himself as imposter into their fragile family.

He had been obstinate as a child, pursuing science to be exactly what his father wanted. He read everything, in every language just to be true to his father's belief that learning, education and reading were the things that gave mankind value.

He had suffered so much in those days. But he held on. Then, with his discovery of the lensing effect in the Earth's Van Allen Belt and the development of LOL, he received that first radio signal, so faint, so curious. The faint signal became a strong signal, and soon it was clear the signal was SIL. The joy was boundless, but quickly soured into doubt by the possibility that the ship was simply automatically broadcasting its signal due to automation.

But SIL was not a death ship sailing blindly. His father had survived. Everyone else on SIL had survived, other than the deaths from disease and old age that were inevitable. Commander McVee had created the non-Earth-reliant space habitat he had envisioned. George had reconnected with his father, and had become involved in SIL. He had had half of his life to spend with his dad. He started to cry. The weight of his father's death broke through his shock. Memories toppled over each other, straining his heart beyond its limit of loss. He lowered his head and cradled it in his hands as wave after wave of sob overcame him. He hit a lull in the tears and was staring at nothing in particular, hands still partly covering his eyes. Under the beam in front of him, right next to the Eye's edge, he saw a red glow. It was faint, and he wasn't sure he saw it at all. Then it was gone. He removed his hands from his face and looked more intently and it came back. Then was gone, then came back.

He looked under the beam and found a small radio signal tracking device. He knew it well from what he had gone through with the security team. The device, when used on Earth, allowed one to find it with a margin of error of about twenty inches due to the global satellite surveillance network. SIL was outside of the envelope of satellites, so he didn't know what kind of tracking it allowed off planet. As he was quite familiar with this device he knew how it worked. He reached down and removed it from the beam and stuck it in his pocket. To do that he had to reposition himself, and from his new location, he saw another one of the devices. He took it too, and searched all around the area and found five others, seven in all. With all of them in his pocket he realized he should return to the Overseers and report his findings. But he wanted to take another moment in this place to be with his father.

He returned to his perch and, as if tears were part of that location, began again to cry. With his muffled sobs he didn't hear the slight noise that came from behind. He was lost in grief one

Second Pass

moment, and in the next a hand grabbed him from behind with another holding a knife to his throat.

* * * * * * *

When George left for the Eye, Su Lee and Toby went to get Ali, leaving Malanga and Elizabeth with the Commander's body, Jun-Jun and the cocoon surrounding Willa. There were other finders assigned to different duties, but Malanga had to give her personal attention to these three. Willa was starting to protest being held captive in the now clear mass, and Jun-Jun was recovering normally, as she knew from the continued freelocking experiments under her care. He had stayed outside in space 72 seconds, which was far less than the 89 second length record, but it was enough to leave him unconscious for almost an hour.

Malanga was aware of her unique position. What she had witnessed was beyond anything ever done by anyone in the medical profession in history. She saw that the effects of prolonged life on SIL were reversing many of the signs of aging in the oldest citizens. She also saw that there were community responses to events. For example, many years earlier, when the exercise tray was first developed, only a few of the members of the crew actually used it. And while there were immediate results in the bodies of those who were exercising, as expected, she noticed that there were subtle changes in the bodies of all members of SIL, with more pronounced changes in the bodies of those who were working in the Eye Chamber.

This new plant was fascinating to her, for it dramatically changed the dynamic between plants and human health. This plant clearly had potent health impacting properties, but it seemed to have a consciousness, a willful investment in the health and well being of the humans who had worked with the plant. She intended to start to run some experiments to determine if this sentient connection was between the plant and humans in general, or just those who had worked with, and developed relationships with, the plant.

She was also eager to explore the implications of freelocking. The more she became involved in the experimentation process, the more it interested her. With this recent application of the technique, and the fact it allowed them to find Ali and to learn that SIL was being sabotaged made her keenly aware that freelocking was a tool, not just the demented folly of youth. For those who had done it, there were profound changes of psyche and personality.

She looked over at the Commander's body and felt regret. All of these new things, frontiers of medicine beyond every projection ever made of what space-based experimentation and application may have provided, he wouldn't be here to know about. She knew the Commander much better than anyone knew, and had been the closest there was to being his wife. Her own grief was larger than she could comprehend, and was, she knew, the one part of the human condition for which there was no cure other than time and reflection. But she didn't have time to take time. She would weep later.

* * * * * * *

Toby and Su Lee jetted through the dye vats and found the removable back wall to the storage room. They entered the netherworld between SIL's layers of skin. Su Lee gasped when she saw the repeated geometric shapes made by the support beams. They seemed to stretch forever, toward a far horizon in every direction. She realized how easily one could become lost in this labyrinth. Even though there was a system of numbers and colors to mark the different regions of SIL, these details were small and only existed as markings on the bases of each beam where it joined the others. She felt a fear grip her like nothing before. It was kin to such things as claustrophobia and agoraphobia, but was neither. The fear was that of disorientation, perhaps like what would happen when a pilot was blinded by nightfall or a storm and lost compass orientation, or when someone was lost in a snow storm. The uniformity of everything in sight erased the uniqueness of self identification.

"Are you okay?" asked Toby, seeing how pale she had become.

"I think so," she replied, "I feel panic wanting to take over. This is a very different kind of environment than I've encountered before."

Second Pass

"Just keep close to me, and touch me whenever you need to. Touch will reorient you to something relative to your self." He put an arm around her shoulders and gave her a squeeze.

They jetted on, with him checking the butts of the joining beams every now and then to get his directions. Eventually they came upon the area Jun-Jun had told them Ali could be found. In the distance they saw one of the beams that seemed a bit fatter than the rest, but otherwise unremarkable. As they neared it the thick shaft became lumpy and finally showed that Ali was bound tightly to it.

The space around him was slightly yellow from the pollen that had collected around him. Toby and Su Lee hovered just outside of the pollen haze and looked at Ali, who seemed to be sleeping. His face was beautiful. His thick black hair curled gently in tufts, and his smooth, uncreased eyelids, closed over his eyes, were outlined on the bottom by a perfect ridge of evenly spaced lashes. His nose was flat and broad, and his mouth was full with lips that appeared to be partly turned outward as if in a sensual kiss.

Toby reached forward to touch him and retracted his hand quickly. "Ouch!" he yelped. "That pollen dust feels like radiation exposure burn!" He shook his hand, rubbing it with the other.

Ali's eyes opened and a smile came across his lips. He looked far away for a moment, and the yellow cloud expanded to encircle Su Lee and Toby. Toby instinctively backed away to escape it, but it engulfed him too quickly. His skin prickled slightly, and then felt a warm glowing. "What the hell?"

"It will protect anyone I tell it to," Ali said. "It asked if you were okay and I said yes. But it will not let anyone I don't want to get near me. That's why she left."

"Who is she?" asked Su Lee. "Did she hurt you?"

"Well," Ali said, trying to rationalize, "she tried to. Well, not really hurt me, but to scare me. I knew she wasn't going to kill me with the knife." He looked down at the straps wound around him and then looked back at Toby. "Could you..."

"Of course," Toby and Su Lee said together. They found the ends of the straps and untied them, balling them up as they unwound them. Toby nodded to Su Lee with a wink as they did, and the two of them took many opportunities to give Ali little tickles as they did their work. Ali just threw his head back and laughed. His laughter was like a beautiful music, the kind of music a small waterfall would make if it sang.

Once free, Toby took Ali by the hand to lead him away from the area, but Ali pulled his hand free. "You are going the wrong direction," he said.

"No we aren't," replied Toby, "we are to get you back to Malanga right away."

"But we can't go there first," Ali protested, "we've got to help the Commander."

Su Lee and Toby looked at each other sadly. Ali didn't know the Commander had died. In fact, the announcement hadn't yet been made to the Overseers or Assembly, much less the general population of SIL. "The Commander is dead," said Toby, humming as he delivered the news.

"I know," said Ali, rolling his eyes at the silliness of adults, "he told me so himself. He needs us to go help his little boy."

"What do you mean?" asked Toby.

"He came to me through the plant dust. Well," he wrinkled his nose to try to figure out how to describe what he was meaning to tell, "the dust can shape itself. It turned into him, and he could talk to me that way. He said he was dead, but not gone yet. He is going to stay for a while, just to help until the Chinese people come. But his boy, the man called George, is in trouble now and we have to help him."

"What about the Chinese people?" asked Su Lee. "When are they coming?"

"Oh boy," Ali said with a disgusted click of his tongue followed by a forced sigh. "They are coming to take over SIL, but that isn't for a while. Common, we have to help Georgie!" He yelled at them over his shoulder as he jetted away in the direction of the Eye. Toby looked at Su Lee and shrugged and set off after Ali.

They flew through the maze of beams, Ali traveling far faster than either of them felt was prudent, but he would not slow so they were forced to keep up with him. He seemed to know exactly where he was going, and Su Lee started to feel a sensation of fun rather than gnawing panic. She caught up with Ali and was traveling next to him, enjoying the wind their quick movement was creating. Toby soon joined on the other side of Ali and the three sped through the widest part of the openings between the beams.

"This is fun!" said Toby. "How did you learn to find your way around out here, Ali?"

Second Pass

Su Lee looked over to hear the answer and saw that Ali's eyes were closed tight shut. She screamed and Toby looked over, seeing what she was seeing.

Ali only smiled. "I can't find my way when my eyes are open," he said. "The plant dust is leading me. Try it! If you just let it in your mind it can talk to you."

Su Lee refused to close her eyes, but couldn't argue with the fact that Ali has been traveling at high speed for quite a while, going between beams and periodically turning, without hitting anything. Toby tried to close his eyes and let the plant in, but there was no result.

"I can't do it," Toby said. "How do you let it in?"

"You know silly," he said teasingly, "like you found me. You let my real self in your mind and you were here with me."

Toby realized he was talking about following the essence and tried it. Again it didn't work. "Nope," he said, "nothing."

"Stop!" said Ali. "Quiet," he whispered. He had slowed to near hover and then turned off his jet, motioning to the others to do the same. They did, and followed Ali as he started to swing from beam to beam with his arms. They rounded a corner and saw ahead the back of a person who was obviously holding a knife at the throat of someone in front of them. There was the sound of George's voice.

Toby took Ali's shoulder and got his attention, motioning him to fall behind. As they did, the cloud of yellow dust left them and started toward George and his captor.

* * * * * * *

George sensed movement from behind and kept talking to distract attention. He knew as well that he had to keep facing away from whoever was approaching. "I can help you," he said. "Whatever you want from SIL, I can make it happen."

"You are useless," spat the voice. George identified that he was being held by a woman. He also saw out of the corner of his eye that her skin was red with a rash.

"Not so useless as you might think," he said calmly. "I can at least help you with that rash. It looks like radiation burn, and if you don't treat it quickly, it will make you very..."

"Shut the fuck up!" she snapped. "Don't try to help me now after you've done everything in your power to harm my entire family."

George recognized the voice, but couldn't place it. He had spoken to so many people since he arrived, the voices were all becoming confused. "If I've harmed your family, I did not intend to."

The knife cut slightly into his skin and he inhaled. "Didn't intend to, hah!" she said. The force of emotion behind her words made the knife move, stinging him. He saw a droplet of blood float up past his right eye.

He didn't know what to do. He sensed that the entire world was coming to an end. His father was dead and SIL was falling apart. His father's dream was becoming a nightmare. He wanted to be with Liz, to embrace her, and to hold their son. He wanted his life to be a different life, one belonging to someone with no famous family, no ambitions, no notoriety. He felt tears welling in him and fought to control his emotions.

Suddenly there was a different feeling in the air around him. His skin started to tingle and burn slightly. His captor let out a moan of pain and the knife loosened on his neck. "Fuck!" she said.

She turned her head away from George and caught sight of the three behind her out of the corner of her eye. She slashed George's arm deeply with the knife and gave him a sudden stab in the side. The knife went between two of his ribs and punctured his lung. He spasmed in pain and cried out. Having momentarily disabled George, she pulled something out of her left pocket with the left hand. It was a canister which she held up next to George's head and sprayed a quick mist. He immediately crumpled into unconsciousness. Then she did the same in the direction of Ali and sprayed a mist into the air. As soon as it reached them, Toby and Su Lee went limp in the air, unconscious. She turned and sprayed it at George, who was instantly rendered unconscious by the mist. Ali realized that he was not affected by it, but pretended to be and let his arms float up into the sleeping position of weightlessness, closing his eyes.

Inside of his head the plant showed him what was happening. The assailant reached into her waist pack and pulled out a radio device. She looked around to get her bearings, and then jetted about ten meters to the outer hull of SIL, pulling out a wire with

Second Pass

a suction device on the end. She attached it to the inside of the hull and waited an instant, then seemed content and pressed a button.

"Stevens, this is Becka, I have problems."

"Becka, damnit, you aren't to break silence!"

"I have four hostages, one is the Commander's son and he is badly wounded. I can kill them all if you want."

"No!" shouted Stevens. "Under no circumstances are you to harm McVee Junior! You had specific instructions!" He was in a rage.

"Listen to me," she said through clenched teeth, "I am doing what I have to to keep fucking alive. I'll kill them all, you fucking bastard, unless you can figure out a way to get me some help here."

"Okay, Becka," he said more calmly, "I know you are alone there and I appreciate what you are doing. Have you placed the markers around the Eye?"

"Yes."

"Are you able to hide for a few days until the other shuttles arrive?"

"I thought I was hiding, but somehow two of them found the boy. I don't know how."

"What is the situation exactly with your hostages. George is injured, what about the rest."

"I sedated them with the spray. They'll be out from that for about 6 hours."

"Okay," he was thinking. He needed three days until the large shuttles would arrive, but he needed her to be free to do more of the preparation. "Put patches on all of them, just below the right ear on the neck. That will keep them unconscious until you take the patches off. Secure them wherever you need to so they won't be found. As for George, Jr," he said with a sigh, "leave him somewhere he will be found. He cannot die, do you hear me?"

"His lung is punctured and his arm cut at the shoulder. Neither of those wounds will kill him unless they get infected." She detested Stevens more than anyone in her life. He had been ruthlessly cruel to her and her husband, creating a financial dependence on him they would never be free of. She would much rather have stabbed him than George, but the wounds inflicted were her only option to subdue him while she dealt with the others.

"Do it," Stevens barked, "and then go to the CommLink and for fuck's sake disable their communications!" The link clicked off.

She looked over at the mass of floating bodies. George had several shimmering balls of red around him, with more forming. She first went and applied a tourniquet at the very top of his arm and saw that the blood stopped flowing from that cut. She bound his ribs with a long scarf she had, and trussed his ankles and wrists, joining them together behind his back.

She then turned to the others and dreaded getting anywhere near the boy and his cloud of yellow. Her skin had broken out so badly in reaction to it she was now seeping clear liquid and, in some places, small amounts of blood. The reaction was confined only to areas of exposed skin, however, so she could cope with it for now. Anticipating the burning pain of entering the cloud, she got three patches out of her waist pouch and jetted toward them.

Reaching Toby first, she applied the patch, and while doing so noticed the coiled straps he had stuffed into the carrying compartment of his jetpack. She got them out and bound him in the same manner as George. She then went to Su Lee and did the same. When she turned back to Ali she panicked to see he, and his cloud of yellow poison, had disappeared. Hanging absolutely still in the air to listen, she heard nothing other than the beating of her own heart.

She decided to deal with finding him after she had the others secured and hidden. She threaded a single strap through the ties that held wrists to ankles on all three of her hostages, and proceeded further from the Eye area of the outer ship. She decided to place them near the water distillation area, since it had the loudest continuous sound on all of SIL, just in case they woke up and tried to attract attention by making noise.

She looked at the straps and decided she needed to make it more secure if she were to haul them half way around the outer perimeter of SIL. She yanked open the Velcro connection and continued about her business for another full fifteen seconds before she realized that there had been no sound when the Velcro was opened. She examined the Velcro patches and found nothing unusual about them, then proceeded to push them together and tear them apart several times. No sound at all, even though she could feel the fibers overcoming their friction connection with

Second Pass

each other. "Damn it!" she yelled in frustration, and stopped cold.

She could not hear. The problem wasn't the Velcro, it was that she was totally deaf. Her hands flew to her ears and she felt them, reaching inside with her fingers. There was a sticky residue all around the inside of her ear, and when she pulled her finger back out and looked at it, there was a bright yellow jelly on it. She opened her pack and found a pen and tried to reach into her ear canal with it to dig the stuff out. There was no change. She was deafened by the goop in her ears. She would need some type of swab to clean them out. Knowing her condition was not permanent she ignored it as best she could and trundled off with her three lifeless bundles trailing behind her, running into beams every now and then.

Chapter 23

Solange Malanga returned to her quarters exhausted. Jun-Jun was completely restored after his freelocking work, and had returned to his own quarters for the night. The Commander's body was placed in a cryotank until George returned to make some of the fundamental decisions. The fact he had not returned from his mission to intercept the saboteur from placing a bomb near the Eye concerned her. Andrew Stetler had sent a team of 8 to find him and found nothing. There was no bomb anywhere near the Eye, nor was there any sign that there had been. She wondered if the information delivered by Jun-Jun had been some sort of delirium, but she was unwilling to challenge him about it until he was stronger.

When the team returned empty handed, and another team failed to find Ali, tensions were extremely high. Toby and Su Lee had not returned either, and could not be found. Malanga was getting criticism for having sent them based on information received from freelocking, and at the same time others were demanding that she have Jun-Jun, or one of the other freelockers to repeat the exercise and find out where everyone was. Malanga had not known what to do, for to placate either side was to inflame the other. At one point she had excused herself and gone to the Chapel, just to get away from everyone.

While in the Chapel she performed an intuitive trance, tracing the essences of Ali, George, Toby and Su Lee. The result was clear visions of the life-saving plant, and a strong sense that everything was fine if she would only wait out the not knowing. She sat in the Chapel for nearly an hour, which, for her, was an eternity. When she left she chose to go through the gallery where there was a display of photographs of SIL taken by Hubble IV during the last pass and also during the current one. She took interest in the trail of matter following SIL through space. Her musings were interrupted by an urgent alert that came from the Finding Chambers.

She entered the chamber to find a fourth bed occupied by George, Jr. He had been found by engineers floating in a corridor near the sewage processing plant. She had tended him, drained his collapsed lung and mended his wounded upper arm, and eventually brought him back to semi-consciousness. He would not speak until they were alone.

"My father is still here," he said in a rattling voice with constant coughing to clear his lungs. She saw he was delirious and humored him. She patted his head lovingly and he continued. "There was no bomb, only tracking devices around the Eye. She doesn't know I've removed them. My father has showed us the way through the mist and the dust. She sedated the others, and can talk through the walls." Then he fell back asleep. She was now certain he was delirious, and put him into deep sleep until the following day. BQ had made her aware that Liz had demanded a private CommLink conversation with him, and she'd asked BQ to deliver the message that he was busy but would link to her in the next 24 hours. Liz had agreed.

She and her select group had decided to keep the news of the Commander's death from the Overseers, and she had reported to Machmood that he had suffered a stroke and was in a coma. That kept them away, made Machmood acting Commander, and got everyone off of her back for several days, if it turned out she needed the time.

Sleep came quickly to her, sleep so deep it held no dream. Her nose started itching and running in sleep, and she awoke sneezing into the open air. She reached for her absorption swab, waved it around in the area of the sneeze to collect all of the droplets of phlegm and then placed it back against the clip hook that held it. But it was grabbed out of her hand. Her eyes flew open.

Beside her bed floated Ali, with his finger pressed against his lips. She was startled, but did not cry out. Instead, she looked at him and waited. Her gaze calmed him and challenged him. She was, by remaining silent, offering nothing with which to fill the space of this encounter. He could have done nothing, said nothing, and left, leaving the encounter empty and unfulfilled. Or he could do anything at all, which proposed a supreme challenge for this child.

He took his finger away from his lips and reached out to her. She pulled him to her as he began to cry. He cried softly at first, but the storm within him grew from her permission into a raging typhoon. He sobbed violently, pounding her shoulders with his fists. Eventually the storm passed and he fell asleep in her arms. She tucked him into a spare sleeping sack and bathed his face with a warm wet cloth, removing the tear salt from his skin so it wouldn't be irritating in the morning. She placed his sack next to hers and returned to her dense, total sleep.

She woke to find Ali stroking her hair. He sat with crossed legs, floating in front of her. She gradually opened her eyes and looked at him, again offering him space to fill. This time he spoke.

"Toby and Su Lee are being kept asleep for 6 days," he began, "from patches on their necks. Dr. George has been cut and is going to be left to be found so he won't die."

"We did find him," she said softly, "yesterday. He won't die. He will be well again."

"The Commander spoke to us out of the plant dust," he said, then wrinkled his eyebrows, knowing that these words would not make sense, so he backed up. "The plant protects those who care for her, and everyone they care for. It sent dust, yellow dust, to follow me when the angry lady took me. The dust can decide if it will help you or make you sneeze and itch. The Commander, after he died, was able to organize the dust, make it in his shape, just bigger. He could speak that way. He said the Chinese people were coming. I think they are coming to take over SIL."

Malanga considered this. She knew well of the Commander's offer to receive 750 people on SIL via the new Chinese super shuttles, but that he would only allow half of them to be Chinese. She also remembered that there would be 51 shuttle loads of new supplies to build extensions onto SIL so that, by next pass, thousands more people could come. He had offered her methods of Finding as the means of exchange payment for all of this. But he had later told her Mr. Hwan had violated his trust and the exchange was cancelled. She let none of this reflect on her face. Ali continued.

"The angry lady has to kill people to feel powerful, and to make everyone scared. She is very frustrated that the plant won't let her kill people."

"Why, then," Malanga wondered out loud, "would she insist on attempting murder repeatedly and exclusively in the Eye Chamber where the plant resides?"

Ali closed his eyes. His head tilted slightly to the side and a wan smile overtook his lips. When his eyes opened he spoke. "She has brought some people here who are trying to help her take SIL. She is making everyone scared so that more people, the strongest, will be put into security groups, to hunt down the murderer. That will mean the ones with strong arms from the Eye Chamber will

Second Pass

leave, and others will be killed. Then, to get enough people to keep the Eye Chamber going her people will volunteer. That is why she killed Madam Jiimson-Marsdon, so she wouldn't be the one in charge to choose who comes to help." His voice shot up an octave abruptly at the end of this and he began to cry. He loved Willa more than anyone.

"She is not dead," Malanga said, "she lives stronger than ever. But why did the, uh, angry woman try to kill you?"

Ali looked blankly, shocked by discovery, as if he were learning for the first time she had tried to end his life. He got a worried, confused look on his face, then closed his eyes as before, tilting his head and calming his face. Malanga performed a mental EMP as he did this, and saw he was in rapid communication inside of his brain. He opened his eyes and continued. "I am the link to the plant, she thinks. If I'm gone, the plant can't interfere with her plans. She didn't tell the man about the plant, she's too afraid."

"What man?" asked Malanga.

"The man called Steven. She talks to him through the outside wall of SIL."

"When you close your eyes, who do you talk to in your mind?" she asked.

"I don't talk, I listen," he said tersely.

"So true," she laughed, "to whom do you listen?"

"The plant." He looked at her and saw she was about to ask more questions, and he wanted to keep telling her things. "Don't ask about the plant now, it isn't important yet. What is important is stopping the Chinese people from taking SIL away, and the man Steven from coming here."

"Ali," she began, "I will let you talk about whatever is the most important thing. But I have one question about the plant. May I ask it?"

He pursed his lips, then sucked them between his teeth. "Okay," he said, "one question."

Malanga smiled at the businesslike quality of this child, seeing a great leader in him. "Does the plant talk to you, or show you pictures of things?"

Ali thought about this. It wasn't easy to describe. "It doesn't really do either one," he said with hesitancy, "it just lets me know things."

"Like now things, or future things?"

"That's not one question," he said flatly, looking at her with disappointment.

"You are right," she admitted, "but let me explain what I am trying to figure out. If the Chinese people are coming, and if Stevens is coming, I want to know if the plant can show us when, and how to prepare, or if it can only tell us things about now."

He closed his eyes and tilted his head. He took a deep breath in and when he breathed out a cloud of yellow mist came out of his nostrils. She attempted to back away from it, but it grew too quickly and soon enveloped her. She felt her skin tingle and her muscles calm. When Ali started to speak it wasn't his voice, but the voice of the Commander. But Ali's mouth wasn't moving. She suddenly realized that the Commander was speaking directly into her head through the yellow cloud.

"Sweet Solange," he began, "you are my beloved in death as you were in life. There is much you must understand. I have betrayed my people in an effort to protect them. SIL is much smaller than China, and my error was to think that distance protected us."

She wanted to talk to him, but when she tried to think to him she could tell she wasn't making contact.

"Speak normally," the Commander's voice said in her head, "I will hear you."

"George," she started to cry, "I love you so. You didn't betray anyone, ever. But what is happening?"

"You and everyone on SIL are in grave danger. It is my fault. I denied the Chinese all access to SIL, thinking I could do that, but they are bigger, stronger, and I am convinced they are coming to take SIL, kidnap you, and steal what they think is immortality from you."

She gasped at the thought. "But I..."

"You will have to be smarter than they are. You cannot be bigger."

"I have ordered that the docking ports be permanently altered, so no known ship can dock."

"I know that," she said, "you did that before this pass began."

"I have done it again, since then. Bryant is making it so. The stolen shuttles can access both portal opening configurations by using the adapters from before. The Chinese can only dock with the original configuration. The new portal configuration will be

Second Pass

such that none of them can dock with us. Bryant will only give it out to those who are to be trusted for future shuttles that will be built by next pass."

"You have always been clever," she said. "What do we need to do?"

"You must find the one who is trying to kill. She is working with Stevens, and was on my son's security team. I do not know her name. She came here with her husband."

"Becka Masters," said Malanga. "I know who she is. Ali has just told me why she is killing."

"Listen to him, he is the voice of Truth. What he thinks is the plant is beyond any plant. Trust him only, but do not let anyone know he holds this Truth. If he is exposed, he will be killed."

"But she already knows he has the connection to the plant."

"She thinks the plant will only protect people if he is here. She only thinks the plant is preventing her from taking over the Eye Chamber, nothing more."

"Why does she want the Eye Chamber?"

"Hwan thinks in Chinese terms. He is convinced that Finding refers to plant essences you've discovered or that were biologically engineered here on SIL. For him, with thousands of years of herbal medicine as part of his cultural heritage, he thinks the reversal of the aging process comes from the plants. He had hired Stevens to infiltrate SIL, place people in the Eye Chamber and then take samples of all of the plants."

"But how can Stevens and his crew possibly take over SIL? There are more than a thousand of us."

"I don't know the exact plan. And now that I'm dead, I can't find it out. You will have to figure it out. That is why you must protect Ali at all costs. He alone will be able to know what is going on."

"How can I protect him?" she asked with a bit of exasperation, "and how can I get the Overseers to listen to what he says?"

"I do not know." Ali's body convulsed and his eyes snapped open. He looked around the room and started to cry.

"What happened to me?" he said, terrified.

Malanga gathered him in her arms. "The Commander used your mind to speak to me, that's all."

"I don't want him in my mind," Ali cried. "Get him out!"

"He won't be doing it again," she said, "I assure you." She took him into her arms and rocked him back and forth until he calmed. She felt such compassion for this child, who was so frightened, and had such responsibility thrust on him. "Ali," she said quietly.

"Yes Finder Malanga," he replied, breathing spastically as the tears subsided.

"We need to talk about some things, some very serious things."

His hand twisted her shirt absentmindedly. "Wh—what things?" He was so afraid.

"Nothing bad," she said calmly, "but they are serious. You know that there are people who are trying to take SIL. You are going to be very important to them if they know you can know things from the plant. I need you to play a game with me, a game of pretend."

"I like playing pretend," he said, wanting to be eager but shy of it.

"In this game of pretend, you will tell me the things the plant lets you know, but nobody else. With everybody else you will pretend that the plant can't talk or make you know things at all."

"But everybody can see the yellow stuff the plant keeps around me. They will know."

"Yes, that is a problem. Let me see about that. Stay here for a moment." She jetted to her kitchen and looked around. "Come in here Ali, will you please?" she yelled to the other room.

Soon he was at her side. "Watch this," she said. She took some sugar and put a drop of lemon juice in it, and then grated some of the lemon's rind into the mixture. She had him taste it, and he loved the sweet lemony taste. Having gotten his approval, she put it into the heat compressor and raised the temperature to 300 degrees Fahrenheit. She then had him drop it into a vat of cold water. The result was hard, yellow balls of lemon candy.

She dried them on a towel and gave one to him. "Here, what do you think?"

He tasted it and smiled. "Very good! Can I have some more?"

"Yes, young man. In fact, you must have one every hour that you are awake."

He looked suspicious. "Madame Marsdon doesn't like me to eat too much candy."

Second Pass

"This isn't candy!" She made a comical outraged face when she said this, making him laugh. "You have a rare disease, a *deadly* disease, and if you don't eat this every hour for the rest of your life, you will die a horrible death." She tickled his stomach with this last line. He howled with laughter.

"You're silly."

"Me? Silly? How can you say that when I'm saving your life?" She made large motions with her hands, playing the pompous doctor to his delight. "There is only one side effect of this medication, other than saving your life, that is."

His eyes got wide in mock fear. "What is that, Finder Malanga?"

"It will make a yellow cloud of dust follow you everywhere you go. Some people will be allergic to it, others will not. But you will always be surrounded by a cloud of yellow."

"Yay! I get yellow dust!"

They laughed and played. Ali felt much better about everything, and Malanga knew this would buy her time. Eventually there would be questions as to what exact disease he had, and if it was contagious. Contagion was one of the biggest fears on SIL. There was a knock at the door of her quarters. She jetted to the door and opened it. Ali came into the room after her and shrieked when he saw Willa in the doorway, along with Hermes Whipple.

"Do come in," said Malanga. Willa buzzed right past her, going directly to Ali.

"Are you all right?" she asked.

"Yes," he answered. "Are you?"

"Excuse me," Malanga interrupted, "how did you get out of the cocoon? How did you know where Ali was?"

"We are connected now," said Hermes. "Everyone the plant has saved will always know exactly where the others are."

"That is what I was trying to tell you from inside of that thing," said Willa. "We know everything about each other at all times."

"Uh oh," said Ali, waving his hands around the air. He jetted to the kitchen and came back with a little plastic bag of the yellow candies. "It looks like they will need to take their medicine, to save them from their very terrible disease."

Malanga looked at the two of them and saw that they, too, were surrounded by a cloud of yellow. This would make her job much easier, showing that the 'contagion' factor had to do with having been saved by the plant. It was going to be hard to convince Willa to take candy every hour. "Let me explain," she began.

When she had finished they had decided many things. Ali would be in custody of Malanga at all times. They would immediately post a volunteer sign up station for new workers in the Eye Chamber, and everyone who volunteered would be placed in a training program that would be under the supervision of Arthur Stetler, the former head of Security, and Willa Jiimson-Marsdon. The training would take place near the waste removal chambers on the opposite side of SIL from the Eye Chamber.

Commander McVee's body would be hooked up to life-support systems to keep if from decay, and to create a political situation where Machmood would continue temporary duties of Commander, but Bill Bryant would take control of SIL for the expressed purpose of assuring all access to SIL was tightly controlled.

Malanga called a private meeting in her quarters including Paul and BQ Dunn, Sylvia and Bill Bryant, McKenna, Tom and Shandor Robinson, and George, Jr. The meeting decided the course of the future of SIL. The meeting was kept completely secure and, with luck, no one would ever know it took place.

Chapter 24

Liz and Woody had waited for nearly two hours by the large CommLink screen. George was coming, Sylvia kept assuring them. Strangely, there was little talk between Associated and Earth, and Liz and Woody were also silent. Liz had tersely announced to everyone present upon her arrival she had nothing to say except to George. Period. And then she had remained silent.

Woody had not questioned Liz's demand for complete privacy, and had prepared the situation at Associated accordingly, giving all technicians the day off and then locking all entry doors to the CommLink area. He had also had security come in and completely sweep the area for any listening devices, an effort matched by the programmers who had worked round the clock to make sure there was no infiltration through computer connections.

Sylvia came onto the screen and announced that George had arrived and, as George came into view on the screen, she could be seen jetting across the room and exiting, closing a door behind her. Woody made sure the link was secure, then left. Liz and George looked at each other.

"Hey there," said Liz. "It's been quite a week. You look like you are holding yourself together...," she looked at him and smiled. "Well, you and some gauze and tape. Is there pain?"

George smiled, so fond of her his heart ached much more than his wounds. "You've been a rock, Liz. An absolute rock."

Liz felt emotion rise in her throat, but mastered it and calmed. "George, we need to talk. I know some things that are, well," she couldn't categorize them. "The Chinese Chairman has contacted me."

"What? Again?"

"Yes, again," she said. "He threatened SIL if I don't play a disk for you. It is apparently an explosive device that can only be played once without incident. He wants to bring me to SIL, but will not bring us back home afterward."

"My father said they were the answer in his last words," he sighed, squashing an emotional surge. "You'd better play the disk," he said with resignation.

Liz looked through the window and motioned to Woody to play the disk. He placed it in the slot and pressed the play button. Liz had expected something to show on the screen, but instead it was just an audio recording of a conversation between Hwan and the Commander.

"This is Commander McVee," his father's voice said.

"Ah my friend," Hwan's replied, "it is time for us to make our final contract."

"It is."

"This is being recorded, as I'm sure you are recording on your end, to assure what we speak of here can be verified later as a valid contract."

"We are recording as well."

"So, my friend, what is your answer."

"SIL, at this point in time, cannot accept the help of the Chinese people in the population or development of SIL. We do not trust that your motives are clear."

There was silence on the disc. George was shocked at the abruptness of his father, but not at the content. His father was independent first and foremost.

"There is no negotiation?" asked Hwan. "You introduced me to your Finder Malanga with promises of great things to help my people. We are most interested in what you have to offer us. Surely something of what we have offered is of interest to you."

"Oh, be very certain, Hwan. What you offer is exactly what we want and need. We could use materials to build expansions onto SIL. We could use the workers, and the money. It would make me very happy to, by next pass, be able to house an additional three or four thousand inhabitants on SIL."

"Then why are you eliminating the possibility of all exchange?" His voice now changes on the disk from friendly diplomat to menacing villain. "Why would you place SIL in such a vulnerable place, knowing we can reach you with an army of workers to accomplish any task we may wish to accomplish?" His use of the word army was not lost on Liz or George, and apparently not on the Commander either.

"You will send no army to SIL. And we are not as vulnerable as you might suspect." The commander's voice now grew louder and more firm. "The most important fact to understand is that we are a sovereign nation, and are not willing to be a pawn in any game, nor a stepping stone to space domination. We are to be respected, regardless our small size."

Second Pass

"You have our utmost respect," Hwan said too quickly to be believable. He paused for several uncomfortable moments. "Perhaps we can scale back our negotiation."

"I'm listening."

"We have already loaded 23 shuttles with the materials to build housing for an additional 1200 people. We could deliver these materials to you in exchange for information about the health practices Madame Finder Malanga has developed. In fact," he sounded excited in a phony carnival barker way, "we can make our first delivery and bring her back to lecture to our scientific community, then return her when the last delivery arrives."

Commander McVee laughed spontaneously. "You think we would allow you to take her to China? That is outrageous!" He roared with laughter. When it died down he continued. "No, you can send your scientists here to study with her. There is no sense in her demonstrating her techniques in a gravitational environment. Her work is based on a weight free atmosphere."

"I'm afraid we do not have the time to gather our scientists."

"Well then, it looks like my first assessment of the situation stands. There will be no exchange."

"We do not consider this conversation over, Commander McVee. We will make contact again when you have had more time to think."

The sound on the tape stopped, but suddenly Hwan's face appeared on the screens in both CommLink facilities. "And so our Chairman has contacted Madame Elizabeth, mother of the child of the Commander's son." He looked at the camera directly, his fat face filling nearly the entire screen. "As our Chairman has said in this contact, we have no control over the vulnerability of SIL in space. A non-Earth-reliant colony is of great interest to the people of China, and we remain dedicated to pursuing the extraordinary advances in health care your Finder Malanga has invented. We ask you to allow cooperation between SIL and China."

The disk went blank; screens returned to the video conference mode.

"I believe SIL is going to be attacked by China," Liz said bluntly.

"I don't know," said George, "while the Chinese intelligence is good, we have already begun a process that will make it impossible for them to dock. And Sylvia and BQ have created programs that will completely erase the systems memories that run SIL's different environmental and life-support works. Only those who have lived on SIL before the last pass will be able to operate her systems manually. The Chinese wouldn't have a chance even if they were able to dock and board."

"What about Malanga?" asked Liz. "It seems she was somehow in on this. Might they attempt to kidnap her?"

"I will speak with her presently. I don't think they would get much out of her if they tried. She has mind control skills that are extraordinary."

"What's going to happen, George? Why does the Chairman call me and threaten me? What does he think that will accomplish?"

"They obviously think you will influence me to let them come to SIL. In their mind the son takes over for the father."

"Oh come on, they can't be so incredibly dense? I mean, the man is leader of the largest nation on Earth. They acknowledge other forms of government, other systems. He said it himself, they are a very old country. They know how the world works. It just doesn't make sense."

"Unless," George said with an air of depressed weight, "they think they can force me to do something by threatening you and Georgie. That might very well work wonders on me."

She hadn't thought of that at all. She hadn't considered that she and her son might be in jeopardy. "That makes me more angry than it does scared," she said, her lips a thin white line. "That anyone would harm a child to get what they want."

"I don't know that they would harm you, but they may well threaten you."

"Do you think they are the ones behind Masters and his group?"

"Well, I'm sure that Stevens is behind them. Perhaps they are in bed with him as incentive to make him do what they want. Stevens has always been completely vulnerable to any sort of temptation. He is a very weak man. I should never have allowed him to interview us when we returned from SIL that first time." He thought about that for a few moments.

"What should we do? Why not allow them to deliver the materials they have prepared, and even send some workers? There will be a full 18 years before SIL returns again. In that time the Chinese group would be the minority by far. How much damage could they do?"

Second Pass

"Well," George was feeling tired, his shoulder aching, "things here are very unsettled. We haven't let people know my dad is dead yet. Machmood doesn't know he's really in charge. There is a terrible amount of resentment against the new arrivals. Hell, BQ and Paul have never been welcomed here in all the time they've been here. Even their daughters are treated like some kind of lower class citizens. It is this kind of unrest that makes it really easy for an outside force to come in and take charge."

"George," Liz bit her lip to keep it from trembling. "I want to come to SIL. I want to bring Georgie and be there, even if the Chinese take over. Whatever happens, I want it to happen to us together as a family. I can't bear to be here away from you." She started to cry quietly.

George saw her crying, and saw how brave she was. "I want you here too," he said. "But if you come here, then they will have access to the ship. They have 70 vehicles that could all arrive. I believe they do have 23 shuttles loaded and ready to go, they are arrogant like that. But that means, also, that they could load a fighting force of nearly 11,000 men on the first trip. We wouldn't stand a chance. And the rest of the world would have to sit by and watch, unable to do anything."

"Well, at least unable to do anything in space. Remember, George, that the United States still has a superior arsenal of weapons on Earth, and the current administration is rather trigger happy and hates the Chinese. I don't think they would sit back and do nothing. But I believe there is another way."

"What is that?"

"The other shuttles," she said. "What if the Chinese go there and then are prohibited from boarding SIL because they don't have the proper adapter to dock? It is clear that the Chinese must have some plan to meet up with the other shuttles. Maybe I could come on the Chinese shuttle and somehow get onto the other shuttle." She stopped herself, realizing that what she was saying was simply ridiculous. Her tears returned, now flowing freely. "I just can't accept there is no way for us to be together again." She sobbed.

George hung in the air, his arms and chest aching to hold his partner, to comfort her. He was as bereft as she at the thought of being separated. "Liz, let me get together with everyone here, my team. We have to tell the population that the Commander is dead, and install Machmood as the new Commander. But before we do that, I will meet with McKenna, Gould, Robinson and the others. We will figure this out." He didn't know what they could do, but there was something he felt that prevented him from losing hope. "Keep close to Woody," he said, "you don't have security anymore. I'll speak with you in a few hours. Can you and Georgie stay there at Associated?"

"Yes," she said, "we can. And we will. I'm so frightened, George. I will stay here. May I speak about this with Woody?"

"Yes. I trust him completely. He's got a good head on his shoulders; maybe he can come up with some ideas."

Liz thought about what the Chairman had said about finding out the specs for the docking port alterations, and his threat that she wasn't to tell George, but somehow to get them. She didn't want to do anything behind George's back, but she felt, for the moment, that she shouldn't speak of that. George noticed her hesitation, and sensed something else had remained unspoken.

"Is there something else?" he asked. "Did you want something more?"

"I'll talk to you in a few hours, George," she said looking intensely at him, "I have to go now." She pressed the disconnect button so quickly she was sure George would figure something was wrong. It was her attempt to speak in a way other than words. And that little gesture reminded her of something she and George had discussed and planned for more than fifteen years before.

* * * * * * *

George went directly from the CommLink center to the Finding Station. His father's body was still on a life-supporting system in the main room. It wouldn't be suspected he was actually dead, though it was clear that he was in grave condition. Malanga was with him when George entered the room. She looked up and he could see the glittering of hundreds of miniscule droplets of tears around the two of them.

"You really loved him, didn't you?" George asked rhetorically.

She looked at him and, though she was startled by his sudden appearance in the room, she was too numb to jump. "George," she said softly, "he was the closest thing to a husband I'll ever have in my life. I love him more deeply than anyone knew."

Second Pass

"I can only hope that my recognition of your relationship can help you now. For all purposes you are my mother, Solange, and we are a family in mourning. That the others don't know or understand hurts, I know." He jetted gently to her and they embraced. Neither one cried, though. There was a different kind of comfort each was experiencing that made tears inappropriate for the moment. They were discovering each other in that embrace, a discovery that made their entire realities shift and realign.

"How is Liz?" asked Malanga.

"She is scared," he said. "The Chinese have threatened her. I believe she is in serious danger and there's not a damned thing I can do about it."

"George," she said, pulling her head away from his shoulder so she could look into his eyes, "I need to talk to you. There are things with the Chinese you don't know about. Nobody knows about. Things your father and I..."

"I do know," said George. "I just received a message from Hwan, a recorded conversation between him and my father. They discussed you. That is why I came here. I believe you are in as much danger as Liz."

"Pawns in a chess game," she said with resolution. "Tell me, George, what kind of a woman is Liz?"

The question surprised George. It seemed out of place. "What do you mean? In what way are you asking? She is remarkable in so many ways."

"Well, I was thinking less of her capabilities and more of her manner," Malanga said. "I want to understand how she operates and reacts."

George knew that this question would, from anyone else, irritate him and make him defensive. That it hadn't had that effect surprised him, almost as if it should have offended him somehow and didn't. But he knew he needed to answer, and his answer had to be accurate. "Well, she is direct, honest. She doesn't like waste of any kind, including wasted words. Some people find her abrupt, a bit callous I suppose, even rude. But she knows her mind and is not willing to put up with any nonsense."

"Wow!" Malanga laughed this word in a single burst. "I'd give anything to witness her conversations with the Chairman. He is pure nonsense and waste."

"I believe the word you are looking for is bullshit." He laughed bitterly.

"I wasn't going to say that." She looked at the Commander's body and sighed. "But how does she react under stress? She is a remarkable scientist, which takes patience and poise. At the time she developed her mapping system it was a man's world. How did she handle it? The sexism and everything?"

"Well, it was because of it that she was able to do her work," he explained. "She had made a concerted effort to get a position at Associated, and was so intent on working there she took a job that was way beneath her skill level. She put up with the mistreatment she got by keeping to herself. When the guys found she wasn't going to even acknowledge their lewd flirting, and she didn't seem to have any fuse whatsoever when they slighted her, so they soon ignored her. And that's how she did it. If someone needed anything, she always knew exactly where it was to be found. If there was extra work, or work nobody wanted because it was grunt work, she did it without complaint or question. This way she gained access to every division, and gained trust universally, but without anyone even realizing what she was doing. When she announced her mapping system it caught everyone by surprise."

"Well then, son," she said with a smile, "it seems my daughter-in-law has every quality I could ever dream of. When you talk to her again, let her know that she and I will be great friends one day."

George thought this was a bit strange, small talk of this kind in the circumstances. But he also knew that Malanga was always doing something other than what she was doing.

"George?" Malanga asked.

"What is it?"

"Do you have any way of getting information to her without anyone realizing that is what is happening?"

"How do you mean?" he asked.

"I need to explain things to her strategically," Malanga said. "You see, I believe she and I will be under a particular kind of attack by the Chinese and I need her to fully understand what is happening. But I need the information to be given to her without anyone realizing that anything at all is going on between us. She and I need to be pawns in each others games without anyone suspecting we even know each other."

Second Pass

"There is a way," he said. "We did develop a contingency plan for communication when we were being watched, particularly when one of us is on a screen. I've been under much observation in my life, and I'm often interviewed on the autovision, or in the news or just lecturing. So we did develop a sort of private system. What do you need to tell her?"

"Unfortunately for you, it is necessary you not know anything at all that I am telling her. For your own safety."

George didn't like this at all. "I have to know! What are you saying? She and I have no secrets!" There was more emotion in his voice than he intended.

"Calm down," she hummed, "it isn't what you think. There are things the Chinese want from me and they will go to extreme lengths to get them I'm afraid. I need her to understand some of the things that are happening here, and in the Eye Chamber. When I am gone, what I leave behind will not be the whole story. I need to leave the missing pieces with one person, and I think that person is Liz."

"Why not Elizabeth, or Toby, or one of your Finder apprentices?" he was sweating. This talk of Malanga not being around left him feeling unsettled and threatened.

"It can't be anyone that has direct ties to me. I have to make sure that if the Chinese do come here, and take over SIL, that they are defenseless against the environment here and will be forced to leave because they can't survive." She looked at him, beseeching his understanding with her eyes. "I need someone to be able to come here after they've left and make it come back to life again. SIL's future must be assured beyond this current threat from the Chinese."

"When you put it that way," he said, "I have to agree. And of everyone in the world I know, Liz is the only person I'd trust with that kind of information."

"I'm glad you see that. I'm glad we agree."

"What do you need to give to her?"

"I'll send something to Woody. I'll send many, many things. Within it will be hidden the information and I need to let her know where to look."

"She and I will be speaking again on the CommLink in a few hours. I can do it then." They talked about how they would set up the transfer of information for about twenty minutes, until they had worked out a plan.

"I should tell you about the Chinese, George," Malanga continued, "about what has happened."

"We need to have a meeting," he said, "that includes a very select group of people. If SIL is to survive, these people must join together. I want to call a summit here in about an hour. I want to hold the meeting at Paul's residence. I'll need you and Toby; Elizabeth Dunn will already be there. But other than that, no one else."

"Agreed. But Toby is gone. We cannot find him or Su Lee."

"Where were they?"

"They went to find Ali, when you were at the Eye to get the bomb. They never returned."

George didn't have time to deal with this information. "We can do it without them for now. I'll need you more than ever now. Meet me at the Dunn's in an hour."

"I'll go transmit what I have to get to Liz through Woody, then I'll be there." George took a last look at his father's body and jetted out of the chamber.

* * * * * * *

One benefit of being detested on SIL as Paul and BQ were, was that their living quarters were far from the general area set aside for living. They had been put nearer the environmental maintenance facilities. The advantage was that people could travel to their home from any number of routes, none of which would be suspected as having their quarters as its final destination. Each of the people coming to meet with George had been instructed to travel a different path to get there.

Elizabeth greeted each one as they arrived, inviting them into the main living module where they took places around the room. Some used the Velcro tethers, others just the foot mounts, while others chose to simply hover. Tom and Shandor arrived together, and a bit early. Shandor had taken a liking to Erica, Elizabeth's twin sister. His hopes to run into her were dashed when he learned that she was in the exercise room. He and his dad were in one corner talking idly about the differences between Earth and SIL.

Solomon Gould had come through the education center to get there, mainly because of his interest in education, but also because he had never been on that side of SIL. He was impressed at how easily the children seemed to focus on their work. His analytical mind wanted to draw some conclusion from that, like children on SIL had fewer distractions or that learning and survival were more obviously linked even in the young mind's concept of the world, but just as he was settling into these thoughts a ruckus arose. One of the boys, at the urging of his friends, had reached over with his foot and kicked one poor girl's leg, sending her spinning in spirals away from her desk module. It took several minutes for the teacher to settle the snickering boys, soothe the girl, and discover the culprit and send him out of the room for discipline, which he went to skulkingly. It was a very normal classroom scene.

Gould's entrance was accompanied by some old chum chatter with Tom, that quickly was reduced to extreme sorrow over the many friends they shared who had recently been murdered by Stevens and his men. Gould had spent his entire adult life developing Associated, and Tom had assisted him from over at MIT. Sorrow became anger, then resignation to find these culprits and bring them to justice. As they were speculating just what this justice might be, McKenna arrived.

He came into the room and was saying his hellos when BQ and Sylvia turned up at the door. The only ones missing were Paul, Malanga and George. Malanga had said she would be a little late, just five minutes or so, and please wait for her to begin. Paul was at work in the lab and was going to have to sneak past Machmood to get over to the meeting. His plan, should he for some reason not be able to accomplish that, was to get sick and have to return home. BQ was also ready to call him with an emergency regarding one of their daughters if he was considerably late. As it turned out, Malanga, Bill and Paul arrived together. Everyone waited for George.

By the time he arrived the tension was palpable. Elizabeth prepared to take her leave, but he asked her to please stay, so she did. "Thank you all for meeting me here in the middle of the afternoon. I have to make sure everyone in this room understands the whole picture of what we know about what is going on. And I am going to rely on you all to tell the rest of us what each of you knows. We must prepare to defend SIL. But first allow me to bring you up to date and explain why I think this is necessary." He proceeded to tell them about his conversations with Hwan, what he knew of his father's negotiations with him, and the calls to Liz from the Chairman. Malanga added what she knew about the Chinese; many faces in the room were wide-eyed with incredulity.

Sylvia then discussed what she knew of the shuttle, and she and BQ explained what the plan was for the old space station and the two stolen US shuttles. They played a tape of Liz's explanation.

"So it is clear that the Chinese are willing to invest amounts of money we cannot imagine, and manpower and machine-power on the same scale, apparently to learn the trade secrets of Finding," said George.

Tom Robinson then indicated he wished to speak, and was recognized by George. "We have one leg up on this situation with the old space station," he began, bringing the first good news of the meeting. "I have been able to activate the video and audio surveillance on the old station. We cannot tap into the shuttles, but there is plenty of chatter happening between the crew and the group working on the old station."

"An interesting point," said BQ, "is who exactly is on those ships. I've given an in depth look at the make up of the hijack teams and they are elegant in structure. One thing for sure is that they are after the synthetic diamonds on one of the old planetary probes and our own Eye. Karen Smith is a master faceter, who worked in the diamond industry in South Africa for many years. She was expelled when it was found she had been taking stones."

"What is not clear," said McKenna, "is what exactly they are after. With Smith on board it would seem logical that they are aiming at faceting the stones for the buyer, who then intends to sell them, but the numbers just don't work out. We have intercepted communiqués stating they are being paid $20 billion for a total of about 63,000 carats of diamond. This is nearly $31,750 per carat, which is ridiculous."

"I believe they are after the Eye itself," said Malanga. "They clearly are interested in the ways of Finding, and it is a logical extension that the Chinese would think in terms of herbs as a basis for medicine. I suspect they want to take the Eye, render SIL dead and make their own orbital body."

"That does not make sense," said Bill. "They have the capacity to just come to SIL with their plethora of large shuttles, capture it, and live here. To have gone to the trouble of developing crafts that can extend the window of accessibility from four to six

Second Pass

months, they know the only repercussions for taking SIL would be here on Earth."

"If that is what they were going to do," said Shandor, "then why go to all the trouble to destroy the shuttle fleet and hijack the old space station?"

George cleared his throat in an obvious way to get the attention. "Whether or not we know what their motivation or plan is, we still need to defend ourselves. I do think it is clear that whatever they are doing, our best interest is served by preventing it." He looked around the group to see if there were any ideas. "Does anybody have a plan of action to produce?"

"I don't have a plan," said Tom, "but I have what is part of a plan. Not only am I able to control the old space station's surveillance, but also all other ship functions. In the day of that station, Houston had control of every onboard system. And what that means to us is that I can cut off the energy that is being generated by the nuclear power plant on board. By doing that we can force them to use up their fuel."

"Can you disable the power plant completely?" asked Gould.

"Not exactly," Tom said getting some papers out of his sack, "there was a safeguard put in place that protects the nuclear power plant. But I can permanently disable nearly all other systems. So, in effect, I can disable the power generators coming from the plant, and all life support systems. They could create some workarounds, but it would take days to do that, and require resources they may not have. Which reminds me, does anyone have an inventory of what supplies were on those shuttles?"

"I've got them here," said BQ as she rifled through her things, occasionally sending a pencil floating listlessly away from her. She handed the list to Tom who immediately looked it over.

"Meanwhile," said McKenna, "I believe I have an idea for a defense. As we know, they are currently about 2.78 million miles from here, extracting the diamond from the probe. Once we have confirmation they have launched to come our way, we should disable the fuel supply at that point. That way they will never get to us."

"I disagree," said Paul, "we need them to get to us. We need those shuttles.'

'What for?" asked Gould. "we are already too far to reach Earth."

"It gives us some sort of vehicle to get around in," Paul answered. "Even if we just use them locally, they give us leverage. And we have a large fuel reservoir here that we continuously replenish."

"We do have some other vehicles," Elizabeth said shyly. "We have the collection pods."

"What are those, young lady?" asked Gould. "I'm not familiar with all of SIL's resources."

"When there are meteorites or other space debris floating around out there we use them to go capture it and bring it into our mineral plant to extract what can be used."

"Good point," said McKenna. "I had forgotten them in my calculations. They do give us some mobility and could contribute to the element of surprise. But before we get to actual strategic planning, do we know for certain that they intend us harm?"

"Didn't they plant a bomb near the Eye?" asked BQ.

Malanga and George looked at each other. "I'm sorry," George said, "I didn't have time to update you all on that situation. When I got to the Eye there was nobody there. I discovered that what was planted there was not a bomb but a series of 7 location transmitters." He reached into his pouch and produced them. "I know these because they were used by my security team. And," he said with a snide look, "that same security team seems to be our enemy right now."

He passed one of them around and the group looked at it briefly. "Does anybody know how these operate up here?" he asked. "On Earth they work in conjunction with the GPS network, and while we are within the satellites, they aren't focused here. Would they work up here?"

Bill Bryant took it in his hand as he spoke. "A single one will not do much good here, since there isn't any programmed data that give it a relative location. But the signal can be picked up by the shuttle and with six others, they would be able to get a fix on whatever was inside of the parameter marked by these. Where exactly were they positioned?"

"They were pretty much in a circle around the Eye," George said, "as much as the network of structural support beams would allow. Any ideas why they planted them there?"

"Again everything is pointing to the Eye Chamber, and the plants," said Malanga.

Second Pass

"Look," McKenna said, "we are getting off of the point again. We must remain focused on the task at hand. What evidence is there that they plan to attack us? Or to harm us in some way?"

"Becka Masters," said Malanga, "is working with them and has succeeded in killing one person, and tried to kill several others."

"Liz told me that the Chinese Chairman has given veiled threats to the safety of all of us on SIL," said George. "I think it is pretty clear they mean to harm us."

"And how do we know there is a direct connection between the Chinese and the renegade group who stole the shuttles?" McKenna asked.

"Again," said George, "Liz, in her conversation with the Chairman, pretty much confirmed the connection. It was all veiled, hinted at and the like, but it was very clear to her."

"Well then," McKenna said with a new, harsh look on his face, "it is now time for SIL to come of age it seems. Before I became President I had endured many tough political battles, and knew people were, shall we say, quite set in their ambitions. But once I held the office I found in short order the type of decisions which must be made. We here on SIL must now make similar decisions."

"What kind of decisions are you referring to?" asked Sylvia. "How to protect ourselves? We have no armed forces. We have no defenses."

"Then we have to eliminate the enemy before they get here," he said. "We have to kill the people on the shuttles."

BQ let out a little grunt of pain and sadness. She grabbed Paul's hand and held it to her breast. "Do we have to kill them?"

"Yes," McKenna said, "we do."

"But what about the Chinese?" asked Bill. "They are coming and will certainly be following the progress of the shuttles."

"I am also afraid," said George, "for Liz and my son. We no longer have a security team. I'm afraid the Chinese will have no trouble kidnapping them, or harming them if it serves their purposes."

"My plan takes all of that into consideration," McKenna said. "They will not realize until too late."

"Then," said Malanga, "we had better hear your plan."

"As Dr. Robinson has told us, we can control the systems of the old space station from here on SIL. I propose the following. When the shuttle group leaves the probe to start in our direction, we create a power boost for three minutes, accelerating them suddenly with a force of 9 to 12 Gs, which will kill everyone on board almost instantly. Then we fire retro rockets and keep them on track to arrive at SIL as planned. We send a crew to the shuttles on the small vehicles you have here, and have them pose as the original crew, who will be disposed of."

He looked at George with concern. "Here is the difficult part of the plan for you son," he said kindly, "you must have Liz and your son accompany the Chinese as if they are joining you here as requested. They will think her presence grants them access to SIL, and you will give them adapter specifications which will cause them to outfit their QY fleet with physical docking ports that will allow them to dock with the shuttles, not with SIL. They will think they will be able to dock SIL, however.

"When they arrive they will be instructed to first send their diplomatic mission, along with Liz and your son, to one of the shuttles to discuss the coordination of their arrival on SIL. We will speak of this up front, so it will not be any form of surprise to them. When this group, which will certainly include Hwan, reaches the shuttle, our small vehicles will have come around from behind and sent a load of debris backwards up the exhaust nozzles of the main engines of their ships and into the thruster rockets as well. If any one of those rockets is fired, it will cause the ships to damage themselves in the case of the thruster rockets, or destroy themselves if they attempt to fire the main booster rockets. Liz and your son will be brought onto SIL in the small vehicles, and then SIL will use its own thrusters to move away from the QY fleet. They will then be told about their thrusters and boosters and we will let them decide what they will do."

The room was silent. This was the first experience any of them had with considerations at this level, or with a person who was as brilliant a strategist as McKenna. He looked around the room into each person's eyes. Satisfied that he had their attention, he now needed to know if he had their trust. "What do you think of my plan?"

"It will work," said Bill simply. "It will give us total control."

"But won't they know the shuttle has been tampered with?" asked Malanga. "The Chinese are certainly monitoring it very closely."

"At the distance from which they are viewing it," said Gould, "which will basically be from Earth's surface, the fact that the

Second Pass

trajectory of the vehicle is on course will give them nothing to see, accept the acceleration."

"Yes," said Sylvia, "and that acceleration will be picked up by the computers on both shuttles, and by the Chinese."

"Actually not," said Tom with a broad smile on his face. "My son, Shandor, became an expert at computers in his young life. With the type of interface the old station will be forced to have with the shuttles, and the access we have to all of the systems of the old station, we can alter the computer telemetry readings going to the shuttles so that they read as if the speed is consistent."

"But how long will it take for the occupants to actually die?" asked BQ. "If they realize something is happening, will they have time to alert the Chinese?"

"At 6-Gs or higher, they will loose consciousness in about 12 seconds," said Malanga, "and be dead within 2 minutes. Those 12 seconds will give them ample time to alert the Chinese."

"Well," Tom said, "I had thought of that. What we will do first is increase the oxygen supply for several hours, which we can start in an instant from here at any time, which will make them very drunk. That will be taking place while they finish whatever they are doing with the probe vehicle. Then we will start to change the mixture of air to include carbon-dioxide by halting the air refiltration systems and suddenly cutting back the oxygen. This will make them pass out. That way when the acceleration occurs they will not be conscious."

"Tom," said McKenna, "remind me to never have you on my enemy's team."

"There is one major problem," said Sylvia, "Machmood. We must tell him the Commander is dead." She looked at George with a wince. "I'm sorry. I didn't mean to sound so..."

"It's okay," George said with a sad smile, "what we are talking about is exactly what he would want us to be discussing. Please go on. What about Machmood?"

"Well, we have to tell him, and when we do, he will become the Commander," she said. "He will have to make the decisions, and, being so new to his position, he will surely want to have the Overseers consider every option, who will want it to pass through the Assembly. It will take time."

"I have a proposal," said McKenna. "As Chairholder of the Assembly, let me talk with him privately. What you all don't know is that at the time of the last pass, just as my term as President was ending, he contacted me. He and I built a liaison of convenience at that time. I believe I can convince him to allow me to run this operation."

"We must make a decision," said BQ, "as to our reaction to McKenna's plan." She took a deep breath and held Paul's hand tighter. "I can't stand for anyone to die. I have been opposed to killing all of my life, and this plan is very difficult for me to even think about, much less support. But," she held her lips tightly together as a tear floated up from her eye, "I have to say I am behind it. It seems like the only way we can save the lives of everyone on SIL." She buried her head in her husband's shoulder and cried. Elizabeth came to her mother's other side and embraced her, as Paul did the same.

There was little further discussion, and all agreed to go forward to enact the plan. Bill Bryant took the GPS devices from George and studied them, finding that they might be able to guide a missile to themselves, precisely the sort of missile guidance the Chinese had.

Meanwhile McKenna had a private talk with Machmood, who became angry and belligerent when the proposal was made to have him even temporarily turn over any of his new power. McKenna then reminded him of some of the things he had proposed years earlier to discredit Commander McVee and usurp his power. Once McKenna made it clear he would not hesitate to make this information available to everyone on SIL, which would result in Machmood being replaced by Erica Pimmit, he backed down completely.

Meanwhile, the mass of documents Malanga had sent had all been received by Woody, who didn't know what to do with them, or why she would suddenly send them. The cover note said only 'Woody, these documents will be important later. Keep them for Liz when she asks.' He printed them all out and bound them by volume, knowing that Solange Malanga never did anything without good reason. Malanga took George aside and told him that she had sent some very important documents to Liz, the ones she had spoken to him about before. He was to arrange in their next CommLink to make her aware of a particular book. He said he would figure out how to do that.

George and Sylvia returned to the CommLink and opened a new session. Liz was waiting for them. When the last CommLink

Second Pass

conversation had ended, a call came to Woody's office phone from Hwan who commented on their conversation, letting her know that even with the secure CommLink the Chinese had seen and heard everything. She had waited with knots in her stomach since. Hwan had renewed the demand that she get the docking specs without George knowing.

"Liz," George said as soon as her face appeared, waiting the few seconds for her to hear him and respond. "We need you to do some things for us here on SIL."

"I'll do whatever you need."

"I want you and Georgie to accept the offer of the Chinese and come to live here with me."

"But if I do, it will put everyone in danger."

"They won't hurt either of you if they are bringing you here," he said.

"I will not let anything happen to our son," she said harshly. "And I won't have him be a pawn in any political game."

"We are already pawns in this," he said, "we have been all along. I need you to do this. I can't live without you for 18 years Liz! I won't live without my son knowing me. I did that with my father, and I can't allow it for him."

"Okay, George," she said with a sigh. "We will come." Then she thought about her assignment to get the specs for docking SIL. If she didn't have them, they would never allow her to come. But they had forbidden her to let him know she was getting the information.

"But what were you saying earlier today about them not being able to dock?" she asked him, returning to the subject. She knew that somehow the Chinese were able to see everything she did, and was not going to risk telling him they wanted her to get the plans for the docking ring adaptations. As she spoke the words she turned her head to the side, as if brushing something off of her cheek with her shoulder. It was a movement they had set up with each other to communicate that something was going on other than what was being said. George's eyes changed slightly when he saw the gesture.

"The docking ports are being altered," he said, waiting for her to give him further signs. He brushed his forehead with the back of his hand, as if waving off a stray hair or pesky fly. This meant that what he was about to say was not the whole truth. "We have created an adapter ring so that any ship attempting to dock would have to have the counterpart ring to dock."

"What kind of adaptation?" she asked, knowing that he was now giving false information.

"Well, when we first suspected danger of being approached, we created one adapter ring configuration for the arriving shuttles from Earth. What we have done is make alterations to that adapter. Now that the two remaining Earth shuttles, or I should say, US shuttles, are out there and possibly coming back, they will not be able to dock, even with the adapters from before. It is our only defense." He brushed his nose and blew as he said this. "Sorry, there's something floating in the air here that's bugging me. Hang on a second, I'm going to change position. It must be dust or something."

Liz and George had rehearsed this over and over. Any movement having to do with the shoulder, a shrug, adjustment of bra strap, rubbing of cheek to shoulder, meant there was something that person needed to say but couldn't say. Any gesture of clearing anything away from the face meant what was being said was not to be taken as truth, and if either one of them blew, it meant they were lying and needed the other to pursue the topic and perpetuate the lie. If they somehow indicated the area behind or under it meant to look further, dig deeper. They considered telling this to Masters, but George argued that they needed their own completely private means of communication. Liz was now very happy she agreed, as much as she had liked and trusted Masters at the time.

"What is the new adjustment?" she asked. "I mean, could it be worked around? Could someone figure it out?"

George smiled; she was giving him the opening he had asked for. "Well," he said as he adjusted the camera to his new location, at one point looking down and behind him as if he was clearing himself of some obstacle in his new position, "we completely reconfigured the opening, making it smaller and no longer round. For a person to pass through this opening he would have to turn slightly sideways..." he went on with the explanation, giving information that could be understood by a skilled engineer and then built so that the specifications could be met and another ship could dock. Except that what he was saying was not the truth at all, she knew, and the false impression would no doubt make docking completely impossible if it were in place.

Second Pass

She looked behind him, straining her eyes to see what was there, knowing from his gesture there was more for her to discover. At first she saw nothing, simply the wall, a small opening to stow things in, some junk in a string bag, a grease pencil erasable board for messages with nothing written on it. She started to panic thinking she wasn't seeing what he was intending to show her. She had the capacity to zoom in on the picture from her end in a way that would not be detectable to anyone who was picking up the signal. She zoomed in on the background, and then adjusted the focus to different areas. She did a zigzag pattern across the background, sweeping back and forth across the picture, each time lowering her focus slightly. She saw nothing out of place in particular. It was a cluttered space, obviously used to store the personal belongings of those who spent much of their time at the CommLink. She saw mostly Sylvia's personal belongings.

Just as she was about to give up, her view passed by the string bag and she noticed a book. She stopped the panning and zoomed in closer. There was something about it that seemed oddly familiar to her. She looked at the title and nothing rang a bell. It was a technical manual about operating the CommLink. Quickly she realized her recognition was because it was the exact manual Woody had referred to when he was making sure the link was completely secure. *CommLink Operations - Administration.* She looked down to her right and saw the same manual there, and thought that it probably meant nothing at all. But it was in a string bag of Sylvia's personal belongings, not with the other manuals.

She looked again at it and noticed that the last three letters on the cover had been colored in by blue ink, as if someone had been bored and doodled on the book. The letters 'i - o - n' were thus highlighted. She wrote this down and zoomed back out. George was still talking.

"...so that even though the opening is smaller, nearly any size person will pass through it, except the largest body types..." he was giving her plenty of time.

She again did a sweep of the background, but this time saw where all of the books were kept. The complete set of CommLink manuals were over to the left, and only the administrator's volume was out of place. She zoomed in to the books and looked at them in order. There was a full compliment of five volumes, none was missing, nor was there a blank space. She examined the five books: Installation, User, Configuration and Integration, Glossary and, where Administration would be was another book, however, that was the same color as the others, but not from the series. She zoomed in on the title. '*Biobotanical Quisling in the Eye Chamber.*' She knew there was significance here; that George had moved the books intentionally, but she had no idea what the meaning was. She noticed that the book was by Paul Dunn.

There was something strange about the book. It was the same basic government manual as the others, black ink on white paper. The fact that, in the book that was misplaced in the string bag, the three letters had been inked over would not have been noticed if she had not been looking for it. She considered the book that was out of place—administration. If this were significant it would mean that she was to look into the administration of something— SIL, Associated, the Chinese government. It was clear he wanted her to think about that. The administration of SIL would now pass into the hands of Machmood, which was a very big change. However, she now realized, none of the communications with the outside world had included him on any level. She suddenly wondered if he even knew the Commander was dead.

Beyond SIL, the entire administration of Associated had been murdered by Stevens, apparently, who was their chief administrator. This, too, was consistent with the current situation. As for China, it was the Chairman himself who had contacted her repeatedly, not the lesser politician Hwan who had contacted George and his father. Administration was significant no matter where she looked.

During their many years together, they always left notes for each other in as cryptic a language possible. Held over from the early days of Internet communication, it was now part of every day life to use truncated symbols to represent larger concepts, substituting single letters or numbers to represent the words the sound of them represented. For him to very subtly accent the letters 'i', 'o', and 'n', she could only surmise he was trying to tell her to keep her 'eye on' administration, or administration that was out of place.

Satisfied that she had part of the puzzle figured out, she left it for the moment to focus on what had been substituted. She looked again at the title and realized she did not know what the word 'quisling' meant. She reached into her purse and got out her personal computer pad and typed the word in and asked it to give her the definition. The display read: "/quisling/ *n.* 1 a person cooperating with an occupying enemy; a collaborator or fifth columnist. 2 a traitor." She looked again at the book, zooming in on it. It couldn't have been an actual book, not by that title. As she zoomed she saw that the second word was actually a piece of paper wrapped around the binder of the book with the word 'quisling' printed on it. It wasn't actually the title of the book at all. By changing this word she realized he was trying to tell her something about a traitor. The book was compiled by Paul, George's best friend on SIL, and perhaps in the world. She was certain Paul was no traitor, though she would remember to be careful around him. But then she realized that the words Biobotanical Quisling held the acronym BQ, who was Paul's wife.

Taken together, she was to keep her eye on the administration, and there was a substitution of some sort, which perhaps had to do with the Eye Chamber or the biological work done there. Paul had been a biobotanical engineer and had been eager to go to SIL to further his experiments and theories. Perhaps George was telling her that BQ and Paul had information about some sort of substitution in the Eye Chamber, or a traitor there, or in the administration. She gave up. It was too much.

George had stopped and she interjected, "It is just hopelessly complicated, George. I don't think I'll every understand it."

"Well, it's really quite simple Liz," he was putting fake anger into his voice. "I hope you will have recorded what I just told you (hand brushing the face again) so you can learn how we've adapted the docking ports. If you don't, (he looked down and back) how will you ever come here?"

She took a second. She needed more information, so she brushed her hand through her hair, arranging it – the signal for needing clarity for understanding. "I understand the basic principle of the need for an adapter, and I think I understand how it is configured, though I'm not an engineer. It is just all so complicated. What is the governing principle here? Is it the physical size and shape of the opening, the electrical connection, the atmospheric pressurization, the biological makeup of the body? What?"

He smiled, loving this brilliant partner of his. "Don't worry about the electrical connectors, the physical environment or the bodies that need to pass through the docking connection. And, as far as the atmospheric differences, we will be able to control them. What we are most worried about right now is not what is coming, but our end of it – if we are ready to accept them. We have limited but adequate resources for those of us who are here, but not for any others. I don't think the Chinese understand what life on SIL is actually like. I mean, no matter how friendly an environment, if we aren't organized, we can't be good hosts."

"Okay, George," she said, "I trust you. I have to go get ready though. Can I talk to you more later if I need to, and if I have time?" She asked this figuring that she would study everything she could get her hands on and try to find out what he was saying to her, but she may well have to get more from him. She was frustrated and terrified.

"Of course you can Liz," he said. "In fact, I will need to talk to you later. We will have some protocol for the arrival we will need to go over with you and with the Chinese."

"Okay, George. I love you."

"I love you more than life," he said with a kiss.

Chapter 25

Malanga called all of her apprentices to the main room of the Finders Chamber. They took positions as they entered the room in no particular order. Seven of Malanga's nine apprentices were grouped together, talking about Toby and Su Lee. In another part of the room were her four department heads, all silently waiting for her to begin. Ali was next to Malanga, which drew not a little attention. But when anyone looked too questioningly at him Willa Marsdon-Jiimson's return glare caused them to quickly avert their eyes. On the other side of Ali was Hermes Whipple. Everyone in the room took furtive glances in the direction of these three, who positioned themselves away from the others, mainly because of the yellow cloud that surrounded them.

"We have been unable to locate Toby and Su Lee," Malanga began. "I've asked Hermes, Ali and Willa to join us today because of their encounter with Becka Masters." She looked around the room. "The yellow cloud that surrounds them is pollen from the plant that saved their lives. I have asked Tanya Lee to document and study all aspects of this plant, so please cooperate with her should you make any observations."

"I know that often apprentices have a keenness to their skills when they are first developing," Tanya said, "and I hope you will turn the focus of these skills toward these three. Anything at all that you notice must be documented. I realize this is a time of extreme stress on SIL, but hope you will manage to assist in my research in any way you can."

Malanga held her hand up politely to interrupt Tanya. "Excuse me, Finder Lee, but I must interrupt." She waited a moment, then continued. "We have several tasks before us and I need to make some assignments today. First, we must find Becka Masters before she attempts to kill again. My fear is that she will strike away from the Eye Chamber and the plant will not be able to protect the victim, or save more lives. Second, we must find Toby and Su Lee. I have had multiple scans of SIL conducted, and we are finding that the vibration of their essences has ceased, yet I choose to believe they are still alive. Ali assures me they are, based on a conversation he overheard. Ali?" she gestured to him. "Please tell them what you told me."

Ali twisted his fingers in his tunic and kept his eyes downcast. "She was talking to the wall through a phone and said she was going to put a patch on them that would keep them unconchents until she gave them another drug."

"I believe you mean 'unconscious' Ali," Willa said. "You must forgive him, he is quite young and does not have a perfect command of vocabulary."

Ali twisted his fingers more violently, and pressed his lips hard together. He looked up at Willa with extreme apology in his countenance. Malanga interceded. "You're doing fine Ali," she said kindly, "I find that word a bit hard to pronounce myself." She giggled, as did the others. "Please continue."

"Well, that's really all. I mean, besides when she said that she had to keep them all alive."

"Ali, how did she make them lose consciousness?" The question was asked by Josephine Winston, a biochemist responsible for the coordination between conventional medicine and Finding.

"She sprayed them with a spray that was going to last six hours," he said. "Then she put one of these things on their necks."

"What kind of thing was it? Can you describe it?" Josephine asked.

"Well, it was kind of, well..." he made a very funny face. "I know!" he said excitedly. "I have the one she put on me. It didn't stick because of the plant goop on my neck." He reached inside of the pouch on the front of his jet pack harness and pulled out a square patch. "This is it. She was going to make me go uncon... shoos, ohw, I can't say it right."

"That's okay, Ali," said Josephine, "I know what you mean. May I take it and do some tests?"

"Sure, I guess so, I mean if..." he looked toward Willa, who nodded stiffly. "Here." He gave it to Josephine.

"There are a few other things we must discuss," Malanga said, moving things along. "We learned that Masters had recruited several people who were going to volunteer to work in the Eye Chamber, as you will remember from yesterday. They have been apprehended and are currently being kept in a secure area near the waste filtration plant. I need those of you with specialty in psychology to go interview them and see what can be found out. We also know that the Chinese are going to try to learn the methods of Finding. Each of you is a potential kidnap target. The

Second Pass

Chinese are expected to send several large shuttles in the QY class vehicle, as they call them. We do not intend to let them dock on SIL, but should they, we must not let them know who you are. So I want you to return all of your Finders guild robes, whether you are apprentices, in the directorate, or even if you are in the regular medical corps. We will keep all of your clothing here, and you are to wear everyday clothing. I also want you to always be with someone else from this guild, either finder or medical, so we can protect each other."

There was a bit of chatter, including the comment that working as a team didn't help Toby and Su Lee. Malanga put an end to that right away. "I need some volunteers to do another free-lock to find Toby and Su Lee, and also some to find Becka Masters. We will need two different teams."

Jun-Jun's hand shot up; Malanga looked over to him. "Jun-Jun, I am sorry, but I must insist you not be part of either of these teams."

He started to argue, but Malanga stayed firm. She was worried about his overall health and she didn't want to risk it. He was as disappointed as his parents were delighted.

* * * * * * *

Ronald Stevens sat strapped into his seat in the main passenger compartment of the shuttle. He did not like sitting next to the pilot, mostly because he feared the openness of space. He preferred being strapped into his seat for a similar reason—it made him feel connected as gravity did. He simply couldn't dwell on the unconnectedness of space, of weightlessness, or of his unpredictable future. His lust for position, power, money and recognition had led him throughout his life away from the very comfort he desired. Entitlement would suffice if community did not embrace him, as it couldn't do someone who constantly needed to be aloof in superiority.

He had controlled everything, and was on the verge of becoming one of the wealthiest men alive. When the light blinked on, summoning him to engage his listening device, he was disturbed. He did not ask anyone to call him. In fact, he had specifically forbidden any radio communication, even between the shuttles. He flipped up the switch.

"You know damned well I've forbidden radio communication," he snarled into the microphone.

"You have forbidden?" asked Hwan's voice with sarcastic irony. "And whom have I reached? God Almighty? I simply wanted to speak to a little man named Stevens; a sniveling runt of a lowly human. I believe I have the wrong connection!" He ended this with an abrupt snort of mirth and condemnation.

"What the hell do you want Hwan," he asked angrily. "I think I deserve a bit better treatment than that." He truly hated Hwan, not because of his detestable characteristics, but because he needed him and his money.

"Oh!" said Hwan with surprise. "It seems perhaps I did get Stevens after all."

"What do you want?"

"I wanted to tell you that there has been a surprising development, much in our favor," he wanted to draw this out as long as he could, both to confound Stevens with suspense, and to most fully disobey his rule of radio silence. "But, before I tell you this amazing turn of good fate, I must say that your rule for radio silence is patently ridiculous. We have in our control every space vehicle there is. We have all of the shuttles that exist in the world, and you are leading the space station by its proverbial nose. SIL, which will be ours in short order, is in such defenseless disarray they could do nothing whatsoever even if they were to know the exact details of our plans. In fact, they probably don't have the manpower to monitor random frequencies to find that we've spoken at all, much less the ability to unravel our decryption. Relax, my friend, relax. Just float, weightless, untethered, far from the pull and the crush of Earth's demands."

Stevens felt panic rise in his body, like a powerful drug shooting through his veins. "What the fuck is your news?" he yelled, hands trembling, cold sweat forming on his neck.

"Ah, the news," Hwan said luxuriously, "yes, I'd almost forgotten it. It seems that the mother of little Georgie, wife of this generation's recently orphaned Dr. McVee, has decided to spend the next 18 years with him on SIL. Or at least she thinks she will. Unfortunate that she will find herself in completely other circumstances so soon after her arrival."

"That's great," mumbled Stevens. "We didn't need her anyway. Who cares?"

Second Pass

"Ah, but you truly do not grasp the whole situation, poor thing. It will never cease to amaze me the truncated view of life you Americans have. You do realize, though, that what comes together quickly does not last long? That is true for nations as well as any of man's accomplishments."

"I do not need your pontificating, Hwan. If it weren't for American ingenuity you would not have a space program."

"Well then, if we are so ill equipped, perhaps you don't need our money either."

Stevens couldn't mask the sound of in-taken breath, a gasp of shock. Hwan hadn't ever threatened about the financial aspect of their agreement before. It had been clear from the beginning that Hwan needed his team and their expertise just as much as he needed Hwan's money.

"So," Stevens said coolly, "are you suggesting you no longer need our services?"

"Ah," Hwan cooed, "so it appears we have each other by the testicles. Such a strong basis for relationship, don't you think?"

"We should just focus on the task, not on trying to like each other. Our mutual hatred may just help things go more smoothly."

"How true," said Hwan. "And so we shall proceed. Barbs and jabs aside. How long until you have extracted the diamond from the probe?"

"About three hours," he said with a smile. "And then it will take us another two days until we reach SIL."

"And here," Hwan said mechanically, "is where we do agree about radio silence. Once you push off from the probe, we will not communicate further until you are next to SIL's waste disposal facility. That is the point of surprise, taking them from behind. That is your favorite thing, isn't it? Approach the waste removal site?" Hwan laughed uproariously at his crude humor. He too enjoyed anal sex, but Stevens did not know this, and so he loved to rub his nose in it, so to speak.

"Yes," Stevens snapped, "we do agree. So, other than to tell me that the little bitch will be with you, what else?"

"Only just that," Hwan said calmly, knowing he would end up with everything he needed and never having given a dime to Stevens and his crew. "We will use her to guarantee entry into SIL, even though she has dutifully gotten full specs for us on the docking port adapters."

"Good," Stevens said, relieved the conversation was coming to an end. "I will speak to you again when we arrive at SIL." He switched off the radio speaker and changed to the inter-shuttle device. "Smith," he said.

"Yes Stevens," she replied.

"I've just spoken to Hwan, there is a change in plans. As soon as they give you the diamond, start to cut it into 1 and 2 carat stones."

"I thought we were to take it out and simply clean cut the edge for placement into his greenhouse ship."

"Apparently he has changed his mission," he said with glee. "We will prepare the stones for sale on the open market."

* * * * * * *

As the final housing released, the diamond started to float outward from the probe. Dave Masters looked over at his brother, Steven. In the privacy of their sleeping quarters they had waited for Marty Wellington to fall asleep and formed their own plan. Steven Masters had been bested and humiliated by Stevens a few too many times. He had kept his mouth shut and played along because he knew his moment of revenge would arrive. The two brothers discussed their plan over and over, not about to let the promise of extreme wealth divert them from their revenge against the abusive Stevens. They would have their wealth, but Stevens would be made to pay. As the diamond floated up, Dave took it carefully in his hands while Steven opened the sack in which it would be stowed to carry back to the old space station. Marty was busy looking over the other devices in the probe and grabbed some extra wires, circuits, transistors and things that would be needed to fully assemble the gem cutting station.

They finished their work and fired their guidance jets in small bursts to propel them back toward the old station. Jiimson saw the flashes from their jets and notified his team to prepare the recompression chamber in Shuttle A for the three to return from their EVA. Stevens was busy working with Mackelroy on the flight path back toward SIL.

Karen Smith had taken advantage of the distraction of the EVA, which everyone was paying close attention to for most of its 6 hour duration, and gotten together with Kaplan and Martin to finish their preparation of the cutting station. When it was complete, with the exception of the parts they would use from the probe, there had still been close to two hours left before the EVA would be finished. She invited the two of them to join her in a weightless orgy in the old space station. She was unaware the EVA had been completed nearly an hour ahead of schedule, and her male friends were simply too intoxicated with sex to care.

When the three were safely back inside of Shuttle A, the signal was given to fire the main thruster jets of both shuttles simultaneously, starting the voyage to SIL. All of the onboard communications, along with the orgy, were being monitored on SIL. Gould had worked with Paul, Tom and Shandor to break through the computer links between the old station and the two shuttles and had created a series of workstations, each one displaying the computer screen of the different computers in the shuttles. They were able to watch every single key stroke and mouse click as it occurred, as well as hearing all communications.

For the past hour the mix of carbon dioxide into the breathable air of shuttles and station had been slowly altered, making everyone a bit drunk, and a bit sleepy. As the EVA crew entered the recompression chamber, where they would have to wait for nearly an hour to prepare their bodies to re-enter the shuttle atmosphere, a very rich mixture of carbon dioxide was put into their air. Dave Masters vomited immediately, and his brother helped him clean up. Marty Wellington fell asleep.

Karen Smith threw her head back in the ecstasy of climax and fainted just as the SIL computer was engaged by the Shuttle thruster rockets to blast them into their new trajectory. The rest of the crew of all of the three vehicles joined Smith in unconsciousness as the rockets blasted. The sudden burst of movement crushed everyone against the back wall of whatever module they were in, and killed them instantly. They never knew there was any problem, nor that their lives were about to end. They just died in a tangle of flesh, blood and anything that wasn't secured in place at the time of the thrust.

BQ turned away from the video screen of the inside of the old space station. She couldn't lose her compassion, even for people who were ruthless killers and criminals. She was secretly glad for Karen Smith, however, who had died mid-orgasm. It was a fitting end, and exactly what Smith had prayed for all of her life—that she would die having sex.

After the three-minute burst, the ship slowed to a normal rate and preceded the two day journey toward SIL where they would rendezvous with the fleet of Chinese QY shuttles.

Chapter 26

"Greetings members of SIL," Hwan's voice boomed throughout SIL suddenly. People stopped mid-task to listen, looking quizzically at each other. Becka had managed to slip into the communications control room and insert a remote controller. She, hanging mid-air next to Su Lee and Toby, still unconscious from the powerful sedative four days later, was delighted it had worked. BQ and Sylvia were in the CommLink chamber unaware that his voice was being sent throughout SIL. "We are the diplomatic envoy from the People's Republic of China. We bring hope to those of you who are trapped on SIL against your wills. We also bring supplies."

"And probably an army hidden in the ships," said BQ sarcastically as she listened to the voice on the usual CommLink speakers. "How many ships are with him?" she asked without turning her head.

Tom looked at the radar screen and counted. "It seems there are twenty or more. It is an impressive presence."

"Well at least they can't dock," said Gould. "Is our team in place?"

Sylvia checked the cameras on the other side of SIL where the space station and shuttles were hovering, then the link to the cameras on board. They had gotten to the shuttles via the collection modules and activated the link to SIL so there would be two-way audio/video communications. George waved at the camera, aware of the question. "All here and counted for," he said, as First Officer Bryant came up behind him and waved. Paul's red hair could be seen in the back ground.

"My new friends," Hwan continued, "we will need your help, if you are to receive our help. You must make the leadership of SIL realize that you demand to be allowed transport back to Earth. You have a democracy on SIL, and so you must let them know your wishes. We will be meeting with your leaders very soon on the old space station, and they must come with full knowledge of your will. We give you two hours to comply."

"Commander Hwan," said Sylvia politely, "the people on SIL cannot hear your words."

He looked fiercely at her through the screen. "Yes they can," he said crisply, "I have gotten control of your communications. Check your monitors; I believe you will see some very excited members of your community there." Sylvia turned around, as did everyone in the CommLink chamber, to see the bank of monitors. There were people jetting everywhere, they were talking and some yelling. In the temporary living quarters there were signs of tremendous activity as some prepared to pack their things and leave.

"How did you get control of our communications?" she said to him. Then, cutting off the audio on the CommLink she said to the others with her, "turn off all sound into SIL immediately!"

Tom and Gould, not very adept with the system, were trying to shut it off, but had no way to see if it had worked until Hwan spoke again.

"It is futile to try to override the interruption to your system," he said, "And, people of SIL, I think you should be aware of the fact that those in charge are trying to prevent you from knowing what your options actually are."

There was the sound of banging against the communications module outer doors and voices demanding to be let in. The loudest voice was that of Machmood. "Let Machmood in," shouted Sylvia, "but no one else." She turned back to the CommLink, and switched on the microphone system so her words, too, would be broadcast throughout SIL. "Okay, Hwan. It is clear you are not here in a friendly way at all. I think it is important for everyone on SIL to know that SIL is being approached by you without authorization, and that you intend no good for her inhabitants."

"What the hell is going on," shouted Machmood. "I want to know who that man is."

"He is Commander Hwan, chief negotiator for the People's Republic," said Sylvia calmly. "Apparently he and Commander McVee had agreed for some exchange after the window of opportunity for the US shuttle fleet had closed."

"Why haven't I been told of this?" he demanded, veins standing out on his forehead and neck. "I demand an explanation!" His voice thundered with a force none of them had ever before encountered.

"We have just learned of it," said Sylvia, "and as you have just become acting Commander yourself, there has been no time to brief you."

"Where are they?" he said in dismay, pointing to the screen showing the interior of the shuttle where Bryant, George, Paul and the others were. Sylvia quickly shut off the sound so Hwan couldn't hear what he was saying. "Is that Paul Dunn!" He was in a rage, which did not surprise BQ at all, but made the others look from one to another.

"We have a very dangerous situation," said Sylvia, "and you need to be brought up to date on it."

"Allow me to explain," said Tom, who knew Machmood better than anyone there from his early days on SIL. "In the last days of Commander McVee's life, this situation arose. We all believed he would recover and we were so focused on the pending crisis that there wasn't even time to alert the Overseers or the Assembly. Then he died this morning."

Machmood was both frustrated and flustered. He couldn't blame them, but he also felt the burning need to exert his new authority. "All right Robinson," he snorted, "but be quick about it!"

Tom proceeded to explain, as if it had all just happened—about the two shuttles driving the old space station and the execution of their crew, and the planned ruse by placing the SIL team where Hwan's counterparts should be. Machmood listened, and as he heard the complexity of the situation he became relieved that all of these people were in place and a plan had been formulated. He suddenly dreaded being Commander, the very thing he'd dreamed of for decades.

Meanwhile, Gould was noticing that another couple of collection modules had launched. He pointed to the screen so BQ could see. Neither of them indicated outwardly their surprise when they switched on the internal cameras and saw that one of them contained Malanga, and the other contained four workers from the Eye Chamber along with Ali who, due to his young age, was dwarfed by those surrounding him, even though it was Ali who was clearly in command of them. There was another person in the small vehicle with his back to them. Gould and BQ merely exchanged wide-eyed looks and quietly got Sylvia's attention so she, too, would see. They were interrupted by Hwan; Sylvia switched the microphones back on.

"I've instructed my person to disconnect my voice from the rest of SIL," he said. "I want to speak with George McVee. I know the Commander is dead, and I will speak with him only."

"I'm afraid he's already gone to the shuttle to ready for the diplomatic meeting with you."

"Ah yes," he sneered, "all because you have changed your docking ports so that you can control who docks on SIL. Very clever, but not clever enough. I have his woman here, and their son. I intend to bring them together on the shuttle in a short time. But first, I want to explain why we are here."

"Commander Hwan," Machmood's voice said suddenly, "I am Commander Machmood, instated just under an hour ago upon the death of McVee." His purposeful omission of the title was meant to tell Hwan that all earlier agreements were null and void and that he and Commander McVee had no love lost between them. "I am the Commander of SIL now, and you will speak to me alone, not young George Junior."

Hwan laughed out loud, enjoying the show of force and mocking it. "You are no more Commander of SIL than I am Chairman of the Republic, though I admire your tenacity. I will discuss nothing with you at all. However," he held his hand up against the sputtering coming from Machmood, "I will concede that you are indeed Commander of SIL in the future. And let me spell out that future for you, and for your friends there." He reached to the side and had a brief conversation. "Pardon me, but I was deciding whether or not to let all of SIL hear what I am about to say, and we have decided not to let them know. Cattle go so much more peacefully to their slaughter in ignorance."

Sylvia's heart rate increased. This was the first direct threat he'd made, and to her it indicated that he had some sort of military force with him. She clutched her elbows with her hands, and BQ put a reassuring hand on her shoulder.

"We have tried to learn the secrets of the ways of Finding, but your predecessor refused us access to Madame Malanga. We have, as a result, brought our best scientific minds, as well as our most knowledgeable herbologists to study what you have developed on SIL. The ships with us are carrying materials with which to build our own little SIL - two of them in fact. One will be smaller and will only be a plant greenhouse, or Eye Chamber, as you call it. It will be built onto the existing old space station. This will serve to preserve your plants, or the ones our people deem to have healing properties, while we build another, larger one."

"You cannot succeed," said Machmood with a snort of his own, "you need the Eye. Without its refraction capabilities the plants cannot grow."

"How true," Hwan sneered, "but you see, we have gotten the large ellipsoidal diamond from the old probe to use for our smaller one. It is being cut to fit into place on the old station as we speak."

Sylvia turned off the audio uplink. "So that is what they were doing with the shuttles." Then she turned it back on.

"But you will have no such device in your second chamber," said Machmood with a victorious grunt.

"We might have brought an army with which to overtake SIL," Hwan continued calmly, "but they weren't practical and we have no real weapons for that kind of assault as of yet. So instead, we will be taking the Eye itself, to fit into our newly built facility. Once it is gone from SIL, of course, it is only a matter of time before you will all die."

"You have offered transport to those on SIL who want to return to Earth," said Gould. "They have taken you seriously."

"I will do as I've said. They will return to Earth. They will be held in a camp in China and not allowed any communication with the outside world. We will study them and find out exactly what space environments do to people. They can do that, or they can remain on SIL and die."

The CommLink screen went blank.

* * * * * * *

Liz was strapped into her seat with little Georgie attached to her front with Velcro straps. The trip had been an exhausting ordeal, beginning with a frantic rush of packing. Sienta had been more helpful than Liz could imagine a person could be. The two women had not spoken of the possibility that neither the two of them, nor George, might ever return. Liz had considered that she might not be able to come back until the next pass, at which point Sienta would be into her mid-70s, so she had deposited half of the savings she and George had managed over the years into an escrow account in Sienta's name. She also had added Sienta's name to the deed of her house, with an addendum to her will that should anything happen to her the house and her entire estate would belong to her beloved companion, Sienta. The money was nearly a half million dollars, not much to live on, but considering Sienta's age and the government benefits that would come to her in just three years, she could live comfortably for about ten years on the amount before she would have to do something to extend her cash flow, like selling Liz's house. The government provided Liz and George transportation to Beijing on military transport—an extremely loud cargo plane, and a very rough ride. Georgie had howled half of the time and slept the rest. Upon their arrival in China they had been treated coldly at best, and their possessions were thoroughly searched with many items removed, she knew not why. Hwan had sent an aide to greet them, along with a translator. Both were young women who never smiled, seemed uncomfortable around Georgie, and acted bored with life. They deposited them in a room at the United States consulate where they received the first warm welcome of the entire trip. But that was very short lived, as another car arrived just two hours later to take them to the space launch facility where they waited for two days in a very small room for the launch. They were fitted with space gear and fed space food as if there were some sort of adjustment period the body needed before eating the diet. Georgie hated everything fed to him; Liz hated life.

When they boarded the large QY shuttle, Liz was fascinated. The vehicle was nearly 550 feet long with a wingspan of over 300 feet. It was mounted on a cluster of rockets with multiple thrusters, creating a field of nearly two dozen nozzles on the bottom. The entire assembly reached over 700 feet into the air, and the elevator system for mounting the monstrosity was rustic and exposed to the elements. They were put in a compartment away from other passengers, with five armed guards. Liz thought the entire sense of security around them was absurdly overdone, and the formalities were stifling to her. As they lay on their backs, strapped to their launch chairs, the screen in front of her flickered to life and the Chairman was there smiling at her.

Their conversation was short and brief. He welcomed her and her son to China, thanked her for her cooperation, and made some flowery, poetic statements about international relations and SIL that were patent bull shit. She simply smiled through it all. In the end, he asked if there was anything she required and she said she would like to have her baby carrying harness with her and its counterpart chair for her son so they could sit together on the trip, rather than next to each other as they currently were. The Chairman got a puzzled look in his eye which turned into a broad smile and he simply said yes. Then the screen want black. A few moments later, much faster than she could imagine possible, the harness and chair were delivered and fitted on them. The exchange had changed things with their armed guard, who saw that the Chairman himself spoke to her. She realized they must have understood English, which she and the Chairman spoke, because they had displayed minimal facial reactions to the different parts of their conversation and, when she was making the request, one of them had started speaking in rapid, though hushed, Chinese into his lapel.

The take off was usual, and Georgie had screamed in terror at the sound and jostling of take-off and climbing away from Earth's gravitational pull. It was the moment that weightlessness was achieved that he got a peaceful, curious look on his face, and started to giggle. From then on Liz talked to him, answered his myriad of simplistic questions and got him eager to see his daddy again. The guards then also started to loosen up and began to speak among themselves in Chinese, and with Liz and Georgie in English. That part of the trip was quite pleasant.

Hwan came back to check on her several times, but mostly avoided speaking directly to her and addressed the guards about her more than talking to her. It was annoying, but Liz much preferred being referred to in the third person than being directly addressed by the grotesque man. He did refer to her as 'Doctor' which she appreciated, but that confused the guards enormously.

She sensed a change in the atmosphere. Guards were speaking into their lapels constantly now, many people were moving around doing methodical tasks, and the video programs on the little screens were terminated. Hwan's face appeared and he spoke in Chinese, obviously addressing others on the shuttle. She thought she heard the word SIL but couldn't be sure if that was even what they called the orbital body in Chinese.

The friendliness of the guards recoiled to humorless mechanical function; English was forgotten. They indicated to her she was to get Georgie and put his space suit on, and she was to do the same. She struggled to get Georgie, who now thought everything was a fun game, into his ill-fitting suit, but did, and then put on her own. They were then led forward. She had trouble holding Georgie and both of their bubble helmets, while also navigating weightlessness.

"Put on your helmets," Hwan commanded when they were presented in front of him.

"Where are we going?" asked Liz.

"We are going to make our first meeting with the diplomatic mission from SIL," he said. "We going see daddy?" asked Georgie while he batted away his helmet.

"Honey," Liz said, "we are going to see daddy, and you have to wear this to see him."

"I don't want hat," he said, lip trembling in advance of manufactured tears, "no hat!"

Hwan came close to the boy and spoke directly into his startled face. "You will put on the helmet and you will do so quietly...NOW!" Georgie was too frightened to do anything but comply. "You see," said Hwan, turning to Liz, "we Chinese know how to deal with future generations. Come."

They were led through a maze of passageways with clumsy moments of over exaggerated results of ill timed weightless movements, and finally into a smaller vehicle that was inside of their cargo bay. Again strapped in, the vehicle was locked airtight, and the cargo bay doors opened. Liz could see SIL in the distance, and saw above it the strange sight of the two shuttles docked tandem on the old space station. The smaller shuttle jerked free of the metal clamps holding it in the cargo bay and the thrusters fired giving them a jolt. They maneuvered clear of the QY and went the relatively short distance to their target, and then docked onto the old space station. She saw a little flicker of light off to the right of the old space station and watched it intently. Just before the vehicle she was in turned to obstruct her view, she saw that there was a small vehicle circling behind the old space station and recognized its markings as coming from SIL. This gave her a small sense of relief.

Hwan was sitting, looking very contented indeed throughout this entire side trip. He was in charge in space, and he liked that very much. Here there was no Central Committee, no Chairman, no protocols decided by others. Here he was the top man and, in his mind, this is how the world ought to be. He had been the third child his parents produced. The first two, girls, had been sold for foreign adoption and the births not recorded, as was the most common practice in Chinese families. It was the male child that had value, and when he arrived his parents were so thrilled they had treated him like a king. In a world of so many people, with such strong traditions and long, long ladders to climb toward any kind of stature at all, being in charge was all he thought of.

Second Pass

In their small shuttle were three guards, a pilot, copilot, Hwan, his secretary, the one who had met them in the car, Liz and her son. Liz didn't know exactly what to expect, but did know that much had gone on to prepare for the arrival of the Chinese on SIL. She was prepared for anything.

The docking was very smooth, almost unnoticeable. The copilot was sent to the rear of the transport vehicle to prepare to open the docking door between the two ships. Hwan was right behind. The door opened and the pressure changed enough for Liz to feel it in her ears even with the helmet on. The copilot and Hwan floated upward into the station, then went the secretary and one of the armed guards. Liz and Georgie were next, and Georgie was put through first. Liz followed and after her another of the armed guards entered.

"Daddy!" said little Georgie as he attempted to swim in space toward George who jetted smoothly to him.

"Hello there big boy!" he said hugging his son. "And look at your mommy!" He jetted around to Liz and hugged her with one arm while Georgie clung to him.

"Where is Stevens?" asked Hwan. "And where are the Masters?"

"They won't be joining us," said Bill Bryant. "In fact, there is a major change in plans." As he said this, George jetted himself and his family back next to Bill. Paul and Andrew Stetler came past them and went to either side of Hwan, grabbing him by the arms.

"What are you doing?" shouted Hwan. "Let me go!" His two guards, without the benefit of jet packs, tried to make their way over to Hwan, but were unfamiliar with fighting in weightlessness and managed to send themselves spinning out of control. The secretary and copilot just hung there in space unsure of their next move. Paul and Andrew handed Hwan over to Bill, who disabled his speaking devices, and jetted to the two guards, using a shocking weapon to render them unconscious. A couple of other people from the SIL team disabled the speaking devices of the other two as well. One of them, in perfect Chinese, radioed to the shuttle that they should return to the QY.

George managed to get Liz and Georgie into another part of the station. As they went through the interior of the old space station George explained to Liz that they were going to take a collection pod back to SIL. He pulled Georgie's helmet off, and then took off his own, as Liz took hers off.

"What is going on?" demanded Liz, shaking her head to free her hair. "Hwan isn't anyone to threaten, George. He is dangerous."

"And hello to you too," he said, kissing her. She shrugged him off; Georgie clung to him. "We are basically under attack, as you well know. We knew bringing you here would at least assure he wouldn't destroy SIL without some sort of diplomatic interaction."

"But there are many QY vehicles with him. I don't know what he intends, but it is clearly not friendly."

"We know," George said, "and we are ready for him. He thinks his crew on the space station is ready to deliver him a large diamond which he intends to use to start a new, smaller Eye Chamber. He then plans to build another larger structure and take the Eye." He saw her realize what this meant. "Yes, everyone on SIL would die." He smiled at her and took her cheeks in his hands. "That isn't going to happen, Liz. These people here are amazing. We've got probably the best minds alive working together here."

"I saw one and maybe two of the small vehicles SIL uses to collect space debris circling around behind the space station on our way here from the QY. Are they part of the plan?"

He looked puzzled. "Well, we are planning to use those, but there shouldn't be any coming here now."

* * * * * * *

Hwan had not sent the proper signal to the QY sub-shuttle, which was the actual signal for them to retreat. The order they had received had not been a voice they recognized as his, and he had left unquestionable instructions that he and only he would be giving them instructions. Lun Wang fired the small rockets to move the sub away from the space station docking bay, and imitated a departure. Once out of sight of the portal windows he then turned his vehicle around and started to go to the far side of the station when he noticed a small SIL vehicle approaching from behind.

He directed his vehicle in its direction and got close enough to it to see a woman inside. He recognized her as Madame Malanga,

Second Pass

the one Hwan said was absolute top priority. Wang knew Hwan planned to take her back to China and get from her all of the healing secrets she held; and that she was the most valued prize of this mission. He positioned himself between her small shuttle and his larger one.

She saw she was blocked and began to maneuver away from him when a light came from his vehicle and suddenly her controls were inoperative. She tried to engage her retro rockets and they would not respond. She tried to radio to SIL but the radio was blocked. Her complete attention was on her various controls so she didn't notice that the cargo bay of his vehicle was opened now and the large robotic arm was approaching her vehicle. When it grabbed a stabilizing bar and took purchase, the clank and jolt made her snap her head around. She couldn't see what had grabbed her, but felt she was being pulled toward the larger shuttle.

Wang manipulated the robotic arm to deposit her vehicle into his ample cargo bay and then shut the doors. He then began the trip back to QY, radioing that he was returning with a captive, and that something was wrong; Hwan had not given him the proper signal to return to QY.

Inside her small chamber, Malanga did a meditation. In it she alerted Erica, Jun and all of the other apprentices she had developed contact with. Once she had established the connection and an alert with them, she then put herself into a coma so she couldn't be questioned.

Chapter 27

Inside of the storage chamber was crowded. The decision to hold the people planning to sabotage SIL there had been made so quickly that several aspects were never considered at all. Each member of the group displayed shock when they were isolated, and some mixed outrage with that shock. Once in the chamber together, conversations revealed that each believed he or she was the only one secretly spying for the Chinese in exchange for a variety of rewards. All had been recruited by Masters. But when they compared stories, it soon became evident they were all being misled and manipulated, and, most suspected, the promised rewards were never to materialize. The effect of this was resentment against Masters and a distain for the Chinese, yet they also had a sometimes violent opposition to the authorities of SIL. They had been betrayed on all sides.

The chamber was hot nearly all of the time, and was periodically filled with the awful odor of the waste processing facility nearby. Sleeping sacks were easy to move into the area, but the Velcro attachment mounts weren't so easily installed. In addition, without knowing how long they were to be detained, details of daily living like food, bathing and bathroom facilities became crises to deal with, and life became a crisis to crisis mania.

Willa saw what was happening and stepped forward to become the administrator of the detainees. She felt it her duty to keep an eye on these people, and felt deeply betrayed by them. The idea that the Eye Chamber would be violated by anyone made her livid, but that they would infiltrate the Chamber in a time of need for the purpose of allowing the Chinese to steal it rendered her white-hot with rage. But over the years she had become a master of self-discipline, and her rage was not evident to those under her supervision.

They had been held in these close quarters now for several days. Interviews had been conducted by Finders and Finder apprentices revealing many common psychological factors. The most interesting one to Malanga had been that they were each either the product of a couple, or in a relationship, where each member of the couple had a strong affiliation with one of the two political parties, and the other had the same for the opposite party.

Second Pass

Oddly, however, is that there was no particular party affiliation, neither Firster nor Born, which determined the willingness to undermine the security of SIL. It seemed that Masters had taken advantage of the political turmoil in the family to be able to make promises they would find appealing.

Willa and Malanga, along with Ali, had made a conscious contact with the essence of the plant that had mutated into a sentient protector. It had been named *chambali malangeye*, and was called Chambali by them. The Chambali would allow telepathic visualization to anyone who was sincerely dedicated to the well being of the plant itself. Its curative properties, however, were not fathomable to any of the scientists or botanists assigned to study it. When any of its properties was studied at a molecular or chemical level, there was nothing at all unique about its makeup. The clear gel it emitted to heal wounds was simply sap, and appeared no different from the sap of any other leafy tree. There were chemical components that were specific to it, but they did not hold any special curative properties. Yet, when it came in contact with an individual's blood, it developed stem cells and white blood cells holding the DNA of that person. Likewise, there was no central location from which the telepathic properties emanated; it had no brain center. Willa did not like this at all, but Malanga found comfort in it.

Willa had telepathically asked the plant if she could take some cuttings and allow them to take root for the purpose of placing them in the chamber holding the detainees, and the plant happily allowed this. One immediate result was that any time anyone was angry with Willa, even internally, they would be overcome with some allergic reaction to the cloud of pollen that surrounded them whenever she was near, rendering them helpless to do anything more than blow their nose, rub their eyes or scratch their skin.

As Willa entered with the food containers, several of the people started sneezing and scratching. Others stayed away until the food was served and she had left the chamber. They all agreed she was not one to trifle with as the rumor of her mortal wound and miraculous recovery inside of a cocoon of goo made her seem something of a freak to them.

But they had heard the words of Hwan that had been broadcast throughout SIL and were emboldened by the presence of the Chinese. In their private talks they had determined that while the Chinese had not been loyal to them, their presence would distract their caretakers. In the event SIL was invaded or captured by the Chinese, they all agreed to hide their animosity for their earlier betrayal and become cooperative with them, hoping to be in good favor of the new authority on SIL. Some even hoped to return to Earth and start over, tired of the type of life SIL provided.

They had prepared a plan to break free of the chamber and attempt to make a radio transmission to Hwan. As Willa turned to leave the room and opened the doors, they rushed forward. They had been stripped of their jet packs, but used the force of pushing with their legs to make themselves like human bullets. Over twenty bodies flew through the air toward the doorway. Willa was knocked to the side as they overtook her, flying out of the chamber and into the hallway. One man turned to attack Willa, raising his fist to hit her. A shoot from the plant's root shot across to him and wrapped itself around his arm. It got tighter and tighter until blood was forced through the skin of his hand as he screamed in pain.

Willa hit the commpatch on her wrist and radioed to Sylvia that the detainees had overpowered her and were freely traveling through SIL.

* * * * * * *

"We must find Su Lee and Toby," Elizabeth said to Jun-Jun. "Malanga authorized the free-lock before she left."

Jun-Jun didn't know what to do. He was willing to do the free-lock, but something felt unsure in him. "I don't know, Erica," he said hesitantly, "it just doesn't feel right. So she said I shouldn't do it. I know she authorized it but not for me, and that isn't what feels wrong. I know its okay to do it; I just feel that if I do then something bad will happen."

"What could happen?" asked Erica, coming into their family main room. "What are you two talking about?"

"Malanga wants us to free-lock to find Su Lee and Toby. And Jun-Jun feels that something bad will happen if he does."

"Yeah," Erica said with a sneer, "like you might not wake up. I remember that very well."

"Erica," Elizabeth said sharply over her humming, "we have learned quite a bit about freelocking since then, and it has become an effective tool for us to use."

Second Pass

"So kill yourself, what do I care?"

"Don't be like that," Jun-Jun said, also humming. "I don't fear for my life. I just feel that something will go wrong when I'm out there, something I need to be here for. It is a very strong feeling."

"I wish Malanga were here," said Elizabeth. "I don't know how to make decisions."

Erica felt herself calming. She still had a crush on Jun-Jun and felt jealous of her sister now that they were both apprentices. "If you feel that way," she said quietly, "maybe I could do it."

Her sister looked at her intensely. She hadn't considered that Erica and Jun-Jun were the ones who had originally created freelocking. "Are you sure you would like to do it Erica?"

"It would be your first time," said Jun-Jun. "I don't know if it would be wise..."

"It isn't my first time," she said defiantly. "I've already done it twice."

"When?" asked Jun-Jun.

"Without you," she snapped, "I did it without you. After you nearly died, but were alright, I had to try."

"Erica," Elizabeth said seriously, "if you have done it before, then I would be in favor of you trying. But if you haven't, I don't think it would be a good idea."

"I did it with Marcus," she said. "And I want to help. Ever since you became an apprentice you are different," she said to Jun-Jun. "I'd like to be part of things too."

Elizabeth and Jun-Jun looked at each other. They both knew Erica had been left out of things, not because she wasn't wanted, but because so much had happened they didn't have time to all get together much. "If you will do it," Elizabeth said, "we would love you to help. It is very important to find Su Lee and Toby. We tested the drug Ali had on the patch he gave us and Su Lee is allergic. For a normal person it will keep them unconscious for about 6 days, for her it could be for much longer, if it doesn't kill her."

"What do I do?" she asked.

"I thought you said..." Jun-Jun started.

"I mean, once I'm dead, what do I do? How do I find them?"

"We will guide you telepathically to her essence. You just concentrate on everything you know about Su Lee or Toby and go out of your body and kind of float around. You will be able to see through the walls and everything. Just find where they are and then tell us once you are back."

"Sounds simple enough to me," she said as she went to her room. "I'll get my warm clothes. It'll just take a minute."

* * * * * * *

Ali watched as the larger shuttle cargo bay swallowed Malanga's transport vehicle. Shandor, watching from his seat behind Ali, became angry. He switched on his personal commpatch and spoke into it.

"Dad, come in. This is Shandor."

"Shandor!" Tom's voice said after a few moments. "Where are you? I need you to help us in the CommLink Chamber."

"Can't do that dad," he said. "I'm with Ali, on my way to the space station."

"What the hell are you doing..." he was cut off by Shandor.

"They've kidnapped Malanga."

Sylvia swung around when she heard this. "What do you mean, they've kidnapped Malanga?" she said into the master microphone.

"Malanga was in one of the small collection pods from SIL on her way to the Space Station and the QY small shuttle captured her with their mechanical arm and put her in their cargo bay. It is on its way back to the main QY shuttle now."

"Damn it!" said Sylvia under her breath. "Shandor, listen to me. I need you to be our eyes out there. We mustn't allow them to have Malanga, or to use her for leverage. I am going to develop a plan and then contact you. Follow that shuttle, and learn everything you can about their configurations and capabilities, even if it is only visual for the moment, it will have to do. Now, cut off communication and wait until I get back to you."

Ali and Shandor looked at each other. Neither was prone to wait for instructions, not while Malanga was in jeopardy. Ali focused with renewed intent on the controls of their small vehicle. He steered it to a position behind the space station from which they could watch the shuttle holding Malanga and the large QY vehicle.

Shandor had been part of the team that was to place the location devices found near the Eye in the propulsion jets of the

Second Pass

QY vehicle. When the SIL radar had shown an entire fleet of QY vehicles, Machmood and his team had quickly made a few hundred of the devices, which were rather simple. He had brought a few dozen with him. He got out the sack containing them and studied it while his mind was working on a plan of his own.

"What are those?" asked Ali.

"These, my friend," he said grandly, "are location devices placed on SIL by Masters' team. At first it was believed they were bombs, but it turned out they were just markers – that could be used to guide bombs."

"There are so many! They must have planned to completely destroy SIL." Ali was alarmed.

"Actually, they only planted 7, all around the Eye. We made more of them. We are going to put them into the jets of the QY fleet. That way, if they launch a bomb, it will blow them up and not SIL. But," he said, opening another satchel he brought with him, "these are our own bombs." He held up a fist-sized device with wires coming out of one end. "I intend to connect these bombs to the devices and then," he pulled out a small commpad activator, "I can use this simple every day item to blow them to bits!" He laughed gleefully at himself.

"So," Ali said slowly, turning the ship and firing the jets, "we have some work to do while Sylvia comes up with her plan."

"Yes we do, Ali. Yes we do." Shandor put away his things and pulled out an electronic pad to make notes on. They made a list of all of the QY vehicles they could see on the radar, and figured out an approach that would keep them well out of eyesight of the windows of the vehicles. They were small enough to avoid being detected as anything more than space junk. And they began to place the rigged bombs into the fleet.

* * * * * * *

Jun-Jun and Elizabeth were just inside of the docking portal. Erica was greased and heavily clothed in the warmest clothes she could find. She hadn't said much as they prepared for the freelocking. Instead she was remembering her previous experiences and contrasting them with this one. The others had been blatant acts of revenge and rebellion, spurred on by her anger at herself that she had removed herself from working with

Jun-Jun. Recognition from him was a thing she swore she did not need, while inside she ached for his affection. The rivalry between herself and her sister over the years had become palpable once they had reached puberty. With a very small community of perspective suitors on SIL, she was bitter beyond expression that Jun-Jun had ended up working closely with Elizabeth. She expected this experiment to be the culmination of all of her best efforts to win back Jun-Jun's attention and gain some respect from her sister. But it felt awkward and internally still. There was no victory—only fear.

Jun-Jun had grown quite a lot in his apprenticeship. Mostly he learned that each person has profound effect on those around him in life. The impact of self on others was unavoidable, and even retreat from another will have an impact on them. With this realization came responsibility—the responsibility to help, to heal, to communicate and to benefit society. The road to learning such lessons was decorated with exercises of self-examination, in particular looking at the various encounters with others earlier in life. Naturally, then, he had looked at his entire relationship with Erica, as well as his own maverick experimentation with freelocking. The result was that he understood how much she needed to be recognized by him, and how deserving she was of an amend. He hoped including her in this crisis would begin the road to mending their relationship.

Elizabeth had always hated having red hair. She hated it because it linked her to her father, who was rejected by Machmood and other conservatives on SIL, and because it linked her to Erica, who was rebellious. Elizabeth wanted everything to be good, to be pleasant, to fit. She was herself quite conservative, and hence an outsider to her own family. As a young child she believed that the distain the other children showed to her and her family had to do with their red hair, mostly because that was the characteristic most often, and most easily, teased. She had intended from a young age to be the best, to be the unquestionable, credible standard bearer in all of her endeavors. And she had been. But as she looked through the thick plexi and saw her sister's red hair amid all of the gray grease, thick protective clothing and colorless void of space, she suddenly thought that maybe, just maybe, family was somehow more important than anything else. And if she lost her sister during freelocking, she would have lost the opportunity of her life to get to know the very person who would always be closest to her—her twin.

Jun-Jun indicated by gesture rather than speech that he was ready and looked in at Erica for the hand signal of readiness. It came; he pressed the outer latch opening control, and watched. The outer door retracted sideways into the outer hull of SIL. Erica was jerked outside of the docking tube by the vacuum of space. She hugged herself in a ball as the tether pulled taught to maximum reach. Her head flew backwards, and her eyes opened in fright. Her body spasmed into a limp position and her eyes fluttered shut. Elizabeth hit the timer, preset for 70 seconds.

Jun-Jun and Elizabeth went into their trance state. They concentrated on the essences of Su Lee and Toby. Elizabeth found her sister's spirit voice and urged her to follow the essences. Jun-Jun was unable to find Erica's spirit voice, but was suddenly able to hear Toby's. He projected all he heard to Erica, creating great cones of life force to help guide her to the source of the voice. Toby was showing Jun-Jun a limbo state, a stasis of muted sensual access, and a foreign lack of desire to reach the sensory world of reality. Jun-Jun realized that Toby was himself in a trance that went beyond the mere effect of the drug; it meant Toby knew they would be coming and was determined to help.

* * * * * * *

Erica floated at first outside of her body with a strong urge to stay close to it. She recognized this familiar feeling, and knew she had to break the bond with her manifest self to find Su Lee and Toby. Suddenly Elizabeth was inside of her head, telling her to follow the essence. She sensed Su Lee and Toby strongly, almost as if she could hear their voices. Jun-Jun was in front of her, reaching out his hand. She took it and the instant of contact she was pulled quickly forward, her sister on her other side. They flew outside of SIL and she saw the fleet of QY vehicles, but also saw Malanga in a collection pod inside of a cargo bay of one of the QY shuttles. She panicked, wondering if anyone knew this. People were opening the pod and pulling, treating her roughly. As she started in the direction of Malanga she was jerked away, her view suddenly back at SIL.

She saw SIL not as the lentil-shaped ovoid of its outer hull, but like a geometric sponge with every internal chamber exposed. *Follow the essence! Follow the essence!* The dual voices of Elizabeth and Jun-Jun spoke in near unison, but had a slight echo quality because they weren't exactly synchronized. She found the essences, which were now like parallel wisps of smoke – one bright green and the other lavender. They were long and intertwined, but never mixed. She saw inside of the Eye Chamber and heard the voices of each plant, like metallic chimes and sweet little voices of pixies, singing a chorus of encouragement. When she was aligned with the green and lavender path the chorus was punctuated with "Ooooh! Aaaah! Uuuummmm!" sounds, but if she was distracted several little voices became slightly hysterical with "No, no, no, no, noooooooooo! Go back! Not that way! Ni-ni-ni-ni-ni-ni-ni-nieouuuu!" with always the chorus in the back ground.

One of the plants showed her its face, and from round cheeks blew a trail of yellow dust that twined its way around the green and lavender trails. She followed, moving faster than she knew possible. Looking frantically into every chamber, but continuously pulled by the essences. It pulled her into the Eye Chamber and suddenly she was on a crash course with the Eye itself. She approached and passed through it so quickly that she didn't have time to recoil. Inside of the Eye she turned to the left suddenly in a dizzying movement that blurred her vision. She was then flying between the girders and beams that supported the outer hull of SIL and held everything in place. She followed and followed, arching with the outer curve of SIL. She was both inside of SIL's hull and outside of SIL. She saw that she was coming toward the CommLink Chamber. Inside of the chamber were Sylvia, her mother, and some of the, older men who came during the current pass. But her view was not allowed to linger on them. She saw, knew, arrived, understood all at the same moment. Su Lee and Toby were bound to two beams just outside of the CommLink chamber wall, between the inner and outer hulls of SIL.

She flew to them, seeing that what she had thought were the twin trails of green and lavender were instead simply the two people seen out of time and space, out of reality. Like the trail a hand leaves when it moves quickly, lit brightly against darkness, the trails were actually the time stamp of their movement to their

Second Pass

current locations, and the result of their existence in the lives of other animate and sentient forms.

Suddenly she saw a reddish-pink trail leading away from them. She tried to stay with them but was pulled by the new trail. She turned to look at where it was leading her and saw nothing. There was absolute cold, still blackness. She started to scream as she was swallowed by the void.

* * * * * * *

Hwan struggled against the straps that held him. His mouth was covered and he couldn't make more than muffled sounds. One man guarded him from across the chamber. He was in a side compartment of the space station that had some machinery bolted to the side near the middle of the room. He looked closely at the machinery, which seemed oddly familiar to him. Every curve of it, each joint, was familiar, yet he had never seen it before. He searched his memory for the source of this familiarity.

Upon closer scrutiny he saw there was something floating up from one corner of the table like base. It was floating like smoke that never dissipates, waving slightly back and forth, but only very slightly. It was as if it wasn't meant to be part of the table, but was stuck to it. He looked where it was connected and just saw some brown-black paint that had dried but was partly flaking off. He stopped still. It was hair, human hair. What held it to the table was dried blood. Suddenly he looked around the chamber more closely and saw that one side of it had much of the dried substance spread all over it. There was dried blood nearly covering one wall.

Then he remembered. The machinery was the gem-cutting rig that Karen Smith needed. He had only seen mechanical drawings of it before, never the actual equipment. He looked back at it and suddenly felt sick. The hair was blond like Karen's hair. He was in the chamber she was to have been working in. The blood. The hair. He knew she was dead.

He started to slam his body back and forth, making as much noise as he could. He screamed beneath his gag. The guard looked at him with contempt and spoke into a microphone on his wrist. "Our captive is restless, boss. What do you want me to do?"

The guard listened to the voice being broadcast into his ear by the electronic device he was wearing and then said in response, "No problem." He started in the direction of Hwan, who stiffened to ready himself for whatever the guard had been instructed to do. He knew if he were the one giving orders of what to do with a noisy hostage, the hostage would be killed or rendered unconscious. He hoped for the latter.

The guard got within talking distance and said, "I will remove your gag to hear what you want to say. But McVee has said he will be in to speak with you soon, so most anything you would want will have to wait." He reached out and pulled free the Velcro gag.

"You cannot hold me!" bellowed Hwan. "I represent the People's Republic of China and am being held against my..." The guard put the gag back on to silence him.

"They said you might start spewing bull shit," he said blandly, "and you did." He came closer and smiled. "I just don't want to hear it." He returned to the other side of the chamber.

* * * * * * *

The QY shuttle pilot called back to his QY ship and explained that he was given the instruction to leave without receiving the proper code from Hwan. He was going to hover near the space station to see what developed but instead apprehended a small shuttle vehicle from SIL that was carrying a lone woman, who he believed to be the prime target of their mission, Madame Malanga. He had captured the vehicle and went to question the woman and found her unconscious. He was bringing her back to the QY for medical assistance, not knowing if he had harmed her in some way.

She was indeed the prize of their mission. He radioed to Hwan to tell him they had apprehended Malanga. But their radio contact was not received or responded to. They tried again, and then tried to reach anyone at all with Hwan's party. They received no response whatever.

Chen Chang Lo was first officer of QY 1, the lead vehicle of the fleet. He had been in the Chinese space program, and had been the second citizen to go into space. As such he achieved superstar status overnight, and, possessing of a healthy ego, he quickly translated that into many conquests. He was unmarried and very handsome, and played both sides of the field. His bisexuality was not recognized simply because the Chinese culture, for as ancient and wise as it was, did not acknowledge any sexual orientation other than heterosexual. Consequently, he had a field day in the underground gay and bisexual subculture of China, and was able to have as many women and men as he wanted as well. All was well until just three months ago when he discovered that he had been exposed to HIV. While still not sick, he had been given this mission to remove him from the general population, since his philandering was well known, so he wouldn't infect as many people.

He realized his assignment was both prestigious and an imposed exile. He was angry about the latter, but in terms of the former, he intended to make as much of an impact as he could. He seized this opportunity to declare himself in charge of the mission and radioed to the other QY commanders that all orders would come from him from this point forward, until they heard again from Hwan.

"Fellow Citizens," he began, speaking only to the other QY commanders on a confidential circuit, in a private conference, "it seems that our beloved Commander Hwan has been detained, or is perhaps harmed. He does not respond to our attempts to contact him. The QY1 shuttle was dispatched from the space station without proper instructions from Hwan, and we can only speculate that he has been compromised." He waited for any comments or questions, but none came. "We need to ready our armed force for infiltration of the space station and, from there, of SIL. We must also ready the rockets so we can retrieve the large diamond from SIL."

He continued to give orders. At his command, 240 armed men got suited and ready for battle. Forty of them were put into each of three shuttles and dispatched from their base vehicles. They started toward the space station.

* * * * * * *

George entered the chamber where Hwan was being held, and instructed the guard to remove his gag. Paul, Stetler and Liz were with him.

"Well, if it isn't the whole family," said Hwan jovially, as if he were sitting in his own office. "What brings me such an esteemed visit?"

"We find it unfortunate that you choose to compromise SIL and put us in a position to defend her," George began. "You do not have the support of the global community. Why would China want to place herself out of step with the world's leaders and population?"

Hwan smiled wanly. "And what makes you say such a damning thing? We have offered you supplies enough to build many more living units onto SIL. We have agreed to open the expansion of SIL population to the entire world, giving China far less that what would seem an equitable representation in the emerging population of SIL. And for this you make these accusations? I am offended on behalf of my great nation!"

"And it would be this great, beneficent generosity that makes you plant an intruder on SIL to commandeer our communications, murder our citizens, kidnap our doctors, and who knows what else?"

"How can you accuse me of such a thing? I am a simple man. I cannot possibly conceive of such elaborate plots. I believe," he smirked, "you have been watching far too many autovision productions, son."

"Do not call me son!" snapped George.

"Please excuse me," Hwan said, sincerely apologetic, "I had not considered your recent loss. I meant it only as a figure of speech." The two men looked at each other for a long moment. George was not able to forgive the error; Hwan would not grovel. It was Hwan who broke the silence. "I believe that, according to international rules of engagement, you cannot detain me in this way. I have made no aggression against SIL that would make my imprisonment appropriate."

George reached into his pocket and produced a small disk. He put it into his commpatch and turned the volume up so everyone could hear. Out of the small speaker, Hwan's voice filled the air:

"And let me spell out that future for you, and for your friends there. Pardon me, but I was deciding whether or not to let all of SIL hear what I am about to say, and we have decided not to let them know. Cattle go so much more peacefully to their slaughter in their ignorance. We have tried to learn the secrets of the ways of Finding, but your predecessor refused us access to Madame

Second Pass

Malanga. We have, as a result, brought our best scientific minds, as well as our most knowledgeable herbologists to study what you have developed on SIL. The ships with us are carrying materials with which to build our own little SIL – two of them in fact. One will be smaller and will only be a plant greenhouse, or Eye Chamber, as you call it. It will be built onto the existing old space station. This will serve to preserve your plants, or the ones our people deem to have healing properties, while we build another, larger one."

"You cannot succeed," Machmood's voice says, "you need the Eye. Without its refraction capabilities the plants cannot grow."

"How true," Hwan sneered, "but you see, we have gotten the large diamond from the old probe to use for our smaller one. It is being cut to fit into place on the old station as we speak."

"We will be taking the Eye itself, to fit into our newly built facility. Once it is gone from SIL, of course, it is only a matter of time before you will all die."

"You have offered transport to those on SIL who want to return to Earth," said Gould. "They have taken you seriously."

"I will do as I've said. They will return to Earth. They will be held in a camp in China and not allowed any communication with the outside world. We will study them and find out exactly what space environments do to people. They can do that, or they can remain on SIL and die."

Hwan listened to his own voice and realized his opponent was clever. He had been told that George was already on his way to the space station during that conversation, which meant they were either lying about George's whereabouts, or have the capacity to communicate between SIL and the space station outside of his network's ears.

"So you have chosen to expose all truths here," he said menacingly. "In that case, I will warn you that you are dealing with much more than you are prepared to deal with."

"We'll take our chances, Hwan," George said.

"Where is my crew then?" Hwan demanded. "I insist on speaking to Mr. Stevens, or any of the others. Where are they?"

"They are dead," George said, enjoying the look of shock that briefly crossed Hwan's face before his professional composure regained control.

"My forces will be infiltrating this station and SIL very soon unless you cooperate," Hwan said, not missing a beat. "You may have killed my people, but we will prevail in the end."

George wondered just how much Hwan knew. He needed to find out what strategic edge they held. "We have no military force on SIL," George began, "what can we do to prevent this conflict? You want the Eye, but you cannot have that. What else do you want?"

"Give me Malanga and the contents of this space station and we will spare your lives," he said.

George was relieved. Hwan didn't realize that his crew had been killed before they began to work on the large diamond from the probe, and he didn't know that Malanga had been apprehended already. This gave him tremendous leverage. He was sure that the CommLink Chamber on SIL was buzzing with excitement and strategic planning at this very moment.

* * * * * * *

As the three QY shuttles achieved open space, Ali and Shandor watched from behind the fleet and saw them. They quickly planted the rest of their bombs into the jets of the QY ships and reversed their initial approach to circuitously return to the far side of the space station without being detected. Shandor was looking with binoculars at the ships and saw that each was filled with armed men.

As he was watching the direct link to SIL was activated. "Come in Shandor," Sylvia's voice said.

"Shandor here," he replied.

"Shandor, I'm giving you to McKenna," she said. "He has developed a plan and will be leading our effort from here on."

There was a short wait until McKenna's voice came over the speaker. "Shandor," he said, "I have always liked you, ever since the first day we met in Cambridge. In fact, if you will remember that day, I promised you safety and reliability, and today I will make good on that promise. But you will have to help me."

"I will do anything I can sir," Shandor said, remembering first seeing this man from his wheelchair, just after he had first arrived on earth.

Second Pass

"Hwan is captive on the space station, and does not know that his own people have captured Malanga, nor does he know that we took out his crew before they could perform the refitting of the diamond from the probe vehicle. This gives us tremendous advantage, and we have a plan. But first, tell me what you have discovered."

"They have 3 shuttles coming from the QYs and each one has several armed military in them." He said this as evenly as he could, though it was difficult with such excitement flooding through him. "I took it upon myself to build some electronically activated explosive devices, connected to the new location indicator beacons we constructed to imitate the ones left around the Eye. I have placed one of these on the main fuel tank of 17 of the QYs. They are magnetized to the outside of their hulls."

"Shandor," McKenna said sternly, "in a battle you must not go rogue, son. That means you cannot just go and do something without others knowing you are doing it."

"Sorry sir," Shandor said, "and then, I'm not sorry at all. Those bastards should all die!"

"Just calm down," McKenna said, "Now listen to me. We must operate as a well coordinated team. What you have done gives us further advantage, and I am very grateful that you did it, but you must agree to always keep me informed of anything you do from here out."

"I will, sir," he said with tight-lipped compliance.

"How are your devices detonated?"

"With a probing radio impulse. When the devices send out their beacon impulse it does nothing. But if we, or the Chinese, broadcast a probing radio impulse to find the exact location of the beacons beyond their own transmitted signal, it will detonate."

"And how much of a charge is in each bomb?"

"Enough to blast a hole through the hulls and ignite the fuel, but not enough to destroy the ship on their own. I couldn't get anything stronger out of..." he realized that the fact he was stealing supplies was now known.

"We are on a secure channel, Shandor," McKenna said, "and I will not tell anyone what you have stolen. That is why you stopped, isn't it?"

"Uh," he stammered, "yes sir?"

"I will say I authorized you to make the bombs, and I'll get Machmood to agree."

"Thank you very much," said Shandor, relieved.

"Is there anything else I should know?" McKenna asked.

"Well, only that each one can be operated independently. I sequenced the frequencies so they would be independent. And I placed them on the other end of the frequency range from the current beacon frequency. I figured they would use one close to that range for their own probing impulse, so this way they are not likely to be able to detonate them by accident."

"Well," McKenna chuckled, "I sure am glad you are on our side! Well done. Now, here is our plan. We will have to get Malanga back, that is our first priority. But we need to find out how many armed men they have brought with them, and if there are others coming."

"We can only look in the windows. I doubt we can find out how many of them there are from here."

"Yes, but you can position yourselves in a place to hear their communications," he said. "Each of the collection pods is equipped with an enhanced antenna. You've got to have a transponder with you to have achieved what you have with the bombs, so you can use that to be our ears into the QY shuttles. I am going to assign you a unique frequency and have one of our Chinese experts on this end to translate everything you pick up. I need you to position yourselves so that you are not seen by the fleet but can pick up all of their internal and inter-fleet comms. Can you do that?"

"Yes sir," said Shandor. "But what about Malanga? We know which QY she is in. Do you want us to get in there after her?"

"Slow down, tiger," McKenna said with a laugh. "That comes later. First we have to try to break down Hwan. Take your position and start listening, son. Over."

Ali and Shandor talked briefly about what they had to do. They decided they needed to be ready to retrieve Malanga, and organized with the other two men with them how they might do that.

* * * * * * *

When Elizabeth and Jun-Jun pulled Erica in from the free-lock, she was very far gone. She had only been out for 52 seconds when her body monitor registered abnormal brain readings. She had died only 6 seconds before that, and the readings indicated that if they didn't pull her in right away, there could be brain damage when they revived her.

They worked frantically on her, but she wouldn't come around. They kept doing intercept stimulation on her heart and lungs as they flew through the corridors to the Finding Chamber. When they got there she was connected to some advanced machinery and eventually, her life signs started again.

When she first opened her eyes, Elizabeth let out a cry, seeing the absolutely brain-dead gaze coming from her sister. She performed a brain scan and found almost no activity. It was as if she had experienced a brain surge that overloaded her. Desperate to know what to do, they were discussing out loud everything of relevance they had learned from Malanga.

Suddenly there was loud shouting in the hallway outside of the chamber. Elizabeth and Jun-Jun looked out and saw a group of angry people storming past them. Elizabeth recognized them as the people detained for wanting to sabotage SIL. She radioed instantly to Sylvia, and were told that Willa might be hurt and to go check. Elizabeth did not want to leave her sister.

"Wait!" said Jun-Jun. "That's it! We can take Erica to the plant in the Eye Chamber. It heals people all the time."

"Even better," said Elizabeth, "we will take her to where they were held. There are two of the plants there. We can take her and check on Willa."

They gathered Erica and again sped through the halls. This time, when they got to the waste reduction facility, they found Willa in another cocoon of clear fluid and when they put Erica near one of the plants, it immediately spat out its clear gel to cover her as well.

Chapter 28

The group found its way to the CommLink Chamber on a path of destruction. Anything they could break or mistreat on their path was destroyed to the best of their frenzied ability. Had you asked any of them why they were causing such damage, none could have replied. The mob just grew in size and fury the closer they got to the CommLink.

Inside the Chamber, Sylvia, BQ, Gould and Tom watched their progression through the halls of SIL on the security video screens. They had secured the door from the inside and were confident it would not be compromised, but Gould pointed out that the crowd, if denied any satisfaction, would get more rowdy and perhaps turn from breaking objects to harming people.

When the first of them arrived they tried to pound on the door, only to find out that extreme movement caused an equal and opposite movement; they went flying away from the door. On their path they knocked into several of the others and for a moment there was a ballet mêlée. Once they realized they could not break the door down, their anger turned to rage.

"Let us in!" someone shouted. "If you don't we will tear this door apart!" They started to pick at every edge where fingers or simple tools could find purchase. A few joined elbows to form a chain of bodies so that those at the ends of the chain could grab hold and stabilize themselves while the ones in the center used their legs to try to kick down the door.

Gould and Tom found some straps and tied the inner handles together with them. They had made it so that the only way to enter would be to take down the entire double door structure. But these were the inner doors to the CommLink itself, and the mob had to break through two other sets of doors, similarly rigged, to get to those.

"That should hold them for a while," Gould said. "What is the status of Malanga?"

Tom looked doubtful. "How can you just ignore that racket? They are driving me nuts."

"Conditions of battle, my friend, conditions of battle," Gould said. "Just ignore them and they will eventually implode. Hopefully that will take enough time for us to make some progress with the QY problem."

Second Pass

"I'm getting low level life signs from Malanga," BQ said. "Either she is in a deep sleep, or she is close to death. But it puzzles me. Her vitals went from normal to quite subdued in an instant."

"Not difficult to understand at all," said Sylvia. "She is doing what I would do in the same situation if I could—she has put herself into a deep trance-like state, an almost self-induced coma. Finders can do that, and always do that when they need to conserve energy."

"Or," said Tom with a smile, "when they don't want to be interrogated."

BQ suddenly understood. "She can't help them learn anything, even through torture. It is perfect; they need to keep us in the picture if they are to have any hope at all of understanding our culture."

A loud crunching sound came from the outer rooms. Gould checked the security monitors and shook his head. "Got through the first layer kids, now they go for the second."

"Are the locators all in place?" asked Tom. "Once they are positioned we can show our force; scare them a little."

"Not yet," said Sylvia. "First we need to know that Malanga is safe. BQ," she said quickly, "get Ali on the comm."

BQ hit the switch and a red light blinked on. She then pressed a lever and spoke into a microphone. "Ali," she said, "come in. This is BQ."

A moment of static focused into the child's voice. "What do you want? Do you have a plan for us?"

"Not exactly, Ali," she said, "hold on a second, I'm giving you to Sylvia."

"Ali," Sylvia said, "do you have exact coordinates for Malanga?"

"Mrs. Bryant," said Shandor, "Pardon me for intruding, but I can help a bit more than Ali. He is concentrating on driving. And, yes. We have exact coordinates on Malanga. Or at least on which QY she's in. Other than that, we do not know if they have moved her somewhere out of their docking bay."

"Right," said Sylvia, "We need to keep that QY in view at all times. And we need to isolate the location tracking device from that one so we don't blow it up."

"I've done that," said Shandor, "but I am afraid we might have a problem."

"What is that, Shandor?" asked Sylvia.

"The QY she is currently in was one of the ones that dispatched a shuttle and we can see that the three shuttles each have some military personnel in them. I suspect that the QYs they came from are housing military force rather than building materials."

"Do you know how many shuttles each QY can hold? We haven't gotten much useful data on the ships."

"Negative," Shandor said. "We know they can hold at least two, but only because the shuttle that captured Malanga docked and another shuttle was launched from the same QY. From the relative dimensions they could each hold up to 6 shuttles. But that is only from a rough estimate of the length on each side of the docking bay. They are long enough to hold 3 each. But there may be other storage in those bays."

"Right," she pursed her lips in thought, "if we could just get inside of them," she said almost as if thinking aloud.

"Ma'am," Ali's voice said hesitantly, "we do have the ability to see inside of one of the cargo bays."

"How so?" asked Sylvia and Tom simultaneously.

"The collection pods have nine external cameras, three of which are on robotic arms. They are operated from inside of the pod. You can link the pod's computer to one of the secondary CommLink display screens."

"But they are operated from inside of the pod," Sylvia said. "Malanga is unconscious."

"But she is not out of reach," Ali said. "Find Willa, or one of the Finders. They will know how to reach her."

"Of course!" said Sylvia. "Good idea Ali. I'll get right on..." she stopped as she remembered the vigilante mob outside of the chamber. "Let me work on that," she said, deciding not to burden Ali with her peril.

* * * * * * *

"My men will know by now something is wrong," Hwan said, "and they are instructed to use force whenever necessary to achieve our ends. So, if I were you, I would release me immediately so I can call off my dogs, as it were."

"Forget it, Hwan," George said, "I've seen enough of you in action to know that most of what you say is just talk."

Second Pass

"Yes," he said, "regretfully the art of diplomacy is mostly negotiation. I personally detest negotiation. It takes so unbearably long to accomplish what a swift twist of the genitals can do instantly."

George ignored him for the moment, and turned his attention to Stetler. "Would you keep our guest happy? I must go attend to some business." George jetted toward the door, then turned back to the room just before he exited. "And if happy is too hard to achieve, quiet will do just fine." And he jetted out the door, closing it hydraulically behind himself.

Paul caught up with him and stopped him. "So he doesn't know that his original crew is dead, that Malanga is in their custody, or that they have dispatched three shuttles filled with soldiers."

"All true," said George, "and for the life of me, I'm at a loss. What do we do now?"

"Well, George, I'm no military man, but I do believe we need to get rid of those three shuttles, and perhaps even most of their fleet." He stopped and listened to himself. "Damn, I've become a blood thirsty, war-monger!"

"Not at all," said Bill Bryant, who had joined them. "Desperate times require..."

"I need to talk to McKenna," interrupted George. "He's the only one who has any experience in this kind of thing."

"I agree completely," said Paul. "What do you think, Bill?"

"I never thought that being First Officer would make me have to think militarily," he said quietly. "But I must say I agree. We need to talk to McKenna, and the women."

"The women?" George and Paul said together.

"Yes," he said, "the women. They always know what to do."

* * * * * * *

McKenna had not been missed, nor had anyone realized he had left the CommLink Chamber's suite of rooms. But he had, exiting the rear entrance into a side hallway. He was still largely unfamiliar with weightless existence on SIL, but, as in all things, was learning quickly. He could hear the sound of the crowd and was once again astounded at how uninspired mobs were. The secondary entry into the CommLink was not hidden, nor did it try to be. It was simply a logical alternative egress, well marked for easy access and clarity. Yet the group was focused on the entry at the other end exclusively.

So many times when he was president he longed for anonymity in a crowd; how helpful it might have been. But on SIL, though visible, he was simply another old person. Should anyone have recognized him from his presidential days, he had grayed and even whited far from that recognizable picture of youthful energy. He joined the crowd in the rear, gradually increasing his personal volume and animation to match those around him. He made sure to join in some rhythmic chants and have some encounters in which he was able to commiserate with those around him on one idea or another. He gradually then raised his voice above the others, peppering his comments with calls for new direction every now and then.

"They put Communications on auto broadcast!" he yelled, causing instant agreement from some even before they could digest the words. He repeated it, then moved to another part of the crowd and asked what the ruckus was about, what 'auto broadcast' meant and why their leaders would do such a thing. People answered him with enough persuasion that he then joined his voice to theirs, repeating the phrase until it became truth. "Eye Chamber!" he yelled, then jetted to the other side and yelled it again. Others started yelling it, and the words became sentences.

"They are in the Eye Chamber!" "They can hide in the Eye Chamber!" "The Eye Chamber is what they need to protect!" Gradually the mob started to move in the direction of the Eye Chamber. When it turned a sharp corner into the central axis of SIL, he lost himself again and then returned to the same side entrance to the CommLink Chamber he had left from. Still, nobody had even noticed he had gone.

"Look at this, Sol," he said to Gould. "Everyone seems to have left for the Eye Chamber. Listen..." There was silence outside of the door.

"Thank God," said Sylvia, only slightly distracted from her current focus. "They won't find much there except a hostile plant that will certainly tame the likes of that crowd."

"You know," said McKenna, "you are absolutely right! It looks like they won't be a problem anymore." He then called everyone's attention. "We need to have a conference between all parts of this command," he said, pointing to the various speakers,

Second Pass

video screens and electronic messages. "Sylvia, will you set that up right away?" It wasn't a question in the slightest, and Sylvia got right to the task.

Within two minutes there were video links to the space station, the collection pod Ali and Shandor were in, themselves in the CommLink Chamber, the central command of security offices on SIL, the main chambers of Assembly and Overseers, the Finders Quarters, and even a link to all of the cameras on Malanga's pod.

"Here is the status as I see it. Please correct me if I am wrong, but only after I've finished the rundown. More important immediately is the combination of all of us, not the exactness of details. As soon as we have a picture of the whole, then we'd better turn our focus to exact detail, but not before.

"Seventeen of twenty QYs have been armed with bombs, the other three have location beepers in place on their retro-rockets. Malanga is inside of the QY that Ali has marked, and all surveillance cameras on her pod are now being broadcast and monitored in the CommLink Chamber on SIL, with broadcast interface to all points of our command. Ali and Shandor are hovering out of sight, watching Malanga's QY and the three shuttles. Three shuttles containing a total of a few dozen presumably armed men are now hovering between the old space station, which we will call SS1, and SIL. Hwan is held captive on SS1 and has just learned that Masters, Stevens and their crew have been killed, but does not know three shuttles have been dispatched from other QY ships. The band of detainees is angry and have gone off toward the Eye Chamber. Willa Jiimson and Erica Dunn are cocooned to heal. The collection pod Commandeered by Ali to save Malanga also holds controls for the detonation of the bombs. Am I missing anything?"

"Yes," said Tom, "I don't know how you missed it, but the control codes for detonation have been transferred to SS1 under the care of First Officer Bryant."

"Good. Anything else?" McKenna asked.

There was mumble of discussion but no body spoke up. He continued. "We will have to eliminate the three shuttles containing military men for two reasons. We need to show we have fire power and will use it, and we need them to launch another couple of shuttles so Ali can get inside of their cargo bay to retrieve Malanga. Which means we need them to open the QY on which Malanga is being held."

"Isn't that a bit drastic?" asked BQ.

"Not at all," replied Bryant from SS1. "He is absolutely correct."

"But that will be intentionally taking lives," she insisted.

"BQ," said Sylvia quietly enough to seem quite calm but loudly enough for everyone to hear, "we are at war. Our lives are at stake. We must turn advantage in our own favor."

"Excuse me," a new voice said. Everyone looked around, and all except George were shocked to see it came from Liz. "I believe we need to eliminate Hwan, and do it in such a way that his troupes will know he is gone and we have taken him out."

"Why?" asked McKenna directly.

"I have spoken with him and with his superior, the Chairman of the People's Republic. It is clear to me that he has taken on more power than was assigned to him, and that his followers are uncomfortable in large part with his sudden flagrant display of that power for his own arrogance."

"I agree," said Bryant.

"This is Sylvia Bryant, and I concur with Liz. I, too, have had some dealings with this man and he is not fully in control of his faculties. I believe that our action would be supported by China, were they present to make that choice."

"Then China must be contacted," said George. "We must signal our intentions to them, and alert them of the developments here."

"How can we do that?" asked Gould. "We are only in intermittent communication range through LOL and we do not know what the reception of signal capacity is in China."

"Immaterial," said Tom. "McKenna?"

"Yes?"

"Washington has immediate, direct, 24-hour CommLink with China, is that not so?"

"That is so," he said with a smile, "and you know damn well I am the President who made it so!"

"Then we need only communicate on a secure channel with Washington and they can handle communications with China."

"Hmm..." Machmood said, causing everyone to turn to him or to the screen he appeared on that was near them. "I think the United Nations would be better. Relations with China aren't what they were in your day, McKenna, and you are all forgetting that nobody on Earth knows the Chinese even came here at all. The UN will know best how to treat this."

Second Pass

"Good point," said McKenna. "Now, are we in agreement? We will contact China through the UN and then proceed to take out the three shuttles, hopefully causing a launch of more ships, specifically from the Malanga QY. And we will eliminate Hwan in a way that is apparent to the QY fleet." They all nodded.

"Wait!" shouted Stetler. "You are forgetting about the hostages being held somewhere here on SIL and the detainees. What about them?"

* * * * * * *

The darkness convulsed at its center like a bed sheet flipped in the air before floating to rest on a newly made bed. Dark within dark, shades of black distinguishable only by sense, not sight. A vast silent ripple of time not ready to continue in the direction it started going brought a change in the deep current of becoming. The darker part of the shadow found within it the essence of life; a spark ignited new possibility and glowed slowly to animation.

Sound spread so thin as to hold only muffled hints of meaning began to form an ever-hesitating rush to consciousness. Where darkness was total it became the defining absence of an object to reflect light, the between of things that, by being nothing, served to give definition to the things that dared to be. Then all was acceleration. Nothing becoming something; light now the piercing intrusion where reality allowed emptiness; sound now the deafening roar of life took over the void. Light. Sound. Pain. Truth. Harsh Truth.

Erika woke with a start only to find her nose pressed against a moist surrounding – clear, but in the way. She pushed at it with her hands, bound at her sides in the same clear gel. She saw beyond the confines of her cocoon the rippled distortion of Elizabeth's face, and next to her Jun-Jun. She remembered. Freelocking, then death. She stopped her futile pushing.

Jun-Jun was the first to see Erica come back to life. He nudged Elizabeth. They looked at her and waved. Smiling, like people welcoming visitors on a train platform waved to the windows of the incoming train, seeing the face through the windows. Erica couldn't move her arms enough to wave back, and tried to open her eyes in a comical expression as she blew her cheeks round.

"What is she doing?" asked Elizabeth. "Do you think she is uncomfortable?"

"Boy, you really don't know your own sister, do you?" asked Jun-Jun in rhetorical assessment of their relationship. "She does that when she catches someone watching her. It means she is fine."

"How long do we need to wait until she comes out of the cocoon?"

"Don't you remember? It will dry up when the time comes, like it did with Willa before. I hope it isn't long."

As they spoke the form of Willa next to her also came back to life. Willa wriggled, like a worm crawling on a slick surface. She bent her body one way, then the next, all the while rubbing her chin against her collar bone and shoulders, one side then the next. She continued with complete focus until a small tear started to appear in the gel. It separated at her stomach and began to tear upward. When the tear got to the level of her heart the entire cocoon deflated and became just a thin film of clear material, which she brushed from her arms.

"Well," she said contentedly, "here I am. All better!"

"How did you do that? I mean," stammered a startled Jun-Jun, "are you ready? Don't you have to wait until it goes away on its own?"

"Well," Willa said as she blew a small fragment of the paper-like material from her lip, "I figured that I felt better and really wanted to be out of there. If it weren't done with me, then it would have put me back to sleep and regenerated itself. I think it is a bit too conservative in its estimate of my healing ability."

They laughed at her absolute confidence, and the sharpness of her delivery. Willa looked at Erica and pointed at the gel around her. "See there," she said pointing at the outer surface near her waist, "it is starting to pucker a bit. I think she's done." She moved her face just inches from Erica's face and spoke loudly. "Just wiggle back and forth, dear," she shouted, "bend as much as you can at the waist." Erica started to move slightly, with great effort. "That's right, but more. And move your chin on your shoulder to break it up. When you do you will be able to breathe out and get some air in there. It will signal the cocoon to release you."

Erica doubled her efforts and started to rock her head back and forth, from shoulder to shoulder. She found it funny and fun,

Second Pass

and started doing it like a dance, getting wilder and wilder. She didn't notice when the gel started to evaporate and open. She kept dancing back and forth and was suddenly free of the gel but kept on dancing.

"This is fun!" she said. "Come on, guys. Join in!" At which they all laughed.

"Enough!" Willa said sternly. "There is no time to play when you have important information to give us. And where are those horrible people who were trying to kill me?"

"Oh, them," Erica said. "They went to the CommLink and couldn't get in and then went to the Eye Chamber. Don't worry about them. The plant was waiting for them." She turned to her sister and a tear formed on her eye. "Lizzie," she said and started to cry. "I'm so sorry."

"It doesn't matter," she said, "it only matters that you are okay. I was so worried about you."

"So was I," said Jun-Jun. "I'm sorry I scared you before. Now I know exactly what you felt like that day. It's terrible!"

"Su Lee and Toby are near the CommLink, right through the wall. There are there so Becka can keep track of what everything. She also has a device that can tap into the main system."

"We know," said Willa. "That is why they all tried to revolt against me. They heard what Hwan said."

"Jun," Erica said, "you must go get them right away. Su Lee is having a reaction to the drug Becka gave her. Toby is fine."

"How will we get them though?" Jun-Jun asked. "Everyone is either on the Space Station or involved in some sort of security preparation. Did you see if Becka had a weapon?"

"She does have weapons, more than one," Erica said.

"But," announced Willa, "I have the best weapon of all. The plant! And I have an idea. Come with me."

She jetted out of the room quickly and they were all on her tail. She went first to the room where they had held the detainees, and got one of the plants she had left there. With it under her arm, she then sped to the CommLink Chamber outer door.

"This way," said Erica, going down a side hallway. At the end of the passage was a vent for circulation. She held her fingers up to her lips and pointed with the other hand. The screws had been removed and the vent was being held in place by a non-drying glue gum. Willa put the plant over the vent so its roots were facing the vent. She then produced a bungee cord with hooks on each end and held it in place by hooking it to the vent itself.

"Now," Willa said, "if you will all help me communicate with this plant. Erica, show it the face of Becka and the scene you saw, where Su Lee and Toby are, etc. Jun-Jun, you show it that Becka is the enemy and needs to be separated from the others. Elizabeth, you send protection and health awareness to Su Lee, showing the plant that she is ill and needs help and that she is beloved and to be protected. I will show the loving toward Toby, and tell the plant to release them both from the drug that has infected them." She looked from one to the other. "Ready?" They nodded. "Go!"

* * * * * * *

Becka was getting worried. She had tried to reach Masters and Stevens, to no avail. She tried to get some message from the QY fleet or from Hwan, even though Masters said he wasn't to be trusted. But she heard nothing from anywhere. She didn't know what to do, and was getting hungry.

She looked again through the packs that had been with Su Lee and Toby, hoping there was some sort of food or drink, even though she had looked many times before. Again, as before, she found nothing. She was still looking when the root of the plant came through the vent and slowly circled around her ankles. It was loose and fit under her pant openings so she wouldn't see it even if she looked. Another shoot traveled up the outside of her back, about two centimeters from her clothing and followed her spine. When it got between her shoulder blades it split off a shoot in each direction following her arms, and continued to grow toward her head as well. Just behind her head it formed a blossom and two leaves. The leaves spread outward, each roughly the size of the palm of a hand. The blossom opened up and a puff of pink dust was emitted. It engulfed her head just as the leaves clamped on either side of her head. Simultaneously the shoots took hold of her wrists and ankles, while the main shoot became thick and strong, an actual tree trunk.

Becka felt light-headed and sexually aroused suddenly. She blinked her eyes and started to reach with her right hand to rub them, but her sleeve seemed caught on something. When she

Second Pass

turned her head to look she found that something was holding her head still. She struggled and then felt her ankles and wrists being tightly bound. Her head was held straight so she couldn't see what was making it impossible for her to move. She screamed, but her scream only came out a whimper as the pink powder drugged her. In her last moment of consciousness she looked in the direction of the two captives and saw they were covered with clear gel, and inside of it they were blinking their eyes awake.

* * * * * * *

Entering into battle with an enemy with no known weapons erases much of the fear soldiers face on the eve of conflict. Yet within the three shuttles there were many sweaty palms; fear of death is not the only consideration. Behind the backs of the leaders there was talk of the morality of slaughter. When people are simply sitting ducks there is no sense of coming victory, but just the dread of having to live with yourself for the rest of your life.

For the leaders, men who had given up identity to achieve power, the questions were different. They would be famous, for one. Every Chinese citizen who had traveled in space was a superstar, and even those peripherally related were held in high esteem. China will have acquired SIL, the hottest territory that existed, and would hold hope against aging with the Silian medicines taken from Malanga. The depictions of the battle would be constructed by the best animators in China, with emphasis on the extreme danger SIL presented to their men. The propaganda machine would spin the tale of grave danger with the public, and would purposefully confuse the line between danger traveling in space and the dangers of battle.

The three shuttles hovered in orbits matching SS1 and SIL. Their imperceptible creeping toward SIL built up tension in the men. Nationalistic music played and there were individual video monitors on the back of each seat with a choice of channels. Selections were different documentary shorts on aspects of Chinese history, the space program, inspirational speeches by the Chairman, and some music/video montages of the homeland juxtaposing symbols of imperialism with sensuous women. The men nervously flipped between the channels.

There was still no word from Hwan, which worried the leaders. They spoke on secure communication systems to each other in conference. It was decided that if they did not hear from Hwan within the hour, they would attack SIL's antennae, with particular importance on the main link to the LOL. Every quarter hour there was another attempt to communicate with SS1, but all they received in return were messages in perfect Chinese that everything was well with the diplomatic mission and to please await word from Hwan, which was promised to come very soon. While they realized they were victims of some sort of misinformation, they couldn't be sure if it was coming from Hwan in his attempt to spin the entire mission in his favor, or if they were being toyed with by the enemy.

Suddenly they saw a small vehicle depart from the far side of SS1. They could not see its origin, but suspected it had been docked in the old docking portal system used for uploading supplies and downloading waste when the station was in service. They watched as the vehicle traveled slowly in their direction.

As it approached the first of the three shuttles, which had taken a V formation, it slowed to match their speed exactly and, appearing to stop in front of them, turned to face their control console windows. The first officer gasped when he saw Hwan in the vehicle. He waved his hand wildly, and went on the ship's intercom to announce that Hwan was apparently finished with the diplomatic mission. The small ship turned and then went toward the second shuttle.

Communications about this development were flying back and forth between the three shuttles and eventually the entire QY fleet. Cheers erupted from the tense soldiers on all three shuttles, and from the other occupants of the fleet.

When the small vehicle got to the second shuttle it was a bit closer. The pilot was able to see more details of the ship and passenger through his window. He, too, waved frantically, and was puzzled when Hwan did not return his wave. He then saluted him, a gesture always returned by Hwan and returned with great fanfare, delighted to have his authority recognized and returned. He instead saw Hwan's face grow flushed and his head move back and forth in short, quick movements. He leaned forward for a closer look at what seemed very strange, but the vehicle turned and traveled to the third shuttle.

Second Pass

When it turned he activated the secure conference channel and reported there was something wrong. He was a serious person, and all of his life had been told he needed to relax, to loosen up. Because of that, the response he got was more of the same. His protests became greater proof that he was allowing his sober view of the world prevent them from their celebration.

At the third shuttle the vehicle was brought nearly touching the nose of the shuttle. The pilot was able to see clearly that Hwan was gagged and strapped to his chair. He stared in shock as Hwan's eyes bulged in his attempt to draw attention to the peril he was in. Hwan's little vehicle then turned and sped off neither in the direction of SIL nor SS1 nor the QY fleet. He was traveling toward open space. As it went it turned so it was facing them, traveling backward.

As the pilot pressed the button to switch to a channel directly to the main control room in QY1, Bryant pressed the button to the devices on the three shuttles. They exploded almost in unison, parts speeding off in all directions. The partial torso and head of the pilot of the third shuttle flew outward from the blast and struck the window of Hwan's collection pod. Hwan screamed.

The QY fleet was not sure at first what it saw, but soon realized their shuttles and all the men on board had been destroyed. An alert went to the entire fleet that they were under attack and the remaining men were instantly to ready themselves for boarding more shuttles.

* * * * * * *

Ali and Shandor could only see the glow of the explosions, but knew that their opportunity to enter the QY with Malanga on board would come very soon. They readied their ship and adjusted their space suits, locking their helmets into place. McKenna had made it clear that no matter what, they were to enter the cargo bay of the QY as soon as it opened.

The four others in the small vehicle were also in their EVA suits, ready to rescue Malanga. They had not realized the mission might include battle or even death, but they were more than ready to face that if it was demanded of them. Living on SIL for all of their lives had prepared them for this mission and the potential battle better than anything else could have. The constant threat of hull breech, whether by accidental collision by space debris, sabotage or some mishap from within SIL, made facing potential death a routine thing. All had kidded about exposure to space with each other as children, and anyone found with space-phobia was mocked relentlessly; it was worse than sleepsack wetting.

They did not know which of the four shuttle cargo bay doors would open, or when. They waited in relaxed silence. Ali was at the controls and had guaranteed everyone, including McKenna, that he had the skill as a pilot to do this mission. Even though he was a child, he had, indeed, been one of the most skilled collectors of space junk for the coffers of SIL and had been able to travel farther in less time than any of the other pod pilots. The joke was that if they were as small as Ali they, too, would be able to travel so fast.

Suddenly one of the doors started to open. Light from within the bay shown outward in sweeping slices across space. The light picked up the floating debris from the exploded shuttles and showed as three dimensional wedges with sparkling interiors.

"Watch for chunks and dead guys," said Shandor.

"Very funny," Ali replied. "Don't worry. This pod was made to go into meteorite storms and come out shining brightly. Hitting an arm or a leg won't slow her down at all."

"You all set?" he said, indicating with a tilt of his head toward the QY cargo bay.

"All set," Ali said, flipping the thrusters on, "here we go!"

The sped forward, feeling the extreme jolt of sudden movement in space. That very movement had killed Masters and his group, but it did nothing to the six of them who were all strapped tightly into their seats.

The large door opened, and Ali sped his craft up to the opening, but managed to stay in the shadow. One of the shuttles, like the ones they had just destroyed, floated down from the bay and was facing away from them.

"Too bad we don't have a spare bomb," said Shandor. "I'd love to shove it up that baby's ass."

As soon as the shuttle cleared the door, a burst from its main thrusters sent it forward. In its wake, the small pod entered the large chamber. Having just launched a vehicle into space, the bay was empty of people. All attention in the control room was on the shuttle that had been launched and the two others being prepared in separate bays. Ali docked his pod quickly and quietly

Second Pass

and let the others out. From watching the abduction of Malanga, they knew her vehicle was in the other cargo bay on that side of the ship. As luck had it, the cargo bays weren't divided on one side of the ship. This way there could be easy travel the length of the bay, and one end of it or the other could be opened. It was a masterful design, perfect for an invading party.

The four of them saw Malanga's pod in front of them at the other end of a long bay. There were hundreds of places to hook tethers, and thousands of Velcro foot holds. They traveled the length of the bay in just under two minutes, and arrived at the other pod. They looked inside, expecting to see it empty, but instead saw Malanga inside. When they tried to open the door, it was stuck.

"Ali, this is Brutus, Malanga is still in there," he said. "But the door is stuck."

"Go to the other side," Ali said.

Sumu Migamu, who at age 17 was the youngest other than Ali, had gone to the other side and tried it, but it was stuck too. "That's stuck too," Brutus said.

"Then go to the back," Ali instructed. "You know where the rear robot arm comes out of the pod, between the two rear thrusters?"

"Yes I do," Brutus rolled his eyes, "I designed the pod, Ali."

"Really!" the youngster said, truly impressed. "Wow! You thought of everything."

"Thanks," Brutus said with a chuckle, "what do you want me to do there?"

"Well, you go in through there. The robot arm can be manually...well, I guess you know what it can do."

"Only problem is, boss, that I'm way too big to fit in there."

Ali realized that his body was much, much smaller than any of theirs. "I'm sorry," he said. "Uh, I could come over there if you need me."

Brutus, who was actually named Bob but was renamed by his amazing build, had shoulders wider than many passageways on SIL and had to sleep with only his feet tethered because his shoulders were too wide to fit between the mounts for sleepsacks. He conferred with his team. Looking at them with suits on made it difficult to see who was larger or smaller. Sumu was slight, but was not the smallest. Joe Culbertson, one year his senior was rather muscular as well. Germaine Shamir, the other member

358

of their team, was a fragile young woman, but at age 18 had developed a handsome bosom. To the young men it seemed that she was all breasts. As Culbertson looked the group over he saw instantly that Shamir was the probable person who could fit.

"Germaine," he said into his microphone, motioning her over to him.

"What is it Brutus?" she asked.

"Come here, please," he said.

"What is it? You can ask me from there." Her delivery was peppered with teenage annoyance at the older man.

Ali's voice broke into the conversation. "He needs to know if your boobs are too big to fit," Ali stated matter of factly. "But my dad told me girls boobs were soft and squishy when you aren't wearing any bras. So, do you have on your bra? Could you squish them to the sides to fit through?"

The others, including those in the CommLink Chamber back on SIL were paralyzed with laughter. Even Germaine, who had been known to be extremely self-conscious about her ample bosom, was doubled over in laughter.

"Yes," she said, "I can fit." She knew for a fact she could fit because she and her boyfriend had been almost caught having sex in a pod by her father, who had come to the collection depository to find out why she was so long out on a collection run. She had been caught in lies many times. As he approached the pod, her boyfriend blocked the view of the rear of the pod as she slipped out the back end, near the mechanical arm.

"What should I do?" she asked.

"Go in through the back and find out why the doors are stuck. If you can't open them, then you can drive the pod yourself."

She entered the rear of the pod and traveled the short distance to the front control seats. "Uh," she said, "um, Ali?"

"What is it, Germaine?" Ali said.

"Malanga is inside of some sort of clear jelly. She has been suffocated by them, I think."

"No she hasn't," Ali said, "it is the plant. It is protecting her."

"But what can I do? She can't be moved."

"Are the rear controls free? Can you get to them?" Ali asked.

"Yes, they are free," she said. "But I don't think I want to drive a dead body. I don't think I can do that."

"She isn't dead," Ali said. "The plant puts that on people who are injured or in trouble to save them. She is alive, trust me. But you have to drive the pod. It's the only way. You other guys get back here right away so we can leave."

The other three came back to the pod and got in. They floated away from the interior of the bay as Germaine used the reverse thrusters to propel the other pod backwards into the open end of the bay. As she did, a man in an EVA suit came out. He was yelling into his microphone, and the door to the cargo bay started to slowly close. The man walked toward the pod Germaine was driving.

She saw him coming and that the doors were closing. She gave the spin thrusters a quick tap and the pod turned on its axis inside of the large cargo bay, so she now pointed toward the open end. The man reached the back of the pod and started to bang on the back of it. Germaine took the controls to the robotic arm and opened the rear compartment, which was below the man. The doors opened and the arm came out and up behind him. He was so intent on shouting commands into his microphone and banging on the pod he didn't notice.

The doors were now about half way shut, and were at a 90º angle from the sides of the QY, enough room for the pod to escape, but soon would be closed too far. In a single movement, Germaine grabbed the man by the crotch with the mechanical robot arm and pulled him, screaming in pain, away from the pod, holding him away from the back. She hit the thrusters and flame shot out of the back of the pod, catching the man on fire as the pod sped forward and out of the QY. Before she got past the doors she threw the burning man against the spare fuel tanks of the QY.

As she sped away, the doors of the cargo bay slammed shut. Thirty seconds later there was a huge explosion and flash of light as the QY fuel tanks burst into flame and destroyed the entire ship. They did not notice another explosion at the same time.

* * * * * * *

Word had not gotten to anyone that Hwan was in trouble. Feeling emboldened by that fact, and furious over the fact that some of their fleet had been destroyed and men killed, the second in command made the decision to fire the rockets that were electronically guided to the locator beacons placed around the Eye. The plan had been to capture Malanga, which they had done. She would be able to teach them how to grow the plants that sustained life on SIL, reversed aging and made all sorts of medicines. If the capture was peaceful, then the Chinese would quickly build a small version of the Eye Chamber using the diamond from the space probe. Then, more slowly, build another large orbital body and gradually move all of the SIL plants to it. But if anything went wrong, as long as they had Malanga and the diamond from the probe, they could begin to build and blow up SIL, retrieving the Eye itself and holding it in storage until the larger facility could be built. When he saw the three shuttles explode, knowing that Hwan was free in the pod, he decided he'd had enough of SIL and all of the trouble that she had brought.

There were three rockets, each trained on one signal from the 7 beacons. In other ships were four more. His were designed to hit in equal points around the Eye. The explosive charges on the rockets wasn't great. It was enough to penetrate and destroy the metal holding the Eye in place, but nothing more. There was a fire retardant on them as well, so there wouldn't be extensive damage. He released the rockets and watched with satisfaction as they came into his vision in front of the ship. But then they all seemed to stop and hang still in space. They then fired tiny rockets to adjust their trajectory and suddenly were facing away from SIL.

"What is wrong with the rockets?" he demanded from his engineers. They did not know, but watched with wonder as the rockets sped back past their QY and away from SIL.

Suddenly there was a huge explosion, coming from the QY that held Malanga. His heart sank, thinking he had somehow shot down their own ship, and killed Malanga in the process. He was wrong, as he soon found out.

One of the rockets passed the rear of his QY, stopped again and turned. This time it was aimed at the rear fuel tank of that vehicle. When it hit there was a small jolt and a small explosion. The outer wall of the QY had been pierced, but nothing more. The nose had nicked the fuel tank, and started a leak, but the flame retardant made it so it did not ignite.

The second two rockets went to the next two QY vehicles, which were flanking the first. When they hit their targets the rockets penetrated further and twin, simultaneous explosions

Second Pass

ripped through those QYs. A burning piece of debris from them flew against the tail of the first ship hit and ignited the fuel. Its burn was slowed by the extreme cold of space, but eventually, about ten seconds later, hit the large fuel tank and the QY was blown to pieces.

Chapter 29

The fourteen vehicles that were left had begun to communicate with SIL when they realized they needed to surrender. They reported in with a cacophonous deluge of spoken Chinese, from calm to hysterical. Between the crews on SS1 and SIL, the messages were deciphered. The entire military force brought on the QYs had been destroyed in those four vehicles. Those other 14 held materials and about 100 workers, set to build in space.

Machmood interviewed each one, with the help of an interpreter, and determined that only ten of the remaining Chinese were likely to cause any trouble at all on SIL. They were placed on the old space station, which was disconnected from the US shuttles. They were given enough food, water and oxygen to live for about two years. The station was then sent back into the low earth orbit, and a communication was sent to the Chinese government that they could be retrieved as soon as the Chinese could reach them. No mention was made of Hwan or the loss of life, and a conference with McKenna was scheduled for one month later to discuss the 'successes and problems' with the Chinese mission to SIL. A formal thank you to the Chinese government for the material and supplies it donated to SIL, along with a disclosure that they had developed space technology that prolonged Earth's accessibility to SIL, was sent, with copies going to all of the major news agencies. There would be many more Chinese space heroes.

* * * * * * *

Willa arrived at the Eye Chamber to find all of the detainees floating in a pink cloud, oblivious and in drugged bliss. She gathered them up and they were sent to the space station with the others. Though they didn't complain at the time of their transport, they would be upset when the drug wore off. Each was given a letter explaining their situation, along with a visa for their arrival in China.

* * * * * * *

Second Pass

George and Liz came out of the Assembly room, where a joint meeting of Assembly Members and Overseers had invited them—along with the Bryants, BQ and Paul Dunn, Solange Malanga, Willa, Tom, Gould, Shandor and Ali—for a debriefing and unraveling of the events that had occurred. They had been invited to stay on SIL with their son, or be placed on the Space Station with one of the US shuttles so they could return to earth when they got close enough. Along with that option came a crew of four who could fly the shuttle, land it, and help them fight off any of the others on the Space Station who tried to avert their arrival in China by gaining access to their shuttle. They were also offered a place on SIL, Commander McVee's large suite of rooms, if they wanted to stay. They said they needed to think about it.

"Excuse me," a voice said behind them. They turned and saw Malanga floating there with Paul and BQ. "Before you decide, we would like to give you a little tour."

"A tour?" George said with surprise. "I believe I know SIL inside and out."

"As for me," Liz said, "I will have plenty of time for a tour if we decide to stay. Right now we really need to be alone to talk."

"I understand that," said Malanga. "But there is something you need to see, something that may alter your decision."

"She is right," said Paul. "You will want to consider this."

"Well," said Liz, "then so we must!"

They went to the waste processing plant and got into one of the collection pods. Georgie was thrilled to ride in the 'baby space plane' as he called it. They came around SIL's lower hemisphere to where the Eye was. From outside of SIL it was just a dirty dent with a sparkling gem in the middle. It didn't give any indication of the beautiful chamber just inside. In fact, the entire outside of SIL was unremarkable and plain.

They then went around the upper hemisphere, but instead of following it around took a tangential route away from SIL. Malanga started to speak.

"Over the years we have seen many developments on SIL. Everything here becomes something, and nothing is predictable. Your father's vision was indeed that of a lunatic, and he was arrogant and wrong to risk the lives of so many just to prove a point to NASA. But that turned into the greatest development in the history of mankind.

"We Silians must always be prepared for instant death, and unknown developments. While we have made many discoveries on SIL, we have also beat the odds in ways we cannot always be sure of. We are a small community, and a viral epidemic could quickly kill us all. A small fire could rob us of our oxygen and suffocate us. In short, we simply cannot offer a reliable environment.

"I've noticed something in the last twenty-six years that we need to show you as you decide to stay or not." She turned the ship around. SIL was now in the distance, and they were looking at her from the side, the Eye perpetually facing the sun to the left, and the outer rim facing outer space away from the sun. The sun-side shined and the light refracted from the Eye shown in strong beams going off in every direction.

"Look at the pretty!" said Georgie. "Mommie! Daddy! See the pretty!"

"Yes," agreed Malanga, "it is a magnificent view. But look to the other side of SIL."

They looked and saw what appeared as lumps of corrosion, stuck to the outer hull like barnacles to a ship's underwater surfaces. Coming out from it was a trail of pieces of dirt, dust, ice and small rocks. This trail formed a tail and reached nearly ten miles into space. It was in the shadow of the ship, and was not readily visible unless your eye was directed there.

"Citizens of SIL do not know this debris is forming, nor that it has attached itself to SIL," Malanga said.

"Have you tried to remove it?" asked George.

"We have," said Paul, "with no success. It is organic, George, not just mineral. And it is fusing itself to the hull of SIL. It is porous on the outer surface, but becomes solid and rock-like where it has fused itself. At the point of fusion it is neither metal nor rock, but a hybrid that is both."

"You see," Malanga said, "we don't know what this will do to SIL. It may eat through the hull and kill us all, or it may enter SIL and bring disease, or some other unknown threat."

"But isn't it years before it will actually enter the inner part of SIL?" asked Liz. "Won't you know more about it by then? Couldn't you deal with it on the next pass, and evacuate if necessary?"

Paul and Malanga looked at each other. "You are right," Malanga said. "It will take years."

Second Pass

"It will eat through the outer surface of SIL, and do that in over one third of the outer surface of the hull, in exactly twelve years."

"Six years before the next pass starts," said George.

"Exactly," said Malanga.

At the end of the tour they left George and Liz to discuss their future. About an hour later, the two of them returned to the Assembly Chamber.

"Have you made your decision?" asked Machmood.

"We have," said George, holding Georgie with one arm, and encircling Liz's waist with the other. "We have decided to stay on SIL, and to make it our home."

About the Author

While working as the electronic communications advisor for Al Gore's first Presidential Campaign, Ken Ludden followed Gore's lead and read the book "The Drama of the Gifted Child" by renowned child psychologist Alice Miller. That book inspired him to find a way to reach out to teens in an effort to help them understand how very young children have a limited view of the adult world, a view that can hinder later development until it is understood. At the time, Ludden was working as a senior editor at the Charles Stark Draper Laboratories in Cambridge, Massachusetts and so began to do research on a story line that would create a scenario in which a child would be exposed to a parent until the age of 6, then not see the parent again until young adult hood.

Space Industries Laboratory (SIL) was the result of the research, and Ludden's first book in the SIL Series (Drs. McVee) was written. The popularity of the book and its characters compelled Ludden to keep writing, and now, Second Pass, has been completed.

Ludden completed three years of course work at Colgate University with a concentration in Art History (Primitive Art/Gallery Curation), and then he finished his Bachelors Degree in Art History at Boston University in 1985. He has written a syndicated column (Dear Diva) from 1993 through the present. Dear Diva has appeared in magazines and newspapers in New York, Miami, Washington, DC, San Francisco, and St. Louis in the US, and for a limited time in St. Petersburg, Russia, Budapest, Hungary, and Prague, Czech Republic. He also published Mary Go-Round! In Washington, DC as a magazine serial over the course of a year, and it developed an enthusiastic and wide following. It was later turned into a television pilot and will begin its journey to become a television series in 2005.

Ludden is a resident of San Francisco, and is a Feature Writer for Spectrum Newspaper there, as well as its Entertainment Editor. He is also the senior correspondent for QTV Newsmagazine on San Francisco local channels.

Other publications include:

- "May These Images Respect and Reflect...", exhibit and publication of photo/poem selections of historic black America from 1947. Spring 1996
- Dear Diva™ advice column in weekly publications in Washington, DC, New York City, NY, and Miami, FL, San Francisco, CA, and St. Louis, MO; 1993 to Present, covering writings on 114 different topics (totaling over 1200 questions from his readership answered)
- Mary Go-Round serial story for Michael's Entertainment Guide, 52 consecutive issues carried the on-going story; 1993-1994
- Remembering Rudolf Nureyev Ballet Review, Winter 1993
- Fonteyn On Video Ballet Review, Fall 1991;
- A Stretch in Time Ballroom Annual, May 1990;
- Interface Documentation Sled Testing Series (SICBM 18-volume series for
- the United States Air Force);
- Publications Style Guide (SICBM Air Force);
- Office Management Procedures Manual (Gilette);
- IBM Project Coordinator Investigation Publication Guidelines (IBM); and
- 18 HUD MIPS User Manuals; and CRS User Manual and System Administrator Manuals for Mainframe and PC applications (Equal Housing Compliance Review System).

Printed in the United States
21453LVS00001B/147